Blood of the Beast

M. Ward Leon

For my Joanie & Sweetpea

"911 operator. What's your emergency?"

"Oh my God, there's blood everywhere! It's Doctor Meriwether—he's been killed! Come quick!"

"Ma'am, are you sure he's dead?"

"Yes, I'm sure! He has no head!"

When Detective Sergeant Johansson arrived at the doctor's office, the rookie-uniformed officer who got there first was standing outside the front door. As Johansson approached the officer, he saw the kid throwing up into the bushes.

Johansson called out, "Hey, rookie, this is a crime scene! If you have to do that again, next time, throw up in your hat."

"Sorry, sir…It's just that I've never—"

"Where is he?"

The rookie pointed and said, "Last room on the left, room six."

Johansson made his way through the lobby, where Mrs. Ponser, the receptionist, was giving details to Detective Wilson, who looked up at him, shook his head in disgust, and pointed down the hall to where the headless body of Doctor Meriwether was lying. Once Johansson passed them, Wilson continued to question the receptionist.

"Now, Mrs. Ponser, you said he paid with cash, is that correct?"

"Yes, he said that he only had a company credit card and couldn't use it."

"Could you show me where you keep the cash, Mrs. Ponser?"

She pointed to her desk where, on it, sat an empty cash drawer, "There. It looks like he took all the money."

"Did he mention what company he worked for?"

"It should be on his forms; let me see." She said as she walked over to her desk.

Wilson quickly followed and told her, "Please be careful not to touch anything. Fingerprints, you understand."

"Oh, sure. There they are."

After slipping on a pair of rubber gloves, the detective picked up the clipboard with the forms and started to peruse all the names on the sign in sheet.

Detective Sergeant Johansson has been on the Bemidji police force for over nineteen years and in homicide for the past eight. A recent widower, who tipped the scales at a little under two hundred and sixty pounds, he was balding with more hair under his lip than on his head. It was common knowledge that he'd been wearing the same three suits since he joined the homicide squad. He was tough, cantankerous, and old school. He played it strictly by the book, and he was quick to tell you that there wasn't too much he hadn't seen when it came to the evil men could do, but even he wasn't prepared for what he was about to see.

As Johansson made his way down the hall to room six, everywhere he looked, all he could see were stuffed animal heads and photos of the good doctor posing with his trophy kills. If it weren't for the overpowering smell of Listerine and the occasional piece of dental equipment, you'd think you were in Teddy Roosevelt's rumpus room.

As he entered room six, Johansson looked at the wall opposite him, where, mounted among the heads of a Zebra and an African Oryx, there was the head of Doctor Meriwether. He was still wearing his Orascoptic HiRes Dental Headlights with built-in Loupes. Doctor Meriwether had a Mona Lisa grin on his face and a hint of yellow fabric protruding from his mouth. Johansson called out for the M.E., who was still examining the body in the hallway, to come to extract the object.

"Hey Doc, come here. What's he got stuffed in his mouth?

The medical examiner walked over to the mounted head and, with a pair of standard medical ring clamps, slowly started to remove the yellow fabric. "Ah, let see what this is." He got the crumpled cloth out and began to unfold it. "It appears to be a canvas flag. See," he stated, as he held it up.

It was a small flag, measuring approximately 12 x 14 inches. Johansson looked at it in bewilderment. "What the hell? Kind of looks like a pirate flag, but what's with the skull and cross monkey wrenches?"

"I have no idea," He said, as he placed the flag into a clear evidence bag.

"Okay. Thanks, Doc. Can you ask Wilson to come in here?"

"Sure," The medical examiner said, and he walked out into the hallway just as Detective Wilson walked past. The M.E. whispered to Wilson, "Good timing, he was just asking for you."

"You wanted to see me?" Wilson said.

Detective Johansson held up the flag and asked, "You ever see a symbol like this?"

"Yeah, I have. I think it's a logo for a French eco-terrorist group."

"A French what?"

"A French eco-terrorist group," Wilson repeated. "I can't pronounce the French name, but its name translates into English as the Monkey Wrench Gang."

"Where did you hear about them?"

"Well, Johansson, maybe if you watched something other than ESPN, you might learn more than every Twins player's batting average."

"Fuck you, Wilson."

"I'm just saying."

"What in the hell is a French eco-terrorist group doing killing a dentist in Bemidji, Minnesota?"

"My guess is, they don't like big game hunters, or, at least, they didn't like this big game hunter…or maybe they just don't like Minnesota dentists."

"Call Johnson back at headquarters, and get him on to this French Monkey Fist Gang; have him find out everything he can."

"Monkey Wrench Gang."

"Huh? Whatever!"

Johansson held up the clipboard to Wilson and said, "Ten bucks says he's our guy."

"Who, Lewis Clark?"

"Read the whole name," Johansson insisted.

"Lewis N. Clark."

"And his company."

"Corps of Discovery Expedition, Inc."

"Lewis and Clark. This guy is a real comedian, a real smart-ass. See if there are any cameras in or around the building. There are probably some somewhere in the area, so have some uni's check them out. Also, the receptionist said that he took back the cash he paid with, so there's no chance of lifting fingerprints from them. Let's hope he left some on these forms; have the lab give them the once over."

Wilson nodded, "Right," and got to work.

Johansson sighed and shook his head. "Fucking French."

As the sun started to rise over the Etosha National Park in Northern Namibia, the members of Doctor Jimmy J. Meriwether's hunting party were late leaving camp for the third day in a row, because the good doctor was once again fumbling around and trying to get organized after having gotten totally shit-faced the night before at dinner.

Doctor Jimmy J. Meriwether, loving husband, devoted father, successful dentist and hunter extraordinaire, hailed from Bemidji, Minnesota. Dentistry was his profession, his family his love, but hunting, hunting was Jimmy J's passion. Nothing got the old juices going like blowing the shit out of something. Doctor Meriwether had hunted the four corners of the world, killed just about one of each of God's creatures, and had their heads to prove it. He was getting close to sixty-five and thinking of selling off his practice, just so he could devote more time killing things. Jimmy had silver hair and blues eyes—he had been told by many of the ladies that he resembled Paul Newman—and was in, basically, excellent health. He had no real vices, other than maybe drinking a bit too much, but he always said he could quite anytime he wanted to—it's just that he didn't want to.

Doctor Meriwether's big game guide, Karl Olsen, had seen them all before; rich doctors, lawyers, bankers and rich corporate assholes from America, who came to Namibia on safari, spending tens of thousands of dollars to show the world and prove to themselves how manly and macho they were by killing the largest land mammals on earth.

Karl Olsen was born and raised in Otjiwarongo, Namibia, a small city of twenty-eight thousand in the Otjozondjupa Region. Translated, Otjiwarongo means 'the place where fat cattle graze.' Karl's father was a cattle rancher, as was his father and his father's father before him; almost seven generations of Olsen cattlemen have worked the Otjiwarongo land.

Karl never enjoyed the ranching lifestyle. He discovered at an early age that he had a natural knack for tracking, and he enjoyed hunting, so he chose to pursue a career in guiding safari parties. The pay was great, the hours were easy, and there wasn't any of the backbreaking work associated with ranching, especially as the lead guide. With the exception of guiding, Karl was very much a lazy soul. He was overweight, tipping the scales at a whopping four hundred and twenty-five pounds, he was balding, and he would never walk if he could ride. Olsen drank like a fish, ate with his mouth open, and never covered his mouth when he coughed or sneezed. He had a full grey beard that was stained orange down the whole length below his bottom lip from chewing tobacco juice. His clothes were always wrinkled and looked as if he had slept in them, which, of course, he did. He rarely bathed and smelled like a French whorehouse when he did from an access of cheap cologne. He was a pig, but he was, without a doubt, the best tracker in all of Africa.

During late Spring, sometimes it would take a couple days to find the big game, but today, almost immediately after entering the hunting area, Olsen found fresh elephant tracks. And within minutes of finding the tracks, they had a huge herd of mixed elephants in front of them, including cows, bulls, and calves.

As Doctor Meriwether and Olsen proceeded to stalk the herd on foot, a young cow came walking directly towards them. They thought she might alert the herd, but, luckily, the cow stopped and trotted back to the others. Olsen froze and stood motionless for a few minutes just to be certain. Fortunately, the herd wasn't spooked and they continued. A few minutes later, two mature bulls moved to the edge of the herd and started to approach them.

Karl knew this was the doctor's best chance to get a shot off, so he indicated to the doctor to take the larger of the two bulls. The dominant bull spotted them and was starting to make aggressive gestures; he would soon start to charge. "Take your shot, now!" Olsen said. The doctor raised his .375 Holland & Holland Best Quality Bolt Action Magazine Rife that he purchased in London for a mere thirty-two thousand British Pounds. He took careful aim and fired. The mammoth bull dropped where it stood, and, with that one shot, Doctor Meriwether's hunt was over. Moments later, as Doctor Meriwether was proudly standing by his kill, he said, to no one in particular, "Well, that was $58,000 well spent."

The doctor posed for a couple of trophy photos, had the tusks, feet, and tail cut off for souvenirs, and left the carcass for the vultures. Then it was back to camp for some lunch, champagne, and a quick nap. Then he and Olsen would spend the next two days fishing on the Zambezi River, relaxing and savoring his good fortune. Three days later, just before he boarded his flight back to his home in Bemidji, Minnesota, he posted a photo of his latest kill on Facebook.

Doctor Meriwether's office looked more like an exhibit of big game hunting than a dentist's office. There were rhino heads, assorted antelope, deer, lion, and tiger heads on his walls; the floors were adorned with a variety of exotic animal skins, including zebra, tiger, and leopard; and there were dozens of photos of the doctor posing with all of his kills, showing how proud he was of all of them.

Karl drove the good doctor to the airport himself, this was the fourth safari he and Jimmy J. had partnered up for— plus J.J. was a huge tipper. As Karl's Land Rover pulled up to the KLM terminal at the Windhoek Hosea Kutako International Airport, the curbside baggage porter ran up the car with a luggage cart and opened Doctor Meriwether's door.

"Good day, sir. May I help?"

Meriwether smiled, handed the porter his ticket, and said, "Yes, thank you."

Olsen placed the car into park and rolled out of the Rover to give his patron a bear-hug goodbye. As Meriwether turned to say goodbye, he heard a large thud, and there, lying next to the left rear tire, was Karl Olsen, dead. Seeing him lying there, it reminded Meriwether how oddly similar Karl looked like the pachyderm he had just bagged days before.

The porter returned from checking in the bags to see Meriwether kneeling next to a large man on the ground. Looking up at him, Meriwether said, "He's dead. What do we do?"

"Well, unless you want to get tangled up with a police inquiry and miss your flight, I suggest you go to your gate, now." The porter handed him his ticket with the luggage tags. "Don't worry, sir, I'll take care of everything." He said as he held out his hand.

The doctor nodded, handed the porter a fifty U.S. Dollar bill, and then headed off to the KLM departure gate.

When Meriwether was out of site, the porter went through the fat man's pockets, gathering all the cash and removed Olsen's Rolex watch, a gold necklace and two gold rings, leaving his drivers license and credit cards in his wallet before he called air security.

On the airplane, before they closed the door, Doctor Meriwether sent a text to his wife: "*Had a great time. Got an enormous elephant trophy. The best safari ever. And Karl died. See you soon. Love JJ.*"

The man known as Rodin, one of the dozens of action team leaders with the North American branch of Le Gang de la Clé de Singe, a United Nation's-labeled eco-terrorist group, had just left a covert meeting held in the Flat Iron Building in lower Manhattan. Normally, the action leaders would hold meetings virtually over the Internet on 'Dark Websites,' but this particular meeting required several of the team members to meet face-to-face, as they organized and planned the latest upcoming combat missions against the abusers of Mother Nature, code name: Assisi.

On those rare occasions where face-to-face meetings were needed, they would be held in different locations so as not to give law enforcement an opportunity to capture its members—sort of like the floating crap game held in the 1950's and made famous in the play *Guys & Dolls*. They could be held anywhere from New York City to Lima, Peru.

Le Gang de la Clé de Singe had decided to set its sights on big game hunting organizations, big game hunters that kill animals and even endangered species for sport, and those who profit from selling any items from those creatures. Le Gang de la Clé de Singe had no issue with people hunting for food and, in even in some cases, for the culling of herds for the greater good and survival of the species, but killing for sport had to stop.

Rodin's team, designated code name 'Red Team', was to initially travel to Africa the following week to start their campaign against poachers, hunters, and safari outfitters. They were to take actions that would be spectacularly newsworthy, to get people talking, and to make people scared about hunting for sport.

Rodin's number two man was an Icelander, who called himself Odin after the God of war and death; he was from Reykjavík, Iceland. Odin became involved in environmental causes in high school by protesting Japanese whaling ships from being allowed refueling privileges. He then became more active in groups like Greenpeace and Sea Shepherd; finally, he yearned for a more aggressive action orientated organization like Le Gang de la Clé de Singe.

Le Gang de la Clé de Singe took its name from the American writer Edward Abbey's novel *The Monkey Wrench Gang*. The story is a fictional account of four environmental warriors, while they liberate parts of Utah and Arizona from evil road-builders, miners, and rednecks. Le Gang de la Clé de Singe was formed in Paris by two brothers whose father was the CEO of the French oil giant, Elf, which was involved in the Great Oil Sniffer Hoax of 1979.

Jean Paul and Philippe Renault were two spoiled rich kids, who wanted to shake up the establishment and piss off their father all at the same time. They started out with some college friends by organizing protest marches, which grew more and more violent over time, and as the oil scandal grew larger so did the movement. Eventually, there were clashes with riot police, who would fire off tear gas and rubber bullets and then start making arrests as the protesters fought back. Some protesters began throwing rocks and bottles, which were sometimes with Molotov Cocktails. Soon the police escalated to live ammunition, killing dozens of protesters, some as young as fourteen. The Renault brothers never dreamed that what started out as a way to piss off their father would evolve into a movement of international outrage. Over time, they extricated themselves out of the group, as Le Gang de la Clé de Singe became more and more militant and violent. They unwittingly achieved their goals beyond their wildest dreams.

As Rodin and Odin were strolling up Fifth Avenue to 34th Street before going their separate ways, Rodin charged Odin with giving the other members of the team their assignments, the procurement of travel documents, and all the necessary equipment. Rodin leaned into Odin and said, "So, you good?"

"Yeah, I'm good. Where you off to?" Odin asked.

"Oh, I have to see a dentist."

"Everything okay?"

"Yeah, just a little pain I need to get rid of." He smirked.

At four fourty-five in the evening, the reception area was empty. He could only see a lone woman sitting behind the counter; she looked to be reading a magazine. The office seemed like every dentist office in the world, with the universal smell of the combination of antiseptic and mouthwash. And then there was the inevitable sound of someone getting a new filling: the whirl of the high-speed, high pitch drill that makes one arch their backs nervously while waiting for the possibility of the drill bit touching the nerve. Then there is the switching to the slow grinding drilling, which always sends the patient pushing themselves lower into their seats, praying for the ordeal to be over.

He could see that the receptionist was deep into the article about the English Royal Family, and she didn't notice him standing in front of the counter until he spoke, which gave her quite a start.

"Hi, I have an appointment with Doctor Meriwether."

"Oh! I'm sorry, I didn't hear you come in," she said, as she quickly tried to hide the magazine.

"I'm sorry, didn't mean to frighten you. I'm in town on business just for the day—I'm flying out tonight—but I have a killer toothache."

She tapped a couple keys on her computer, looked at the man, and smiled. "You must be Mr. Clark."

"That's right, Lewis Clark."

"Do you have insurance, Mr. Clark?"

"I do, but, unfortunately, you're out of my network."

"How would you like to pay?"

"Would cash be acceptable?"

"Cash? Wouldn't a credit card be more convenient?" The receptionist looked surprised.

"Well, it would, except I only have my company credit card with me."

"Okay, well I'm guessing it should be just a simple filling, which would be a total of three hundred and twenty-five dollars."

Lewis reached inside his front right pants pocket, pulled out a large wad of bills, and counted out the exact amount. Handing it to her, he said, "There you are."

"Thank you, Mr. Clark, and here is your receipt. If, for some reason, it's more than a filling, then you can settle the difference with the doctor afterward. Why don't you have a seat in the waiting room, and the doctor will see you in a few minutes. In the meantime, can you fill out these forms, please?"

"Of course. Wow, this is some office you have here. The doctor must be some sort of big game hunter. Did he kill all these animals himself?"

"Oh yes, Doctor Meriwether is quite a world-famous hunter."

"I can't wait to meet him."

"Mr. Clark, what time is your flight? Depending on what the doctor finds, you might not get out of here for at least an hour or so."

"Oh, not until eleven, I have plenty of time."

Clark went into the empty waiting room and sat down opposite of the receptionist; Judge Judy was on the TV. The best he could tell, the case involved a woman who lent her man-friend three hundred dollars, and he never paid her back, claiming he thought it was a kind of gift for his love-making skills.

The receptionist was preparing to leave, as it was almost five o'clock, and the patient that was in with the doctor when he arrived was leaving as well. She was a middle-aged woman, wearing skintight blue jeans and an over-sized gray jersey that had the word PINK printed on it. Her cheeks were so swollen from having all of her wisdom teeth pulled, she looked like a chipmunk that was storing nuts for the winter.

"Would you like me to leave the TV on for you, Mr. Clark?" the receptionist asked.

"No, thank you."

"Alrighty. And, please, if you would leave your paperwork on my desk..."

"Sure thing."

She picked up the remote, aimed it at the TV, and then Judge Judy was gone. She walked back into where then patient rooms were and shouted, "I'm leaving now Doctor Meriwether. I'll lock up on my way out. Don't forget you have a patient, a Mr. Clark, to see you."

A voice from down the hall responded, "Can you send him back, Mrs. Ponser? To room six."

"Mr. Clark, the doctor can see you now, straight back to room six."

He got up and proceeded back to room six. As he passed the receptionist, he stopped. "Thank you, Miss, and have a good evening."

"Thank you, Mr. Clark. Hope everything will be okay with your tooth; Doctor Meriwether is the best."

He continued down the hall to room six, where he saw Doctor Meriwether setting out some instruments. As he entered the patient room, he heard the front door being locked.

"Please, come in and have a seat; I'm afraid it's just me. My assistant's baby isn't feeling well, so she had to leave, but, I can assure you, I can handle everything myself. Now, what seems to be bothering you, Mr. Clark?"

Mr. Clark smiled, "You are, Doctor Meriwether. You are."

KLM flight 6059 landed at Jomo Kenyatta International in Nairobi, Kenya at 11:09PM. He was tired from his eighteen-plus hour flight from Minneapolis when he went thru customs. The customs agent asked all the usual questions: was he here for business or pleasure; how long was he planning on staying; is he bringing any large sums of currency into the country; and where in Nairobi is he staying? After passing thru customs, he was met at the airport exit by Odin and three other team members: Hazael, a Syrian from Aleppo, Pelé, a Brazilian, and Lu Wei from Nantong, which was just north of Shanghai. Rodin shook each one of their hands. "Gentlemen, how is everyone? Good to see you all again."

Hazael smiled. "We're all good and ready to go."

"Are the others here as well?"

"Yes, you're the last to arrive."

"I do apologize; I had to see a dentist."

Pelé looked concerned. "Is everything okay?"

Rodin smiled, "Oh, yeah. I just had to head off a nagging problem. Shall we go?"

Odin led the way to the car parked out in front of the KLM passenger pick up and drop off area. Leaving a parked car was supposed to be illegal, but nobody was ever towed or ticketed here, you might have your vehicle stolen, but nobody ever got a ticket. Rodin threw his duffel bag into the back of the Toyota Fore-Runner, and, as he was climbing into the shotgun seat, Hazael asked if he wanted to drive. Rodin just smiled, settled into the seat, and closed his eyes. "I'm good, thanks."

The Toyota turned left out of the airport and onto Mombasa Road, heading north toward the central business district. As Hazael drove, Rodin started to remove parts of his travel disguise—a false beard, colored contacts, and the ponytail extension. After traveling ten miles on Mombasa Road, they turned right onto Kenyatta Avenue until they reached the Sarova Stanley Hotel. The five-star hotel is the oldest hotel in the city, having been established in 1902 by English businesswoman Mayence Bent when the city was just a railway stop. As they pulled up, the valet rushed to open Rodin's door. "Welcome to the Stanley, sir."

"Thank you."

"Can I help you with your bags?"

"Thank you, no. I just have this small duffel bag."

"Very good, sir."

As they headed into the lobby, Hazael held out a key and said, "You're already checked in. Do you want to head up to your room?"

"No. If you all are up to it, why don't we all go to the Exchange Bar for a quick nightcap?"

Odin asked, "Do you want me to get the others?"

"Nah, it's late. We'll all get together in the morning. I just need a beer and some time to relax."

The Exchange Bar had a presence to it that no other bar could boast. The first thing to hit you was the rich red palate; it almost seemed to have a texture of its own. You were surrounded by smooth leather, polished by years of use, and by glossy, shining mahogany. As they entered the bar, they passed by a photo of Ernest Hemingway and his wife cuddling a lion cub, and further down the wall, in a corner, is a small print of Saint Francis of Assisi; Rodin points to it. "Assisi. Must be a good sign."

The group of four were the only ones in the bar. "Are we too late?" Rodin asked the bartender.

"No, sir, please sit anywhere. Are you gentlemen interested in eating? I can place an order with the kitchen."

Rodin looked at the others; it didn't look like there were any takers. "No, I think we'll just have drinks. I'll have a beer, whatever's cold. Guys?"

Odin asked for a Diet Coke, Lu Wei and Hazael both ordered scotch & water, and Pele had his signature drink, a Caipirinha. They sat by the window, gathered around a small mahogany table. When the drinks came, Rodin raised his glass and purposed a toast: "To a successful mission." An energetic group response of "Here, here" followed.

Detective Johansson and Detective Wilson met back at the Bemidji, Minnesota Police Station, the morning after the gruesome discovery of Doctor Meriwether. Just as Johansson sat down at his desk, the phone rang, "Hello? Oh, hey, Doc. Yeah, okay. Thanks, Doc and send up the report when you get a chance. Bye."

Wilson was standing by Johansson's desk. "The coroner?"

"Yeah, Meriwether was shot in the heart with what looks to be a 9mm, then beheaded. I guess that's a blessing of sorts. He also said there was a letter found in his pants pocket from that French outfit. He's sending that and the report over in about an hour."

"I called Interpol last night to see what they could tell me about the Monkey Wrench Gang."

"Yeah? What did they have to say?"

"Well, it seems that the group started around 1979 in France. They're named after a book about a group of environmental activists in the Southwest. Two French brothers, whose dad was a big cheese at a French oil company, started the group. It started out as just some small-time protest group but quickly grew into a worldwide movement.

Over the years, they have gotten more and more bold, aggressive and violent. They have no qualms about using violence. They've sunken Japanese whaling ships and several pirate fishing vessels, after rescuing and freeing the people on board, who had been virtual slaves; most had been held captive for years.

There's a kind of a weird Robin Hood thing going on. They attack any person or organization that they feel are anti-environment with a vengeance. It seems that they are well-funded by anonymous donors from all over the world. A lot of the groups operate autonomously, so, if they get captured, they only know a small portion of the puzzle. Some of the leaders of the so-called 'cell' or 'fringe groups' have even committed suicide when captured, so as not to give away secret information."

"Fuck me, man."

"Yeah, they make some of these other world environmental groups, like Greenpeace and Sea Shepherds, look like wimps."

"So, it sounds like they might be going after big game hunters now, if Meriwether was indeed a target of this monkey gang."

"Could be. It will be interesting to read the letter that Meriwether had on him."

"Let it be known that, from this day forth, Le Gang de la Clé de Singe declares a proclamation of war against all Poachers, Big Game Hunters, all Big Game Safari Outfits, as well as anybody anywhere in the world that targets, kills, profits, and/or supports the killing of any animals that are endangered or any animals that are hunted for sport. Be forewarned: do so at your own peril. You will be hunted down and pay with your lives. Be it man, or woman, there will be no exceptions and no mercy; we will show no quarter. You have been warned."

"Holy shit!" Johansson said half to Wilson and half to himself.

"They've sent this message to all the major news outlets about a half hour ago. It's gone viral, worldwide, in a matter of minutes. You can imagine the reaction they're getting. Especially from the NRA."

"They must be going apeshit."

"And every gun club, hunting organization, as well as all the right-wing militia nuts—everyone is going off the freaking deep end. The NRA has declared its own war on the Monkey Wrench Gang, saying that they're not going to be bullied by any French pansy outfit. They're encouraging their members to go out and hunt in packs."

"It's going to get ugly, fast."

"I went online and found that the State Department has just issued a worldwide warning to all big game safari hunters overseas to be extremely careful, and they're even warning big game hunters here in the US to be vigilant. They're asking people to postpone their hunting trips until they can evaluate the situation. Uncle Sam is taking this very seriously, and, of course, the French government has condemned the group's actions."

"People are going to be freaking out; I can imagine a lot of innocent people getting shot just for being in the wrong place at the wrong time. I bet these Frenchies are hoping these hunters will start panicking and shoot each other, thinking the other guy is a terrorist. And moose season starts next week."

"Merde."

"What?"

"Merde. That's French for shit."

"Not funny, Wilson. True, but not funny."

"Excusez moi."

"Asshole."

Rodin met the others in the hotel lobby around 0800. "Morning all. You boys had breakfast yet?"

Odin nodded. "You?"

"Yeah, I had room service. A couple eggs, toast, and coffee. Where are the others?"

"They've left already; said they'd meet us there."

"Good."

Lu Wei held out his iPad with an email marked URGENT. As Rodin scanned it, he said under his breath, "Those motherfuckers." The email had information about a group of Kenyan poachers that recently killed five bull elephants by poisoning them in the Simba Hills National Reserve. They had tainted salt licks with oranges that were laced with cyanide, which caused them to die a violent, agonizing death.

He looked at them and said, "Gentlemen lets go to work."

The Toyota was ready and waiting for them in the hotel driveway, doors open and the valet waiting by the driver's door with the keys in hand. Pelé took the wheel, Rodin, Odin and Hazael sat in the back, with Lu Wei riding shotgun.

Lu Wei was looking at his iPad when he turned to Rodin, "Say, what was the name of your dentist?"

"Why do you ask?"

"I see where a big-time game hunting dentist from Bemidji, Minnesota met a rather messy and untimely death. It's raising all kinds of hell in the States. It's got everyone, from the U.S. President to the UN Secretary-General, talking about what barbarians we are and what to do to stop us."

"Well, like they say, there's no such thing as bad publicity."

"Did you really mount his head on the wall?

"It seemed like a nice form of poetic justice, don't you think? Hanging there between his Zebra and African Oryx trophies, I thought he looked in his element. Anyway, people are talking, and hopefully, soon, they'll think real hard before going out and blasting the shit out of anything that walks for fun. I just wish that fat fuck Olsen hadn't dropped dead before I got to him."

Pelé adjusted the rearview mirror to see the passengers in the back seat and announced, "Next stop: Simba Hills National Reserve."

The drive to the Reserve took just over nine hours. Heading south on the Mombasa Road, they skirted another National Reserve, Tsavo West National Park. Off in the distance, to their right, they could see snow-capped Mount Kilimanjaro. They had prearranged a rendezvous point with six other team members to meet up at 1800 hours three miles due east of the small village of Mkomba.

When they arrived, they parked their vehicle next to an olive green Land Rover Defender 110, a mile and a half away from Mwaluganie Elephant Sanctuary, at the bottom of the hill where the camp was set up. The men had set up a cold camp: no tents, no fire, no footprint; they wanted to appear as if they had not been there. Come morning, two members would take the vehicles north on the coast to a safe house in Mombasa and await the pickup call; could be a day, a week, or a month.

In the back of the Land Rover, patiently sitting, was Buster, a pure breed American Leopard Hound, who Rodin had used on several previous missions. Buster would accompany him out into the fields and lay by his side, waiting any number of commands—he could attack either human or beast, he could be called upon to do tracking, and he was an overall team morale booster. Rodin gave a short whistle and Buster leaped out of the back window, standing at attention with tail wagging and eyes locked on Rodin, waiting for a command. Rodin looked down at him and said, "At ease." Buster sat down. Rodin knelt and barked at the dog, "Come." The dog ran into his arms and gave him an exuberant, face-licking greeting. "Good boy, Buster. Good boy."

After a few minutes, Rodin composed himself and recovered the military decorum, as did Buster. Rodin looked around and greeted the other members of his team. Rodin recognized and had worked with all but two of the men; an African American from Birmingham, Alabama, who called himself Vulcan, and a Hungarian named Liszt. Both were fairly new and were assigned to his team to gain combat experience and be evaluated under fire.

Not everyone is cut out for field warfare. Some are asked to be reassigned to less aggressive assignments, and some ask to be reassigned after finding out that they aren't cut out for frontline action. That night, everyone was just making small talk while double-checking their gear; off in the distance, they could hear the sounds of an elephant herd, as well a rowdy pack of hyenas mixing it up with a pride of lions over a recent kill. More often, lions lose out to the hyenas because there are so many in the hyena's pack, however the odds tip to the lion's favor if there's a male lion nearby.

Rodin could see that both Vulcan and Liszt seemed a little uneasy with all the animal activity, as well as the prospects of the upcoming action. They were sitting close to each other, not saying much. Rodin walked over and sat down between them. "You boys okay?"

Liszt smiled. "Yes, sir, just a little anxious. It's my first time out in the field with a small team."

"What sort of assignments have you participated in?"

"Mostly covert actions against big oil companies. You know, drilling rigs, refineries and pipeline shutdowns; that sort of thing."

"Gotcha. Anything up close or mostly distance?"

"Sir?"

"Up close, you know, hand to hand."

"Well, it did get pretty hairy on Rig 88 in Prudhoe Bay, near Deadhorse."

"Yeah, I heard about that; nasty stuff. You were on that detail?"

"Yeah. Seemed like they were waiting for us; we lost three that night. They lost eight, and, after everything, the big boom had to shut that puppy down. They never did reopen it."

"How about you ,Vulcan, seen any action?"

"Not with the Gang, but I did six tours in Iraq as a Ranger sniper."

"Thank you for your service."

"Thank you, sir. I heard you didn't serve when called."

"No, I didn't. It was a different time and different war. Although I can't say either Viet Nam or Iraq were justified wars in my opinion, not that that lessens the bravery and honor of those who served. I did, however, serve in the French Foreign Legion; we were involved in several humanitarian efforts where combat was required."

"How long did you serve?"

"Twelve years. Then I was recruited into the Gang."

"You ever kill anyone, sir?"

"Yeah. You being a sniper, I know you have."

"Yeah, but I'm not like some of the other guys in my unit, where they bragged about the number of kills they had. Even though the guys I killed we're considered bad guys, I guess they probably felt that they had God on their side, just like we did."

"All through history, it's been one God versus another God, and it's the poor warrior who pays the ultimate price. I just hope everybody's God appreciates the effort."

Liszt settled on the ground and laid his head on his knapsack. "This time, no God's involved."

Rodin turned to Liszt as he started to walk away. "Well, if you do feel the need, you can pray to Fauna, the Roman Goddess of animals, if it helps. Now you boys try and get some sleep, we're up at first light. I'll be taking the first watch; Lu Wei will take the deuce."

The horizon was starting to get a golden hue, as the sun was on the verge of peaking over the savannah plains; in the sky, there wasn't a cloud anywhere to be seen, which usually meant they were going to be in for another scorcher. The team started slipping into their ghillie suits and wrapping their rifles in tactical sniper veils. Even Buster wore a specially designed ghillie suit made especially for 'Dogs of War'.

Rodin checked the team to make sure they were fully prepared; they were going to spread out along a half a mile line and lay immobile, possibly for ten to twelve hours in sweltering heat.

"Did you all remember to put on the Rid-A-Tick patches? Those little bastards' bites can kill you if left untreated." They all nodded their heads affirmative. "Okay, and are everyone's radio headsets working?" Again, all reacted affirmatively. "Now, listen up. Odin is going to stay up here and be our spotter, code name Red Flyer. He will be giving us updates and locations on any targets. Feel free to take small doses, but stay frosty as things can happen quickly. Don't worry, he knows where everyone will be and will be keeping a sharp eye out. If you feel, at any point, that you need to abandon your post, you must communicate with Red Flyer; you do not just abandon your position. Is that understood? Any questions?"

Odin said, "As you make your way to your positions, I will be checking with each of you to make sure there aren't any last-minute glitches with your headsets before you get to your failsafe marks. I'll be communicating with you all during the day. Good luck, men."

The men silently started to make their way to their predetermined positions. Keeping low, they walked for half a mile till they reached the tall grass, then crawled for another mile until they reached their positions where they settled in. The five-man team formed a semi-circle; Rodin and Buster were the center-point. Along the way, Red Flyer checked in with them all, making sure their headsets worked. The sun was slowly rising in the sky by the time Red Flyer alerted the men of all the wildlife in their vicinity; there was a small herd of elephants meandering onto the fringes of their designated parameter to their left, as well as giraffes, zebras, gazelles and a few impalas, but no predators.

Odin sat high up in the canopy of one of the three Acacia trees on top of the hill, overlooking the plains below where his team hid. He primarily relied on his Steiner 10X50 binoculars, but, just to be safe, and to have an extra pair of eyes in the sky, Lu Wei operated a French Aerospatiale C.22 drone, which was equipped with two Hero four Black GoPro cameras and two Aster missiles in the event that any shit hit the fan. The C.22 could stay up for twelve hours and even had night vision capabilities.

Every team member was equipped with an M2010 Enhanced Sniper Rifle, a rifle the U.S. Army had developed to give extra range and help snipers in a mountainous and desert terrain like Afghanistan. It had a computerized scope that could mark a selected target, and uses a special trigger that doesn't pull until it's sure the bullet will land where intended. The effective range is over one thousand two hundred and fifty yards.

By one o'clock, the temperature was clicking one hundred and one degrees in the shade, and there wasn't any shade for the men out in the field. Each man had a Camelback Ambush One Hundred Oz. Antidote Pack filled with a special concoction for anti-dehydration; even Buster carried a special pack that he could drink from.

At 2:45, Red Flyer placed a call, "Attention Red Team, looks like we have bogies heading your way, coming in at 10 o'clock. Red Team, confirm." Each of the team members acknowledged.

"Red Flyer, more details please." Rodin inquired.

"You have a green Toyota pickup with what looks like four targets. They look heavily armed, and they are heading toward the small elephant herd to your right at about 2 o'clock."

"Red Flyer, I see them. Red team, wait for my command."

They all replied, "Roger that."

"I will assign targets."

The pickup stopped about a quarter mile from the herd of mostly female and baby elephants. Four men got out of the vehicle; each was carrying an AK47 and slowly made their way towards the herd.

Rodin assessed the targets and quickly gave instructions, "Red 2, blue shirt. Red 3, brown shirt. Red 4, plaid shirt. I will take the ball cap. Red 5 backup. Understood?" All confirmed. "On my order."

The four men found cover behind a small clump of toothbrush trees. As the elephant herd neared, the men rose up from their crouching position and started to aim their weapons. Rodin calmly said, "Fire." There were four flashes, and, in an instant, all four men were dead.

"Red Flyer, this is Red 1. Assessment."

"Red 1, hold position; we have another vehicle heading in your direction. Looks to be a faded red Ford F-650 flatbed with three men in the back and two in the cab. ETA four minutes."

"Copy that, Red Flyer. Red Team this is Red 1. Get ready for round two. I will assign targets."

The red truck approached cautiously, as the men standing in the back were looking for their compadres and watching the herd of elephants start to drift away from their direction. Of the five, only two had AK-47's; the others carried machetes. They stopped their truck next to the pickup; the driver and passenger searched the pickup while the others started to spread out, looking for their missing colleagues.

"Red Team, listen up. Red 2, driver. Red 3, passenger. Red 4, cameo pants. Red 5, khaki pants. I'll take grey beard. Copy?"

They all copied.

"On my mark."

The man with the grey beard spotted the bodies and started to yell out their names as he ran towards them. The others followed, and, as they reached the pile of the dead, Red 1 gave the order, "Fire." Five flashes, five dead.

Once again, Red 1 said, "Red Flyer, this is Red 1. Assessment."

"Red 1, you are all clear."

"Red Flyer, copy. Red Team, advance." With that, they stood up and made their way towards the trucks and the victims. Buster walked by Rodin's side until they were about fifty feet away from the bodies, when Rodin sent Buster to investigate to see if, by chance, anyone was faking death; they weren't.

They laid out the nine men neatly in a row; arms folded across their chest, and each with a yellow flag of the black skull and crossed monkey wrenches attached around their necks. They placed, inside each of the men's pockets, the 'proclamation of war' issued by Le Gang de la Clé de Singe, as well as copies inside the cabs of both trucks, where they found oranges laced with cyanide in the back of the Ford 650. They rendered each of the men's weapons unusable; then they policed the area, making sure that they left no clues or evidence. On the way back to base, they even picked up after Buster just in case someone tried to retrieve a DNA sample. Then they headed back up the hill to rendezvous with Red Flyer. Mission accomplished.

Detective Wilson walked over to Detective Johansson's desk with the CSI report, and, by his body language, Johansson could tell that there wasn't a lot he could expect in the way of good news.

Wilson plopped the folder down on Johansson's desk. "All they found was one index fingerprint on the clipboard that doesn't belong to any of the employees or regular patients, and our lab and the boys at the FBI are running it now."

"Well keep a good thought: at least it's something."

"We need some kind of break; the press is relentless."

"Oh, I forgot to tell you, we're getting a couple of special visitors meeting with us this afternoon."

"Batman and Robin?"

"You wish! No, two guys from Interpol."

"Really? Interpol."

"Yeah, apparently they've been chasing this Monkey Fist Gang for years."

"Monkey Wrench."

"Whatever. They'll be here around three. An Inspector Morris from London and a South African, Inspector Volker. You available?"

"You bet. Wouldn't miss it."

"Great, I want—" Johansson's phone rang. "Johansson. Really? That's interesting; that's fucking interesting. Okay, thanks. Yeah, yeah, real funny."

"What?"

"That was the results of our unidentified fingerprint."

"And?"

"Well, it turns out that Elvis isn't dead after all, he apparently has joined the Monkey Fist Gang."

"Monkey Wrench."

"Whatever."

"So the fingerprint found at the murder scene of Doctor Meriwether was really that of Elvis Presley?"

"Yeah, I don't know how they pulled that off. These guys are a bunch of real freaking comedians, except I ain't laughing."

Once the Red Team reached camp, they were out of there within minutes. Odin had radioed the pickup team, and they were waiting for them by the time the team reached the bottom of the hill. The Red Team stowed their gear, and they were gone. Mad Max, the pickup team leader said to Rodin,

"Man, that was quick. I was expecting to be waiting around for at least a week. How did it go?"

Rodin, looking at his GPS, said, "Mission accomplished. I'm sure it will be all over news outlets within hours. Odin, did you send out the call?"

"Yeah, just about the time you reached camp."

"Excellent. We might as well kick back; it's about fifteen hours till our next assignment, the Kizigo Game Reserve." He picked up a walkie-talkie. "Team, I just wanted to say how very proud I am of everyone. I know how tough this job can be, but take solace and pride in that we saved a lot of elephants' lives today. Now, it's a long journey to Tanzania, so everybody try and get some rest."

The two vehicles took separate routes as a precaution; they had a preset rendezvous point and would plan to meet up at the river just south of Wangama.

When Rodin's vehicle reached the Kenyan border at six o'clock, the border outpost was vacant, the Tanzanian guard posted opposite of his Kenyan counterpart just waved the Toyota thru the checkpoint without bothering to stop them. At seven o'clock, Max clicked on the radio to try and catch the news on BBC radio.

"Good evening, I'm Nigel Williams, and this is the BBC World Headline News. Our top story this hour comes from the Mwaluganie Elephant Sanctuary in Kenya, where the bodies of nine known poachers were found shot to death. The eco-terrorist group known as Le Gang de la Clé de Singe has claimed responsibility.

"The men were found with yellow flags bearing the skull and crossed wrenches around each of their necks, along with a letter of declaration of war. Worldwide commendation is pouring in as many..."

"Well, looks like the message is starting to get out," Max said.

"Let's hope so," Rodin said as he reached over and switched the station over to Radio Kwizera, a soft jazz station. Then he pulled his ball cap down over his eyes and drifted off to sleep.

Max looked over and said, "Sweet dreams."

A short burst of snoring was Rodin's only response.

Rodin's real name was Todd Styles, your typical surfer boy from Southern California. He was just over six feet tall, had long blond, sun-bleached hair, an athletic body, and was who many thought could have been a true surfing champion if it wasn't for the Viet Nam War.

In 1969, while attending classes at Santa Monica City College, Todd attended an anti-war protest that turned violent, and he was arrested for the first time. After that, he started breaking into government buildings, setting files on fire, regularly scrapping with police, burning draft cards, and, in general, being a real pain in the government's ass. Finally, he made the FBI's hit list, and they issued arrest warrants, so Todd did what any patriotic antiwar protester would do: he ran away to Canada. He was lucky he had a distant uncle living in Montreal who agreed to take him in.

He lived in Montreal with his uncle for almost seven years, doing odd jobs on ships traveling up and down the Saint Lawrence Seaway, while still working with anti-war groups protesting the Viet Nam War. Then in 1974, Todd was almost arrested; he managed to elude the police by just a couple of hours. Having learned to speak French fluently while living in Montreal, he decided to go to France and try to go underground. He made his way over to France by working on a supertanker as a merchant seaman. He worked in France for several years, doing mostly menial labor jobs; he worked as a waiter in Nice, a bouncer at a nightclub in Paris, worked on a fishing vessel out of Brest and a librarian at the Université Jean Moulin 3 in Lyon, always-just one-step ahead of Interpol.

He had thoughts of turning himself into the police; he was tired of being on the run and always looking over his shoulder. One night, while having coffee at a cafe with a friend in Lyon, his friend jokingly said, 'Dude, why don't you just join the French Foreign Legion. Hell, they don't care what you've done."

Out of desperation, he decided to go and see if, in fact, they would accept a fugitive of the law. So, in 1978 he walked up to the recruiting center, knocked on the door, and was immediately invited to see if he could pass a battery of exams to see if he could qualify. The first three days were devoted to the teaching the new recruits just what they are getting themselves into and the terms of their five-year contracts that they are required to sign. Then, for the next two weeks, they undergo psychological and personality tests, logic tests, medical exam, physical condition tests, motivation and security interviews. Then, if they pass, they sign the contract. The same week, he passed all his tests and was accepted into the Legion. No questions about his past were asked, so he took the oath and became a French citizen.

For someone who was so antiwar, he found that the difference between the US Army fighting in the Viet Nam War and what he was doing in the French Foreign Legion was somehow more just in that he played more of a peacekeeper role rather than the aggressor.

In 1982, he was part of a peacekeeping operation of a Multinational Force in Lebanon during the Lebanese Civil War along with the 31st Brigade. He spent two years there and was lucky to not have fired a shot. He did see combat in the Gulf War, as his Legion force, comprising of 27 different nationalities, was attached to the French 6th Light Armored Division, whose mission was to protect the Coalition's left flank. During the Gulf War, they operated in support of the U.S. Army's 82nd Airborne Division and provided support for the units bomb squad. After the cease-fire, he helped clear mines alongside a Royal Australian Navy Clearance Diver Team Unit. His war ended after a hundred hours of fighting on the ground.

After several more peacekeeping deployments to Sarajevo, Bosnia, and Herzegovina in 1993, Rwanda, Central African Republic and Congo-Brazzaville in 1997, Todd had seen enough. It just so happened that when his latest contract was coming to an end, he read an article about a French group of eco-terrorists called Le Gang de la Clé de Singe, or 'The Monkey Wrench Gang.'

The article told how an international organization had decided they had had enough with playing by the rules; many countries considered them as pirates, thugs, and gangsters. They sank whaling ships, blew up oil rigs, attacked deforestation logging camps, assaulted company headquarters, and, on occasion, kidnapped their leaders. Unlike Greenpeace and Sea Shepherd's, thèse guys didn't hesitate to take lives when they felt it was just. Their belief was that corporations have been destroying and killing nature for profit for generations, so now Mother Nature's declaring WAR. It's payback time!

Todd had seen the massive destruction that man is capable of doing for pure greed, and how unable or, more likely, unwilling governments have been to curtail the corporation's gluttony and selfishness. After reading more articles and doing a lot of research on the group, he started writing letters to the editors of newspapers and international magazines, all in favor of the group.

At the end of his latest contract, he walked off the base he was stationed in at Brazzaville, the Capital of the Republic of the Congo. The Legion offered him transport back to France, which he declined; after saying goodbye to his comrades, he just walked out of the base gates, carrying all his worldly possessions in the duffel bag hoisted on his shoulder. He was a quarter mile from the base, when a woman, who strongly resembled a young Meryl Streep while wearing a black beret and a camo shirt, blue jeans, and black Converse high-tops, approached him. As they met, she smiled and asked in a French accent, "Todd?"

"Oui. Et vous êtes?"

"Je suis Venus. Parles-tu Anglais?"

"Yes. Can I help you?"

"I hope so," she said, as she unbuttoned her shirt and revealed a yellow tee shirt with a black skull and crossed monkey wrench logo on it. "Where are you off to?"

"Nowhere in particular as, to be honest, I really haven't given it much thought. I was going to see where this road would take me. By the way, nice t-shirt. I like it."

"I thought you might. We were really impressed with your writings and articles, and we're hoping that you would be interested in joining our little group."

"As a writer?"

"Well, if that's how you feel you best can contribute to the cause, we always need good writers to help tell the outside of the story, but we thought you might want to take, let's say, a more active role."

"That sounds more my speed."

"Great. There are some folks I'd like you to meet, if you're interested."

"Lead on."

She waved her arm and gave a whistle that would make anyone hailing a cab in New York City jealous. An old beat up red Toyota 4 Runner pulled up, with two guys sitting in the front and one guy in the back. She opened the rear driver side door and indicated for him to get in first. He walked to the back of the vehicle, opened the back hatch, and threw his duffel bag in, slammed it shut, then slowly walked back to her. She watched him and was impressed at his deliberate movements and nonchalant attitude. As he passed her and climbed in, she joined him and shut the door. She half turned to him and said, "Todd, I'd like you to meet Connie, B-Reel, and Sassoon."

The driver looked to be in his late fifties, long gray hair pulled back into a ponytail, wearing tattered blue jeans and a black Converse t-shirt. He glanced in the rearview, smiled, and said, "Hey man, I'm Connie."

The man sitting in the front passenger seat was a twenty-something black man with dreadlocks, wearing sunglasses and JVC headphones that were hooked up to his Sony Walkman. He had on a Hawaiian shirt with khakis and was sitting half turned in his seat. He held up two fingers, showing a peace sign, "Yo, welcome to the dance."

Sitting next to Rodin in the back seat was a small fat man wearing a French beret, black, plastic, round-rim glasses, and sporting a rather large mustache. He was wearing an off-white linen suit that was extremely wrinkled and looked like it hadn't been cleaned in several weeks. He smiled and nodded, "Bonjour, mon ami. Je suis Sassoon."

The SUV pulled away and headed west towards the port of Pointe-Noire, the second largest city following the capital, Brazzaville. It was a seven-hour drive over dirt roads and through mostly plantation fields of cassava, a starchy tuberous root that was a major source of carbohydrates in the Republic of the Congo.

Over the next seven hours, they got to know each other, and they discussed many things, but mostly they were vetting each other to see if they were a right fit together. Todd liked the fact that four totally different individuals were united by different reasons but for the same cause. He was curious about their reasons for joining such a militant group.

"So, guys, why did you decide to join, Connie, where you from?"

Connie never looked into the rearview; he just kept his eyes on the road as he spoke, "Bozeman, Montana. I worked as a ranch hand for several cattle ranches in and around Bozeman pretty much my whole life. Well, for me, it was when I was working on the Flying B Bison Ranch that the government had approved the construction of an oil pipeline to transverse the whole ranch. The building of the damn thing was bad enough, but then, because of shoddy workmanship, of course, there was a massive oil spill, which killed several dozen bison and a large portion of the ranch was rendered useless. The oil company received a slap on the wrist, and, when a bunch of us protested, we all got thrown into the hoosegow."

"You got arrested just for protesting?"

"Well, that and maybe all the damage we'd done to their pipeline and equipment might have something to do with it too," he said, laughing. "So, after I made bail, I hightailed it out of there, headed up to Saskatoon, and joined up with some like-minded fellas who don't like big oil as much as me. Hey, I've been over whole the world fucking with these bastards and enjoying every minute of it. I met up with my main man B-Reel about two years ago when we were messing with Exxon on one of their offshore drill rigs in the Gulf of Mexico. Right, man?"

"Right on, right on, my brother." B-Reel patted the gray-haired hippie on the shoulder; he turned down his Walkman slightly and picked up the story. "Ya see, me and my man, Connie, and four other brothers were paddling out in the dead of night to do a little sumpin' sumpin' to try and slow down production, ya know, a little sabotage. Right after we planted some C-4 plastic on two of the rig's legs, all of a sudden, out of nowhere, came six Zodiacs filled with oil company goons; they came guns-a-blazing. A bunch of our brothers was shot and panic ensued. As we were making our get-away, we capsized; two of our mates didn't make it, and I would have been a goner if it hadn't been for my main man, Connie. He kept his cool and helped me and two other brothers back to the mother ship."

Connie kept looking straight ahead and said sheepishly, "It wasn't no big deal, man. We all helped each other."

"Sheet man, you the man! And just as we was bushwhacked, Connie even had the moxie to set the timers.

As we made it to safety, *Ka-Boom*" B-Reel threw his arms out in an exaggerated gesture. "And that mother came a-tumbling down. It was a thing of beauty."

Todd looked at the two men sitting up front, shook his head, and said, "Wow, that's the kind of commitment and dedication I'm used to from my time in the Legion, very impressive."

Venus sat forward, leaned toward Sassoon, and touched his leg, "Tell Todd about the Parc Forestier et Zoologique de Hann affair."

The diminutive man blushed and smiled as if he was asked to reveal an embarrassing secret. He fidgeted in his seat and looked out the window.

She tapped his leg again, prodding him, saying, "Go on, don't be shy."

He turned his head to her and nodded okay. He looked at Todd and spoke softly, "Well, Monsieur, I was working at a private Clinique Vétérinaire in Dakar as one of three veterinarians. We handled everything from domestic animals, to farm, and the occasional wild animals. You see, the Senegal zoo was too poor to have a veterinarian on staff, so, on occasion, we would be called upon to attend to the animals. I was the newest member of the staff, as I had just graduated from veterinary school in Paris and wanted to start my career with some adventure and not just attend to cats and dogs. So when I heard about a position in Dakar, Senegal, I took it. Then, one day, I was called upon with great urgency to come to the Parc Forestier et Zoologique de Hann, as one of the male lions had been injured. This was to be my first experience working at the Zoo, but, when I got there, I could see that the cat had been badly beaten. His attendant claimed that the lion had attacked him while he was feeding him, and that he feared for his life. I talked to several witnesses, who said that he was teasing the lion and that the man was the aggressor.

After attending to the lion, I went around and noticed that many of the animals had been abused. I went to the proper authorities and lodged a formal complaint. All I received was, as you say, the runaround.

It turned out that we at the clinique would get calls to come out to the Zoo once or twice a month for an injured animal. My fellow doctors and I continued to complain to the officials as well writing letters to the newspaper, but to no avail. It wasn't until one day I was visited by a man from Le Gang de la Clé de Singe, who said that he had read some of my letters and articles and said that he could help. I had, of course, heard about the organization and was weary because of all the wild stories that I had read about them. I told him that I didn't think I wanted or needed their help. He said for me to think it over, and he would, on occasion, stop by to see if I had changed my mind.

Several weeks passed, when I received a call from the Zoo saying that one of the chimpanzees had died. I was prepping for surgery on a farmer's ox, so one of my colleagues went there and brought back the body to do an autopsy on the poor thing. We found that the young chimp had been beaten and strangled to death. Two days later, the man from the Gang came by again, and I finally decided to ask for their help.

One week passed with no calls from the Zoo, then two weeks, a month, and six months—nothing. I had heard from people at the Zoo that several of the attendants had quit suddenly, and they were replaced with more caring and responsible people. It seems that the people who left had been relatives and friends of the Zoo's officials and that was the reason that they were protected. But, it was months later that the story of what persuaded them to leave was revealed.

It seems that, late one night, the three men who were responsible for the mistreatment of the animals were abducted at gunpoint and taken to one of the lion enclosures at the Zoo. One of the men who were responsible for the teasing and torturing of the lions was stripped naked, bound and gagged, restrained to a chair with his legs spread open and had honey poured on his genitals. A female lion was released into the cage. The lioness, I'm told, went directly to the man and proceeded to maul and nearly castrate him, before she retreated back into her enclosure. The other two men observed this and were told that if there were any more abuse of any kind to any of the animals, they too would face a similar punishment. The next day, all three men resigned, and the man who was mauled was taken to the hospital and soon died of an infection. The case is still unsolved.

I was later contacted by the man from Le Gang de la Clé de Singe, asking me if I would be interested in joining the group, as they are always wanting to have people from the medical field, both doctors and veterinarians. I was, at first, uncertain, but, the more I thought about how best that I could serve abused, injured and even endangered animals, I decided to join the noble cause. So here I sit, mon ami."

"Wow, that's quite a story, my friend, I can honestly say that I'll never eat honey again without thinking of you."

Todd sat quietly, just absorbing his fellow passenger's stories while staring out the front window. For the next two hours, with the combination of the monotonous scenery of vast fields of farmland, meager roadside villages and small patches of undeveloped forests, and the warm air of the open windows had him nodding off into a sound sleep. When he woke up, still in the fog of dreams and reality, he was discovering that he had, at some point, rested his head on Venus' shoulder. Once he emerged into total conscious, he bolted upright. He apologized, "I'm sorry. I hope I didn't discommode you."

Venus smiled. "Not at all. Sleep well?"

"I did, I guess I really needed it." He leaned forward and said to Connie, "I don't know about anybody else, but I sure could use a pit stop."

Connie peered in the rearview mirror. "There is a petrol station about ten minutes ahead, can you wait?"

"No worries, I appreciate it."

Cruising on the N1 heading west, they were skirting the suburbs of Loubomo, the third largest city in the Republic of the Congo. As they approached the intersection of the N1 and N3, there was a Total petrol station. As they pulled up to the pump, Todd noticed a café.

"Hey guys, let's get something to eat; I'm buying.

Connie said, as he got out of the vehicle, "You guys head on in. I'm meet you all inside."

Everyone piled out and headed over to the La Croissanterie Café, stretching and shaking out the road trip aches and stiffness. The place smelled of greasy hamburgers and fries, and they grabbed a booth by the front window. The waitress sauntered over, handed them menus, and asked for their drink orders. When she left, Connie came in and decided that squeezing six people into a four-person booth was a little too cozy, so he decided to drag a chair over. Todd noticed that in the corner sat an old-time jukebox, so he reached into his jacket, plopped down a hand full of change, and asked Connie to go and surprise everyone with his choices. As Connie stood up, he said, "I'll have a cheeseburger, fries, and a Coke. Be back."

The waitress brought the drinks and took everyone's order, as Connie was dropping what seemed to be a ton of coinage into the juke. As he walked his way back to the booth, Steppenwolf's 'Born to be wild' filled the room. They spent the next hour listening to classic rock from the sixties and seventies—Hendrix, Janis, the Doors, and Jefferson Airplane. At one point, Todd said, "Far out man, I'm like tripping on an old LSD flashback. I got a buddy in Jamaica, Buzz, who is still stuck in the '60's, living the hippie life."

Once they were back on the road, all were feeling content, and they sat in silence until Todd turned to Venus and asked, "So, what brought you here?"

She smiled and looked out the window for several minutes, and then she started to speak softly. "I come from a small town just outside of Odessa, Ukraine called Yuzhne; it's a port city on the Black Sea. My grandfather owned a small fleet of fishing boats; my grandfather's grandfather had handed it down to him. About eight years ago, the government declared private fishing fleets would become part of a state-owned commercial venture. You had no choice, those that refused were harassed, damage to equipment would occur, so called 'accidents' happened to crew members, and a few even were killed—my grandfather was one.

To fight back, a small group of resisters started to publicly protest by marching in the streets, clashing with the police. We tried to bring world attention to our cause, but there was very little outcry worldwide. It seemed our cause was so small, compared with all the other injustices in the world, that ours was a lost cause. Until some of us started to fight back using tactics that the State had used against us: we sabotaged their equipment, harassed their crewmembers. We were called thugs and terrorists, and we had to go deep underground. Then, one day, a man simply called Mars, you know, like the Roman God of War, came to us and offered us assistance in our struggle against the State.

For several months, we wreaked havoc against the state-run fleet, but soon the Ukrainian government sought help from the Russians. We had to disband, so me and several others from Yuzhne left and joined the Gang, and here I am."

By the time they reached the port, Todd was convinced he found a cause he could believe in and one where he could use the skills he had learned in the Legion. One thing that was required was that he had to change his name, so as to keep their real identity a secret. The main reason was to protect their family members from being harassed and hassled by law enforcement.

Venus said, "Have you given any thought to your new identity?"

Todd thought for a few minutes. "Rodin."

Connie looked in the rearview mirror. "The sculptor?"

"Yeah."

Venus held out her hand and said, "Welcome to the cause, Auguste Rodin."

He took her hand. "Just Rodin, you know, like Cher or Madonna."

She smiled and said, "Gentlemen, I'd like you to meet Rodin."

Detective Johansson and Detective Wilson sat on a park bench facing Lake Bemidji just a few feet from the water's edge, sharing a double portion of crispy pork belly bruschetta from their favorite Italian Restaurant, Tutto Bene. They often came to Paul Bunyan Park whenever they found themselves stymied on a case. The park was a favorite with the locals and the tourists, for the locals because of the beauty and serenity of the environment, and for the tourists because of the giant statues of Paul Bunyan and Babe the Blue Ox.

From behind them, they heard footsteps approaching. "Detective Johansson? Good afternoon. I'm Inspector Morris, and this is Inspector Volker. We're from Interpol. We were told we could find you here. Thank you for taking the time to meet with us. I hope we're not disturbing your lunch?"

Johansson looked up to see two men wearing identical black suits, white shirts, black ties, and sunglasses; they looked to be right out of central casting for the movie *Men in Black.*

Wilson and Johansson stood up and shook hands with both men; Johansson introduced his partner, "Pleased to meet you both. This is my partner, Detective Wilson, and no, you're not disturbing our lunch. Have a seat."

"This is a very beautiful park. Reminds me a little of some of the parks in Cape Town, except we don't have huge statues of a scruffy-looking bloke and his blue cow in any of our parks," Volker said.

"Ox."

"Sorry?"

"It's a blue ox, not a cow, and I wouldn't go around making that mistake to any of the locals. Could get you into all kinds of trouble, if you catch my drift."

"My apologies, no offense intended."

"None taken. But just know some people around here are a bit touchy when it comes to Babe."

"Quite right."

"What can we do for you folks at Interpol? I can't believe you came all the way from London for Doctor Meriwether."

"To be brutally honest Detectives, we don't give a toss about the poor doctor; we're only really interested in getting any useful information or leads about Le Gang de la Clé de Singe. Aside from all of the Islamic terrorist groups, this group is one of our top priorities."

"Well, there's not much to go on. I brought you a copy of what little we know," Johansson said, as he handed Morse a folder. Both Morse and Volker read the scant police report and the coroner's statement. Volker smiled and said, "Elvis."

Wilson took a bite of his bruschetta. "Yeah, this guy's a real scream."

Morse, still reading the coroners statement, said, "This is the first time we've had Elvis involved; we've had Andy Warhol, Mao Tse-tung and even JFK, among many other A-listers." Morse started to hand Johansson the folder back.

"Keep it. So, they've used this gimmick with the fingerprints before?" Johansson offered, holding up his hand.

"All the time. It's pretty much the same story; they don't leave anything of value behind, just one celebrity fingerprint."

"Do you think I'm looking for multiple assailants or just this one Lewis N. Clark guy?"

"Hard to say. But I would say, with something like this, my guess would be just one lone killer. The people who perpetrate these kinds of acts are very skilled, usually ex-military and battle-hardened. I'd be checking with the airlines and reviewing any airport CTV videos available. This guy is probably on the other side of the world by now."

"We've already requested the airport security videos, and we've gotten any footage from the security cameras that we found in and around the doctor's office. Unfortunately, all the security footage from the doctor's office was taken. Since you are experts on this terror group, what can you boys from Interpol tell us about this Monkey Fist gang?"

"Wrench."

"Whatever."

Inspector Morse reached into his coat pocket and pulled out a rather thick sealed envelope and handed it to Johansson. "Fair is fair, you shared with us. Here is a small dossier of known members that we feel might be of interest, as well as some information about the organization that might be helpful. I've also included my card and contact information, along with Inspector Volker's, in case you would like to contact us for any reason. I would appreciate if you could email me any photos from the crime scene; we can share them with our folks in the photo lab. You never know, they might see something that you might have missed." With that, Morse stood up and held out his hand. "I'm sorry, Detectives, but we have a flight to catch."

Johansson and Wilson shook the Inspector's hands. "Well, we want to thank you and Inspector Volker for your interest and insight. We will keep you up to speed on our investigation, and I will have the crime scene photos sent to you."

"Good luck with your investigation, detectives. We only wish we could have been more helpful. But you never know, there just might be something in one of those photographs."

"You never know. So, where are you boys off to now?"

"Back to London."

"You boys flew all the way to Bemidji just to meet with us?"

"Well, we'd like to flatter you by saying yes, but, actually, you're the last stop we're making before heading back home. We had a couple of meetings in Washington DC and at the United Nations in New York, and we thought that since we were in the colonies, we might as well hop on over to your fair city and meet with Bemidji's finest."

"Ouch."

"Sorry, old man."

"Hey, we get it. We do appreciate you guys making the effort, and we hope it was worthwhile."

"Every little bit of information helps solve the puzzle."

"Well, thanks again. It was a pleasure meeting you both, have safe travels."

"Cheerio."

Billy Ray Pepper, president of the West Texas Shooters Association in Pecos, Texas, called an emergency meeting of all the club members. It was to be at eight o'clock at the association clubhouse, located on the outskirts of town on South Cedar Street, not too far from the Wal-Mart and Buck Jackson's Rodeo Arena. His message was short and direct: come early and armed!

"Okay, let's get this meeting going. How many here have heard about this attack that our country has come under?"

"What the hell are you talking about, Billy Ray? What attack?" Roy Alexander asked.

"I'll tell you what attack. A bunch of Frenchies terrorists is saying that they're going to kill anybody who goes out hunting for sport. Didn't you hear about that poor dentist up north who was beheaded and had his head mounted on the wall next to his hunting trophies? I tell you what, I think it's a bunch of socialists and commie bastards in cahoots with our own government in trying to take our guns away. Now they have the French involved, too. I bet it's a whole second amendment conspiracy."

The group of sixteen members was defiantly worked up; there was a mixture of anti-Franco slogans and anti-liberal epithets thrown about as the anger grew. There were even calls to go down to the local Democratic Party Headquarters and shoot the place up.

Eventually, calm was restored when Billy Ray held up his hands and said, "Listen up, here's what I propose. We're going to place an ad in the Pecos Enterprise telling those fucking French Commie's to go fuck themselves, and, if they want to come to Pecos and try to tell us what we can and can't shoot, then all I can say is 'Let's get ready to rumble'!" The clubhouse exploded with hoots and hollers. "Now, let's go out back and shoot something!" With that, everyone burst out of the back of the clubhouse where the shooting range was and started shooting at the special targets that Billy Ray had set up of human figures wearing berets.

After a night of blasting the shit out of targets and consuming large quantities of alcohol, it was decided to go as a group whitetail deer hunting on the upcoming weekend in the Cajoncitos Mountains.

A hundred and sixty miles to the west in Fort Hancock, Texas, the city whose slogan is 'Where a fence and hope for illegals ends,' the members of the American Eagle Gun Club were holding a similar anti-French, pro-gun and hunting meeting, proclaiming it's their God-given right to bear arms. Somebody in the group said they thought it was even written in the Bible, maybe in Deuteronomy or Leviticus, that a man has a God-given right to openly carry assault weapons.

After a lengthy discussion and a lot of drinking, they too all decided to go on a members-only hunting trip for whitetail deer out in the Cajoncitos Mountains that upcoming weekend, because it was God's will.

Billy Ray Pepper was considered a bit of a colorful character in Pecos, Texas. He ran for mayor of Pecos six times as the 'Freak Flag' Party candidate, under a number of platform themes like: 'Life is full of regrets. What's one more? Vote for me,' 'All the Way with Billy Ray,' 'With a Great Moustache Comes Great Responsibilities,' and, his favorite, 'Live • Laugh • Love. If that doesn't work, Ready • Aim • Fire.' He garnered only a handful of votes and was never allowed to participate in any mayoral debates. He was, however, able to raise several thousand dollars in campaign donations every time he ran for office, which was his real motivation for running for office.

Billy Ray is the owner of the Pecos gun shop slash bar, Hoot Shoot & Scoot, located out on Highway 17 next door to In & Out Bail Bonds and the strip club, The Boobie Hatch, of which Billy Ray has been a regular patron. Billy Ray has a table set aside for him for lunch between the hours of twelve and two every day, including Sundays. He is currently going through his third divorce to marry the new love of his life, a stripper named Caramel Delight. Caramel's breast size is 38KKK; her act consists of her crawling out on stage and trying to stand upright. For Billy Ray, it was love at first sight.

He was the founder of the West Texas Shooters Association, primarily as a venue to sell more guns and ammo. He came up with the association's catchy slogan, 'While others invest in gold. We invest in lead.' Starting out, the gun club was made up of Billy Ray's immediate family and a few friends, until he put up a billboard showing his then-fiancée, Caramel Delight, in a bikini and holding a Glock 9mm pistol; the headline was 'I love playing with my man's Glock.' Membership tripled within a week, and, after a month, the West Texas Shooters Association boasted over a hundred members. Who says advertising doesn't work?

Born and raised in Fort Hancock, Roger McGuire has been the French teacher at Fort Hancock High for the last twenty-six years. Roger prided himself as a bit of a Francophile: he loves French food, French films, and he even follows the Tour de France every year. On his first trip to France, right after he received his master's degree, his folks sent him to Paris as a graduation gift, where he met and fell in love with Monique, an art restorer who was working at the Louvre. Three weeks after they met, he married her.

He drives a 1993 Renault Clio, which he bought during his second visit to France, for the only time he and Monique actually traveled the entire length of the Tour, and had it shipped back to the States; he has taken a lot of shit over the years for not driving 'Merican Iron. The little shitbox is painted Renault yellow with black racing stripes, although there is nothing racy about the Clio. When he goes hunting, he stands out from the others in the hunting party by wearing a beret, instead of a ball cap or the more traditional cowboy hat, which he also takes a load of crap for.

As much as he loves all things French, he loves blasting the shit out of anything that moves with his AR15 Model 1 assault rifle, even more; be it on the ground or in the skies above. All the razing of Roger stops when he picks up his rifle. He is the best shot of the group, and he's the one who always bags the largest buck.

It was predawn on Saturday morning when a group of twelve men met at the Fort Hancock High School parking lot and carpooled in three cars up to the Cajoncitos Mountains, one vehicle being Roger's Renault. It took about an hour and a half to reach the trailhead where they parked the cars; they unloaded their gear and headed up the trail in search of whitetail. Roger had taking point of the party as usual, which no one seemed to mind since he seemed to have a keen sense of tracking that usually ends up in spotting game.

They were a good three or four miles up the trail from where they parked the cars, so they never heard the five cars carrying the fourteen members of the West Texas Shooters Association arrive at the trailhead.

"Looks like we're going to have some competition," Billy Ray said, as he got out of his pickup.

Mark Landreth, the owner of Landreth Hardware, noticed the Renault and walked over to examine it. "Hey fellas, check this out, a Renault!" One by one, they all congregated around the little yellow car, some peering inside. "Whatcha think? It couldn't be those Frenchies. Could it?"

"They wouldn't be that stupid to show up in a French car," Roy Alexander commented.

"Hey, we're talking about the French here—not your brightest nation. We saved their asses twice in the big wars. Look, there's a field manual on the floor there! These must be the bastards!" Billy Ray quipped.

"Wait, wait, wait, that looks more like a French cookbook."

"What are you, fucking Jacque Cousteau? I say it's those French motherfuckers!"

Billy Ray aimed his Swedish Ak5 and shot the right rear tire out, and then he started peppering the Renault with a full clip of 30 rounds of armor-piercing ammo. When he reloaded, he turned to the group with a smile on his face and said, "Now, saddle up, boys, and let's go get some frog bastards!"

The members of the West Texas Shooters Association were pumped up and raring to go; you could almost smell the oozing of testosterone in the air. These good old boys were chomping at the bit to engage in battle and kick some French butt. Billy Ray said, "Somebody hand me a beer."

Roy said, "Jeez, it's six-thirty in the morning, Billy Ray."

"Whadda you, my mother, Roy? Give me a beer."

The group started heading up the trail, when Mark shouted out, "What happens if we miss them, and they come back? Our cars are vulnerable." They all stopped and looked at Billy Ray.

Billy Ray surveyed the area, then pointed to a cluster of oak trees and said, "Good thinking, Mark. You and Bobby hide over there among those oaks. And if they come back, give us a call."

"Why us?" Bobby asked.

"Because Mark weighs 350 pounds, and you're a terrible shot. If we get into the shit, we'll have to move and move fast and be able to count on every shot. Okay?"

"Are we really ready to kill someone?" Mark asked, looking around at everyone gathered around him. No one spoke for several seconds before Billy Ray broke the silence. "Only if they won't surrender, or if they start something. Now, let's rock and roll."

Roger McGuire stopped the group when he heard the rapid firing coming from down below. He turned to the group. "What the hell was that?"

Buddy Nolan, the high school wrestling coach, said, "Ah, probably just some dickhead's first time out hunting, showing off his new weapon for his buddies."

"Yeah, I guess I'm just a bit jumpy with all the talk about those French killers running around. But just to be safe, everyone keep your eyes open and stay alert."

Pastor Ronnie Campbell of the First Baptist Church nervously asked, "Fellas, maybe we should call it a day?"

"Naw Padre. We came out here to get some whitetail. I'm just being paranoid. Come on, let's keep going. I saw some tracks heading this way." He led the group off to the left of the trail, towards a thicket of trees down into a ravine. "We'll head down there and spread the scents."

They slowly meandered down into the coulee, sprayed the deer scents, took their positions, and waited. The sun hadn't raised enough to reach into the gully, which added to their fatigue after having hiked five miles over hilly and rugged terrain; most of them nodded off where they sat.

Kizigo Game Reserve lies smack dab in the center of Tanzania; it covers over four thousand square kilometers. It sits in Singida Region, and it is next to Muhesi Game Reserve. There are woodland forests sprinkled throughout the open plains of the Kizigo game reserve, and there are dozens of watering holes, springs, and marshy valleys. The main wildlife found there are Eland, Roan, Lion, Leopard, Liechtenstein Hartebeest, Greater kudu, and Sable.

Rodin had received a tip that David Leeway, a prominent racist and bigoted American real estate mogul who once ran for President of the United States, his two adult sons, David Thorndike Leeway Jr. and Richard 'Skippy' Leeway, and his daughter, Sasha Alexis Leeway, were in the reserve on a big cat safari guided by Mwindaji Safaris of Tanzania, who are notorious for hunting lions and leopards.

The buzz on social media was that they had already posted photos of two leopards that they had killed and were looking to bag a large male lion named Wilson, an icon within the park. For the past three years, the Leeway's children had posted dozens of photographs of the three of them smiling and proudly posing with their 'trophys'. They had killed everything from elephants, baboons, wildebeest, Cape kudus and rhinoceros, to hippos. The rumor is that the daughter, Sasha, is the better and more ruthless hunter of the three. The Leeway siblings were actually all stepbrothers and stepsister, as old man Leeway switched wives like some men switch ties. He was currently on wife five.

It was after ten o'clock by the time Rodin and his team reached the Wangama meet up point. A couple of local team members had set up camp; a fire was going, and dinner was ready to be served. Rodin gathered the team around the campfire after dinner and planned out the mission for the next day. The local guide, Zuberi, had spotted the Mwindaji camp just over five miles to the north, and he figured they would be heading towards them as the big cat's prey were all starting to migrate to the south.

Rodin waited until Zuberi gave his download of all the intel that he had gathered before speaking. "Thank you, Zuberi. As usual, you've done an outstanding job. Now, as you know, when we engage the Mwindaji Safari party, there will be a woman in the group, and, from what I understand, she is quite the huntress and an excellent shot. What I want to know is if any of you have any qualms of taking action against a woman; I need to know now. There will be no repercussions, and no one will think any the less of you. I will understand, but I need to know now and not when we get into action. So, speak up now."

The group sat silently, looking at each other for a minute or two before Liszt raised his hand. "I would like to recuse myself if I may."

"Is there anybody else?"

There were no others. Max, the driver, put his arm around Liszt's shoulder, as did Lu Wei sitting next to him, reassuring him that his beliefs were more than acceptable within the group. Rodin, who sat opposite of Liszt with Buster at his feet, got up and walked around the fire, handing out the team assignments. When he got to Liszt, he leaned down and said, "No worries mate. You can help Odin with the drone tomorrow. Besides, we have a man on the inside. As for the rest of you, you have your assignments. Read them and throw them into the fire; we move out at dawn. Come on Buster, time for your walk." He and Buster headed out of camp and into the darkness.

The next morning at six a.m., everyone was up. They all had eaten breakfast, prepared themselves in their ghillie suits, and checked their weapons. Odin sent the drone airborne, and he and Liszt were making final checks on the team radio headsets. The plan was to have a team of five head north to the small watering hole, where the animals would naturally gather to drink, and wait until the safari group comes to bag their unsuspecting prey. But then again, as Rodin would say, "You live by unsporting rules; you die by unsporting rules."

The rules that Rodin played by were that they only would take out the hunters and the safari operators, never the bearers, porters, or any support staff who were just trying to eke out a living, unless they involve themselves into the fight.

They got to their objective at about eight, settled into position, and blended into the environment to wait. Each of them went through the normal radio check procedure, and everything seemed operational. Odin kept the team up to date on the safaris progress via the drone. The other members of the team not out in the field with the 'Kill Team" were being vigilant of keeping watch in all directions, making sure that there wouldn't be any unexpected surprises.

The Mwindaji Safari party arrived just before eleven in four luxury Land Rover T.D.I. 300 Diesels with a pop-up canopy so they wouldn't have to get out of the air-conditioned vehicles to take their shots. There wasn't any game in sight, aside from the occasional family of *Phacochoerus Africanus*; they were more commonly known as the common African warthogs. The bigger game wouldn't come to get a drink until closer to sunset. That meant a long wait for the team, but it was Rodin's practice not to engage the targets until they drew their weapons. They had to make the first move, threatening the lives of the animals. They didn't want to take preemptive action, just in case they had received faulty information; what if this safari actually turned out to be a photo safari and not a hunting safari after all? Best to be safe.

"Red Team, Red Leader here. It looks like it might be a while, so try and get some rest. But remember, stay frosty. Red Leader to Red Drone, Over."

"Red Drone here."

"Keep us posted; we're going to shut down for now. Give us plenty of notice if anything stirs."

"Copy that, Red Leader."

The warm mid-day sun and a strong breeze was very contusive for nodding off and most of the team settled in and fell asleep. Rodin could see the Leeway children sitting in the Land Rovers, looking bored while playing with their iPhones and waiting for the big cats to come for a drink so they can shoot them from the convenience of their vehicles. After an hour of observing, Rodin slipped off to sleep with Buster lying and leaning next to him.

"Well, fuck me!" Billy Ray said, as he spotted the other hunting party down in the ravine; he handed his binoculars to Mark, who was standing next to him. "That's those French sons of bitches. Am I right, Mark? Lookie there; there's one right there wearing a fucking beret! I tell you what." The others scrambled to get their binoculars out or viewed the group thru their rifle scopes. They all stood there looking down into the ravine at Roger McGuire, who was wearing the beret that he bought in the Charles de Gaulle Airport duty-free shop some ten years ago.

"That guy standing there is wearing a fucking beret," Mark noted.

Bobby hastened, "Men, men, just because he's wearing a freaking beret, that doesn't make him a terrorist. Let's not go off half-cocked and do something we'll regret."

"What do you recommend we do, Bobby? Go down there and see if they start speaking French?" Billy Ray said, half joking.

"That's exactly what I'm recommending. I speak a little French; let's go down there and scope this out. If they are the terrorists, then we can go get the authorities, or, if we're forced into a situation, take action and maybe capture them and get the reward. If they're not, then no harm, no foul."

"What if they just start blasting our Asses?"

"Let's just stay claim."

"And don't forget, Billy Ray blasted the shit out of one of their cars," Mark said with a big smile on his face.

"Shut up!" Billy Ray started to take a step toward Mark, when Bobby stepped in between them. "Come on, boys, settle down. Follow me." Bobby led the way down the ravine towards the possible terrorists. Everyone was on edge, their fingers on the triggers of their guns.

As they were approached, Roger noticed them and called out to his friends, "Hey guys, we've got company." The members of the American Eagles, still groggy from nodding off, started to understand what Roger was saying. They began to slowly rise up and turn around to see a group of armed men approaching them. Roger started slowly making his way towards the group heading in their direction.

Bobby held up his hand and said, "Bonjour."

Roger instinctively shouted, "Bonjour." Unfortunately, he continued and said in a very distinctive and authentic French accent. "Comment vas-tu?"

Billy Ray looked at Bobby and sneered "Told ya!" Then he raised his gun and fired six rapid shots into Roger's chest, yelling, "Eat lead, French scum!" Roger was hurled back ten feet by the force of the shots. Billy Ray then turned his gun to the other members of the American Eagle Gun Club, as did all the members of the West Texas Shooters Association. Within seconds, only the law-abiding American citizens of the WTSA were standing; every member of American Eagle Gun Club lay dead.

With mega streams of adrenaline pumping thru their veins, they all started whooping and hollering about the great victory they had achieved over the French terrorists sprawled out dead at their feet. Billy Ray carefully walked over to Roger's lifeless body with his gun at the ready to continue the carnage, just in case this French mofo was just playing dead; he kicked him hard in his side, nothing. He then leaned down and flipped him over to see if he had any ID. He pulled out Roger's wallet and found his Texas driver's license and his Fort Handcock High School teachers' ID card, stating that his staff position was that of a French teacher. Billy Ray stood frozen and, unknown to himself, peed his pants.

Kent Abernathy had been a guide with Mwindaji Safari for over twelve years, a hardened veteran of over a hundred safaris. Born in Johannesburg, South Africa, he came from a long line of hunting and tracking guides, tracing his lineage all the way back to the Boer Wars of 1899. At age thirty-two, Kent was ruggedly handsome, a cross between a Brad Pitt and a young Robert Redford. He was what most would call a man's man; a hard-drinking, educated outdoorsman who loved the ladies, and they loved him. It was no surprise that Sasha Leeway had handpicked Kent to be her personal tracker, leaving her two brothers with John Vorster and Brady Shepstone, each well-experienced guides and each well over sixty years old.

The Leeway Safari was on its sixth day, and Sasha had started sleeping with Kent on day two. So far, she hadn't fired a shot; she was more interested in bagging Kent than big game. Today was the first day she had a taste for blood; she was ready to kill something. As she and Kent waited in the Land Rover T.D.I. for the cats to come for water, Kent was feeling frisky, but Sasha wasn't.

"Mmm, maybe later, Kent."

"Aw, come on baby. It's going to be at least a couple of hours before the cats show."

"Later!"

"Okay, okay. I'll go and check with the others. You hungry?"

"Yeah, I could go for some caviar and champagne."

"I'll tell Abena to bring some by."

Kent headed over to the food truck where the porters were setting up for lunch. "Abena, Miss Sasha would like some champagne and caviar."

"Yes, bwana."

At Mwindaji Safari, all the porters were encouraged to use the term bwana—more as a theatrical term than anything else—especially with the American customers. Most Americans equated the word bwana with old Tarzan and jungle movies as a term of respect and lordship.

Abena was a thirty-four-year-old graduate from Jomo Kenyatta University of Agriculture and Technology with a degree in Animal Health. She had been serving as the head chef at Mwindaji Safari for six months; she specializes in authentic Swahili delicacies like Pilipili ya Carrot,

Meatball Biriyani, and Zarda. The operators found that their clients liked the experience of eating native cuisine, as it seemed to give them a feeling of authentic and exotic safari adventures of historic proportions. Plus, their clients didn't question it when they would charge more than they could if they served up a roast beef sandwich.

Kent checked in with his compatriots, John and Brady, to see that everyone was a happy camper. They were killing time by inspecting their rifles, giving them a last minute once over. When Kent strolled by, they gave him the thumbs up. The two Leeway brothers were fast asleep while listening to music with their headphones, dead to the world, literally would be soon.

Detective Wilson was kicking back, half-asleep in his Barcalounger and watching CNN news late night wrap up, when the announcer dropped a bomb about a breaking news story out of West Texas about members of the West Texas Shooters Association, who massacred twelve members of the American Eagle Gun Club from Fort Hancock, Texas. The attorney for the West Texas Shooters Association said that they had mistaken the American Eagle Gun Club for members of the notorious French Eco-terrorist group, Le Gang de la Clé de Singe, or 'the Monkey Wrench Gang'. The local district attorney said that they would all be charged with second-degree murder. This followed several other hunting incidents involved in mistakening other hunters for being Monkey Wrench Gang members.

Wilson bolted up out of the recliner. "Fuck me." He fumbled for his cell phone and speed dialed Johansson.

"Hey, did you hear what happened down in Texas?"

"Yeah, people are batshit crazy, man."

"Hunters are nuts anyway, and this is just adding fuel to the fire."

"You know, it won't be too long before some knuckle-headed moose hunters around here start blasting the shit out of some geeky-type bird watcher. Then *we'll* be on CNN."

"Yeah, I can't wait. Fucking French."

At a four in the afternoon, the waterhole was starting to see some activity; first, a family of warthogs ventured down to share a drink with a few dozen zebras. Around five, Rodin was awakened. "Red Leader, Red Drone here, do you copy?"

As he awoke, Rodin spoke into his mic, "Red Drone, I read you loud and clear. Over."

"Red Leader, we have a pride of lions approaching from your right at about two o'clock."

"Copy that. Red Group, Red Leader here, acknowledge please." Each of the Red Team acknowledged the call. "Alright, team, stay sharp and remember your targets. Be prepared to fire on my command."

Rodin could see activity among the hunting party; people were emerging from their vehicles with rifles in hand. The two Leeway brothers had climbed atop their Land Rovers, while Sasha and Kent were meandering down closer towards the pool. Rodin saw that Sasha's guide was pointing off in the distance; he assumed the guide must be pointing at the big cats heading down to the pool for a drink.

"Get ready. Looks like it's going to go down soon," Rodin said, as he was following the woman's guide in his sight. His plan was to take the guide out first and then the woman. He noticed that Sasha didn't have a firearm; she was holding a camera with a telephoto lens. That complicated things, as he wasn't all too keen to kill an unarmed woman; he would wait and see how everything developed. If she didn't fire a shot, she would be spared. He would handle the guide and the woman, and that would leave his team to handle the other four hunters; hopefully, the support staff would get scared and run off, not wanting to get involved in a firefight. "Remember, only the hunters, unless the others get involved."

There were three lionesses and four cubs following close behind. They were within rifle range of the hunting party, but the guides were telling the Leeway's to hold their fire until the males appeared. They knew that the males were always known to lag behind, so as to protect the pride because they would be vulnerable while drinking.

'Skippy' Leeway, the younger of the brothers, who had been drinking straight from a bottle of Jack Daniels for over an hour and wearing a pair of Beats studio wireless over-the-ear headphones, decided not to wait. He stood up, laughing, and shouted, "Hey, watch this!" He aimed his rifle and shot one of the lion cubs in the head, creating a fine red mist that sprayed the other cubs, causing all the animals gathered around the pool to scatter away.

Rodin immediately called, "Fire."

'Skippy' received such elated enjoyment in his marksmanship abilities for only a nanosecond, which is all the time it took for the bullet fired by Odin to blow a hole in his head the size of a cantaloupe. 'Skippy's' older brother, David Thorndike Leeway Jr., and the three guides went down like sacks of potatoes. Sasha lay on the ground, motionless. She had inadvertently been struck unconscious when, while recoiling from the sight of Kent being shot, her Nikon D5 camera swung back with such force into her face that, not only did it brake her nose, it knocked out six of her perfectly formed and brilliantly pearly white teeth. Fourteen thousand dollars' and eighteen years' worth of orthodontia, the best money can buy, gone in an instant.

It took only two to three seconds before the porters realized something bad had happened; all seven of them were seen running off into the bush. The pride of lions ran off, leaving the one dead cub lying by the water's edge.

"Red Leader, Red Drone here."

"Red Leader, over."

"All clear, and the lions are leaving as well as the safari support staff. Over."

"Copy that. Red Leader to Red Team, let's go recon." With that, the team stood up slowly and made their way towards the Land Rovers with Rodin taking the point. "Spread out and stay alert," He said as much to himself as to the team.

"Buster, go!" Buster took off to investigate. He sniffed all the bodies and stopped where Sasha lay; he froze and pointed.

Sasha had been knocked unconscious and was lying next to the left front tire of the lead Land Rover, where her brother David was slouched over into the front passenger seat. Sasha was slowly starting to regain consciousness when the Red Team was approaching the hunting party.

Rodin noticed a movement off to his left; he froze, raised his clenched fist as the signal to halt, which everyone did, and trained his rifle in that direction. It was Abena, the head chef of the safari; she emerged with her hands up, approaching Rodin and the team. She smiled and said, "Hey, handsome."

Rodin removed his ghillie headpiece. "Hey, doll. Long time no see. You okay?"

"Yeah, I'm fine." She walked over and gave him a big kiss and a hug.

"Team, this is Abena. She was our inside man. Abena, this is the Red Team; wish we could all get acquainted, but I think it best that you get going."

Sasha heard voices off in the distance as the fog lifted, as well as she felt a sharp pain start in her mouth. She touched her lip with her hand and brought it back to see it covered in blood; she let out a scream. She then saw a scary image of what she could only imagine to be a large dog wearing some sort of camouflaged outfit, growling menacingly, and stalking her in a pointer stance no more than two feet away.

The team, as if in a coordinated gesture, trained their guns in her direction. Sasha slowly sat up; she was crying and sobbing as she looked around, spotting several human-like creatures that looked like beasts from another planet. Then she saw Abena, and she gave a slight smile at having found what she thought was a respite of kindness. She raised her left hand and called out, "Abena."

Abena walked toward Sasha and, when she was within six feet of her, reached behind her back and produced a Glock 38 compact handgun, firing off four rounds within a two-inch grouping of Sasha's heart. She walked over to Sasha, reached down, grabbed dead heiress's right arm, and held it up to show that she was holding a 9mm Glock in her hand. Abena turned back to the group. "The bitch was always armed; she would have taken at least three of you out."

Detective Wilson had just returned to the office from a meeting with the coroner about a drug-related triple murder and the death of an innocent three-year-old bystander, when the phone rang.

"Detective Wilson."

"Detective Wilson, Inspector Morris of Interpol here. Did I catch you at a bad time?"

"Not at all, Inspector. What can I do for you?"

"I was primarily calling to see if you've made any progress with the Doctor Meriwether case?"

"Not really. Every lead we've followed up on has ended in a dead-end street, if you know what I mean."

"Quite right. Well, I might have something, although, I must be honest, it could be nothing."

"Please, Inspector. I would appreciate any help you might be able to give."

"Well, we did some checking at numerous international airports and found that, on the evening of the murder, there was a male passenger on KLM flight 6059 from Minneapolis to Nairobi, Kenya, who was traveling on a bit of a dodgy passport."

"Dodgy how?"

"This man was using a passport that had once been declared stolen from an ex-military man, then reinstated. We're checking up on it. Just thought I'd keep you in the loop as it were."

"What was the man's name?"

"His name is Chase Madrid; it is American issued. We're sending you his passport photo; not much to go on—he has a full beard and glasses. I suspect it might be a disguise, but, like I said, it could be nothing."

"Thanks for letting me know; I'll do some checking on my end too."

"Smashing idea. We'll contact you if we find anything more."

"Same here. Thanks again, Inspector; I really appreciate it."

"Cheerio, old chap."

"Oh, Inspector. Where does this Chase Madrid supposedly live? Minneapolis?"

"California. Oakland, California."

"Okay, thanks. Goodbye."

Wilson hung up the phone and started a search for one Chase Madrid. As he was typing in the name, he said to himself, "What a great fucking name, Chase Madrid. Sure beats the shit out of George Wilson."

George Wilson served with the Bemidji police force for twelve years; he was married with three kids. He married his high school sweetheart, Donna Sue Lofton, right after he graduated from the police academy. He was over six-and-a-half feet tall, with wild, bushy, jet-black hair. When he and Johansson were next to each other, they looked like the original odd couple, but they were the best homicide team the force had, with over a ninety-eight percent arrest and conviction rate. What made them so good was that they complimented each other's strengths and covered the other's weakness.

Rodin placed the dead lion cub on 'Skippy's" lap after they placed him and all the others inside the two Land Rovers. He attached the yellow Monkey Wrench pirate flag to both of the vehicle's radio antennas; then he pinned a letter onto Sasha Leeway's Hermes safari jacket.

This is another warning to all poachers and hunters of big game and endangered species: this aggression against nature will not stand. Be warned that we will target you no matter your economic stature, rich or poor, black or white, individuals or corporations, collectors or purveyors, man or woman.

We can and will strike anywhere and at any time, without warning or mercy.

We have posted a graphic image of a lion cub that Richard 'Skippy' Leeway so heroically murdered onto the Internet.

We're not fucking around; we are willing to die for what we believe in. The question you have to ask yourself is: are you?

Le Gang de la Clé de Singe.

Rodin gathered everyone around. "Let's do one last clean sweep of the area to make sure we've left nothing behind. Abena, better let me have the Glock. Can't have them find you with the weapon that killed Sasha Leeway."

As she handed him the pistol, she said, "I don't feel all that safe with the big cats in the area without it."

"Here." He took the Glock 38 and handed her a Webley MK IV service model revolver, the kind made famous by Harrison Ford in the *Indiana Jones* movies. "You won't be out here long; we'll call it into the Reserve Police as soon as we get back to camp, and we'll have Red Drone keep an eye on you from above. Now, you should get going."

He gave her a kiss on the cheek, and then they headed off in opposite directions.

As the team headed back to base camp, Rodin walked up to Odin. "I need you to take command of the team and get them to the next target. I received a radio communication late last night; I have to handle an unexpected assignment, because the assigned leader has been incapacitated. "

"Roger that, You need any help?"

"Naw, it seems pretty straightforward."

"Where you off to?"

"Singapore."

"Zhù nǐ hǎo yùn."

"And that means?"

"Good luck, in Chinese."

"Kansha." Odin looked quizzically at Rodin. "It's Japanese for thanks. Hey, at least it's Asian."

"How does the defendant plea?"

"Not Guilty, your honor," Billy Ray Pepper said, as he stood in front of the honorable Judge Robert J. Novak.

The "Texas Trial of the Century" was being held in the Salt Flat Justice of Peace Court House instead of being held in Fort Hancock due to all the local and worldwide publicity, plus Billy Ray's faux celebrity status in Pecos.

The courtroom capacity was designed to hold a maximum of eighty spectators; there were over five thousand requests for seats. Demand for entrance to the trial was so great that a lottery was held even among the world press, and several world news organizations were denied access. There were large sums of money trading hands for access, deals being made between networks, and even spots for the gallery being sold on eBay for as much as ten thousand a seat. Rumors were floating around that book deals were already in place with some jurors, although nothing had been proven.

Billy Ray couldn't afford a high-priced lawyer, so he was appointed a public defender. His lawyer was a young kid, fresh out of South Texas College of Law, named Tommy McGrath; he graduated bottom of his class. He always made a joke about it, saying someone had to be at the bottom. But, because Billy Ray's case was so high profile, he had dozens of celebrity lawyers knocking at his door, wanting to represent him for free. So Tommy McGrath was out, and world-renowned New York criminal attorney Jason Parker Ryan, and his defense team of six, was in. Ryan had made his reputation for his defense, and his eventual acquittal, of United States Senator Emmitt B. Hayes from the great state of Mississippi for murdering his wife.

Hayes claimed that he shot her eight times, because he thought she was a deer that somehow had gotten into their thirty-six-room mansion, in an exclusive area of Vicksburg. His defense was simple: it was dark. It had nothing to do with the fact that his wife of over thirty years wanted a divorce because she found out that the sixty-eight-year-old Emmitt was bonking his twenty-two-year-old intern, Betty Sue Burnsides.

Jason's most recent accomplishment was that he won a highly publicized triple-murder case, where the defendant was charged with three first-degree murder charges and the prosecutor demanded the death penalty. The man went free on a technicality, then walked out of the courtroom and killed two police officers. Jason didn't take on that case.

Billy Ray's defense team decided that they would plead not guilty, due to the fact that he committed these acts in the heat of passion and was acting as a patriot in the defense of his country, protecting his and every other American's God-given right to bear arms. The feeling of the defense team is that, since the trial is being held in Texas where guns rule, their best chance for acquittal is to play up the whole gun angle and American patriotism. Jason Parker Ryan was a real media hound and star fucker; he loved being in front the camera, any camera, and seeing himself on TV or his picture in the papers.

Jason Parker Ryan had a near perfect acquittal record—forty-eight wins, one loss. His one loss was when he failed to get his client off for killing his wife and six kids just because she over-cooked his Mac & cheese. While on the witness stand, Justin Mosby, the defendant, showed no remorse and actually laughed when he described how he slit his wife's throat and preceded to kill all six children with a baseball bat.

Ryan objected to the fact that the judge was going to allow the jury to see the eighty-plus crime scene photographs, claiming that they were so horrific that they would be prejudicial against his client. The judge did agree and decided that the jury would be allowed to see two photographs from the scene: one of the wife with her head attached to her body by a small sliver of muscle, and one of the youngest girls with her face so battered that she had no distinguishing facial features; there just seemed to be a mashed up pile of hamburger meat where her face used to be. Jason tried to convince Justin not to take the witness stand, but he insisted, "Dude, it's my fifteen minutes of fame, and I'm gonna ride this crazy train all the way to the end of the line. You can relate to that."

It took the jury a record of just six minutes to return a verdict of guilty on all counts. It was so unprecedented that it was recorded by Guinness World Record as the fastest criminal conviction ever recorded, beating the old record by some eighteen minutes. At the sentencing, when the judge asked the defendant if he had anything to say before sentencing, he said, "Did I mention the bitch burnt my Mac & cheese?"

The judge replied, "Well, Mr. Mosby, let's hope the electric chair can do the same to you."

Rodin stepped up to the customs agent station at Singapore's Changi Airport and presented his passport.

The agent looked at him, then down to his passport, and back to him. "What is the nature of your visit, business or pleasure, Mister Peterson?"

"Pleasure, I'm here to attend the Grand Prix."

"How long are you planning on staying in Singapore?"

"Sadly, only five days."

"Do you have anything to declare?"

"No, nothing."

The agent stamped the passport and handed it back. "Enjoy your stay, Mr. Peterson."

"Thank you. Have a nice day."

With that, he was off to baggage claim, and then hailing a cab to the Ritz-Carlton, Millenia Singapore. By the time he reached the hotel, it was 10 o'clock on Friday morning, and the Grand Prix cars were out on the track and running their initial reconnaissance laps of the weekend. The sound of twenty-two cars out on the track, running around, wasn't very conducive for catching up on much-needed sleep. It was 8 o'clock on Saturday night, the following day in his time, so he decided to have some dinner in the Summer Pavilion, the one-star Michelin Star restaurant that specialized in contemporary Cantonese cuisine. He ordered the specialty of the house: the braised whole South African abalone with Chinese mushrooms in oyster sauce, finishing off the meal with the house dessert, which was chilled green apples with assorted fungi and topped with almond flakes.

By the time he had finished eating his lunch, the cars were off the track and back in the garages for some adjustments and lunch. They wouldn't be running again until later in the afternoon, which left just enough time to catch a quick nap and do a little reconnaissance with the local operatives.

"Interpol, how may I direct your call?"

"Hello, this is Detective Wilson of the Bemidji Minnesota Police Department. Could you connect me with Inspector Morris, please?"

"One moment, please." There was silence for a second, then he was listening to an elevator music styled version of Ozzy Osbourne's "Crazy Train" for two minutes.

"Inspector Morris here."

"Hi, Inspector. This is Detective Wilson."

"Ah, Detective Wilson, how may I assist you?"

"Well, I was just following up on that person of interest, Chase Madrid. I was hoping you might have some more information. We did some checking on our end, but we didn't find much, other than that he is apparently from California, like you said, and he works as a freelance computer software consultant. There doesn't seem to be anything on social media about this guy—no Facebook, no Twitter, nothing."

"You might have gotten information about his father, Chase senior, who we have found to be the computer software consultant. Honestly, Detective, the son, Chase Jr., has proven to be a real mystery for us as well.

However, it's not totally unheard of for some of these ex-military types to stay off the grid, as they say. Most know the pitfalls of exposing oneself on social media, so they just go stealth. So, we're stuck with doing our investigation the old school way, just a lot of more man-hours. It will take a little longer, but we'll find out if Mr. Madrid is involved, and, when we do, we'll most definitely keep you informed."

"There is one other thing. You heard about the killing of David Leeway's children on safari in Africa?"

"Yes, I heard; it is tragic."

"Well, they left another phony fingerprint. I don't know how they got it, but this time they left your American President Teddy Roosevelt."

"How ironic, since Teddy Roosevelt was a huge hunter himself."

"Well, we're looking into how someone would be able to access such a thing. It could be just the lead that just might help give us a break in the case. Detective Wilson, I just wanted you to know that we are looking at every lead and keeping you informed."

"Well thanks, Inspector. I look forward to hearing from you."

Wilson hung up the phone and shouted down the hall for Johansson. "Hey sarge, come here for a second, will you?"

"Yeah, what's up?" Johansson said, as he stuck his head into Wilson's office.

"Sir, where in California does your sister, Sally, go to college?"

"Dublin."

"Dublin? I thought she lived in California; when did she move to Ireland?"

"No Dublin, California. It's about twenty-five miles from San Francisco. Why?"

"So, she's close to Oakland, right?"

"Yeah, why?"

"Think she might do us a favor and do some snooping around?"

"Nothing dangerous?"

"No. No. Just some minor surveillance;, no personal contact. a chance to earn some bucks while going to college."

"I don't want her getting close to this freak!"

"We would never put her in danger, you know that."

"Why not just call in the Oakland PD?"

"Don't want to call in the Marines just yet; at this point, it could nothing. If she could occasionally drive by this guy's house and maybe grab a photo or two. If she thinks, at any time, it's too dangerous or she gets scared, she stops. Period!"

"I don't know; this creep beheaded a guy."

"Okay, it was just a thought. I'll give the OPD a call."

"Well, the least I can do is ask her."

"And if she doesn't want to, then we'll call OPD."

"I call her tonight. Good idea, Wilson."

"Thanks, boss."

Rodin was driving very fast through the streets of Paris, and no matter how bad he wanted to slow down, he couldn't; his foot kept forcing the pedal to the floor. He was heading towards the Arc de Triomphe on the Avenue Victor Hugo; the traffic all around him seemed to be frozen as he weaved his way, missing them by what seemed to him to be inches. As he reached the Place Charles de Gaulle, he performed a power slide that brought the backend of his Lime Green Lamborghini LP610-4 Huracan Spyder around and around, making his Pirelli P Zero PZ4 tires flat spot as he finally came to a screeching halt. He woke up in a start, as it was just a dream brought on by one of the Ferrari Formula 1 cars spinning out on the Marina Bay Street Circuit that brought him to from a deep, deep sleep.

Rodin slowly got up, walked to the window, and opened the blackout curtains in his room just as the sun was setting. The race track was lit up as if it was mid-day, except the light is white light and not the golden light from the sun, the power requirement is three million one hundred and eighty thousand watts with an illumination measurement of around three thousand lux—effectively four times brighter than floodlights in most football stadiums. His view of the city, and especially of the track from his suite on the thirty-second floor, gave everything a surreal feel; it looked like the cars were racing on a slot car track.

He was brought back to reality by the ring of the hotel phone. "Hello?"

"Mr. Peterson?"

"Speaking."

"Mr. Peterson, this is Jia En. I hope I'm not too early." From the tenor of he voice, she sounded like she was in her early twenties. These new millennial volunteers seem to get younger and younger all the time, or maybe he's just getting older and older, probably both.

"Yeah, you did kinda catch me not quite ready. Why don't you come on up, and I'll be ready shortly. It's room 3207; I'll leave the door unlocked."

"Okay, I'll be right up. Bye."

He grabbed his clothes and walked by the door, unlocked it, then headed off to the bathroom to get a quick cold shower to wake up and shake the cobwebs out of his head. He was rinsing the shampoo out of his hair when he heard a voice from the living room. "Mr. Peterson, I'm here."

"Make yourself at home; I'll be out in a minute. Fix yourself a drink if you'd like." No response, so he finished up, dried off, and got dressed. When he emerged, he was wearing a slate grey Armani Collezioni suit, with a white button-down shirt and a Yves Saint Laurent black skull & crossbones bow tie.

He was right; she was young, about twenty-two years old, and she was tall, about 5' 10," with long, straight black hair. She was wearing a black Ralph Lauren crepe sleeveless gown with an open back and slim straps that formed a V, quite sophisticated, quite beautiful.

"Jia En? Hi, I'm Robert; it's a pleasure to meet you. I appreciate your helping, although I want you to understand, up front, what is going to happen tonight. There will be no repercussions if you decide to back out. Do you understand?"

"Yes, I understand. I was told what to expect, and I am totally committed to the cause. I'm here to help you in any way I can."

“You’re sure?”

She didn’t say anything; she just nodded.

“Okay, let’s go.”

They rode the elevator down together in silence without any stops; Rodin assumed that the majority of hotel guests were probably at the racetrack. When the doors opened, in the lobby stood two rather larger Asian identical twins dressed all in black from head to toe, right out of central casting. They both had shaved heads and were, of course, wearing black-rimmed Ray-Ban sunglasses with black lenses. Jia En introduced them as the Chang brothers. She said not to bother with first names if you need to call on either, just refer to either one or both as Chang.

Jia En said, “Everything is ready per your instructions.”

“And the rest of the team?”

“They’ll arrive at the venue ten minues before you give the green light.”

“Okay, let’s roll.”

The Chang brothers led the way, past the reception desk and outside to a waiting black BMW Alpina B7 Bi-Turbo sedan. Jia En and Rodin sat in the back seats with the Chang brothers up front. The driver unleashed the six hundred horsepower beast and showed that the claim of “zero to sixty in less than four seconds” wasn’t just advertising hype. They were all pushed back into their seats by the g-force of the excessive power of the 4.4-liter twin power turbo V-8 engine; it felt like a jet’s take off.

They jumped onto Raffles Boulevard, heading west, then onto Nicoll Highway and eventually merging onto the Keppel Viaduct West, until they pulled off onto the feeder road and ended up at the Republic of Singapore Yacht Club. They were stopped at the guard station, where passenger Chang got out of the car; Rodin could see that some serious negotiations were going on. After about ten minutes and four hundred U.S. Dollars later, they were waved through. They slowly made their way past the West Coast Pier and the Borneo Motors New Vehicle Delivery Centre to a large concrete building with no windows. There was a hand-painted corrugated sign hanging precariously over the loading dock door, denoting that this was the PSA Marine Company. There were several dozen high-end automobiles, mostly BMW's and Mercedes, with a couple Cadillac Escalades parked in the lot.

Once the car was parked, they all just sat observing the comings and goings of the patrons. There were two doormen checking people's passes; this was a by-invitation-only affair. They saw that any interlopers or wanna-be gatecrashers were not tolerated and were asked to leave with extreme prejudice. Rodin saw that there were several surveillance cameras not only on building but located around the parking lot. He said to Jai En, without turning his head, "Cameras?"

She looked at her iWatch and said, "In six minutes, they all will be down."

"Excellent, and back up?"

Still looking at her watch, "Twenty-eight minutes from now."

"Once the cameras are disabled, we go. When we're inside, let me know when the Astro Team enters, then follow my lead. Jia En, stay close to me; things will go down very quickly, and I don't want to have to worry about you. Chang, you boys seem experienced; are you good to go?"

In unison, they replied, "We're good to go, Sir."

"Good. Do you have something for me?"

The passenger Chang opened the glove box and handed Rodin a Glock 38 and three extra fully loaded clips. "Here you go, Sir."

Jia En, still looking at her watch, said, "Cameras down."

"Okay, let's roll."

The jury filed into the courtroom all too somber for Jason Parker Ryan's liking. Billy Ray leaned over to his attorney and whispered, "Whadda think?"

"I think this number two."

"Huh?"

"Never mind."

The bailiff stood up as Judge Novak entered the room and sat down loudly, announcing, "All rise. Court is now in session, the honorable Judge Robert J. Novak presiding. The case of the State of Texas versus Billy Ray Pepper."

Judge Novak slammed the gavel down and said, "Please be seated." He turned to the jury. "I understand that you've reached a verdict. Is that correct, Madam Foreperson?"

A woman in her early sixties rose up, holding a folded piece of paper and said, "Yes, your Honor, we have."

"Would you please hand the verdict to the bailiff, please?"

The bailiff walked over to the foreperson, took the piece of paper, and handed it to the Judge. The Judge opened the folded document, looked at it for a moment, and handed it back to the bailiff. "Please give the verdict to the clerk. Before I have the clerk read the verdict, I want to ask the jury if this verdict is unanimous by all the jury members. So, I'm going to ask each of you to say 'yes' if you agree with this verdict. Juror number 1."

Each juror acknowledged that they did, in fact, agree to the verdict that was set to be announced.

"Thank you, Jurors. Before I have the clerk read the verdict, I want to caution the people in the courtroom that I will not tolerate any outbursts. Do I make myself clear? Will the defendant please rise; Marsha please read the verdict."

"In the case of the State of Texas versus Billy Ray Pepper, on the twelve counts of aggravated murder in the second degree, we the jury do hereby find the defendant, Billy Ray Pepper, guilty as charged."

There was a great uproar within the courtroom despite the judge's orders. "Order in the court! I said order! Bailiffs, please see to it that this court comes to order."

The bailiffs started to move toward the gallery, and the crowd became silent very quickly. Up at the defendant's table, Billy Ray's legs gave way, and he slumped into his seat, sobbing. The sheriff's deputies came up from behind him, stood him up, and placed him in handcuffs.

Judge Novak rapped his gavel to bring attention back to him. "Billy Ray Pepper, you have been found guilty of twelve counts of capital murder, do have anything to say before I pass sentence?

Billy Ray composed himself, stood as erect as he could muster and turned to the gallery, looking at the family members and friends of his victims. "I thought I was doing the patriotic thing. As God is my witness, I thought they were those French terrorists out to kill us Americans, taking away our God-given right to bear arms and kill shit. I'm very sorry to you all, and God Bless ya and God Bless these United States. I guess I'm ready to meet my fate, your Honor."

"Billy Ray Pepper, it is the judgment of this court to sentence you to the maximum penalty under Texas State law: death by lethal injection. May God have mercy on your soul. You will be remanded to the state prison at Huntsville until your execution, of which the date will be set in due course. Deputies, take Mr. Pepper away."

Billy Ray asked the Deputies if he might say goodbye to his wife. The two male Deputies took a look at Mrs. Pepper, who was sobbing and just happened to be wearing a rather revealing scoop neck blouse, decided that it would be a nice thing to do, and said okay.

She tried to put her arms around him, but, due to her ample bosoms, she could only manage to put her hands on his shoulders; she leaned in and kissed him. He said, "I love ya, baby. You go on with your life and forget about me."

"Okay."

"You'll come to visit me, won't you baby?"

"Sure will hon, whenever I can."

"I love you."

"You take care of yourself, ya hear?"

She gave a slight wave to her husband as she slid over to Jason Parker Ryan, who was getting ready to leave the courtroom, and asked, "Say, do you know any good divorce lawyers?"

The two Sheriffs Deputies escorted Billy Ray out of the courtroom; they made their way through the County Court halls, leading to the back entrance where several people were waiting to give Billy Ray support and words of encouragement. As the Sheriffs were getting ready to put Billy Ray into the van that would take him to a holding cell at the county jail until arrangements for his transfer to Huntsville Prison could be made, a young woman in her early twenties stepped forward past the six or seven Billy Ray well-wishers, pulled a Colt revolver from her handbag, and proceeded to shoot Billy Ray in the head. One of the eyewitnesses later told CNN that he could have sworn he heard her whisper, "Vive la France!" right before she put the gun in her mouth and blew her brains out.

Eighteen months to the day of Billy Ray Pepper's murder, all of the other defendants were found guilty of second-degree murder, and all were sentenced to life in prison without the possibility of parole. One juror later stated that it's a shame that they killed a bunch of Texans instead of killing a bunch of them Frenchie's, otherwise they'd be heroes.

David Leeway heard the news of his children's death when several dozen reporters and TV camera crews met him upon landing in Los Angeles. He was quickly whisked away into a private VIP lounge, where two inspectors from

Interpol and half-dozen representatives from the LAPD met him.

"Mr. Leeway, my name is Inspector Morris, and this is Inspector Volker; we're from Interpol. Let me first say how sorry we are about the death of your children. And that we at Interpol are doing everything we can to bring these criminals to justice."

"Tell me, Inspector, just what the fuck does that mean—that you're doing everything you can? I have to tell you, that doesn't mean a whole lot to me."

"I understand, sir. I know it must be cold comfort, but let me assure you that we at Interpol will not let this matter rest. If that means it takes two years or twenty, we will bring these people to justice."

"Thank you, Inspector. I'm sorry to take it out on you. It's just the stress talking. Now, what can you tell me about what happened out there?"

"Well, sir, according to witnesses on the ground, your children were waiting at a watering hole for the big cats to come down to drink, when your youngest son, Richard, shot a lion cub. That's when all hell broke loose; the witnesses say it was like one large volley of fire from a small grove of trees to the East. When the smoke cleared, your three children and the three hunting guides were all dead. Panic ensued and the staff all ran off in different directions into the bush, fearing for their lives, but, up until they scattered, their stories of that dreadful moment are all consistent. There wasn't any warning before it happened. We believe that it was a calculated and highly planned assassination by the French eco-terrorist group called Le Gang de la Clé de Singe, or 'the Monkey Wrench Gang.' The killers knew who your children were and where they were going, so we believe that it was meticulously planned to get maximum worldwide news coverage."

"I want them dead, Inspector! I want them caught, and I want them dead! Do you hear me?"

Volker noticed the veins on both sides of Leeway's neck looked as if they were about to explode from out of the crimson-colored head of the former Presidential runner. Leeway was a dumpy, lumpy man of average height with noticeably small hands and, what looked like, a sleeping marmot for hair upon his head. He was extremely vain and narcissistic and, like so many wealthy men, a bully. Volker led Leeway to a chair, sat him down, and handed him a glass of water before he said, "Mr. Leeway, you mustn't over excite yourself. Rest assured that Interpol and other world law enforcement agencies are working around the clock to bring these people to justice. We will be keeping you abreast of any new developments as they develop. Here's my card, please feel free to call me, day or night, with any questions or if you happen to think of anything you might think is relevant." With that, he stood up, nodded to Morris and they left the lounge, leaving Leeway and his entourage.

Officer Roland from the LAPD asked if there was anything that they could do. Leeway said he couldn't think of anything and thanked them, then, after an elongated awkward pause, they too left.

Once the Interpol inspectors and LAPD left, Leeway pulled out his cell phone and called an old friend. Retired SEAL Team Commander William T. "Wooch" Brown was best known for spearheading several successful SEAL kill missions against ISIS that the American public will never hear of—at least not in their lifetimes.

"Wooch, Leeway here. I'm sure you've heard about my children. I need to see you, as I'm interested in doing some big hunting of my own. You in?"

Rodin got out of the car, walked over to Jia En's side of the BMW Alpina, and opened her door, holding out his hand assisted her from the car. As they were approaching the entrance, Rodin slipped on a pair of non-prescription glasses with a built-in camera, mic, and receiver.

They approached the entrance, and, once there, they handed the doorman closest to Rodin their invitations. Both of the doormen looked every bit the part of goons; they were wearing matching black suits, black turtlenecks, shaved heads, and, of course, black wrap around Ray-Ban sunglasses with earpieces like the Chang brothers. The one holding the clipboard asked their names. The other brought his wrist up to his mouth and whispered their names into a microphone; he then nodded to them, opened the door, and said in a monotone voice, "Have a pleasant evening."

Once inside, Jia En was taken aback by the smell and sight of the enormity of all the endangered animal skins, elephant tusks, rhino horns, shark fins, and even the large variety of living species that were alive and caged: everything from baby orangutans, exotic snakes, lizards, birds from the Amazon Rain Forest, to a five-foot-tall California Condor. Rodin whispered to her, "Just be cool; look disinterested and follow my lead."

They casually started walking among the vendor's booths as if taking inventory of what was available, while, in the back of the large auditorium, the auctioneer was getting ready to start the bidding. Rodin was softly speaking as if to Jia En, but he was actually speaking to the Chang brothers via the transmitter within his glasses. He was pointing out where all the live animals were within the crazy maze of vendors and where the armed guards were stationed. He was preparing, and hoping, to save as many of these endangered species as possible during the raid. The Chang brothers alerted Rodin that the rest of the team had arrived and were in position.

Rodin casually glanced at his watch as he and Jia En walked to the bar. The bartender sauntered over and spoke in broken English, "What you have?"

Jia En smiled and asked for a vodka tonic with a twist of lime; Rodin said, "White Russian." The bartender smiled and started to prepare their drinks just as the overhead lights started to flicker. Rodin looked at his watch and whispered to Jia En, "Any second now. Stay close."

The entire room was suddenly thrown into darkness, at which point there rose an anxious cacophony of dozens of different languages all asking the same question: what's going on? The confusion ceased when the lights came back on. Then, seconds later, fear swept over the room as people realized they were surrounded by dozens of heavily armed men, wearing black balaclavas and dressed in unmarked black military uniforms, screaming at them to get face down onto the ground. During the blackout, Rodin and Jia En themselves had put on balaclavas so as not to be recognized. Rodin moved up onto the auctioneer's podium and raised his arms in the air; he spoke a mixture of English and French with a slight Belgian accent, "Ladies and Gentlemen, Madame's et Messieurs, may I have your attention please. Don't bother trying to use your mobile devices, as we have jammed all services both use of cellular phones and the use of the Internet. We represent an international group known as Le Gang de la Clé de Singe, we are an environmental action movement who wages war against all poachers, big game hunters, and—aw, Hell—we're waging war against you."

There was mostly silence with an undercoating of sobbing and whimpering. "Now, I want anyone who is armed to slowly stand up with your hands above your heads. Any sudden movements or attempts to use your weapons, and you will be shot. Now, please rise now."

About a dozen men stood up with their hands above their heads. Eight members of the team started to go through the crowd and gather up the weapons. Just as the last of the dozen men standing handed over his weapon, a man sprung up from the floor and shot one of the masked men in the back, whereupon no less than three team members opened fire at the assailant, killing him on the spot. As the team member who had been shot started to slowly get to his feet, there was a collective gasp in the room. People couldn't believe that he was still alive after being shot in the back at close range. He turned to the roomful of people, shrugged, and whispered with a smile in his voice, "Gilet pare-balles," meaning 'bulletproof vest.'

"Alright, are there any more heroes in the room?" Rodin shouted. "I want everyone to get up, move to my left, and stand against the wall. Now!"

As the people moved to the wall, the team of hooded commandos patted down men and women for wallets and purses, along with any weapons and cell phones. Once they had collected them, all the hostages were led outside to the parking lot except for eighty men. They were the vendors at the event and were told to stay where they stood against the wall.

Rodin spoke to those not standing up against the wall, "You all should consider yourselves very fortunate that you're being allowed to leave. It's because of your ignorance and selfishness that allow this atrocity against nature to occur. Remember, we have your names, and we know where you live. If we find that you continue to participate in this immoral trade, we will take action. Do you understand? Now leave!"

Once outside, the captives saw, waiting for them, all their chauffeurs being guarded by a half dozen black-hooded soldiers.

A large, rotund man in a hooded uniform jumped onto the hood of a silver and blue Bugatti Veyron 16.4, a car capable of reaching speeds over two hundred and fifty mph and with a price tag close to a million pounds, not dollars, the black warrior shouted, "Listen up people! We have all of your identifications, and we know where you all live. So I recommend you all forget what you've seen, or else we'll come to find you late one night and help you forget. This will all be over in a few minutes, so just sit tight. All of you so-called customers, start heading towards the main gate that you entered in from. In a few seconds, there is going to be a small explosion and then a rather large fire, so get a move on. You've got about three minutes. Now go!"

Someone shouted, "What about our cars?"

"Oh yeah, we threw all of the car keys into the bay. I suggest you get going, now!"

As the big man jumped down off the car, he left behind a rather sizable dent on the hood. "Sorry about that," he said to a little old Asian man in the crowd, who looked like someone just kicked him in the balls and probably would have preferred it.

Inside the auction house, all the animals were being evacuated onto a red and white Nordic Tugboat, which was docked just docked a hundred feet away. Once all the live species were safe on board the vessel, petrol was poured over all the illegal and endangered products. Rodin estimated the value of everything to be well over sixty million dollars.

He walked towards the men standing against the wall, flanked by two soldiers on either side of him. There were eighty vendors standing against the wall. when one of them stepped forward. A man with a German accent shouted out, "What are you doing? Are you crazy; you can't just burn everything; do you realize how much all this is worth?"

Rodin stopped and said, "Yes, I am crazy, and yes I do know how much all this is worth, and I am going to burn everything."

"Do you have any idea who you're dealing with, do you know who I am?"

"As a matter of fact, I do, Baron Von Drumpf. If my memory serves me right, you come from a long line of so-called German aristocrats, who have profited from the misfortunes of others, be it taking advantage of human beings, like your family did during the Nazi regime when your family stole millions of dollars of priceless artwork from the Jews, or, now, profiteering from the suffering of endangered animals."

"Lies! I will not stand here and be insulted by the likes of you, just tell us what do you expect, an apology, money, what?"

"I expect you all to die, Baron." Rodin nodded to the men with him and they opened fire, killing all eighty vendors with the exception of Von Drumpf.

"You're not going to kill me, too?" Drumpf said sweating profusely.

"Not today Herr Von Drumpf, but soon. Very soon. But first, I want you to take this letter and release it to the press; let them know what you've witnessed here, and let the world know we're tired of this exploitation of animals. Do you understand? Oh, and once you've done that, I suggest that you try and find a safe place to try and hide where I won't be able to find you. I don't think you can, but you can try. Now go." Drumpf took the letter and ran as fast as his stubby little legs could go.

When everyone was at a safe distance, Rodin gave the signal to the demolition team. There was a small explosion, and, in seconds, the entire building was in flames that lit up the evening sky and could be seen for miles. The mass of captives had, at first, slowly started meandering toward the front gate, but, when the explosion occurred, full-scale panic broke out. People began to run, some tripping over others, and a few actually fell into the bay. There was little that the fire department could do, since its fire trucks were stuck due to all of the immovable parked cars that were sitting so close to the building. Some cars caught fire from the immense heat, and all the boats that were docked in the bay hampered even the fireboats. One crewmember on the fireboat said it was one of the most magnificent fires that he's ever seen in his twenty-plus years as a firefighter.

SEAL Team Commander William T. "Wooch" Brown and David Leeway met on board Leeway's yacht, the

Lunar Eclipse, a five hundred and seventy-eight-foot vessel. He spared no expense when it came to designing his mega-yacht. Onboard luxuries include an infinity pool with a thirty-foot glass wall that doubles up as a cinema screen—so he can watch all of his movies while enjoying a swim. Other amenities onboard include two helipads, two swimming pools, a disco hall, twenty-four guest suites, a mini-submarine, a gymnasium, a spa, a massage room, and even a missile defense system.

"Commander, so glad that you came."

"I'm sorry that we have to meet under such dark circumstances. Please, accept my deepest condolences."

"Thank you, that means a lot. Are you able to help me?"

"Quite frankly, I disapprove. And if this ever comes back to me, I will disavow any knowledge of such an operation. Do you understand?"

"Yes, of course."

"Well, I have been through several layers of contacts and have been able to assemble a strike team of the top ex-military and mercenaries available. They are the very best, and they are very expensive."

"Money is no object. Whatever it takes to bring these thugs to justice. And by justice, I mean dead."

"You understand, this is no quick mission; it could take months and possibly years. Are you prepared to wait to get results? These people will not be rushed. It may be your money, but it's their lives."

"I understand."

"Good. I will have someone contact you in a day or two, if that's good."

"Excellent. Wooch, can I offer you a little something to drink?"

"A Whiskey would be nice."

"Whiskey it is. I have a little something special to sort of celebrate on this occasion. Yamazaki, fifty-year-old, third edition, 2011 release. Ever had some?"

"Can't say that I have."

"Well if you had, you'd remembered I guarantee it."

Leeway walked over to the bar in the salon and asked William, his majordomo, to pour two whiskies. Turning to the Commander, he asked, "Neat?"

"Yes, please."

The Commander walked over to where Leeway was standing received his glass, then took a sip. The look on his face was orgasmic. "Oh my God. This is incredible."

"I'm glad you like it. It's very rare; only one hundred and fifty bottles were ever produced, and I own sixty of them."

"Expensive?"

"Oh, one hundred and twenty thousand dollars a bottle, give or take. Would you like a bottle?"

"David, that's very generous, but I couldn't."

"Don't be silly. You're doing me a very large favor. Please accept a bottle, as just a token of my eternal thanks."

"David, you're too kind."

"Nonsense. Now, let's go down for some lunch, and you can tell me all about my strike team."

Detective Wilson had just taken out the Swanson Chicken Parmigiana TV Dinner from his oven and sat down at the kitchen table, when his cell phone rang. "Ah, shit. It never fails."

The Swanson Company, famous for TV Dinners, had long ago dropped the "TV" from the name and now just called them dinners to class up and bring a bit more cache to the 'hey you're a loser' meal category.

The Chicken Parmigiana was his favorite of the dozen or so Swanson meals. They claimed that they topped their breaded chicken cutlet with rich tomato sauce and mozzarella cheese, serving it with a side of pasta and mixed vegetables for the full Italian experience! Wilson had never been to Italy, but he knew this TV dinner hadn't truly captured the full Italian experience—well, not any Italian experience he envisioned anyway.

Ever since his wife of forty-four years, Linda, passed away four years ago from a tough bout with breast cancer, he poured his everything into his work. He didn't much care about the everyday details of his life like gourmet dinners; the fifteen-year-old Dodge Dart was just fine, and the ninety-nine dollar two-forone suits he bought off the rack served thier purpose, thank you—even if he bought them eight years ago. It was all about the work. He was one of the best Homicide Detectives in the department and recognized in the state of Minnesota.

"Yeah, this better be good. You know this is my Chicken Parmigiana night."

Johansson said, "It's Brad Devin."

"What did that scum bag do now?"

"His wife, Janie, killed him."

"Fuck."

"We're down at the station."

"You got her?"

"Yeah, she's in interrogation room one, and she says she's willing to talk without her lawyer."

Wilson sighed. "I'll be right down. Thanks, Johansson."

Brad Devin was a day worker. He would stand outside the local Lowes or Home Depot and try and pick up odd jobs from contractors or just plain people who need brawn and no brains. With Brad, you usually got what you paid for: not much.

He'd had a long history of using his wife as a punching bag and, occasionally, as an ashtray. He had been in and out of jail for assault and battery, spousal abuse, and public drunkenness for years. Brad was a real lowlife; his passing would bring no tears to anyone, and even his mother thought he was a real dirtbag. Before Wilson moved over to homicide, he had arrested Devin several times for punching out his wife. One time he beat her so bad that she lost sight in her left eye; he got eighteen months in County.

When Wilson got to interrogation room one, Detective Johansson was leaning against the door and checking his emails on his iPhone.

"How's she doing?"

"I'd say in shock."

They opened the door to see Janie Devin sitting, staring off into space. She looked so small and frail. She was covered in cuts and bruises, and the right side of her face was swollen three times its normal size. Only when Wilson spoke did she realize that someone was in the room with her.

As Detective Wilson sat across from her, he reached across the table and touched her hand. She looked up from her deadeye gaze and said, "I just couldn't take it anymore."

"I know, Janie. Did Detective Johansson ask you if you wanted a lawyer present? We can get you one if would like."

"No, I just want to get this nightmare over with."

"Okay Janie...just take your time and tell us what happened."

"Well, for about six weeks, Brad had been drinking quite a bit more than usual. He hasn't been able to pick up much work because of the bad weather. He was spending a lot of money on liquor and beer, money that was supposed to buy groceries. When I mentioned it to him, he got angry and punched me in the stomach, told me just to shut up and get him another beer.

That was last Saturday night. So that night, I waited until he was sleep, and I got my father's old baseball bat that he gave to little Bobby, and I hit him in the head, broke his nose. He went to the ER and came back all bandaged up. He beat the living hell out of me, and he broke little Bobby's arm. Up until then, he had never hurt Bobby. I always thought I could live with him as long as he didn't hurt Bobby. I took Bobby to the hospital and told them he had fallen off his bike. I knew they didn't believe me with the way I looked, and they told me that they had to report it to the police and child services. I wasn't going to let them take my baby away because of Brad. All week long, he would smack me about, yell a lot, and threaten Bobby.

So last night, Brad was all nervous and jerky. Every time he was about nod off to sleep, he would snap up and look around to see where I was. He had gotten a gun from somewhere, and he kept pointing it at me and Bobby, saying that, if I tried anything, he'd kill us both.

I was sitting at the foot of the bed, just watching him, not moving a muscle. It took him a long time to finally fall asleep. When he did, I slowly got up and sneaked into Bobby's room, got the bat, and went back into our bedroom. He was sleeping, still holding the gun in his hand. I didn't think I could get the gun away from him without waking him up, so I hit him in the head again as hard as I could. He was laying on his side; I hit him on his ear, and I hit him again, and again and…"

"How many times did you hit him?"

"I don't know, a bunch of times."

"Janie, we're going to have a female officer take you to the hospital, to have the doctors examine you, and to take photographs of your injuries. Do you understand?"

She nodded. "What about Bobby? What will happen to him?"

"Bobby will be looked after. Does your mom still live in town? Can she look after him?"

"Yes, my Mom still lives here."

"Okay Janie, we'll call your mom and have her take care of Bobby, okay? You go with Officer Brighten. Sally, you take good care of Mrs. Devin."

"Yes, sir. Mrs. Devin, will you come with me, please?

Officer Brighten took Mrs. Devin by her arm, and, as they were leaving, she looked back at Wilson, who whispered, "No cuffs." The two women left the interrogation room and went down to a squad car to head over to Sanford Health Medical Center.

After they had left, Wilson asked Johansson, "Was the ME able to ascertain how many times she hit him?"

"Over thirty. He said his head was just a lump of goo. Want to see the photos?"

"No, thanks. I don't want to spoil my Italian classic Chicken Parmigiana dinner."

Johansson said, "So, whatdya think?"

"I think she should get a medal."

It was after midnight when Rodin, Jia En, and the Chang brothers returned to the Ritz-Carlton, Millenia. As the valet slowly walked over to the car, Rodin asked, "Would you all like to join me in a drink?"

"Sure, that would be a nice way to take the edge off. Come on Chang," Jia En said.

The four of them entered the lobby, which was quite a buzz of activity with a lot of conversation about the goings on at the marina. They walked to the bank of elevators and took it to the twenty-seventh floor to the Chihuly Lounge, which was named after famed American glass artist Dale Chihuly. Rodin held up four fingers as they approached the hostess, who smiled and nodded. She picked up four menus and indicated for them to follow her. She led them past a rather attractive Asian woman, who was playing "Stardust" at the piano to an area that looked more like a living room than a lounge with overstuffed couches and armchairs. The interior lights were turned down low, so the guests could enjoy the fabulous view of the Singapore Harbor.

After they were all seated and handed a menu, the Hostess said, "Jasmine will be taking care of you.. I hope you will have a pleasant evening."

Rodin said, smiling, "Thank you, it's been quite an evening so far. I'm really looking forward to seeing what the rest of this night will bring."

Shortly after the hostess left, Jasmine approached them, asking if they were ready to order. Rodin took the lead. "If you all don't mind, I think Champagne is in order. Jasmine, we'd like a bottle of Dom Perignon and some appetizers. How about an order of Seafood Tau Pok, an order of Chicken Char Siew Onsen Egg, Sweet Potato Puree, and an order of Bonito Jus."

"Very good, sir. I'll get your order in right away."

They sat quietly for a few minutes, contemplating the evening's events. The Chang brothers sat, staring down and looking at their iPhones; Jia En seemed to be lost within the melody of the music and was staring out the window. Rodin was about to speak, when Jia En said, "I've never seen men killed before. It was horrible."

Rodin reached over and held her hand. "It's a terrible thing to take a life, and no one can really prepare you for the enormity of it, the finality, and the ultimate cruelty to steal away someone's being."

"And yet, we killed over eighty people tonight in a blink of an eye. Gone. Everything they were and everything they might have been, gone."

"Jia En, by our actions tonight, we might have saved dozens of endangered species, animals that are being slaughtered for sport, for the pattern of their fur, for man's own selfishness.

You saw how they had some of those animals caged and chained; some of those animals would never feel grass beneath their feet, only the cold, hard steel or concrete of a cage. By living in a five-by-seven-foot pen for decades, animals have been known to go mad, and for what? So some wealthy asshole can show the poor thing off or point to an animal's head stuck on a wall?

You're right, eighty people did die this evening. But if we can make these bastards think twice about profiting off of these poor creatures, then I can live with myself. I sleep very well at night knowing that I am helping the helpless. Now, Jia En, the question you have to ask yourself is: can you?"

Jasmine came with the Champagne and four glasses. "Your Champagne, sir, chilled to a perfect 10°C. Shall I pour?"

"Excellent. Yes, please, if you don't mind."

As she poured, the appetizers were brought to the table in front of the couch and set in a most aesthetic arrangement. Jasmine poured a small amount into Rodin's glass and waited.

"That is excellent Jasmine. If you would, please pour for my guests."

After filling everyone's glass, she asked if there was anything else that she might do for them.

"At the moment, no. Thank you."

"Very good, please enjoy."

Rodin held up his glass to the group and said, "I propose a toast to you all and to the cause. Salut."

"Last night in Singapore, at the Republic of Singapore Yacht Club, a raid was held by Le Gang de la Clé deSsinge to obtain the release of several dozen endangered species, including a California Condor, several Orangutans, a baby Black Rhinoceros, along with several varieties of rare birds and reptiles. Also found were hundreds of illegal endangered animal pelts, skins, along with various animal organs, and dozens of Elephant ivory tusks and Rhinoceros horns. We are proud to announce that all the animals have been confiscated and have been safely relocated to wildlife sanctuaries. The illegal items have all been destroyed, and

the perpetrators have been killed. Over eighty racketeers have paid the ultimate price for their crimes against nature.

Le Gang de la Clé de Singe wants the world to know that this aggression against any and all endangered species, or any animals that are hunted for sport, will not stand. You have been warned, again".

David Leeway threw down the copy of the New York Times that carried the story of the Singapore massacre, as it was being called. All over the world came condemnation of these actions, and the UN has called a special gathering to discuss these acts of aggression. Some were calling for an all-out war against the Monkey Wrench Gang; the only problem was no one knew who they were and where they would strike next. There weren't any known headquarter locations, and no one of any significance had ever been captured; when they were interrogated, they could only give up lower-level-personnel information. The organization was so well constructed that it seemed impenetrable.

Leeway was getting ready to head to his office on Fifth Avenue and Sixty-first Street, up to the penthouse of the building that bears his name, Leeway Towers, when his cell phone rang.

"Leeway, go!"

"Mr. Leeway, this is Angel calling. I believe you are expecting a call from me."

"Angel?"

"Yeah, the Angel of Death."

"Ahh, right."

"Is there somewhere we can meet, privately?

"Yes, of course,.I have a warehouse in Staten Island that's not being used at the moment."

"Perfect. Mr. Leeway, it's best you come alone; the fewer people involved, the better. Now, just tell me where and when."

After David Leeway agreed to arrive alone and gave the address of the warehouse, he called down to the garage to have his Mercedes S-Class Cabriolet brought around immediately.

As the valet was closing the car door, he thought he heard Mr. Leeway udder, "I'm off to see the Angel of Death."

Rodin didn't stay for the Singapore Grand Prix after all; he caught a mid-afternoon flight to Gaborone, Botswana to meet up with the Red Team. Although the security at the airport was extreme, he managed to pass through numerous checkpoints and screenings without too much trouble. Their new assignment would be in South Africa, to reek some havoc with the 'canned' game hunts.

Rodin met the team at Sir Seretse Khama International Airport, after his flight from Amsterdam, with a connection in Malawi and then on to Gaborone on Air Botswana, arriving at 3:30 PM local time. The airport was named for Sir Seretse Khama, the first president of Botswana, and, by most standards, it was a fairly modern airport.

Pelé and Odin were waiting in the receiving area, holding a sign reading 'Picasso.'

"Picasso?" Rodin asked with a big grin. "He's good, but he ain't no Rodin."

"Good to see you, boss. Heard good things about Singapore," Odin said.

"Yeah we saved a lot of precious cargo, and I'm hoping we finally kicked the hornet's nest enough to get peoples attention."

Pelé said, "No doubt about it, sir; that seems to be the only thing people are talking about."

"Good, good. Let's hope things will start changing. So, how's the team? Ready to rock 'n' roll?"

"Affirmative, sir," Pelé said as they headed out of the airport to the waiting vehicle.

They headed north on the A1 towards the town of Mookane, and then they took a sharp right off the highway onto a dirt road that would eventually cross into South Africa. They would travel another two hours, by-passing the village of Steenbokpan, and soon they arrived at the Grootwater Nature Reserve around sunset, where they met up with the other members of Red Team. They would camp the night and then head east to the small nature reserve called Lapalala Wilderness at first light. There, they would engage the owners and members of the South African Big Game Association, which has been raising lions for the express purpose of having wealthy, and mostly American, hunters kill them. The animals have been raised in captivity around humans, so they did not fear man. In fact, they approach the hunters, thinking that they would be fed. Instead, they got killed at a mere thirty-five thousand dollars a pop.

Late in the afternoon, Rodin called the men together to go over the game plan and explain why they were at this particular Reserve. They had just finished having an early dinner; the sun was hanging low in the orange sky, just about twenty minutes before it would drop behind the hills.

"Men, every year hundreds of lions are bred in captivity by the South Africa Big Game Association for the purpose of being placed onto their private game reserves for slaughter. We got reports this morning that eight lionesses were released two days ago, literally a day before their clients arrived—in fact, four were released as the plane was landing just down the road. The hunters, and I use the term loosely, shot the first lion probably within half-an-hour of landing; one lion was shot while hiding in a hole, another leaning up against a fence.

Their clients, I won't say hunters because there isn't any hunting involved, are told that it's very dangerous—that these are wild animals…and, of course, they believe it. They want to believe it so they can feel like big men. The guide's pump up their egos by telling them, 'You got so lucky, that was such an amazing shot.' They give them slaps on the back and say, 'You're such a hero, look at what you've done— you've killed the king of the jungle.'

It's all just a lie. These poor animals are raised to be killed; they don't have a chance, and it's not fair nor legal. It's known as canned lion hunting, but it's more like shooting fish in a barrel than a lion hunt.

You all have your assignments. Tomorrow will be a little different than our other assignments, as we will not be wearing our ghillie suits. Instead, we'll be wearing South African Protrack Anti-Poaching Unit uniforms. Any questions? Okay, so tomorrow we will suit up and win one for the lions. And don't forget to apply the camo paint on your faces or, as Pelé likes to call it, 'War Paint'."

Sally Johansson sat parked in her 1968 VW Micro Bus on Brockhurst Street, right across from the Hoover Elementary School in Oakland, California, staring at number 980 Brockhurst. A modest two-story home painted grey with white trim, there was a low chain link fence, and the only notable feature that made it stand out from the other homes was that there was a porch swing.

Sally had driven by and had parked to observe the house for over a week without seeing anyone come in or out. Today, she thought, she'd just knock on the door to see if anyone was home; she would say to whomever that she was lost and ask for directions. She had thought of asking her roommate, Rachel, to go with her, but Rachel had to study for a Poly-Si test, so she would just do it herself.

She got out of the van and crossed the street, opened the gate to the fence and walked up the five steps to the porch, and rang the doorbell. She could hear movement inside the house and a voice shouting, "Coming."

As she waited, she slipped her hand inside her handbag and held on to a small can of Pepper Spray Pocket Defense Spray that her brother, a cop, told her to carry it at all times. He kept telling her that she wasn't back in Bemidji, and that Oakland can be a rough town. She countered with, "Yeah, well, I haven't heard of anyone having their heads chopped off and mounted on a wall out here."

The door opened and a little old man in his eighties said, "Yes? Can I help you?"

"Hi, I'm sorry to bother you, but I'm lost and my phone's GPS isn't working. I'm looking for the Dimensional Outlet Furniture store; it's around here somewhere. I've been driving around and around. I'm supposed to meet my boyfriend there. Would you happen to know where it is?"

"Oh, I'm sorry. I don't, but I do have a local map of the area from the Chamber of Commerce. It's a couple years old, but it might have your furniture store on it. Won't you come in?"

"I don't want to be a bother."

"No bother at all. In fact, I would appreciate the company. Please."

Sally relented and entered the house. As Sally entered the doorway, the man peered out as if to see if anyone was watching, then closed the door. Sally followed the man down a small hallway into the living room. The man gestured to the couch. "Please have a seat. I'll go look for the map. Be right back. Can I get you something to drink? Tea, soda, water?"

"Oh, no, thank you. I really appreciate your help."

"Well, I haven't helped yet. Be right there."

As she settled on the couch, she was startled by what she saw on the walls: a various assortment of mounted animal heads. They were mostly small creatures like a raccoon, fox, and even a coyote—at least, she thought it was a coyote; it could have been a dog. She gripped her Pepper Spray tighter and had it at the ready.

Two doors down from the Reynolds Shipyard Corporation on Edgewater Street, about a mile north of the Verrazano-Narrows Bridge on Staten Island, stood the abandoned Leeway Warehouse Complex. It once housed US Government materials that were being designated for shipment to Afghanistan during Operation Enduring Freedom in 2001 to 2014. Since 2014, the warehouse complex had been abandoned.

The black Mercedes S-Class Cabriolet pulled up to the main office entrance of the complex, and David Leeway sat waiting for the Angel of Death to arrive. Approximately fifteen minutes later, a Lorie Metallic Blue Supercharged LR-V8 Range Rover pulled up nose to nose with Leeway's Mercedes. A tall man with short military style haircut, wearing Ray-Ban aviator sunglasses, blue jeans, a t-shirt, and an Air Force A-2 leather flight jacket got out and proceeded to walk over to the Mercedes' driver's side door.

Leeway rolled down his window and asked, "You Angel?"

"That's me. It's a pleasure to meet you, Mr. Leeway. Let's talk."

"Let's go into the office, if that's okay."

"Sounds good."

They walked into the office's main entrance and past the abandoned reception area, where a large Mercator projection global map with the name Leeway Industries imprinted over the map hung. David led the way toward the back, where there was a large conference room with a view of Bay Ridge, Brooklyn across Gravesend Bay.

David gestured for the man to have a seat. "Please, have a seat."

"Thank you, sir. It's sufficed to say that the least you know about me and my team, the better. We will do everything we can to keep your name out of this operation, but shit happens, mistakes are made—usually not on our end—but they do happen. So again, the less you know, the better. Have all the financial accounts been set up as you were instructed?"

"Yes, everything has been followed to a tee."

"Excellent. Now let me explain something to you, and I want you to fully understand this. Most likely, you will never see me again, nor will you probably ever hear from me again either. We will not be rushed, Mr. Leeway; we will move at the pace that we feel is appropriate. We have a saying: 'speed kills.' The results you are looking for may take a month, a year, ten years; there is no way of knowing. We are dealing with a very elusive enemy. I can't say how long this process may take, and, even then, it could take years to build up enough trust to get the information we need. Also, there may be times when you will be asked to provide additional funds for unexpected expenses; please comply quickly. We are not requesting money for parties or frivolous items; they will be for necessities. Do you understand?"

"Yes, I totally understand."

"Good. Now, if at any time, you decide that you don't want to continue with the operation for whatever reason, all you have to do is call the number on this card and say 'red light.' Got it?"

"Red light. Got it. How will I know if you've been successful?"

"Watch the news, Mr. Leeway, and not that fair and balanced crap, but the real news."

The Angel of Death stood up and shook Leeway's hand. "Goodbye, Mr. Leeway. It was a pleasure never to having met you."

Jeffery Foster and his guide, Jason Hamilton, walked along the well-worn trail that dozens of others hunters had walked before him. The guide by his right side gave a low whistle, as a large, dark-manned lion walked just a few meters away and then slowly turned and approached them. The lion stopped and looked at the two men as if he recognized them. Foster raised his 30-06 Remington and fired. A single shot rang out and echoed over the Lapalala bush, sending up a flock of Cape sparrows into the sky.

The force of the bullet made the three-hundred-pound lion cartwheel around, dropping to the ground momentarily. Shocked and confused, it roared, got up quickly, and limped off into the bush.

"Shoot him again! Shoot him again! Shoot him again!" Hamilton frantically shouted, as Foster reloaded and fired blindly into a group of Camel Thorn trees. They tracked the big cat, following the trail of blood splatter it had left for a couple hundred yards. They found the big cat lying on its side, dying behind a Camel Thorn tree. Jeffery Foster walked up to him, and the lion lifted his head and gave him a look of betrayal. Jason said for Foster to put the beast out of its misery, which he did.

Foster, laughingly, said, "King of the jungle, my ass." Then, he leaned down and kissed the lion on the head.

Hamilton patted Foster on the back and said, "Right, mate. *You* are the king of the jungle. Congratulations."

Their attention was drawn away from Foster's lion by a group of five uniformed men heading towards them. Hamilton recognized the uniforms. "Ah, they're Protrack. They're an anti-poaching unit that operates all around these parts." He raised his hand and shouted, "Howzit!"

Rodin raised his hand in response and shouted back, "Hoe gaan dit!"

The uniformed men fanned out to form a semi-circle around the two men and their trophy. Rodin stepped forward, handed Hamilton a copy of the Le Gang de la Clé de Singe's manifesto, and asked, "Have you ever seen this?"

Hamilton looked the document over, then handed it back. "Yeah, I've seen it, and those geezers best not come 'round here, or they'll get what for, you know what I mean, mate?"

Rodin handed it to Foster. "Have you ever seen this?"

Foster looked at it without taking it from the uniformed man. "Yeah, so what?"

"So, would you gentlemen be so kind as to put these around your neck?" Rodin said, as he handed each of the men the yellow ensign with the black logo of the skull and crossed monkey wrenches. The members of the Red Team lifted their AK-47's and pointed them at the two hunters.

Hamilton threw his on to the ground. "Go fuck yourself."

Pelé fired one shot, hitting Hamilton in the upper right torso, which caused him to cartwheel around and drop to the ground, just like what happened to the lion moments earlier, except he didn't get up or roar.

Foster looked down at Hamilton's lifeless body, dropped down onto his knees, and threw up. He looked at the five men, who were pointing their guns at him, and cried, "Please, don't. I recently lost my wife and have three small children. Please, no, don't."

Odin said, "You said you had read the manifesto, did you not? "

"Yes, I'm so sorry. Please don't kill me."

"The manifesto says no quarter shall be given," Odin said coldly.

"But my children."

"No, your orphans."

Rodin looked at Lu Wei, gave a short nod, and took a shot at Mr. Foster that placed him next to Jason Hamilton. The team laid them side by side next to the lion, and then they placed the Monkey Wrench flags around the two men's necks. In their pockets they put the accompanying proclamation, which proclaimed their ongoing war against all they consider to be transgressors against nature.

They then moved West to where they knew the hunters camp was set up. The report from the drone was that there were six other hunting parties scouting big cats in the vicinity.

There, a dozen or so well-worn paths criss-crossing each other all eventually seeming to head to the main camp. On the way, the team came across several small prides of lions that seemed very accustomed to humans, and, for the most part, they just ignored the team as they passed by.

When they arrived at the camp, it was deserted, so they decided to wait for them to come to them, rather than spending hours tracking every group. They were kept apprised of all the hunting groups whereabouts from the Red Team drone. Off in the distance, they would hear the occasional shot, indicating that some rich bastard's ego had been stroked by the killing of a homegrown lion.

The team settled in and waited for the groups to return to camp. They didn't have to wait long; it was forty-five minutes later when the first pair of hunter and guide entered the camp. Shortly behind them came their porters, who were carrying the body of a female lion. The guide, Ted Harrington, an Aussie from Alice Springs, saw the uniformed Protrack team as they were entering camp. "G'day mate," he shouted out. "You boys out for poachers? No worries here, mate; we have all the proper docos."

Lu Wei stepped forward and said, "Never had any doubt."

Harrington glanced at his watch. "The others should be wandering back pretty soon; care to stay for some lunch? We usually eat right around noon. I think today it's just going to be some meat'n veg, sorry. Care to join us?"

"That would great, thanks."

"Oh, this here is Mr. Andrews, from Tulsa, Oklahoma, USA. He's the bugger who bagged that beauty," Harrington said, pointing to the lion that the porters were placing in the back of a Fourteen-ton baby-poop-brown Steyer 1291 4X4 Expedition Truck. The Steyer had a six-man front cab, hydraulic winch, roof rack with solar panels, awning's on both sides, and all the comforts of home: large kitchen, living room, shower, and bathroom. It had a small sleeping cabin for when the guests needed to take a nap after a hard day of killing shit.

Within an hour, the other four hunting teams appeared, each with their daily limit of kills. One team had shot a giraffe that had wandered onto the nature reserve; the porters would need the help of others to bring that trophy back after lunch. The hunter, William Stringer, a real good-old-boy from Tennessee, had a bunch of photos of him standing with his foot on the torso taken with his iPhone. Said he couldn't wait to text everyone back home in Sneedville, where Mr. Stringer was the assistant manager at the local Hardees.

As lunch was being prepared, the talk was all about the hunts and the excitement of the kills. Stringer was exalting grand tales of his taking down such a unique beast, when he looked around and asked where Foster and Rogers were.

"Oh, we ran across them a couple hours ago. Unfortunately, they won't be joining you," Rodin said, as he and the Red Team formed a semi-circle around the group seated at the lunch table.

"Why not?" Stringer queried, as he took a bite out of the ear of corn he was powering through like a beaver through a pine branch.

"'Cause they're dead."

"Whaddya mean they're dead?" Harrington asked, as he began to stand up.

"Everyone stay seated! I want all you porters to drop what you're doing and stand over there," Rodin demanded as he pointed off to the left of the makeshift kitchen area. The seven porters did as they were told.

"Gentlemen, we are not members of Protrack. We are members of Le Gang de la Clé de Singe, or, if you prefer, the Monkey Wrench Gang. I am sure that you have heard that we are at war with any and all sport hunters and killers of endangered species. We have pledged our lives in saving the world's wildlife from self-serving, narcissistic buggers like yourselves."

"Look, if it's money you want, I'm wealthy. I can give you anything you want. How much?"

"No, Mr. Andrews, we don't care about your money."

"Then what do you want?"

Harrington looked down at his half eating steak and said, "They're here to kill us."

It was over in seconds.

Rodin looked at the porters and told them to go get all the kills out of the truck and lay the hunters and guides beside each of their kills. The Red Team placed the yellow Monkey Wrench flags around each of their necks, along with a copy of the manifesto in their pockets.

Odin asked one of the porters, "Can anyone of you drive the truck?"

A short, elderly man, wearing baggy khaki shorts and a dirty wife-beater t-shirt, said that he could.

"I want you to take the truck and all the porters and go to Ellisras, you understand?"

"Yes, sir. I understand. What about them?" The little man said, as he gestured to the guides and hunters.

"No, they stay here."

Ellisras is a coal-mining town about an hour and a half drive from the reserve. The town was named after a couple farm owners, Patrick Ellis and Piet Erasmus. The Red Team knew there would be a police station located there; they figured they had at least three and a half hours to vacate the area before all hell broke loose.

Rodin waited for the porters to leave before they surveyed the location and said to the group, "Make sure the area is spotless. Lu Wei, who shall we say was here?"

Lu Wei looked into his backpack and pulled out a small metal box containing several small envelopes. He thumbed thru them and pulled one out, held it up, and said, "How about Rock Hudson?"

"Excellent choice."

Lu Wei opened the envelope and took out a small piece of tape and removed the plastic backing; he then rubbed the clear tape onto a tin cup and placed it at the head of the lunch table, filling the cup with Mister Pibb.

When Rodin was satisfied that the camp was in order, he announced, "Saddle up, men, and head out."

Sally didn't hear the old man enter the room; she was staring with total concentration at the stuffed heads on the wall in front of her. She nearly wet herself when he said, "Do you like my little collection? Oh, I'm so sorry. Did I startle you?"

"Just a little. I was just admiring your trophies. Did you mount them yourself?"

"Oh no, no. My son did those when he was a teenager, a long time ago. Must be twenty years now; my how time flies. I only put them up recently. You see, his mom helped him when he was a boy scout to get some badges. When he left home for college, I put them away, so they've been in the attic all these years."

"So, why bring them out now?"

"My wife recently passed away, and I was cleaning out some stuff in the attic.I stumbled across these, and so I thought I'd put them up. It's just something to remember them by."

"Oh, I'm so sorry."

"We were married for over fifty years. Fifty-three, to be exact."

"Wow, fifty-three years. That's incredible."

"My son came home for the funeral; they were very close."

"Does he live here in Oakland?"

"No, my son lives overseas. He was in the Army, but now he's a consultant for a bunch of nonprofits. He's a big mucky muck."

"That's nice; you must be very proud."

"Yes, I am. You know, come to think of it, I don't know if he would like me putting these heads up on the wall."

"Why is that?"

"Well, he was a war hero, but now he does work for a lot of environmental groups, and it might not be politically correct, you know. I only really did it so I could have something to remind me of them now that Margret is gone."

"So, I guess he's not still into taxidermy?"

"No, he doesn't even hunt anymore and doesn't like people who do. You know, with all the animals that are endangered."

"I agree, totally. By the way, my name is Sally Johansson."

"I'm Chase Madrid. Nice to meet you, Sally Johansson."

"What an interesting name. What's your son's name?"

"Chase Madrid Jr.," he said, looking down at the floor. Then he noticed he was holding the map. "Totally forgot, I got the map right here. Let's see, what was the name of that store you're supposed to meet your friend at?"

That evening, Sally called her brother and gave him a full download on her super sleuthing.

"This Chase Madrid Jr. has got to be your guy. He mounts heads, and he works for environmental groups. According to his dad, he hates hunting and hunters, and he lives overseas!"

"Nice work, Sis. We'll have Interpol check him out. Just stay away from the old man."

"Aw, but he's a nice old guy."

"No. Not until we check out his son. Promise me."

"Okay, I promise."

Chase Madrid Jr., *a.k.a.* 'the Angel of Death,' was ex-CIA. And with twenty-two years of working primarily in the murky world of covert black ops, he did anything he was asked to do without question. He was responsible for helping to set the detention center in Iraq known as Abu Ghraib Prison. It was during his time serving at Abu Ghraib Prison, that Chase Madrid Jr. obtained the nickname 'the Angel of Death.'

During the war in Iraq, personnel of the US Army and the CIA committed a series of human rights violations against detainees. These violations included physical and sexual abuse, torture, rape, sodomy, and murder. In fact, many of the torture techniques used were developed at Guantánamo detention centre, including prolonged isolation, the frequent flier program—a sleep deprivation program whereby people were moved from cell to cell every few hours, so they couldn't sleep for days, weeks, even months— short-shackling in painful positions, nudity, extreme use of heat and cold, the use of loud music and noise, and preying on phobias.

While at Abu Ghraib, Chase Madrid Jr. ordered soldiers to rape female inmates. Some of the women who had been raped became pregnant, and, in some cases, they were later killed by their family members in honor killings. Not America's finest hour.

Chase was responsible for ordering over sixteen detainees' deaths; eleven soldiers were convicted of various charges relating to the incidents, with all of the convictions including the charge of dereliction of duty. Most soldiers only received minor sentences. Three other soldiers were either cleared of charges or were not charged. No one was convicted for the murders of the detainees, though, and Chase Madrid Jr. was promoted and sent to Guantánamo detention center to help set up their detainee program there.

Once Guantánamo was up and running, Chase was sent back to Afghanistan to coordinate with the locals on how to deal with the growing Taliban problem. His career was on a high trajectory; there was talk of a path to the Joint Chiefs one day, until destiny took a hand.

One day, a United States Senator's son, who was on a fact-finding mission, was killed by an IED while traveling in a convey under Chase Madrid's command. Someone's head had to fall, and Madrid's head was volunteered to be put on the chopping block. Just months before, an assignment had been in the works for his transfer to the Pentagon.

Madrid was fully aware of these sorts of bloodlettings. Hell, he participated in several himself, although you're never quite prepared when it's your head they're chopping off. Not having a place of his own and not being able to stay in government housing, Chase headed home to stay with his Dad in Oakland.

After a couple months of self-pity, anger and bitterness, Chase got a call from SEAL Team Commander William T. "Wooch" Brown, asking him to have dinner with him in the Roof Dining Room at the Yale Club in Manhattan.

"Commander, I'm honored, but I'm not in Manhattan. I'm in Oakland, California, staying with my Father."

"I know, Captain. I know. There will be a first-class ticket waiting for you at the United Airlines ticket counter, and a car will be waiting for you upon your arrival at Kennedy. I look forward to having dinner with you, and, oh, by the way, a jacket is required in the dining room. See you tomorrow night, Captain."

As Chase came down the escalator at JFK, he saw a man in chauffer attire holding a sign with his name on it. As he approached the man, he said, "I'm Chase Madrid."

"Do you have any luggage, sir?" the chauffeur asked.

"No, just this," He said, as he held up an army issue backpack.

"May I take that, sir?"

"No thanks, I'm good."

"Very good, sir. Please follow me."

The limo ride into Manhattan took just over an hour; traffic was its usual snail's pace for that time of the day—in truth, traffic was terrible at any time of the day. Chase fell asleep the moment he got into the limo; he had learned in combat to catch forty winks whenever he could, because you never knew when the opportunity for sleep would come again.

Chase walked up to the maître d' station at the Yale Club and said that he was meeting Commander Brown for dinner. As the maître d' was reviewing his reservation book, Chase was marveling at the old world, old boy clubhouse that was surrounding him. The Yale Club was founded in 1897 with the goal of allowing graduates the ability to continue the friendships they formed at Yale. The Yale Club was the largest Clubhouse in the world and continues to be the largest college clubhouse in existence.

"Ah, here it is, sir: Commander Brown, dinner for two. Won't you please follow me?"

Commander Brown was looking down at his cell phone, when Chase approached the table; he placed the phone down and stood to greet his guest. "Chase Madrid, a pleasure to meet you. Please have a seat. Would you like something to drink?"

"I'll have scotch rocks."

"Make that two, Johnny."

"Yes, sir, Commander. Right away," The maître d' said, as he gave a short bow and left.

"I'm glad you could make it, Chase."

"Well, Commander, to be honest, I was more than a little curious on why you would want to have dinner with a pariah like myself."

"Nonsense. I know what happened and why it was your ass on the line. Someone wiser than myself once said, 'sometimes you eat the bear, and sometimes the bear, why, he eats you.' "

"Yeah, this was one hungry bear."

"Chase, have you given any thought of what you're going to do now?"

"No, I really haven't given it much thought; I'm still licking my wounds. But, I'm guessing that you just might have some thoughts."

Just then, the waiter approached the table with the drinks. "Here you go, gentlemen. Shall I give you a few more minutes before taking your orders?"

"That would be great. Thank you, Ramón," the Commander said. Then he held up his drink towards Chase and said, "Cheers."

"Cheers."

"Chase, have you ever heard of David Leeway?"

Detective Wilson had just turned off of Paul Bunyan Drive and onto Irvine Avenue, heading south and making a left turn into Greenwood Cemetery, when his cell phone rang.

"Wilson."

"Hey, it's me. Where are you?"

"Hey, Johansson. Greenwood Cemetery—it's Thursday, Brad Devin's funeral."

"Oh, yeah. I forgot."

"Can this wait?"

"Well, I heard from Sally, but it can wait until you get back."

"You sure?"

"Yeah, we'll talk when you get back."

"Okay, I should be back in an hour or so. Bye."

Janie Devin, little four-year-old Bobby Devin, and Reverend Thomas stood all alone as the coffin was lowered into the grave. The sky was overcast, adding to the grayness and bleak atmosphere. Janie seemed so small and frail next to Reverend Thomas, who stood over six feet tall. Wilson waited at a respectful distance, until he was sure that the service was over, then walked up to the Reverend and greeted him, gently putting his arm on Janie's shoulder.

Reverend Thomas, closing his Bible, asked Janie if there was anything that she needed and told her that he wanted her to know that he would always be there for her and little Bobby. She thanked him for his kindness and for all he had done; he smiled at her and Wilson, paused, then left.

"Janie, are you okay?" Wilson whispered.

"I'm doing as well as can be expected, for a woman going to prison."

"You're not going to prison; the DA has decided not to go forward with the charges. He called your lawyer this morning; I guess she hasn't been able to get ahold of you, but you're not going to prison."

"Well, I might not be going to prison, but I'm going to Hell."

"Janie, that's nonsense."

"Detective Wilson, what am I going to do now? I've got no real family, just my mom, and she needs more help than she can provide for me and Bobby. Brad's family hates me, and I'm just so lost and confused."

"I know of some really nice folks at *Sheltering Wings*; it's a domestic violence shelter to help women like yourself, and they have children services to help you with Bobby. In fact, I've already spoken to them, and, if you'd like, I can take you and Bobby over there now, if you're ready."

"That would be very kind of you, if it's not an inconvenience."

"Not at all," Wilson said, as they started walking out towards the parking lot. After walking a few yards, Wilson said, as he pointed to his right, "You know, my Linda is buried just over there."

"Would you like to stop and pay your respects? Bobby and I wouldn't mind."

"That's very kind of you, Janie, but I got to get back to the station. Besides, I have a standing date every Sunday after church."

"You know, I did love him."

"I know, but, Janie, love shouldn't hurt."

Chase Madrid was definitely intrigued by the proposition that Commander Brown proposed. The idea of forming an elite-fighting group that answered to no one, had complete autonomy, and with unlimited funds was just what he was looking for. He knew of several people that he felt would be right for this kind of clandestine mission. Ex-military who were outcasts like himself, people who had no definite future and no family ties, people who could be gone for months or years at a time, people who wouldn't be missed. People like 'Night-Train' Johnson.

Anthony Johnson was a Gunny Sergeant with the Eleventh Marine Expeditionary Unit, a forward-deployed, flexible, sea-based Marine air-ground task force, who are capable of conducting amphibious operations, crisis response, and limited contingency operations. He fought in combat operations in Nasiriyah, Al Kut, Bagdad, Najaf, Al Qaim, and Fallujah. He was wounded four times, was awarded the Purple Heart and two Bronze Stars, and was considered for the Medal of Honor.

Anthony was nicknamed 'Night Train,' because of his numerous nighttime operations into enemy territory, which were carried out with such effectiveness, speed, and ferociousness. When the Train roared, the enemy never knew what hit them; it was literally like a freight train roaring through at a hundred miles an hour, leaving nothing but death and destruction in its wake.

Anthony lost out on his MOH when, one day, while on leave in Tehran, he finished having lunch at the Sangelaj Cafe caddy-corner to the Park-e Shahr Library on Behesbt Street. He got into a heated exchange with a couple of US Government contractors, who were harassing a couple of young Muslim women. At the time, he wasn't in uniform and suggested that they move on and leave the ladies alone.

"Why don't you just back off, boy. Just get the fuck out of here before something bad happens."

"Well, you boys are right about one thing: something bad is going to happen."

The police report stated that, on June third, a Mr. Raymond Tillis and Mr. George Hammond assaulted Mr. Anthony Johnson, whereupon Mr. Johnson proceeded to beat the living snot out of them both. Mr. Tillis received six broken ribs, a broken rotator cuff, and a broken jaw, whereas Mr. Hammond had similar injuries with the addition of a broken arm and fractured skull.

The Marines were in a bit of a spot; Anthony was arrested and was initially charged with assault, but two women and three other bystanders gave statements. Although the Marines dropped the charges, the conservative press had gotten ahold of the story and were blowing it way out of proportion, talking about how could an American beat up two US contractors while they were risking their lives to help the people of Iraq? Anthony was tired of all the political bullshit and quit, walked away after twelve years in the Marines, and went back home to Houston, Texas. There, he got a job with the multinational security firm, TXR Security, as a security advisor; it was a fancy name for a bodyguard.

Night Train Johnson was very popular with his clients, especially the celebrities; they all asked for him by name. He found the work monotonous and boring. There wasn't any excitement, and it was just a lot of standing around and looking mean. He missed the danger, the adrenalin rush of combat. So, when Chase Madrid called and asked if he would be interested in a private and secret Black Ops mission, Night Train put Chase on hold, called the owners of TXR, and told them he quit. Tommy Beech, the owner of TXR, told Anthony that, if he does quit, he'd never work in this business again, ever! To which Anthony replied, "That seems fair."

When Detective Wilson returned to the station, Johansson was on the phone with Interpol's Inspectors, Volker and Morris. He said, as Wilson entered the office, "Gentlemen, Detective Wilson's just arrived; I'm going to put you on speaker phone.

Wilson gave a greeting nod to Johansson and said, "Inspectors, good to talk to you."

"And a good day to you both. Hope you are well. I understand you have some information about this Chase Madrid chap, am I correct?" Morris asked.

Johansson looked at Wilson, who nodded for him to take the lead. "Well, Inspector, certain information has come to light that makes me believe that this Chase Madrid just might be involved in our homicide."

"Really? Do tell."

"That's right. We had someone go to Mr. Chase's home in Oakland. He wasn't there but his father was. There were several stuffed animal heads mounted on the walls, and the father was vague on his son's whereabouts. The old man said that his son was involved in working for environmental organizations."

"Well, actually, we were able to do some digging of our own on this Mr. Chase Madrid. It seems that he is ex-military, who was on a fast track to stardom until it seems that he got involved in a combat *fubar* that ended in a US Senator's son getting killed. He was blamed for his death—negligence and all that sort of thing, don't you know. He was quietly booted out of the service, and no one has seen or heard from him in several months. From what we've been able to glean from our sources, he is hardly the type who would take up arms for an organization such as Le Gang de la Clé de Singe. If anything, he would be leading the fight against them."

"So, does that mean we're back to square one?" Wilson asked.

"Afraid so, old chap. But don't despair, these things take time. Something will break; it always does, and it's just a matter of time. Anything else?"

Johansson said with a bit of frustration, "No, that's all for now. Bye."

"Very good, goodbye."

Wilson sat on the edge of Johansson's desk. "So, Sally met Chase's old man in his house? What was that like?"

"She liked the old guy, but she was creeped out when she saw all the stuffed heads on the wall. And then there's the fact that he didn't know where the son was or who he worked for."

"How old was the dad?"

"She said she thought he was in his eighties."

"Well, it just could be that the old guy is losing a bit of the old gray cells, you know?"

"Yeah, I guess."

"You should tell Sally to stay away from Mr. Madrid. It sounds like a dead end. Oh, and tell her if she wants a job as a detective, we would work something out."

"Yeah, that ain't going to happen."

Rodin and the Red Team separately made their way down to the bottom of South Africa in groups of four; they were to rendezvous at a small town on the southern coast called Jeffreys Bay. When Rodin, Sager, and Odin pulled into the Jeffreys Bay Caravan Park, just on the outskirts of town, about an hour before the sun was to set, there they found the other members of the team just finishing up pitching their tents and setting up camp. Rodin and Odin set up their tents and joined the others sitting around a fire pit enjoying some bottles of Castle Lager beer.

It had been over eighteen hours since their encounter at the South Africa Big Game Association, and all the radio stations were buzzing with the news of what they were referring to as 'the Lion's Revenge Massacre.' There were reports that all airports, rail stations, ports, and highways were having extra manpower to try and apprehend this gang of Monkey Wrench killers. South African authorities vowed that these murders would be brought to justice.

"Gentlemen, can I have your attention? We are set to be picked up this morning at zero four hundred hours, so please be ready to go at least thirty minutes before. Buster and I will be checking to be sure you are. I don't want any fuck-ups, so make sure everything is ready to go; make sure all charges are set and nothing incriminating is left behind. Am I clear?" Rodin looked at each man for a nod of acknowledgment.

He glanced at his watch and said, "Okay, it's almost seventeen hundred hours now. I suggest we have some chow and get prepared for our departure. Any questions? No? Good, let's eat."

The entire team had made camp on the easternmost part of the park, as to minimize any destruction to the other camper's tents and RV's when they destroyed their campsite.

At zero three thirty, Rodin and Buster went from tent to tent, making sure every team member was awake and functioning. At exactly zero four hundred hours, eight Zodiac Milpro Futura Commando rafts, which were powered by a 3.0 litre spark-ignited, direct fuel injected, two-stroke OptiMax Diesel Outboard Stealth engine, hit the beach.

They were loaded and on their way back to a mothership sitting precisely two degrees outside the three-mile international limit. When the Zodiacs were a mile offshore, Rodin gave the signal to destroy their encampment. It started with a whisper of a flame, and, within seconds, their entire encampment was engulfed in a blaze that could be seen from over a mile away. They could see people standing around and watching, knowing that there wasn't anything anyone could do. By the time the Zodiacs reached the ship, their camp was burned to the ground. Once aboard safely, Rodin gave the crew permission to go below and get some much-needed rest, while he and Buster went to see the captain of the ship.

David Leeway made up his mind: he wasn't going to sit by and do nothing, that's not who he was. He was a man of action; he was a force to be reckoned with, and he was David Leeway! Maybe, just maybe, he could help flush these assassins out into the open.

He called a press conference at his offices in Leeway Tower in the heart of Manhattan to announce that he was going to Africa to carry on and continue with the big game hunt that his children were on when they were brutally murdered.

"First, I want to thank you all for coming this morning. As you all know, I lost my three children while they were on a big game safari; they were killed by a group of self-proclaimed eco-terrorists. I prefer to call them by what they really are: cowards.

Today, I am announcing that I will be going to Africa on a big game safari, and I challenge these French terrorists to try and stop me. As you all know, the group known as Le Gang de la Clé de Singe, or the Monkey Wrench Gang, are nothing more than a group of thugs and murders, who have decided that they, and they alone, have the right to kill men and women that they deem in violation of rules and laws that they have decreed as punishable by death. Well, this aggression will not stand; I am standing in defiance and say enough is enough. I will not be intimated. They want a fight, so be it," He proclaimed.

One of the assembled members of the press raised his hand, and Leeway pointed to him. "Mr. Leeway, Bill Oakes from the New York Times. What will you do if you encounter these people? And aren't you just daring them to try something?"

"I will be fully prepared to defend myself by any means possible. I am not undertaking this lightly, I can assure you. Unlike my children, who were slaughtered innocently, we will be very prepared and heavily armed. Like I said, I challenge these French terrorists to try and stop me. Yes?"

"Yes, thank you, Robert Lackley CNN. Mr. Leeway, you're seventy-seven years old. Considering your age, aren't you concerned about your health while going on a safari, along with the possibility of a combat firefight encounter?"

"No! I say, bring it on. I dare these cowards to try something; they won't know what hit them. Unlike my children, I will not be an unsuspecting victim. I will be making my itinerary public, and my locations will be announced every day. As you can see, I am very much daring them to start something. Now, thank you all, but I have a lot to prepare for."

As he was leaving, a female reporter from Fox News shouted out, "When are you planning on leaving?"

"I'll be on safari by the end of next week," Leeway claimed, as he left the Skippy Leeway Memorial Conference Room.

He and his personal secretary, Ron Wilson, stepped out into the main hallway and onto his private elevator, moving up to the ninety-ninth floor where his private office was located. The office looked like something out of an eighteenth-century French chateau. He walked over to and sat behind a rather large and imposing Louis XIV writing table that once actually belonged to the Sun King himself.

The desk was piano black with eighteen-carat gold embossed on the leather surface. His entire office was decorated in original Louis XIV furniture; most were taken from museums and then replaced with facsimiles that were either bought directly from the museums or stolen and replaced without the curator's knowledge.

David Leeway's office looked out onto Central Park, and, as he sat behind his desk, Ron walked over to the window to look out at the view. He spoke to Leeway without turning around; a handsome cab had caught his eye. "That went rather well, don't you think?"

"Yes, rather well, indeed. Mr. Leeway, are you sure about this hunting expedition? I mean, it could be rather dangerous."

"Ron, I know what I'm doing. I want..." His intercom beeped and interrupted his train of thought. "Yes, Carol. What is it?"

"There's a Mr. Angel from the Morte Safari on line two. Would you like to take it?"

"Yes, thank you, Carol."

He picked up the receiver and punched line two. "Mr. Angel."

Anthony Johnson and Chase Madrid were casually discussing the upcoming NFL's pro football season, when seven uniformed officers from the California Highway Patrol ordered them out of the blood orange 1969 Plymouth Barracuda they had been sitting in for over two hours.

"Get out of the car and keep your hands where I can see them!" Shouted Officer Ryan, a fifteen-year veteran who looked like he could suit up and hit the ground running as a defensive guard for the Oakland Raiders.

"Okay, okay. We're getting out. I have to tell you, there is a licensed firearm in the console of the car!"

"Keep your hands in plain sight and get down on the ground, face down. Now!"

Both Chase and Anthony did as they were told; they were handcuffed and stood up to lean against the Barracuda. They were frisked, and their identities were run through the system. While waiting for the information to be relayed back to the CHPs, their car was searched and the pistol that Chase had mentioned was found.

Officer Ryan approached them after having given their information to dispatch. "Gentlemen, you were observed sitting in this parking lot for over two hours. You do know that you are on the grounds of the Folsom State Prison? What is the nature of your business?"

Chase smiled and said, "Officer, we are waiting for a couple of friends of ours, corrections officers Brian and Dennis Wellson. We weren't sure what time their shift ended, so we thought we'd just wait for them."

"You didn't think to go inside and inquire about the Wellson Officers?"

"No, sir, we didn't"

"And what about that rather large sign straight ahead of the parking rules; would you please read rule number six please?"

"No loitering in and around parked cars."

"And please read the last line, if you would."

"Violators are subject to a five hundred dollar fine and/or arrest."

"Gentlemen, I am not going to arrest you, but this is going to be an expensive lesson for you both. I am issuing each of you a ticket for violating California statute C.V.C. 22658A. If you do not pay, a warrant for your arrest will be issued. Do you understand?"

"Yes, sir."

The officer unlocked their handcuffs, handed each of them a citation, and said, "You have thirty days from today to pay the fine."

One of the other officers called out for Officer Ryan to come over to his squad car, where they stood and held a brief conversation, occasionally looking at Chase and Johnson. As the officers were starting to disband, Ryan walked back to the Barracuda. "Seems you boys have quite the service records. I myself served in the Corp, and, for that, I thank you for your service. But, gentlemen, please be aware that service doesn't entitle you to any special privileges when it comes to the law."

"We understand, and I can assure you that we weren't trying to take advantage of anyone, but we know ignorance is no excuse and we apologize."

"Noted. Oh, and here's your weapon, Mr. Madrid. I'm glad to see it had a lock on it. Now, I suggest that you wait for the Wellson brothers at some place like the Folsom Hotel Saloon down on Sutter Street."

Chase and Anthony fired up the Barracuda and made their way over to Sutter Street. Once there, they emailed Brian and waited for him and his twin brother, Dennis, to appear. They didn't have to wait long, and, by the look on Brian and Dennis's faces, they weren't happy campers.

The brothers Wellson's father was a huge Beach Boys fan, so he named the boys after two of the original members; he only wished he'd had more boys, but, unfortunately, he was blessed with three girls: Carla, Michele, and Alexia.

"Chase, what the fuck? You got our asses in a lot of hot water. This better be good. What the hell were you thinking, man!"

"Easy, bro. I'm sorry about all the hoopla; Anthony and I got to jawing and just lost track of time. We're the ones that got our asses in a sling; it shouldn't have rolled down on you."

"Well, we caught a lot of shit."

"Well, again, I'm sorry. What can I get you boys to drink?"

As they sat drinking, Chase told the brothers of the opportunity he thought they might be interested in. The brothers Wellson both served under Johnson, with Brian as a demolitions expert and Dennis as a highly decorated sniper.

Brian glanced over to his brother, who gave a slight nod, then said, "So, like, what's in it for us besides the joy of getting back into the shit?"

Chase looked around to see if anyone was eavesdropping, then leaned in close and spoke just above a whisper, "We each get one million dollars—win, lose, or draw—and, if successful, we each get an additional million. Plus, all our expenses are paid, of course, and all equipment will be provided at no cost. And there were possible future bonuses mentioned."

Dennis asked, "Is this the team?"

"No, there are two others that we are trying to recruit; I prefer not to mention names at this point until things are firmed up."

"And when does this operation get started?"

"We're hoping within the month, but you both have to realize that, once you're on board, there's no cutting and running. We want a commitment from you both that you're in for the long haul, for however long this takes and wherever it takes us to get this job done—or until our employer calls the mission off. Understand?"

Brian and Dennis looked at each other and said in unison, "Where do we sign?"

"Don't you need to check with the wives?"

Brian smiled. "Wives, what wives?"

"Oh, sorry."

"Don't be. Dennis and I know we're both a little fucked up after two tours in the Big Muddy. We're just thankful neither one of us had kids."

Chase raised his hand to get the waitress's attention. "Another round for the table," he called out.

Brittany Jones just posted photos of her latest big game kill on her Facebook page with the headline, 'Almost got one of everything on my bucket list, only two to go.' The photo shows a beautiful young woman with long blond hair wearing camo standing holding a dead cheetah in her arms, looking to the camera with a big grin on her face and blood on her hands.

Brittany is a twenty-two-year-old Dallas Cowboy cheerleader with aspirations to get into television. She is hoping that her exploits in big game hunting will get her an opportunity for a hunting show on one of the cable networks that specializes in outdoor programming. She started hunting when she accompanied her father on his big game safaris at the young age of eleven. Killing a rare African white Rhino was her first ever, and it was also the first in her quest to bag the Big 5 African game animals—rhino, elephant, Cape buffalo, leopard, and lion—which she did by the time she was fourteen. Since then, she has continued to kill zebras, White Springbok, hippos, black wildebeest, crocodiles and giraffes, among dozens of various plains game.

Brittany wasn't the sweet, little, innocent Southern Belle image that she liked to put out to the public; she was a cold-hearted, sadistic killer. She would shoot her prey with a massive dose of animal tranquilizer, rendering it immobile. Then, when the poor animal would be laying there, she would taunt it and torture it. When the beast would start to come out of the effects of the tranquilizer drug, she would finally kill it. Several of the safari outfits, having observed her behavior, refused to do business with her. Her reputation was starting to spread, so even safari outfits she hadn't gone out with were declining to accept her as a client.

On the ride back ot camp, she emailed her father: *"Daddy. Got my cheetah! Tomorrow I go for a Sable antelope. Love B."*

Her father immediately emailed her back: *"Brittany. Mother and I are fearful of the eco-terrorists on the loose. Please come home now! Dad."*

"No worries, just two more days. Be home soon. Bye. B"

After hs daughter's refusal to come home, Mr. Jones called the US representative of Wild Times Safaris. "Hello? Yes, this is Sydney Jones. My daughter, Brittany, is on safari in Namibia."

"Oh, yes, Mr. Jones. This is Jerome Phillips. What can I do for you?"

"Oh! Hi, Jerome. Brittany's mother and I are concerned for her safety with all of the goings on with the Le Gang de la Clé de Singe being on the rampage."

"Mr. Jones, I can assure that we have taken every precaution and have even added extra security. There is nothing to worry about. I'm looking at her schedule, and I see that she will be home in two days. Not to worry!"

"Okay, Jerome. Thank you. I'm feeling a little better now."

"Is there anything else I can do for you, Mr. Jones?"

"No, I think we're good. Bye, Jerome."

"Goodbye, Mr. Jones. Look forward to speaking with you soon."

"Was that Mr. Jones calling about his little precious?" asked Jerome's partner, Kyle Tailor, as he walked over to Jerome's desk and sat on the edge. He was drinking his sixth cup of coffee of the morning. "What's he concerned about?"

"He's got his panties all in a knot over that Le Gang de la Clé de Singe-thing, thinking that poor little Brittany is next on their hit list."

"If only; she's such a freaking psycho. It's a good thing her old man is so rich, because he is willing to pay double for his baby to get her kicks torturing and killing animals. Can you imagine being in a relationship with her? I don't think you would ever be able to sleep next to her, knowing that you might wake up dead one day."

"Yeah, she is one freaky chick."

Rodin and Buster were standing outside the bridge of the ship, watching the sunrise over Table Mountain as they were rounding Cape Town and heading northwest towards Muanda, a small town lying on the Atlantic Ocean coast of the Democratic Republic of Congo at the mouth of the Congo River. Once there, they would drive over fifty-four hours across the entire country, some two thousand and twenty-five miles to Virunga National Park, to take care of some gangs of poachers reeking havoc and killing gorillas in Virunga National Park near the Democratic Republic of the Congo and Uganda border.

The captain of the Mary Louise gave Rodin new orders to be implemented after the Virunga expedition. Word had just come down that David Leeway was planning a big game safari in hopes of drawing out the members of Le Gang de la Clé de Singe who had killed his children. The heads of the organization had been informed by reliable sources that this was most likely a ploy to set up an ambush. Details were still sketchy, so they wanted to know if Rodin and his team would be interested in encountering Leeway and whatever forces he may bring. But since they've been on assignment for over two months, they would have the option to decline.

The plan would be that there would be two teams sent to engage Leeway: the Blue Team and Rodin's Red Team. They said that no one in the organization would think less of him and his team, though, if they refused to take on this assignment. Rodin told HQ that he would talk it over with his team and let them know within a day or two.

Odin assembled the Red Team in the galley at thirteen hundred hours for an update from Rodin.

"Men, I received a communication from HQ this morning. Apparently, David Leeway has declared that he will be going on a big game safari, and he has dared us to take action against him. HQ feels that this is most likely some sort of trap to engage us in combat and set up an ambush. I believe that to be that case as well. They have asked us if we would be prepared to take on such a mission, or, without any prejudice against us, if we would rather refuse. We would spearhead the operation and have a second team, the Blue Team, as a backup. I told them that I would want to run this by all of you. I think it best if we have a secret ballot, so if you all would write down either yes or no on the paper that Lu Wei is passing out and then pass the ballots to the end of the table."

Lu Wei passed out the ballots and then collected them, bringing them to Rodin. Rodin reviewed the ballots and announced the results. "Fifteen yeah's zero no's. I thank you all for that. We will be formulating a plan of action to be carried out against Mr. Leeway after our taking care of business in Virunga National Park."

"A bit of gorilla warfare," Odin said.

Rodin smiled. "I like it."

Detective Johansson was putting the finishing touches on an arrest report, involving the killing of two Muslim women by an irate customer who was offended that the women had the nerve to wear their hijabs into a Wal-Mart. The shooter, Mr. Frank Christian, told police that he felt that his life was being threatened and had no choice but to waste 'em. The thirty-five-year-old, a known white supremacist, was booked on two counts of aggravated murder, two counts of intimidation in the second degree, and one federal count of a hate crime.

"I thought them bitches was wearing them suicide vests under them robes. They were really creeping me out, acting all funny and looking like they were figuring out how many they could kill at one time, you know?" However, witnesses told Johansson that the two women were shopping in the vegetable aisles, when Christian shouted to them, "Hey! Take off those fucking burkas. This is America; go back to your fucking country, you fucking fig-eating bitches!" Then, he pulled out a gun and shot them both.

Detective Johansson just left to take Christian over to the County lockup, when the phone rang; it was Inspector Volker from Interpol. "Detective Wilson, good morning. This is Inspector Volker; is this a good time?"

"Good morning, Inspector, or I guess it's evening for you. Yeah, sure, this is as a good a time as any. What's happening?"

"Well, I just wanted to give you an update as to where we stand at the moment. It's still premature in our investigations, but we're rethinking Chase Madrid's involvement into these murders."

"Really, can you tell me why?"

"I'm sorry, I really can't. Like I said, it's still premature."

"You will keep us posted?"

"Yes, of course."

"Is there anything you can tell me that might help our murder investigation of Doctor Meriwether?"

"Like I said, as soon as we are able to, we will. I am sorry. I hope this doesn't make matters worse for you."

"No, it's just frustrating."

"I do understand, old chap. I promise to keep you up to date as we learn more definitive information."

"Okay, Inspector Volker. Please let us know as soon as anything breaks."

"Of course."

Wilson hung up the phone just as Johansson came back into the squad room.

Wilson shook his head and said, "You're not going to believe this."

Brittany boarded the Air Namibia Airbus that was heading non-stop to Paris, France; then she got on Air France flight 8984 to Atlanta's Hartsfield-Jackson for the thirty-one-hour-and-forty-minute flight home. She was seated in seat 2B in first class, enjoying a glass of champagne while she looked at her iPhone and reviewed all the shots from her recent safari, when a man said to her, "Excuse me, I am in 2A. I hate to disturb you."

"No, no. That's quite alright," She said, as she stood up and allowed the man to pass and get seated.

As they settled into their seats, he smiled, held out his hand, and said, "Hi, I'm Angelo. Angelo Della Morte." She thought he looked to be in his early thirties—long dark hair, clean-shaven with a hint of Andy Garcia good looks. She liked what she saw.

"Hello, I'm Brittany Jones." She smiled, as she shook his hand. "Were you here on business or pleasure?"

"Business, but I am very lucky because my business is my pleasure. I'm a photographer for National Geographic. And you?"

"Oh, pleasure. I was here on safari."

"Photo safari?"

"Ah no, hunting."

"Really, we're you successful?"

"Oh, yeah. My prize shot was a cheetah." She thumbed through her iPhone photo gallery until she got to the photo of her holding the dead cat in her arms smiling to camera. She handed him the phone with pride said, "See? I got her on the run while she was going after a Red Lechwe Antelope."

"Mmmm, so you're going home now?" He handed her back the phone.

"Yeah, to Atlanta. And you?"

"Actually, I've been assigned to photograph two newborn Giant Panda cubs that were just born at the Atlanta Zoo."

"Cool. I'm on Air France 2306, you?"

"Why, yes. Yes, I am."

"Great, would you care for some champagne? Oh, stewardess!"

The flight attendant walked over. "Yes, Miss?"

"Could you get us some more champagne?"

"Of course, Miss."

Angelo leaned into Brittany and whispered, "I think they prefer to be called flight attendants."

She smiled and finished her champagne. "Yeah, whatever."

The blood orange Barracuda was screaming down US 15 just on the outskirts of the Mojave National Preserve, heading to Las Vegas and cruising at 140 mph, when Madrid's cell phone rang. He didn't recognize the number, but it looked to be a South African exchange. He decided to answer it through his headset, rather than the car's Bluetooth where Anthony and the Wellson brothers could listen in.

"Hope you fellas don't mind. Hello?"

On the other end of the phone, a man with a Belgian English accent spoke, "Hello. Whom am I speaking with, please?"

"This is Chase Madrid, and who do I have the pleasure of speaking with?"

"I shall refer to myself as Café Noir, for security purposes, if you don't mind. Commander Brown suggested that I might be of some assistance to you and your mission."

"Mr. Noir, what sort of assistance can you provide?"

"Well, sir, I have certain contacts within Le Gang de la Clé de Singe that may be willing to provide information, for a price, of course."

"Of course. Well, Mr. Noir, I am very much interested in your help. How can I get in touch with you?"

"It's best that I get in touch with you. I shall call back in three days time, as I understand you are still in the process of staffing up for your mission. Will that be sufficient time for you to obtain the rest of your personnel?”

“Yes, we should be good to go in three days. Am I to assume that you are a South African, Mr. Noir?”

“Why would you assume that?”

“Because the number that you called me on is a South African code.”

"You can assume what you like, Mr. Madrid, but I will be calling you using a variety of phone exchanges. I look forward to speaking with you in three days, so until then. Unless there's something else?"

"No, I think we're good. I look forward to speaking with you then. Bye.”

He and the Wellson brothers looked at each other, and then, almost in unison, said, “Mr. Noir?”

Chase looked in the review mirror at the brothers. “Commander Brown’s inside man with Le Gang de la Clé de Singe, who is going to feed us inside information. He fancy’s the code name ‘Café Noir’; he can call himself Betty Boop for all I care, just as long as he gives us what we want.”

The conversation was abruptly halted when the radar detector on the dashboard gave out a series of whoops and whistles. Chase hit the brakes and downshifted from sixth down to fourth in order to bring the Barracuda screeching down to a respectable eighty miles an hour. As the hill crested, they saw six Nevada Highway Patrol cars at the bottom of the hill, where they already had four cars pulled over. As they passed by the gaggle of patrol and civilian cars, Anthony waved at the poor souls sitting by the side of the road and getting reamed so that cops can meet their quota of lawbreaking evil-doers.

Anthony leaned forward and turned on the radio to 97.1, a Las Vegas classic rock station where Led Zeppelin was rocking out ‘Stairway to Heaven.’ He sat back and said, to no one in particular, "You guys good with this?" It didn't seem to really be a question as much as a matter of fact. He looked over to Chase. "So who's this Scott Mosby we're going to see?"

"Ex-Navy SEAL, personally responsible for the killing of Rashman Mustafa Ali and several other Al Qaeda leaders, but he was tangled up in the botched raid in Yemen where one SEAL was killed and six others wounded."

Anthony nodded his head. "Yeah, I remember that it was a real cluster-fuck. The fault was laid at the doorstep of the White House for not having a grasp on the details. In fact, the dummy-in-chief tried to lay the blame down the line on the head of the Navy. I guess he doesn't realize that the buck stops with him. Of course, he's more than happy to take the glory when things go right, but he never accepts responsibility when the shit hits the fan."

Brian Wellson asked, "Was this Scott Mosby in any way at fault?"

Chase turned slightly and said, "No fucking way. In fact, he and his squad was responsible for eight of the fourteen confirmed killed that day. No, he just got disenchanted with all the incompetence of the Commander-in-Chief and decided to cash in his chips while he was still in one piece. From what I know, he's one guy you know has your back no matter what shit is going down."

"So, what's he doing since he's been out?" Brian asked, as he finished off his fourth cup of coffee of the morning.

"He is teaching survival courses at the Beta 9 Survival School just outside of Vegas, where they teach SERE classes."

"What the fuck is SERE?"

"SERE, you know, Survival, Evasion, Resistance and Escape classes for paranoid civilians, businessmen who travel to dicey places around the world and, of course, the wannabe military kooks who are always crying that the government is planning to take away their guns."

"Does this kinda gig pay good?"

"You can ask him when you meet him. Why? You thinking of starting a whole new career?"

"Just keeping all my options open, right, Dennis?"

Dennis smiled. "Fucking A."

CNN's Josh Colman and his cameraman, Randy Gaines, had been given exclusive access to travel with and document David Leeway's safari journey, or, as Josh called it, 'Killapalooza'. The whole purpose of this 'safari' was to have David Leeway kill as many animals and draw as much attention to his killing, so as to dare Le Gang de la Clé de Singe to try and stop him.

Leeway was bringing some heavy firepower with him, just in case they were to encounter those assassins that killed his children. He had hired twelve mercenaries to escort him and protect him, plus he knew he had an angel watching over his shoulder, an Angel of Death.

This was going to be a safari like no other in recent times; Leeway had contracted for twenty-two porters, a kitchen staff of eleven, six gun bearers, four teamsters and his ten hired guns, not including three guides and the CNN reporter and cameraman.

David Leeway's personal 737 MAX 9 took off from New York's Kennedy Airport at nine o'clock on a cloudy and rainy morning, a day that, if one was superstitious, had an air of doom, disaster, and death. Their destination was a nineteen-hour flight to Joshua Mqabuko Nkomo International Airport in Zimbabwe.

"Good morning, this is Josh Colman coming to you on board David Leeway's private jet. We have just taken off for our nineteen-hour flight to Zimbabwe to start, what seems to b,e an unprecedented, exclusive journey and safari with David Leeway, who is, what many feel as, tempting fate by intentionally antagonizing the eco-terrorist group known Le Gang de la Clé de Singe, who have claimed responsibility for the killing of his three adult children while they were on

a big game safari. I'm told that we are going to start the safari at Hwange National Park, which is in western Zimbabwe. It's home to large elephant herds, lions, and African wild dogs. The Park has one of the world's largest elephant populations, estimated to be as high as thirty thousand. Leeway told me that the first trophy that he is looking to bag is a legendary bull éléphant named Castor. He seems to be really poking the hornet's nest by going after such an icon. This is Josh Colman CNN reporting."

Virunga National Park was the first national park to be established on the continent of Africa. It was founded primarily to protect the mountain gorillas living in the forests of the Virunga Massif.

Over the years, the mountain gorillas have endured an almost uninterrupted series of challenges. The Rwandan genocide in 1994 displaced millions of refugees, which caused extreme pressure on the park and the wildlife. In 2007, members of an illegal charcoal mafia started to murder mountain gorillas. The motivation was simple: kill the mountain gorillas, and there will no longer be a reason to protect the park, so they would be free to cut down trees and produce charcoal for the black market. Today, one of the biggest threats is poaching and kidnapping the gorillas for private zoos and collectors of exotic animals.

The *Alstonia Congensis* is a tall forest tree, which can grow up to ninety feet in height. They produce numerous hairy seeds, which makes for a very uncomfortable environment when climbing and an even worse one when sleeping in the forest canopy. That's why the team chose mahogany trees, which can reach a height of one hundred and fifty feet, with the trunks sometimes growing more than six feet in diameter; they were harder to climb but much more suitable for their purposes.

The Red Team decided that sleeping and waiting for the poachers up amongst the tree canopy would be smarter than traipsing about in the rainforest, having to avoid the gorillas and the armed Virunga Park Rangers with their Congohounds. As bloodhounds that are uniquely suited to track humans in difficult terrain, like Virunga National Park, they are trained to track, apprehend, and arrest poachers.

It took over four hours for each team member to climb his mahogany tree and assemble their Survivor Asym Universal Camo Classic Hammocks with Monsoon Camo Rainflys. From the ground, unless one was looking for them, the hammocks were not visible to the casual observer. The men stood ready to repel down at a moment's notice, and, as always, the men were in radio contact with each other and the drone pilots.

Pelé and Lu Wei operated the French Aerospatiale C.22 drone from a small farm just outside the Park and near the small town of Bunyuka. They were the eyes in the sky, keeping watch for any poachers and keeping in touch with the Red Team.

After the long grueling road trip from the coast to Virunga National Park and scaling the mahogany trees the team was in no hurry to encounter poachers, they were all exhausted. And with the gentle breeze blowing in the canopy of the trees, everyone was asleep within minutes of a final inspection of their gear and check-in with Rodin. As the sun was starting to set, Rodin reminded everyone that no lights of any kind were to be used, as any light could be seen miles away, and they didn't need any park rangers becoming curious. Besides, the entire team had been issued Aviator Night Vision Binoculars mounted on a Gallet Helmet, which were to be worn at all times once the sun went down.

The jungle came alive with the creatures of the night when total darkness engulfed the rainforest, but the evening's symphony was wasted on the men of the Red Team, who were dead to the world. They wouldn't emerge from the deep sleep until zero-five-thirty, when they were awaked by a radio call from Pelé, who was calling to let them know that Red Drone was airborne. "Rise and shine, Red Team. You have eyes in the sky."

"Roger that, Red Drone. Red Team, muster in," Rodin acknowledged. Within minutes, every member had responded. "Gentlemen, please stand by at the ready. Red Drone, this is Red Leader; we are at the ready," Rodin said.

"Roger that."

The Air Namibia Airbus cabin was completely dark and everyone was asleep, including the flight crew. Everyone, that is, with the exception of Brittany Jones. Brittany was covered with an Air Namibia blanket, and that was all. She had slipped out of all her clothes and raised the armrest between her and Angelo Della Morte, who was sitting in the seat next to her in first class. Angelo had fallen asleep a couple of hours ago after spending much time in conversation with Brittany before and during their meal service, which was surprisingly delicious. It started with a tomato and cucumber salad in a yogurt sauce with salmon, then a good size steak that was nicely seasoned and cooked medium with vegetables and potatoes that were drizzled in a high-quality olive oil and cooked al dente.

After a couple of glasses of wine, Angelo said that he hoped she didn't mind, but he was a bit knackered and would like to take a short nap, as the flight attendants turned down the cabin lights. Brittany tried to sleep, but she wasn't sleepy and was soon got bored and decided that she was feeling naughty, so she took off all her clothes and snuggled up to Angelo. She carefully slid her hand from his thigh to his crotch and began to undo his belt and zipper. Angelo was slowly being drawn out of a deep sleep; by the time he was fully conscious, Brittany had his full erection out of his pants. "Mmmm, want to join the mile high club?" she whispered. Before he could respond, she had his pants down around his ankles and was climbing on top of him, facing him, placing her legs up around his shoulders. Slowly, she slid up and down until they both climaxed, surprisingly without anybody noticing. Brittany was a voracious and athletic lover; after three times and three different positions, Angelo said, as he kissed her, "Brittany, if you want more, you're on your own. I got nothing."

"Oh, you're no fun," She laughingly said, kissing his chest. "You get some rest, and I'll wake you in an hour."

"An hour! I'll need at least four."

"Two."

"Okay, two." And with that, he was out like a light.

Two hours later, the flight attendant, asking if he would like breakfast, awaked him. He looked over to see that Brittany wasn't seated next to him. He smiled and said that, for right now, all he wanted was a nice hot cup of coffee.

Moments later, Brittany came out from the lavatory. She looked all dolled up, wearing faded and torn blue jeans and a white t-shirt with a large head of Medusa, who was portrayed as a beautiful woman with a supernatural aura rather than snakes for hair. Below it, in large letters, was the name, Versace.

She plopped down in her seat and gave him a kiss. "Morning, sleep well?"

"Like the dead."

"Mmmm, maybe later we can see if we can raise the dead."

The orange Barracuda turned off I-15, about fifty-one miles Northeast of Vegas onto Hidden Valley Road and just a stone's throw from the tiny town of Moapa, Nevada. They traveled another ten miles down the dirt road until they saw a hand-painted sign riddled with bullet holes for the Beta 9 Survival School. There were several vehicles parked in the dirt parking lot, mostly pickup trucks and old beater cars. As Chase and the others got out of the car, a man wearing green fatigues came out of a Quonset hut and walked towards them. "Greetings gentlemen. My name is Robert Adams. How can I assist you today?"

Chase met the man and shook his hand. "Pleasure, Mr. Adams. We'd like to speak with Scott Mosby, if that's okay."

"Scott is out until tomorrow, teaching a class on Urban Escape and Evasion."

Anthony looked at Chase and said, "Cool."

"Are you boys interested in taking some of our classes? I can get you a good deal on a group rate."

"Actually, we're all ex-military, and Scott is an old Army buddy. We thought we'd drop by and surprise him," Chase said. "Would it be alright if we came back tomorrow?"

Adams was noticeably disappointed in losing a sale. "Sure, he should be back in around four o'clock tomorrow afternoon, if you want to come back then."

"Thanks, Mr. Adams. We'll see you tomorrow around four."

As they were walking back to the car, Adams asked, "Are you sure you wouldn't like a refresher course; a lot has changed?"

Chase raised his hand and said over his shoulder, "See you tomorrow."

The next day, at four, Chase and the crew walked into the Quonset hut to find Mr. Adams sitting and pitching the school's courses to a young couple with two small children, who were interested in the basic survival training class. "This course is very intensive, and it is almost entirely hands on with very little lecture time. The skills we teach you are a mix of primitive and modern survival skills. Our survival training standard is not so difficult that family and children can't attend." He looked up at Chase and gestured for them to go out the side door.

Chase nodded and waved his hand as an acknowledgment. Outside the hut was a bench where a man wearing urban camo was sitting with his back to them. Without turning around, the man said, "Hey, Chase."

"Hey, Scott."

The group walked around to the front of the bench, where they were a bit taken back to see a man with a bionic right hand cleaning a Glock 19 handgun.

Without looking up, he said, "Chase, are you going to introduce me to your friends?"

"Scotty, this Anthony Johnson, Brian and Dennis Wellson. Guys, this is Scott Mosby."

Scott finished up with the Glock by dropping the magazine into the gun handle, stood, and shook each man's hand. "Gentlemen, it's a pleasure."

Anthony was the last to shake Scott's hand and held on to it to inspect it. He turned it over, held it up close to his face, and said, "Man, this hand is dope. Where did you lose it?"

"Yemen 2013, and I know you're wondering about my hand and if will affect my performance. Well, I can assure you that it won't be." He held up his arm and pulled up the sleeve to show them.

"Scott, that won't be necessary," Anthony interrupted.

"No, no. I think you shouldn't have any doubts, so let me give you just a quick tutorial. This is the bebionic hand; it is a multi-articulating myoelectric hand. It has fourteen different grip patterns and hand positions, including a trigger grip for using firearms. This baby has microprocessors that are continuously monitoring the position of each finger. Any questions?"

Brian looked at the others and smiled. "Ah, I think we're good."

Chase sat down on the bench and asked Scott if he was up for the mission. Scott sat down next to him and nodded. He looked around, as if to make sure no one was listening, and said, "Oh, yeah. I'm tired of dealing with all these wannabe wankers who like getting off playing Rambo on the weekends. I'm ready to get back into the shit. When do we go?"

"Tomorrow, if you're ready."

"I'm ready now."

"Alright. Next stop, Zimbabwe.

Robert Lester, ex-Navy SEAL sniper, was best known for holding the world record for the longest distance kill in military history, three-thousand-four-hundred-and-eighty-meter shot. Lester, a French Canadian better known as the Iceman, because nothing ever seems to rattle him—rumor has it ice water runs thru his veins—is the leader of the Blue Team.

The Iceman joined the Le Gang de la Clé de Singe after three tours of duty in Iraq. He was looking for something meaningful to get involved with, so he first joined up with Greenpeace right after the Deepwater Horizon disaster. He was one of the first who protested big oil rigs drilling in the Arctic Circle, slowing production by jamming their equipment.

Greenpeace did not condone his actions and wasn't prepared to go to bat for him legally. He was arrested for destruction of private property and vandalizing property, he spent close to a year in Goose Creek Correctional Center in Wasilla, Alaska.

When he was released from Goose Creek, he had nothing but sixteen dollars in his pocket and the clothes on his back from when he was arrested. He headed over to the bus stop, where he would catch a ride into Anchorage. Once there, he figured he'd stop at a bar and then figure what his options were. While standing at the bus stop, he was met by a young woman wearing a sweatshirt with the name Sarah embroidered over a Greenpeace logo.

"Hi, are you Robert Lester?"

"Maybe."

"My name is Sammy."

"Your sweater says, Sarah."

"So? My jeans say Gloria Vanderbilt."

"Okay…Well, are you with Greenpeace?"

"Not exactly. My name is Sammy, and I am with an environmental organization that you might be interested in joining."

"What organization would that be? I have to tell you, I'm a little disillusioned in the whole environmental-activism-thing at the moment."

"Have you ever heard of the Le Gang de la Clé de Singe?"

"Shit yeah—the Monkey Wrench Gang."

"Well, as you probably have heard, unlike other environmental organizations, we don't just protest; we kick ass and take names. We don't ask permission; we ask forgiveness."

"Yeah, you guys do some pretty hairy shit."

"That's us, and, as the Marines say, 'We're looking for a few good men,' interested?"

"Why me, man?"

"You're kidding, right? We're looking for people who are tired of playing by the rules and getting nowhere while the other side cheats, lies, buys politicians, and basically plays by their own set of rules. If you want to make a difference—I mean a real difference—and help stop the corporations of the world from ruining the environment for their own personal profit, I have a car right over there. Otherwise, you can stand here and wait for the bus."

Lester saw the bus for Anchorage approaching the bus stop, but he looked at her and said, "Lead on."

She led him over to an old, beat up, silver Honda CR-V, where he noticed two men were seated in the front. He looked at her and asked, "And they would be?"

"My friends, my protection."

"Protection?"

"Yeah, Alaska has the highest rape rate in the country; a girl can't be too careful. Okay?

"Wow, I did not know that."

As they got into the car, Sammy introduced the Iceman to her friends, Tommy G and Jimmy the Chew. Both were veterans of many eco-war campaigns for the Gang against corporate America. They would eventually become part of the Iceman's Blue Team. They drove down the Glenn Highway into Anchorage, to West 6th Avenue across Town Square Park, and to Humpy's Great Alaskan Alehouse, where they all ordered the halibut fish 'n' chips and a large glass of Hopothermia beer. Robert said that, after almost a year in jail, this was the best meal he had ever had. As they sat eating and drinking, Sarah explained what Lester could expect and what would be expected of him in return.

After several hours and several beers, Robert agreed to join 'the Gang.' He was given his solo first assignment as a sort of initiation: he was to pose as a National Geographic photographer and make contact with a young woman who hunted big game and endangered species, but what made her a person of interest was that she got pleasure from torturing the beast before putting them out of their misery. He was given a complete dossier of her social media postings, articles, and affidavits from porters, guides, and other eyewitnesses.

After reading the information, he looked at Sammy and said, "Wow, this bitch is a real piece of work. I'll come up with something special; leave it to me."

Air France flight 8984 landed in Atlanta's Hartsfield-Jackson at Terminal I, Gate 2 at 7:24PM, both Brittany and Angelo were fast asleep and didn't feel the landing, so they had to be woken up by the flight attendant when they reached the gate.

While standing in line for customs, Angelo offered her a ride home, but she said that her parents would be meeting her after customs; he then asked if she would be interested in getting together.

"You bet! Where and when?" she asked.

"How about I meet you at Zoo Atlanta after midnight tonight? We'll have the whole place to ourselves; I got permission to photograph the animals without the hassle of having tourists around. What do you say?"

"Sounds like it could be interesting."

"Okay, I'll be waiting at the Georgia Avenue entrance at midnight. Oh, and dress appropriately; it gets cold out there."

"I'm counting on you to keep me warm." She said as the customs agent called her to his station.

Angelo was called to an agent several stations away, and, by the time he was waved through, he had lost sight of her. He walked out from the customs area to be met by Bill Flannigan, who was holding a sign with his name. Bill is his Zoo Atlanta contact and a Le Gang de la Clé de Singe sympathiser, who is going to let Angelo have full access to the Zoo.

Bill took Angelo's bag and led him to the parking lot where his car was parked. He asked his passenger if he would like to sit up front, but the man declined and said he preferred to ride in the back. Bill asked him if he would like to go straight to the Zoo or go have something to eat.

"Dinner sounds great; what do you recommend?"

"You up for some classic soul food and barbecue? I know a great place, Walter's Soul Food Café."

"Oh yeah, now your talking. Lead on, my man, lead on."

Traffic on 285 was actually moving at a decent pace, when, usually, it moved at a snail's pace and would feel like sitting in a parking lot. Sometimes, it could take over an hour to move a mile. Bill would occasionally try and engage in conversation with the man sitting in the back seat.

"So, what's going on at the zoo?

"I really can't say, and the less you know, the better."

Looking in the rearview mirror, Bill jokingly said, "Oh, yeah. If you tell me, you'd have to kill me, right?"

Angelo was gazing off to the right, never looking at Bill, and said, "Right."

It was because of the tone of his voice and the manner in which he said it, that Bill knew that's what would happen. They rode the rest of the way to the restaurant in silence. After dinner and while on the way to the zoo, there was a call for Angelo on his cell phone that seemed odd to Bill. When he answered the phone, he answered with a different name—not Angelo Della Morte, but Chase Madrid.

"Red Leader, this is Red Drone, do you copy?"

"Red Leader, go."

I have a group of bogies heading your way from twelve o'clock, due North of you, about two clicks. If they remain on course, you should encounter them in approximately forty minutes. Over."

"Copy that; how many? Over."

"Looks to be about twenty, and they appear to be heavily armed. Over."

"Copy. Keep me posted. Over and out."

Rodin radioed his team, "Gentlemen, let's rock and roll." Within minutes, all eight men had rappelled down from their hammocks in the tree canopy to the jungle floor. As they made their way towards the poachers, Rodin was developing his ambush strategy. Taking in consideration the size of the opposition and the terrain, initially, he was going to go with a linear ambush. But because of the size of the enemy, he decided on an L-shaped ambush and set his men in position. They were outnumbered, a little over two to one, but they had the element of surprise. The Red Team settled in and then waited. Red Drone alerted the team that the poachers' ETA was under five minutes.

"Red Team, hold your fire until my command."

They heard them before they saw them. They traveled in three groups, with two men out front as trackers and the two groups of nine separated by six-to-eight feet of space. As the first group of trackers got near to where Rodin and three men were stationed, one of the trackers held up his hand and told the others to halt. Everyone held their weapons at the ready. The head scout, an elderly man with gray hair wearing a dirty red plaid flannel shirt with camo fatigue shorts, looked around. He listened for five minutes and then decided that they would proceed. Rodin wasn't sure if he was listening for the gorillas or if he had heard the team in some way.

The firefight lasted less than ninety seconds, and the poachers got off less than a hundred rounds total. After the shooting was over, the Red Team approached them with extreme caution, which proved to the right thing to do as the head scout, the old man wearing the plaid shirt, was only wounded. He sat up and started firing his AK-47, hitting Pelé in a freak shot that penetrated the edge of his bullet-proof vest seam just under the armpit; it traveled upwards and hit the left common carotid artery, causing him to bleed out in a matter of minutes. The old man was instantly fired upon by the entire team, not much left of him after the shooting stopped.

Rodin rushed over to Pelé, but he was dead within seconds of Rodin's trying to stop the bleeding. They did their traditional laying out the poacher's bodies, placing yellow Monkey Wrench Gang flags around their necks and letters of proclamation, warning others that they will face the same fate as these men if they continue to hunt these magnificent beasts, in each of their pockets. They then canvassed the area, making sure to leave nothing incriminating behind. Rodin picked up Pelé and carried him over his shoulder back to camp.

Back at camp, Rodin instructed the others to return to their hammocks in the tree canopy while he and Lu Wei take their comrade and friend out into the jungle to bury him. Odin, the Icelander and the team's number two, said, "Negative, sir. We're a team, and, as a team, we all want to say goodbye to our friend, too."

Rodin looked at each of them and said, "Thanks, men. Pelé would appreciate this. I know I do. Okay, let's go say goodbye to one of our best."

They took Pelé deep into the forest and laid him next to a small grove of Free Standing Ficus trees—not the kind of tree that charcoal trade would be interested in. The charcoal industry was worth two billion dollars, and the trade fueled many of the gorilla killings, which have been reported as an act of sabotage by people in the charcoal businesses who want to see the gorilla's dead.

After laying their comrade to rest, the Red Team went back to their camp and waited to be called upon by Red Drone. They engaged three more times with poachers in the next four days. After which, they got the call to move out and start to proceed down to Hwange National Park, Zimbabwe to team up with the Blue Team and engage with David Leeway's big game safari. The thought from HQ was that four encounters in Virunga, that had left over forty-five poachers dead, had sent a very powerful message. They kept sending out a couple of three-man teams to keep the pressure on and continue to send the message: don't fuck with the gorillas.

Good morning, this is Josh Colman with CNN, traveling with David Leeway here in Hwange National Park in Zimbabwe. We are preparing to head out today in search of Castor, the Parks legendary bull elephant. David Leeway has stated that he is intentionally hunting big game in order to encounter the people who killed his children.

As you can see, the hunting party in heavily armed for much more than big game; the Zimbabwe authorities are giving Mr. Leeway plenty of latitude, allegedly because of his companies rather substantial investments in Zimbabwe's diamond industry. The nation is one of the world's top ten producers of gem diamonds. Zimbabwe's Prime Minister has stated that he is ready at a moment's notice to send in troops at the first sign of any trouble; he has made it clear that Zimbabwe will prosecute, to the fullest extent of the law, any murderous acts.

This is Josh Colman, CNN reporting from Hwange National Park, Zimbabwe.

Brittany arrived a little after midnight to where Angelo was waiting; he had a Nikon D850 DSLR camera with a 50mm lens and a camera bag over his shoulder. She parked her Silver Mercedes-AMG GT Roadster next to the entrance door.

"Nice car."

"Thanks, it's brand new. Mummsey and Dadums picked it out for me while I was gone. It's my birthday present."

"Oh, it's your birthday?"

"Well, it's really tomorrow."

"Happy birthday, kiddo. Sorry, but I didn't get you anything."

She took a step towards him, put her hand on his crotch, and said, "It's early yet. Are we the only ones here?"

"Yup, we got the whole joint to ourselves."

"How do you rate so high?"

"I know a guy who knows a guy."

"What are you shooting?

"A fourteen-foot Green Anaconda named Bubbles."

"Yuck, I hate snakes. They really creep me out. I thought you said Panda cubs?"

"That's tomorrow, in the day, but tonight it's Bubbles. Come on in, and I'll show you around before we meet Bubbles. Anything, in particular, you'd like to see?"

"Let's go see the big cats."

"Okay, follow me. The big cats are this way," He said as they walked arm-in-arm past the Flamingos, veering left past the Elephants, Warthogs, and Meerkats to where the Lions were. Since lions are primarily nocturnal, they were awake and watching as the two approached. The male lion, Zimba, let out a mighty roar, which unnerved several of the other animals—mostly those that are the lion's natural prey, like the Zebras and the Yellow-Backed Duikers.

As Zimba was pacing back and forth, never taking his eyes off of them, Brittany snuggled up to Angelo and said, "I'm cold. Why don't we go somewhere and get hot?"

"I know just the place." As they started to walk away, he pulled out a flask and asked, "Care for a drink?"

"Sure." She took the flask and took several drinks. "Mmmm, what is it?"

"It's called a Nigerian Chapman. I thought you'd like it."

As they were walking, the air was cool and crisp, but Brittany started to feel warm and then hot. She then felt weak and dizzy, so they stopped and sat down on a bench, where she passed out.

When she opened her eyes, she felt the air was nice and warm and humid. She realized that was lying down and looking up at a large tree branch. She knew that she was inside, but, as hard as she tried, she couldn't move; she was paralyzed from the neck down. She tried to scream, but nothing happened. Then, she heard Angelo's voice in the distance.

"Ah, you're awake."

She could only lift her head a few inches, but she could see him walking towards her and smiling. Again, she tried to speak, but nothing came out. He was standing over her, looking down at her. "It's no good trying to speak. You see, you've been drugged. I used a drug called Ketamine; veterinarians mostly use it, and it causes you to become temporarily unable to move as if paralyzed. It's also called a

Date Rape drug." He smiled, leaned down closer to her, and said, "No, that's not why I've drugged you. Brittany, have you ever heard of Le Gang de la Clé de Singe, the eco-terrorist group? You see, my real name is Robert Lester, and I've been sent to kill you."

Brittany tried to scream, but nothing came out, not even a squeak. Robert stood up, looked around, and said, "You know, I had heard a lot about you, how you like to torture animals before you kill them. How you get your jollies from seeing them suffer, how you like to watch them die a slow agonizing death. Well, guess what babe? It's your turn. It's payback time."

Her eyes got as large as saucers, and she started to cry and whimper. He knelt down and lifted her body up far enough to show her the fourteen-foot Green Anaconda coiled up about twenty feet away. She began to sob and tried to scream, but nothing happened. She looked down at herself and saw she was naked.

"Don't flatter yourself; you being naked is only so Bubbles has an easier time swallowing you. Of course, you'll be dead long before that happens. Anacondas always kill their prey before digesting them. I know that it's cruel, but no crueler than you, Brittany, honey. I would recommend that you try not to fight it, but just go with it."

He stood up, looked over at the snake, and said, "She will come for you very soon, once I leave. Brittany, I just want to tell you that I really enjoyed our time together, and, under different circumstances, things might have turned out different—maybe if you weren't just such a sadistic little bitch. Now, I must go. You see, I have a date with David Leeway. Ciao, baby."

She saw him hang a yellow Monkey Wrench Gang flag on the branch of the tree, along with a note proclaiming who is taking responsibility. Then, he was gone; he didn't even look back.

As she sobbed, she strained to hear a sound, any sound, any movement, but the messenger of death was silent. She laid there for what seemed to be an eternity, until she felt something smooth touch her leg. She started to cry, hysterically, but there was no sound as she tried to scream. As the snake crossed her body and slid over her pubic area, she could see it's green-gray eyes with its black slits. They were cold, dead eyes; as it passed her, it seemed to look into her soul, and she saw nothing, no emotion, nothing. Its whole body passed over her, and then it began to encircle her, its head was next to hers. Once it had coiled itself around her, it slowly started to tighten its grip on her, tighter and tighter. She suddenly noticed that she seemed to have some feeling in her hands; she could move her hands and feet, so she began to resist. But the more she resisted, the more the snake constricted. She began having a hard time breathing. Every time she took a breath, the snake constricted a little more, which made it harder to catch the next breath, until, finally, she felt the excruciating pain of her ribs breaking. She began to lose consciousness. Finally, she decided to just let go.

Chase Madrid and company landed in Harare, Zimbabwe two days after the David Leeway's entourage had arrived. Once they made their way thru customs, an elderly man, holding a sign saying 'Madrid Party' and standing by the exit, met them. As they approached the old man, he smiled and said, "Welcome to Zimbabwe, gentlemen. My name is Moses Kubakwashe; please, just call me Moses. I will be your driver and guide during your stay in my country."

Chase looked at his team, before he looked back at Moses and said, "Moses, we weren't expecting anyone to meet us. Who sent you?"

"A fine gentleman named Mr. Noir, boss."

"Mr. Noir. Have you met Mr. Noir?"

"Oh, yes, boss, yes. As you say, we go back a long, long time. I fought alongside him many years ago when this country was still called Rhodesia, fighting for our independence. We fought on the side of the UANC, the United African National Council, during the civil war."

"Moses, what exactly did Mr. Noir tell you?"

"I am to assist you in any way. I have taken the liberty of procuring you gentlemen equipment, vehicles, weapons, and ammunition. I hope you don't mind. And if you find yourself in need of extra men, I can help provide you with trained professionals. Now, if you will follow me, I will take you to your accommodations."

They followed Moses out of the terminal, across the street and into the parking lot, where they all piled into an old Ford Windstar minivan and headed north on Airport Boulevard. They made their way to the A5 West Highway to the suburb of Kuwadzana, which was on the western edge of Harare Province. Kuwadzana looked like most suburbs in Harare: modest homes, no lawns, few trees, and lots of dirt with little or no plants. The house they stayed in was located behind a Puma Service station on 1st Street; Moses pulled the Windstar into the garage and closed the garage door before the men got out.

"Sorry, boss, but four white men going into a house in this neighborhood would raise some suspicions."

Anthony Johnson started to laugh. "That's a good one, and it's usually the other way around. It's usually black men raising suspicions."

The house was small, extremely sparse in the decorations, but very tidy and clean. They entered through the door leading from the garage to the kitchen, and then they went into the living room. Moses led the way. "Please, gentlemen, make yourselves comfortable. Can I get you anything to drink: coffee, tea or a beer, maybe?"

Chase replied, "A beer sounds good to me."

Moses looked at the others. "Gentlemen?"

They all concurred; Moses smiled and gave a small bow; then he set off to the kitchen. He returned after a few minutes with six beers. After everyone had gotten one, Moses raised his bottle and made a toast, "To a successful and safe mission, cheers."

They all raised their bottles and, in unison, said, "Cheers."

"Now, gentlemen, let me show you what I have procured for you in the way of armaments."

Moses took the men into what was once the second bedroom now acting as a storage room filled to the eight-foot ceiling with boxes of ammunition, grenades, body armor, camo fatigues, AK-47's, and even a couple of rocket launchers. He said, "This is what I have; please let me know if there is anything that you require, and I shall do my best to get it for you."

Chase and the team looked things over, and, between them, they came up with a list of items that felt they needed. Moses took the list, looked it over, smiled, and said, "No worries, boss. I shall have these for you in a couple of hours. Meanwhile, please stay indoors until I return. Feel free to watch TV; we have lots of sports channels, and, if you like, we even have some very interesting soap operas. I shall bring some dinner back with me. Sit tight. I hope you like warthog stew."

David Leeway called a meeting between his security team and Josh Colman and his cameraman from CNN to go over the day's agenda; his safari guide was there as well since he was going to be primarily in charge of where they were going. The head guide, Louis Armour, was a native of Zimbabwe. In fact, he could trace his heritage back six generations, all the way to his family being one of the first to colonize what was then called Rhodesia in the 1890's. His father was a guide, his grandfather and his great-grandfather were guides, so no one knew this country better than him.

David stood in front of the group of nine standing outside the mess tent and spoke, "Men, I want to introduce you all to our guide, Louis Armour. Louis will be charge of all safari operations; he will be posting our agenda every evening and possibly revising it in the AM, depending upon various factors such as animal migration, etcetera. I've asked him to have scouts sent out in advance of the hunting party to observe the animal activity, along with them being paired with a member of the security team, to keep a watchful eye for any potential danger from any eco-terrorists. Today, we're going after elephants and, specifically, Castor; he is a legend within this park. We will be heading out in about an hour. Are there any questions?" There were none. "Very good; everybody stay sharp."

Unlike most safaris that use open-top vehicles, Leeway had decided on eight General M1045A2 High Mobility Multipurpose Wheeled Vehicle 4-Door Hard Top Humvee's with Slant Backs; two of them were mounted with .50 caliber machine guns. Mr. Leeway wanted to show everyone that he's not fucking around.

At ten o'clock, the caravan headed out in search of Castor within Hwange National Park. Their original staging area was Sinamatella Campsite in the Northern area of the park; they started traveling south towards the bush town of Pelendaba. Since they were traveling off-road, what would normally be a five-hour trip on the A8 will now be more like a two-day journey.

Two hours out, they spotted a herd of elephants, but, alas. there wasn't the legend among them. He had thought of killing the Bull of the herd to get a bit on the eleven o'clock news, but he decided to wait; if, by the time they got to Pelendaba, they didn't come across Castor, then he would start the mass carnage just to start rattling Le Gang de la Clé de Singe's cage. He was itching for a showdown, and if it meant killing hundreds of animals to start a fight, so be it.

Gloria Harris's job, first thing every Monday morning, was to walk through the Reptile House with a cage full of white lab rats and feed the snakes before the zoo opened; this way, none of the tourists would freak out when the snakes killed and ate their meals. Most of the snakes ate only once a week, except for Bubbles, who, on average, ate once every four-to-six weeks. It all depended on what they fed her, though, and she wasn't scheduled to have a meal for another week after she had eaten a twenty-pound pig twelve weeks ago.

As Gloria approached Bubble's enclosure, she was shocked to see the size of the bulge; she had never seen anything like it in the seven years that she worked in the Reptile House. What in the world did they feed her? It appeared that the snake hadn't quite completed swallowing its meal; Gloria couldn't quite make it out from where she was, so she slowly started to move towards the enormous serpent's enclosure. It wasn't the hoof of a pig, yet it was a similar color, but it had what looked like spots of bright red coloration on it. As she walked closer, she realized that what she was looking at was a human foot with red toenail polish. She screamed and dropped the cage of rats, which, when she did, the latch on the cage broke open and sixteen rats followed Gloria, as she ran screaming out of the Reptile House, to their freedom.

The Atlanta Police were called and arrived within minutes; as did WSB-TV, FOX5, and WXIA-TV, who always listen to the police scanners. By the time the police had walked to the crime scene, the TV crews were already setting up and broadcasting nothing but conjecture, as no facts were yet known.

Heading up the investigation was the eighteen-year veteran of the homicide squad, Charlie Davis, who thought that he had pretty much seen just about every which-way somebody could kill another human being, but he was wrong.

As Charlie approached the enclosure, the head of the zoo was waiting for him. There were no less than twenty-two uniformed police, four plain-clothed homicide detectives, three forensics members and six members of the medical examiner's team, plus two official police photographers, who were shooting Bubbles from every conceivable angle.

Detective Steve Matchet waved for Davis to come over so he could show him the flag and letter that they had retrieved from inside the snake enclosure.

"Whadda we got, Steve?"

As he handed Davis the letter, he answered, "Read this."

Let it be known that Le Gang de la Clé de Singe declares responsibility for the execution of Brittany Jones, a notorious Big Game Safari Hunter who has knowingly killed numerous endangered species. She is also known to have delighted in the torture and suffering of animals before killing them. Therefore, she has paid the ultimate price for her acts of evil.

Be forewarned: hunt at your own peril. You will be hunted down and pay with your lives. You have been warned.

"Fuck me," Davis said to himself.

"The note says it's Brittany Jones, but we won't know for sure until the ME cuts the snake open. He thinks it will be an easy ID; the girl shouldn't be too digested or disfigured for identification."

"Just to be safe, we should start checking the missing person reports once we get her out of there."

"I had heard about her, and how she liked not only killing endangered animals but torturing them before she finally killed them."

"That's really fucked up, but to go out like this... Wow! I guess we should call in the FBI."

"Already took care of that. And we got a call from a couple guys from Interpol, who want to talk to us in a day or two. Inspector Volker and Morris, out of London."

"Interpol, huh?"

"Yeah, this is major shit, Charlie."

"Yeah, pass the word: until we contact the family, I want a tight lid on this. We don't need those news vultures freaking out Hotlanta, ya dig?"

"Got it."

The Iceman and his Blue Team were camped in the hills overlooking Bulawayo, a city in southwest Zimbabwe and just three hours away from Pelendaba, where David Leeway's hunting party was heading for.

Bulawayo was the gateway to Matobo National Park, home to the Matobo Hill's rock formations and Stone Age cave art. The park included rhinos and black eagles. The Blue Team had set up their camp three days earlier, having hiked in from Botswana; they had been told that the Red Team should be expected to arrive at their camp by sunset.

The Iceman and Rodin had never worked together before, but it was decided that Rodin, being the more senior and experienced, would be in command. He had no problem with being second in command and was looking forward to working with and learning from Rodin, a true legend within the organization.

Just as the sun began to set, the Red Team crested the hilltop to join the Blue Team's campsite overlooking Bulawayo. Several of both teams knew and had worked together on other assignments, so there was a positive sense of camaraderie and fellowship. While the two teams were enjoying the reunion, Rodin and the Iceman started to develop a strategy for a battle plan. They had reports of the size and strength of the opposition, but there was an unconfirmed report from HQ that a Leeway insider had information of a rogue unit working outside the main group, acting as an independent unit. After several hours, they finally decided on their course of action for what they called 'Operation Sacs d'Argent,' translated as *Operation Money Bags*.

The Iceman removed a small flask from his backpack, took a swig, and offered it to Rodin. "Care for a drink?"

"Don't mind if I do. Thanks. Heard about that little snake thing down in Atlanta. Got a lot of people talking, nice work."

"Brought a lot of heat to the organization."

"They can handle it. Besides, I believe that it's going to take shit like this to make people wake up and change their ways. We, and by 'we' I mean the world's endangered animals, are running out of time; Look, man, did you know that there is only one male Northern White Rhino left on the planet? One! When it's gone, it's gone forever. And for what? Because some limp-dick Chinese assholes think that rhino horns will magically give them a hard-on? Fuck 'em. I have no sympathy for any of them; that son-of-a-bitch dentist in Minnesota, those vendors and buyers of endangered products in Singapore, those fuckers who kill farm-grown Lions, for any poachers, or for that rich bitch that tortured and killed the wildlife she hunted. Fuck 'em all. Their lives aren't worth more than the animals they killed. In fact, with all the billions of people taking up space in this world, they're worthless."

"I couldn't agree with you any more, although I'm sure that there are going to be a lot of governments starting to organize against us. They're going to be coming after us with a vengeance."

"Bring it on. Our cause is gathering momentum everyday, and besides, unlike religious terrorists, we don't go on camera and pontificate. We stay anonymous; we work in isolated groups, only knowing our assignments; and we stand for something that has universal appeal: animals. Who are more sympatric: fat-ass, wealthy, self-entitled hunters like the

Leeway brats, or baby elephants? It's a new twist on 'Shock & Aww look at those baby elephants'."

"You ought to be in advertising. Not to change the subject, but to change the subject: what are your thoughts on the rogue outfit that is supposedly roaming out there? Any ideas?"

"Ever hear of Perdix Drones?"

"No, can't say that I have."

"Perdix Drones are U.S. government experimental drones that are designed as autonomous mini-drones to be used for unmanned aerial surveillance. They travel in swarms, are about the size of a Freesbie, and each individual drone isn't controlled separately but, instead, is controlled by a shared collective brain, traveling in leaderless swarms. Each member can adapt to changes and remain coordinated with the other drones. Having numerous drones doing surveillance is tactically advantageous to simply having one large drone, because it is easier for the mini-drones not to be detected by radar. We've decided not to use the big drone when these seem so much more efficient and productive."

"So, they…"

"Think for themselves, right. Now we have gotten ahold of some Perdix Drones and have modified them to not only surveil but to have the capability to defend themselves and even act offensively."

"That's awesome; how did we get them?"

"Can't say and you don't want to know, just in case. We also have got some real techy micro air vehicles, or Bugbot Nano Drones. Some look like a large beetle that can fly, crawl, and hover; we even got a couple that look and act like a bird. We are going to use these to spy on Mr. Leeway and friends, while the Perdix's will be topside, looking for that rogue team somewhere out in the bush. If they're out there, the Perdix will find them."

Moses finished uploading the trailer attached to the van. When he was done, Chase and the rest of the outfit piled into the Ford Windstar and headed west on the A5 for the five-hour drive to Bulawayo Province. For the first hour and a half, everyone was silent, just watching the scenery go by. The two Wellson brothers were crashed out in the back seat. It was a very desolate countryside, rarely seeing anyone or anything. There weren't very many vehicles on the road either, just the occasional semi hauling goods from one end of Botswana to the other.

After two and a half hours, as the van was at the halfway point, the city of Gweru, Moses asked to no one in particular, "Hey, boss, shall we stop and grab a bite to eat?"

Chase was deep into studying a topographical map, so Anthony answered, "Sure. What did you have in mind?"

"We be coming up to a Chicken Inn, a mighty fine fried chicken joint, plus it's near a petrol station. Always good to be topped off when going into the bush, boss."

"Then the Chicken Inn it is, my man."

It was a block off the A5; it looked like any other fast-food restaurant in any other part of the world. They smelled the fried grease before they had even gotten off the highway. As they walked in, they were glad to see that nobody really paid them much attention. A large cartoon chicken head, smiling with a sign that said *luv dat chicken* below it, greeted them. As they walked up to the order counter, Scott Mosby asked Moses, "What's good here, man?"

"Everything is delicious, but I am partial to the Livers with Roll."

"Well, why the hell not? I'm going for the Livers and Roll, too."

Chase had the Chicken strips with Spicy Rice, and Anthony ordered two Family Feasts, which consisted of two whole chickens, fries, and two salads with four rolls on the side. The brothers Wellson each ordered the Chicken Burger with a side order of the Chilli Bean Salad.

After they had finished with lunch, they drove down the block to an Engen Petrol Station and filled the Windstar up, then headed back onto the A5. The rest of the journey was just a boring as the first half of the ride, passing nothing taller than a fence post.

Finally, they approached the outskirts of Bulawayo, passing the Mahatshula suburbs and the Kumalo Aerodrome, where, until 1950 when a new airfield was constructed North of Bulawayo, it served as a Service Flying Training School. After the Aerodrome closed down, the runways were used, at times, for the 'Rhodesian Grand Prix' motor racing events.

They continued on through downtown Bulawayo, merging onto the A8, and eventually making their way to the Steel Works Road heading out of town towards the Granite Quarry Mine where the National Park began. An hour out of town, Moses turned off the Steel Works Road and onto a dirt road that had no signage. They eventually came upon what looked to be a small dam. Moses stopped the van and got out; the others followed.

Chase walked around the van and asked Moses, "What is this place?"

"It is the Khami Dam, boss. It will be a good place to camp for the night, with plenty of fresh water and good cover. Nobody comes up here except during the rainy season, and this is not the rainy season, boss. Mr. Noir should be contacting us soon and giving us directions as to where the Leeway expedition will be. So, what you say, boss?"

"I say, let's set up camp and wait to hear from Mr. Noir."

By the time the sun was setting, Chase and his team were enjoying ice-cold beers and burgers hot off the grill. Nobody had the courage to ask Moses what kind of burgers they were eating, but they had to admit, whatever it was, it was good. After dinner, as Moses was cleaning up, the team got busy going over their weapons and talking general strategies. At eight o'clock, Chase's cell phone rang; it was Noir.

Chase thought about putting it on speaker but decided against it; he stood up and started to walk about. "Hello?"

"Chase, Noir here. How is everything?"

"Good. We set up camp outside Bulawayo, just inside of Hwange National Park."

"I just got word that Leeway's party is heading for a small village called Ndolwane; the coordinates are Latitude: -20.1, Longitude: 27.483333. They should arrive tomorrow sometime in the afternoon."

"Copy that. Anything else we should know?"

"Affirmative. I have it on good authority that the opposition is aware of Leeway's destination as well, so be prepared."

"Copy that; we'll be ready. One more thing, does old man Leeway know we're around? "

"Yes."

"Okay, over and out." Chase turned back to camp to brief his team.

Detectives Davis and Matchet were still going over the zoo CCTV videos, when Charlie's cell phone rang. "Hello?" He held the phone against his chest and told Matchet that it was the Walter with the forensics and report from the ME.

"Yeah, go ahead."

"Well, do you want the good news or the bad news first?"

"Walter, I'm not in the mood."

"Well, we did pull one print that wasn't from any of the employees, and you're not going to believe who's it was. It was Mickey Mantle's."

"You're shitting me. Mickey Mantle?"

"Afraid not. I'm told that this is the MO of this Monkey Gang—they always leave a famous person's fingerprint as a kind of 'fuck you' to the police."

"I'm guessing that was the bad news, so what's the good news?"

"Well, the ME gave a positive ID to the victim; it is Brittany Jones. Any luck with the videos?"

"Nothing yet. Boy, these guys are good. Walter, I want you to check out a Bill Flannigan; he is a zoo employee who seems to have disappeared. Has anyone contacted the victim's family?"

"Yeah, I'm heading back to the squad room now from her parents' place. They were pretty torn up about it. They'll be coming in tomorrow to make the ID."

"I can't image. It's one thing to lose a child, but to lose her by her being eaten by a snake, God. How does she look?"

"Actually, she looks okay. She wasn't in long enough for the snake to start digesting her."

"Thank God for small favors."

"Oh, I almost forgot. Those two inspectors from Interpol called; they said they'll be in tomorrow during late afternoon to speak with you."

"Great, I'm thinking we can use all the help we can get. Anything else?"

"Nope."

"Okay, thanks. I'm going to view the rest of the CTTV video, just in case. Bye."

"Bye, Charlie."

"Good morning, this is Josh Colman with the David Leeway hunting party here in Hwange National Park in

Zimbabwe. This is day three, and, so far, there hasn't been any sightings of Castor the elephant that David Leeway has been tracking but, so far, has eluded him.

"I'm here with Louis Armour, David Leeway's safari guide. Louis, how long have you been a safari guide?"

"I'm a third-generation safari guid., I started going on safari with my grandfather when I was five years old. I've been guiding on my own for over thirty years."

"Is it unusual that we haven't come across Castor in the three days since we've been searching for him?"

"No, not at all. He's very wily; that's why he's survived as long as he has."

"How old is he?"

"He's over thirty years old. To some, he's considered a national treasure."

"And yet you're helping David Leeway to try and kill him?"

"I said to some he's considered a national treasure."

"How long do you think it might take to track him down?"

"We're getting close; it won't be long now. Probably just a day or two. Three days at the most."

"Thank you. That was Louis Armour, David Leeway's safari guide.

"Every day, David Leeway's security forces send out scouts in all directions. They're not looking for Castor or game; no, they're searching for any sign of Le Gang de la Clé de Singe. As each day goes by, the tension grows within the camp. People are on edge, expecting an attack at any moment. It's like being in a war zone.

"David Leeway says, as far as he's concerned, he is just on safari, but he is ready if somebody tries to say different. This is Josh Colman, CNN reporting from Hwange National Park, Zimbabwe."

Inspector Volker and Morris finally received some good news: the flight attendant from Air Namibia Airbus distinctively remembers Brittany Jones and a male passenger, named Angelo Della Morte, who seemed very chummy during the flight to Paris. When asked how she specifically could remember Miss Jones and Mr. Della Morte, she replied, "They pretty much screwed all the way to Paris like rabbits. I guess they thought no one would notice, or, more likely, they really didn't care."

"You know that the name Angelo Della Morte translated into English means Angel of Death? Let's check our database for anyone with that alias."

"Right."

Volker and Morris also received footage of both of them going through customs in Paris, as well as customs in Atlanta. Della Morte looked, to them, like he was wearing some sort of identification alterations, such as height enhancements and body-type adjustments, as well as some facial conversion. He sported a full beard, had long hair with a ball cap, and wore sunglasses most of the time. He seemed very aware of camera placement and rarely did he ever face the camera. He didn't give them much to go on, but it was a start.

Interpol sent in a forensics team to inspect the Air Namibia aircraft in the off chance of pulling any fingerprints or possible DNA samples from Mr. Della Morte. They knew it would be an extreme long shot if they were to be able to find anything since aircrafts usually underwent cleaning between fights. They were banking on Air Namibia not necessarily being too strict in their cleaning routine. They lucked out in a way, as the forensics team found dozens of fingerprints as well as multiple DNA samples, but it would take weeks, possibly months, to process all of the samples. They also contacted the Atlanta ME handling the Brittany Jones case to see if they could collect any DNA from recent sexual contact.

Volker and Morris contacted both Detectives Johansson and Wilson in Bemidji, Minnesota and Detectives Matchet and Davis of the Atlanta Homicide squad to let them know that they had gotten they're first real lead in months. They sent both sets of Detectives copies of photographs of Mr. Della Morte to see if they might be able to provide any further information on the suspect. Unfortunately, neither Detectives were able to add anything to the enquires.

"Right you are, then," Inspector Volker said to Detectives Matchet and Davis. "We'll keep you up to date if there are any new developments. Cheerio."

Aleppo and Lu Wei programmed twelve Perdix Drones for a search and recon mission to see if they could locate David Leeway's group and the support combat team that they had heard rumors about. The Perdix Drones were launched with a slingshot device, one at a time. Once launched, they would circle above until the entire group was airborne. They would then start communicating with each other. There wasn't one drone that was the leader, so they would interact with each other, collecting data separately, and start collating the information before making decisions collectively. Within an hour, they had found both Leeway's campsite and his support team's site, located just a few kilometers from each other.

Rodin planned to send in Bugbot Nano Drones to each of the camps when the sunset began. It was decided that the bird-like drones would be sent to Leeway's camp, since it was set up amongst trees and the insect drones would be more suitable for their support team's camp. The insect drones were no more than three inches long and resembled black beetles; they would send in eight. The insect drones would look like a small swarm, and then, when they were a few dozen yards away, they would land on the ground and crawl towards the campsite. Lu Wei would monitor and control them remotely since they all were equipped with cameras and microphones; as were the bird drones, which Aleppo would be in control of.

The Perdix Drones returned to camp. Of the twelve they launched, all but two made it home safely. Since they don't have a true landing system, they more or less crash landed into catch fencing that the teams set up. In relative costs, compared to the large-scale drones, they could afford to lose a total of eight and still have it be an effective means of surveillance.

As the sun began to set, Lu Wei and Aleppo set their respective drones out into the night to capture intelligence that, hopefully, Rodin and the Iceman could use to plan their attack. It would take the drones a couple of hours to get to their targets; when they started to get close, they would radio back a signal to the operators, who could take control of them using the visual controls and the built-in GPS guidance system. The four bird-like drones, codenamed 'Tweety', were sent out in a staggered release so as not to draw attention to their arrival.

The first bird-like drone arrived and landed on a tree branch overlooking the camp's mess tent, where everyone would gather for meals. Bird numbers two and three were positioned near the tents of Leeway and his guide, Louis Armour. His security team's encampment placed the fourth bird. Once in place, Lu Wei had a separate man assigned to each drone to listen in and keep notes as to what was being said. As did Aleppo with his eight beetle drones, which were consistently being maneuvered around the campsite as a real insect would do; they occasionally would fly about and re-land, especially if someone would walk around.

By one o'clock in the morning, both camps were asleep, and it was the time for a download from all the information that was gathered by the drones to see if there was anything that they could use to help develop a strategy.

Moses was finishing up cleaning the dishes from dinner, when he heard what sounded like a swarm of insects.

Out of the corner of his eye, he thought he saw some beetles landing not too far away. He wasn't bothered by most of the usual things that people tend to have fears of—snakes, spiders, scorpions, or centipedes. No, he had a phobia of beetles. He'd had a severe reaction to the bite of the African Bombardier Beetle as a child that left him with several scars from the boiling hot toxic liquid that it sprays its victim with, burning the skin and causing it to feel like fiery bite or sting.

Chase noticed that Moses was looking all around and acting nervous; something was definitely bothering him. "Moses, everything okay?"

"Yes, boss. I just thought I saw some beetles flying about, and, of all the bugs here in Zimbabwe, African Bombardier Beetles really upset me, as you know. So, if you don't mind, I'm going to my tent."

"No, you go on to bed. I think we'll be fine. Good night."

Chase walked back to the campfire, where the team was relaxing and having some drinks. Anthony whispered, "You know, I don't like beetles either. I prefer Mini Coopers."

Scott Mosby chuckled, saying, "For me, it's spiders, mostly Fiats."

Chase tried to bring the conversation back to the matter at hand. "Look, I had a conversation with Moses about those scars; they were made by African Bombardier Beetles that attacked him as a toddler, which, as a child, I image could be pretty traumatic.

So, let's move on. According to Café Noir, we are just a few clicks East of Leeway's campsite. Tomorrow, we'll start shadowing him, staying just outside of the range, but let's be ready just in case any shit goes down."

After Dennis Wellson finished his beer, he crushed the can against his head, stood up, walked over to the ice chest for another one, and said, "Does Leeway even know we're out here. Cause if he doesn't, and they spot us, they just might think we're the Monkey Wrench Gang and start blasting away at us?"

Chase said reassuringly, "He does know that we're out here. And I've established a safe word to distinguish us from the bad guys, just in case any shit does happen. The code word is 'Skippy', after his youngest son, and, if vocal communication is not an option, we fire off a red flare followed immediately by a yellow flare."

Anthony repeated the safety precautions out loud and went over to where Dennis was standing to get himself a beer, when he noticed a beetle fly up and away into the night. "Holy shit, that's one big ass beetle, man. No wonder Moses freaks out over those motherfuckers."

Chase pulled out his 9mm Glock and said, "Beetles are the least of our problems, guys. I'll take the first watch, then Scott, Dennis, and Anthony. Brian, you take the graveyard watch. We're going to get rocking at sunrise, so, from now on, we have to stay alert. Good night."

Brian sat by the campfire and stared into the fire. Every once and a while, he would notice one of those beetles fly up from the ground and fly off."

Inspector Volker hung the phone up and turned to his partner, Inspector Morris, and said, "Hey, Morris, we got a definite hit from the Air Namibia Airbus and from the snake pit in Atlanta. Guess whose fingers prints they picked up?"

"Jack the Ripper's."

"Oh, so close. No, it was Margaret Thatcher's."

"That's odd. I thought the old girl would have been scared of snakes."

"See, you would've thought so, but apparently not. Now, the fact that she's dead leads me to believe that something's amiss."

"I must say, I concur. I guess we should call the folks in Atlanta."

"Let's wait. Maybe we'll get lucky and get something on this Angelo Della Morte bloke or that missing zookeeper, Bill Flannigan."

"I say we head over to the Red Lion and grab a pint."

"A bit too politico…how about the Feathers?"

"Capital idea, old man. I love their Nicholson's Fish & Chips."

"I'm more interested in sampling some Monkey 47 Gin."

"Right, let's go."

As they made their way to the elevator bank, Detective Sergeant Edwards came running after them. "Inspector Volker, there's a call for you."

"Take a message, Sergeant."

"Ah, sir, it's about Bill Flannigan."

"What about him?"

"They found him."

"Dead?"

"No, sir, alive. In Vietnam. He just passed through customs, sir."

"Hanoi?"

"Ho Chi Minh City."

"Edwards, contact our man in Ho Chi Minh City and tell him to keep tabs on Flannigan and that Morris and I will be contacting him within the hour. Morris, do you like Pho?"

"I really had my heart set on Fish & Chips."

"Right, Pho it is. I know a nice little place on Haymarket called VietCafe."

"Just what the fuck is Pho anyway? It isn't anything with fish heads is it?"

"No, it's a Vietnamese noodle soup consisting of broth, rice noodles called bánh phở, a few herbs, and meat, primarily either beef or chicken. But if you want fish heads, I'm sure they would be willing to accommodate you."

"Not funny."

"Well, it's a little funny."

"Fucking Yarpie!"
"Pom!"

It almost sunset and David Leeway's heart really wasn't into killing the three-thousand-pound male Black Rhinoceros standing less than fifty feet away and grazing on the grassy field. The beast was so docile, it started to wander over to him out of curiosity. When it got to within twenty feet, his guide inquired in a soft voice, "Are you going to kill it or adopt it?"

Leeway had been out on safari for over a week and hadn't killed much of anything—a male lion, two giraffes, four warthogs, and now this beast. The people with him started to question his commitment to bring out the Le Gang de la Clé de Singe by hunting the really big game, threatened wildlife, rubbing their noses in it, and daring them to react. He thought of his dead children, and he pulled the trigger.

The colossal creature landed so hard that the ground actually shook. It was as if someone had dropped a VW Beetle from ten feet in the air. Leeway casually approached the colossus; it was still breathing when he reached the beast. As he slipped another round into the chamber, the Black Rhinoceros raised its head briefly and then died. After the perfunctory staged photos were taken, the porters brought out a chainsaw and sawed off the trophies, leaving the rest for the buzzards, jackals, hyenas, and the rest of the scavengers.

CNN's Josh Colman turned to his cameraman and asked, "Did you get it?"

"Got it."

"Great. Give me a few minutes to write up a lead in; then we'll upload it to the network."

He walked over to Leeway, who was inspecting his trophy. "Mr. Leeway, got a minute?"

"Sure, Josh. Did you get my shot on film?"

"Yes, sir.

"Good. Isn't it a magnificent beast? Its head will be prominently displayed on my Fifth Avenue office wall, as will all the trophies that I bag on this trip. I only wish I could hang the heads of those so-called 'eco-terrorists' on my office wall like they did poor Dr. Meriwether."

"Aren't you concerned about the possibility of encountering Le Gang de la Clé de Singe?"

"Not in the least Josh. As you've noticed, we're traveling with a pretty substantial, heavily-armed security team; I'm actually hoping that they do try something. I want my revenge for their killing of my children; I want a fight. Bastards. Cowards."`

"Would you be available later tonight for a live, on-camera interview?"

"You bet, Josh. I want all the gun-loving hunters out there in TV Land to know that we shouldn't be afraid to go out there exercise our God-given right to hunt."

"I didn't know it was a God-given right."

"Well, maybe not God-given, but, by God, then it is our Constitutional right as Americans."

"Great, shall we say eight o'clock under the large Umbrella Thorn Acacia tree? We'll be set up and ready to go when you get there."

By the time the interview began, the entire party had eaten, the security forces had sent out the scouts, and sentries were set around the perimeter. Josh had pre-recorded his intro, and the link to CNN New York was set; now, all they needed was the man himself to start. As Josh was going over his notes, he heard a strange fluttering above in the Acacia tree. When he looked up, he saw four odd, bird-like creatures perched on one of the branches above him. He had never seen any birds like those, and he wondered if they might have been some sort of bat species. He started to go to his tent and grab a pair of binoculars to investigate, when David Leeway approached him, anxious to get the interview underway.

"Welcome to the Duc Vuong Hotel in Ho Chi Minh City. Do you have a reservation?"

"Yes. Flannigan, Bill Flannigan."

While the young, attractive hotel clerk punched his name into her computer, he gave the hotel lobby the once-over. He noticed a man sitting and looking to be texting on his cell phone in the far corner of the lobby, but Bill gave it no thought.

The three-star hotel was built in 2006; it was ultra-modern and was a steal at only twenty-five dollars a night. The Duc Vuong would suit him fine, until he could find a permanent place to live where his half a million dollars would go far.

He hadn't been back to Vietnam since the war; the last time he was here, the whole place was going into the shitter. He was assigned to American Embassy duty during the fall of Saigon, and the whole city was in utter chaos while thousands of frenzied South Vietnamese were scrambling to get out and escape the Viet Cong's taking-over the country. He was on the last Huey helicopter out of Saigon; There were so many people hanging onto the landing skids as they started to take off from the US embassy's roof, that the pilot ordered him to get them off or they were in danger of crashing. He stomped the hands of several men and even one woman who were holding on, until they released their grip and fell several stories down onto the massive crowd gathered in the Embassy's courtyard.

One unfortunate man hung on for over an hour but lost his grasp and fell to his death while the chopper was several hundred feet in the air over the South China Sea. There, the USS Kirk was steaming offshore, landing the last of the Huey's out of Saigon. Once Flannigan's craft had landed and the refugees got off safely, the flight crew pushed the chopper over the side and into the ocean.

"Mr. Flannigan, how long will we have the pleasure of your company?" She inquired.

"I'm thinking a couple of weeks."

"Very good. May I have your passport and a credit card, please? And how many keys would you like?"

"One will be fine."

"Here's your credit card and your room key; you're in room three-twelve, and here is a key for the mini bar. Please let us know if there is anything else we can do for you." She said, as she handed him his keys. "Do you need help with your luggage?"

"No, thank you. I think I can manage." He said, as he held up two small bags.

As he made his way to the banks of elevators, the man in the lobby, after looking at the pictures that he took of Bill Flannigan, put the phone in his sports coat pocket, got up, and left.

"Skippy?"

"Yeah, Skippy. That was Leeway's youngest son's nickname," Rodin explained to Iceman.

"Oh yeah, I remember now. He was the little shit that shot that lion cub. From the Intel we got from this shadow unit, it sounds like Leeway knows they're out there, which we can use to our advantage."

Rodin waved for Lu Wei, who was packing up the bird drones, to come over. "Lu Wei, have we got anything from the Tweety's yet?"

"Oh, yeah. We got a shitload of great stuff. It seems that there's a CNN reporter traveling with them, and Leeway just gave a half-hour, on-camera interview. We're downloading it now and should have it for you in a couple minutes."

"CNN, great!" The Iceman clapped his hands with excitement.

Rodin started laughing. "You watch. I bet old Leeway will be shooting his big mouth off, bragging and giving away his position and his plans as to where he's heading. Giving us plenty of time to set up our ambush. Poor bastard."

Vulcan, the kid from Alabama, came strolling over with an iPad and knelt down between Rodin, Lu Wei, and the Iceman. "You ready?" he asked.

Lu Wei nodded and said, "Hit play."

"This is Josh Colman coming to you from Hwange National Park in Zimbabwe. I'm here with David Leeway. David, we've been on safari for a little over a week, and, during that time, you've just killed one three-thousand-pound Black Rhinoceros. You said you were going on this massive killing spree of animals to flush out the gang of killers who killed your children."

"Well, Josh, I don't think my killing of a dozen warthogs is going to bring these thugs out, so I've decided to be selective in my hunting. We believe that we will cross paths with the legendary elephant, Castor, tomorrow, and that should ruffle their feathers."

"It doesn't bother you that you're killing these magnificent beasts just as bait?"

"Josh, these murders killed my children, so I'll do whatever it takes, and kill whatever I have to, to flush these killers out into the open. Tomorrow, we will be entering the Sikumbi Forest Reserve. I understand, from my guide, that all signs indicate that there will be plenty of big game. And with any luck, it will be an epic battle of man and beast and then, hopefully, men against those animals.

"David, I know that you never experienced combat. In fact, you avoided the Vietnam War by getting numerous deferments for allegedly having flat feet, so why do you think you have the stomach for combat now at age seventy-one?"

"You fucking little weasel; how dare you bring that up? Are you trying to be funny? I told you, I'm here because

those murders killed my children, and you pull this kind of shit. I want your ass out of here, tomorrow. You understand me? You little punk. When this is all over, I'll have your head on a platter; you can kiss your career goodbye!"

A few minutes after Leeway stormed off from the interview, the four bird-like creatures flew out of the Acacia tree, heading southwest. Josh and his cameraman headed back to their tent to send their interview with David Leeway back to CNN in New York and then to start packing. It looked like they wouldn't be getting the skirmish between Leeway and the Monkey Wrench Gang after all. They were wrong.

Rodin smiled and said to Iceman, "Let's send a 'Tweety' back to Leeway's camp to keep to eye on him, and then let's get rocking on you and your men taking care of those boys over at the other camp. We got a big day tomorrow."

The Iceman stood and just nodded as he headed over to the tents where his men were bivouacked. They were expecting him and were ready to move out when he got there. He looked at each of them, grabbed his backpack and rifle, and, in a low voice, said, "Let's rock 'n' roll."

Air China flight 1492 landed at Tan Son Nhat International Airport on time at twelve-forty in the morning. There, Inspectors Volker and Morris were immediately met by their man, Bao Nghiem, an ex-North Vietnamese Viet Cong Colonel who was now working for Interpol. Bao was a highly decorated officer during the war and had been instrumental in many of the major victories against the invading American forces. He was wounded six times on six different battlefronts—at the Battles of Ap Bac, Pleiku, Van Tuong, la Drang, Khe Sanh, and during the Tet Offensive. He received some of North Vietnam's highest honored medals—the Military Exploit Order, 1st Class, the Brass Fortress Order and the Oppose America Save Country

Decoration, 1st Class, among the dozen or so other campaign and service medals. But to Bao, that was all ancient history; the war was over, and now he enjoyed the intrigue and excitement of working for Interpol.

Bao led Volker and Morris into the airport parking lot and to his brand new Pyeonghwa Promto GS, a sporty little SUV that was built by the Mekong Auto Corporation headquartered in Ho Chi Minh City. The auto was about the size of a Honda CR-V and was quite peppy; it had to be to be able to maneuver the hectic streets of Ho Chi Minh City.

Once they were on their way, Bao told them about the American, Bill Flannigan, who had checked into the Duc Vuong Hotel. He had overheard him say that he was planning on staying for a couple of weeks. On the way to the Duc Vuong Hotel, the three of them hatched a plan that they thought would get Bill Flannigan to start talking. When they arrived at the hotel, Bao stayed with the car, as Volker and Morris thought it better that they not be seen together at the hotel.

"Welcome to the Duc Vuong Hotel in Ho Chi Minh City, gentleman. Do you have a reservation?" The twenty-something-year-old, neatly-dressed clerk asked.

"Yes, the names are Volker and Morris," Inspector Morris replied.

"Ah, here we are. I just need your passports and a form of payment, please. And how long do you think you'll be staying with us?"

As Morris handed him the passports and his Gold American Express Card, he said, "This will cover both rooms, and it's hard to say how long. But it will be at least a week, maybe longer. Depends."

"Very good, sir. No problem," The clerk said as he handed Morris his American Express Card. "I have Mr. Morris in room 212 and Mr. Volker in 218. Here are your keys, gentlemen. If there is anything you might need, just let me know. I hope you have a wonderful stay."

Volker looked at the clerk's name badge and said, "Thank you, Lanh. I'm sure we will."

"Would you like some help with your bags?"

"No, I think we can manage."

They took their bags, headed over to the elevator bank and proceeded to their rooms. There, they just threw their bags inside and rode the elevator back down to the lobby and out the front door to met Bao, who was waiting in the car. Morris jumped into the front passenger seat, and Volker sat in the seat directly behind Morris so as to be able to hear and speak to Bao. Volker leaned towards Bao and said, "I'm famished, old man. What do you say we grab a spot of tea and maybe something to eat?"

"Anything, in particular, you're wanting?"

"I trust you, Bao. Surprise us."

"Very good. Then I'm taking you Quán Cơm Tấm Nguyễn Văn Cừ. They have the best Cơm Tấm in the city."

Morris looked straight ahead and asked, "Bao, what exactly is Cơm Tấm?"

Volker leaned forward from the backseat and assured his partner, "Not to worry, old man. The locals call it poodles and noodles. No, just kidding, it's a rice dish often served with marinated pork, pickled vegetables, an egg, and sweet fish sauce. He's going to love it, right, Bao?"

"Right."

The three of them sat around a small table out on the street, watching the chaos that is Vietnamese traffic. Inspector Morris was pleasantly surprised at how tasty the poodles and noodles were. In fact, he like it so much, he had a second order. Volker teased him ruthlessly for days. After they finished, Volker leaned into the other two and addressed Bao, "Has everything been arranged?"

"Yes, everything is as you asked. We're ready to go."

"Good. Call your man, and let's pick him up."

Moses woke with a start; he felt the cold hard steel of knife against his throat. Vulcan moved close to his ear and whispered, "Don't make a sound, understand?" Moses gave the slighted of nods. He wondered what time it was and which dumbass fell asleep while on guard watch; he bet it was one of the Wellson brothers, probably Dennis. With his knife, Vulcan directed Moses to sit up and then, slowly, stand up. Moses tried to peek out the tent flap, but all he saw was a hint of the campfire. There were no sounds; the camp was eerily still and quiet. Then he heard what he perceived to be the faint sound of a muffled shot coming from the direction of Scott Mosby's tent.

Scott Mosby always slept with a Glock 9mm with silencer nestled and locked in his robotic hand. He was sound asleep in his sleeping bag, when the two intruders creped into his tent. Jay-D was a large Swede from the small village of Hallen, which laid on the shores of Lake Storsjon, a small lake in the lower half of the country. He had been with 'The Gang' for two and a half years and now stood at the foot of the sleeping man, while Willie Tyler, who everyone knew as Cowboy from Terlingua, Texas, slid his Bowie knife under the sleeping man's throat. As Cowboy applied pressure to the man's throat, Mosby was brought out of a deep sleep; he heard a voice with a deep Texas drawl telling him to lie still or he would have his head sent home in a bowling bag.

Scott slowly looked up to see a lean, lanky-looking kid smiling down at him; he then gazed down towards his feet and saw a large man holding an AK-47 in fatigues and with camo paint covering his face. As he laid there, working out a plan on how and if he could survive the skinny kid holding the knife after he took down the fat guy standing in front of him, he was wondering if he had enough mobility within the sleeping bag to get the job done and come out of it alive. He thought about it and visualized different scenarios in his head, but most of them ended up with him dead. Mosby wasn't one to wait and see; he was a man of action, and he wanted to be the one calling the shots and making the decisions—especially when it came to life and death situations. He was counting on the element of surprise working in his favor, and he figured that the shock of the shooting of the fat man would freeze the knife holder long enough to get a second shot off, and, if he was lucky, he'd eliminate them both. Just before he decided to go for it, he, too, wondered which numb-nuts fell asleep on watch duty. If he got out of this alive, he'd cap their ass too.

Jay-D felt a punch-like pain in his stomach. He looked down and saw blood oozing from the wound; at the same time, Scott was trying to bring his hand up fast enough to get a shot off at the man holding the knife, who seemed to be stunned momentarily seeing that his partner had been shot. All was going to plan, except for the fact that Scott hadn't figured on the chubby individual not falling backward but collapsing forwards on top of him, pinning him down so as not to be able to get the second shot off.

The last thing that Scott saw in the remaining seconds of his life, while struggling to get that three-hundred-pound tub of shit off him, was the thin man holding the large Bowie knife over his head. Just before Cowboy plunged the knife downward towards Mosby's left eye, Scott said, to no one in particular, "Fuck me." He felt a sharp sting of pain, then darkness fell over him, and then there was nothing.

Cowboy left the knife in Mosby and jumped up, running over and rolling Jay-D over onto his back to see the extent of his partner's injuries. Jay-D was in a bad way; the bullet had hit an artery, so he bled out and was dead within minutes. As was their practice, he took anything of Jay-D's that could be used to identify him. Afterward, he retrieved his knife from Scott Mosby's head and waited by Jay-D for the signal to move onto the next phase of the operation.

Night Train Johnson was normally a light sleeper; the slightest sound would snap him out of a deep sleep. But on this night, he'd had a couple beers too many, so he was dead to the world when the two intruders entered his tent.

The two intruders were T-Bone from Galveston, Texas and Gianfranco, a small man from Peru, who was a direct descent of the Inca tribe that fought the Spanish explorer, Francisco Pizarro, who invaded the Incan Empire in 1532. Both were longtime veterans of the eco-wars.

T-Bone grew up in Galveston, where his extended family worked on oil rigs out in the gulf. He himself was working on the rigs with his father, when a fire broke out and his father and seven others were killed due to a safety violation that the company had known about but chose to ignore because they felt it would cost too much. That was the day T-Bone joined the MWG. But before leaving Texas, he made a short stop to the corporate headquarters of Midlands Gas & Oil and sent six members of the board of directors, the CFO, and the president to the hospital with multiple broken bones and contusions.

Gianfranco came to join the Gang when his father and four brothers all lost their lives in a copper mining accident. It happened because the chairman of the board decided that the cost of rescuing the men would be too cost-prohibitive and would negatively affect the stock price. He felt that the men knew the risks when they decided to become miners, and, therefore, he put in a minimal effort for the media. Two months after the mining accident, the chairman's car brakes failed while going down the 5N towards Oxapama, and, when his car went off the highway at a high rate of speed and careened into Rio Chontabamba, he was unable to get out and ended up drowning. Foul play was expected, but no suspects were ever arrested; the file is still open as an unsolved crime.

It took a slap on the face to bring Johnson out of his deep sleep; he leaped off his cot and was immediately looking down the barrel of a Remington pump-action Versa Max shotgun. His head was still in a cloudy fog and was having a hard time trying to process the danger he was in, when he heard in a low whisper from, what looked to him to be, a Native American. "Down on your knees and put your hands inside your pockets. Any sudden movements, and your brains will be sliding down the side of your tent. Understand?"

Night Train nodded and then compiled, slowly looking at the shotgun as it lowered at the same rate as he did. When he was kneeling, that's when he saw the other man, who was also holding a shotgun, standing to his left. He thought about asking what the fuck was going on, but these two didn't look like they were interested in carrying on a conversation, so he concentrated on sobering up, fast.

Brian Wellson couldn't stop worrying about brother Dennis who was supposed to be on watch. Brian could only think that either his dumbass brother had fallen asleep or was dead; he was hoping it was the former, as he, too, was kneeling with his hands in his pockets. There wasn't much light in the tent, just some flickering from the campfire outside, but he was able to discern, by the shape of the figure to his right, that she was a woman. She was dressed in fatigues, wearing camo face paint and a ball cap with her hair pulled up and a ponytail hanging out the back. One thing Brian had learned in all his years in the military is that you don't fuck with a woman wearing camo face paint and holding a pump-action shotgun.

Leonor Pesqueria was always picked on as a child in the small town of Estremoz, Portugal, because she was born with a severe case of facial asymmetry, a condition where one half of the face is not equivalent to or the same as the other half. In Leonor's case, the right side of her face was two inches lower than her left side, a condition that could be somewhat repaired, but her family couldn't afford the surgery. She went through her youth being taunted and made fun of. Then, at the age of fourteen, Leonor took her first karate class at the youth center. By the time she was nineteen, she had earned her Advanced Brown— her first Kyu belt. From then on, no one called her names or teased her after she broke the nose of Vinicius Carneiro, the town bully, much to the delight of all of his victims. She left Estremoz for Lisbon at the age of twenty-two, got a job at the Greenpeace, and, within three years, joined the Gang. She took the name Bellator, the Latin word for warrior, and everyone who met her believed it to be true.

Chase Madrid couldn't believe that Dennis Wellson fucked up so royally by not sounding some sort of alarm. If he wasn't already dead, he soon would be, as Chase vowed to do it himself if and when they ever got out of this mess.

Kneeling with his hands in his pockets, he stared up into the face of the man holding a shotgun at his head. He was wearing camo face paint, but he could make out that the man was Asian—his guess was probably Chinese. Lu Wei, holding the Remington shotgun, looked down at the leader of this pack of hired guns, smiled, and mouthed, "You're fucked."

The Iceman was standing off to Lu Wei's left, holding a Colt Government Model .45 ACP pistol. He whispered into his headset and asked the status of each team. They all replied that their mission was accomplished, so he ordered that all captives be brought outside to the fire area. Chase, Brian Wellson, Moses, and Night Train were led out to where they could see why Dennis didn't sound the alarm. He lay face down next to the fire; they could see that he had sustained a head wound, and that he was shot from the front, as most of the back of his head was missing. His brother, Brian, started to run to him but was tripped by Leonor, who said, in a thick Spanish accent, "Just get up on to your knees and put your hands in your pockets!"

"That goes for the rest of you—on your knees and hands in pockets."

Chase looked around to see that Mosby was missing and said, to no one in particular, "We're a man short; where's Mosby?"

The Iceman looked at Cowboy. Seeing that Jay-D was missing too, he asked, "Well, Cowboy?"

"I killed him after he shot Jay-D, so we're a man short, too."

Johnson was getting a real bad feeling about their situation and asked, to whom he presumed was the top dog, "So, whadda ya'll got planned for us?"

"Nothing good," Iceman answered in a cold, monotone voice that gave Night Train a chill down his back. He knew that this wasn't going to end the way they had planned. Dying in combat was one thing, but this was going to be an execution. Knowing if you live by the gun, you'll die by the gun doesn't make dying any easier. Those are the rules. You pay your money, and you take your chances.

Rodin had just put on his ghillie suit and was in the process of putting on Buster's ghillie suit, when Aleppo came into the tent and announced that they had gotten the word from the Blue Team leader: mission accomplished.

"Excellent. Tell the Red Team to get ready to mobilize."

"Yes sir!" Aleppo said, as he turned and ran off to assemble the team.

Rodin had sent word to Leeway's camp, via some native gossip, that a large herd of elephants was seen in the Tsholotsho District, not that far from Bulawayo where they were bivouacked. Rodin had studied Louis Armour, Leeway's head guide's techniques, and he was sure of his route to Tsholotsho to the elephant herd's position and that they would be waiting. There would be ample cover for their attack; the plan was to first surprise them with a quick shoot and scoot to divert them to the main area of attack. They would then engage with the full-on ambush. He had reviewed several ambush options—the linear attack, the L-shaped or the V-shaped offensive—but after considering the terrain, the size of the kill zone and the ease of retreat if need be, he chose the linear attack plan.

Rodin had a small advance team place several IEDs strategically to disable the armored vehicles that were carrying the heavily armed security forces. Then, he had Lu Wei send up the French Aerospatiale C.22 drone armed with two Aster missiles. He had a feeling this firefight wasn't going to be a cakewalk; this was going to be a real battle. As his Red Team gathered around him, he needed to steel them for what was coming.

"Men, we're going to be facing a formable force. Just know that we have faced tougher foes before and have been victorious, plus we have the element of surprise on our side. You all have been in combat and know what to do. Remember, if you get into trouble, don't panic. Stay calm, as, together, we're unbeatable. Are there any questions?"

He looked every man in the eyes; there were no questions. "Good. Let's move out."

"Wooch, go."

"Wooch, Leeway here. I'm calling from Zimbabwe."

"I know; I've been keeping tabs. What's up?"

"I'm just a little on edge. We've been out here for over a week and have had no contact with those French bastards; I thought we would have some sort of sign from them by now."

"You looking for a fight?"

"Well, yeah. That's why I'm out here."

"Don't worry, I'm sure you'll be in the thick of it soon enough."

"What do you know about the whereabouts of my Angels of Death?"

"I haven't had any official communiqué from them, but I know that they should be close at hand and ready to assist if needed."

"I would appreciate it if, if you hear from them, you'd contact me."

"Remember, David, they are acting independently of you and won't be checking in. You do realize that, right?"

"Yeah, yeah. It's just hard for a control freak like myself not to feel in control of everything."

"So, how's the hunting going? I've been watching the reports from CNN. You don't seem to be bagging anything special."

"The word is, we're possibly going to be having an encounter with the prize trophy, Castor, today. If I can bring him down, I'm sure that will bring out those punks."

"Just remember, be careful what you wish for. Well, David, I've got things to do, so stay safe and good hunting."

Josh Colman and the CNN crew were packing up and getting ready to make their way to Bulawayo, the second largest city in the country, located in southwest Zimbabwe. It was the industrial center of Zimbabwe and served as the hub to the country's rail network. They had planned to catch a flight from Bulawayo to the capital, Harare, then back to the States. But, as everyone knows, shit happens.

Leeway was unusually cranky, shouting orders to everyone and, overall, being a real jerk. They had heard from some local farmers that a large herd of elephants was seen north, near the Tsholotsho District, about six miles from their camp. Louis Armour, David Leeway's guide, had planned to send one of his assistants ahead to scope things out and relay confirmation back to camp, but Leeway nixed the idea saying, "Let's just go. I'm ready to get this show on the road, and if killing this beast will bring these assholes out into the open, then the sooner the better. At least it will be on our terms."

Bill Flannigan stepped out of the hotel entrance and was unaware of the two men following him, as he headed east to grab a quick bite at his favorite Indian restaurant, Baba's Kitchen, before catching the midnight showing of Rocky Horror Picture Show at the Cinestar Cinema Quoc Thanh. He was interested in seeing the reaction of the locals to such an American classic.

At ten o'clock at night, the streets were deserted as he reached the corner of Bui Vien and Do Quang Dau; this area of town wasn't known for being a hot spot of activity and was more of a residential neighborhood. He started to get suspicious that he might be in danger when he spotted a midnight blue Toyota van with blacked out windows and its hood open with two guys looking to be working on the engine. Bill had a nasty feeling that something was about to go down, maybe a robbery. He quickly looked behind him and saw two men following him; this was getting serious. He decided to cross over to the other side of the street where three old men were playing Tiến lên, the national card game of Vietnam, in front of their apartment building. They were arguing as one of the men was accusing another of cheating.

Flannigan ran over to them and said, "Giúp tôi! Giúp tôi!" which is 'help me' in Vietnamese, and he no sooner got the words out of his mouth when darkness fell over him, a darkness darker than the Black Hole of Calcutta.

When he started to emerge from a heavy fog-like void, he felt like he was entangled in kelp, as he was wet and cold and unable to move. When he finally did open his eyes, he found himself strapped to a hard, unforgiving wooden chair; he was indeed wet and had a blinding light shining in his face. The space that he was occupying seemed rather small, no larger than twelve-by-twelve feet, and it smelled of oil and gasoline, like he was in an automobile garage; the walls were looked to be rusted, corrugated tin. The light was ultra bight and so close that he was getting uncomfortably hot. He squinted towards the lamp and made out the shapes of, what seemed to be, a couple of men standing behind the spotlight that was shining into his face.

He tried to shout out but could only manage to whisper, "What do you want?"

There was no response. Bill closed his eyes to avoid the harsh light. He could hear a mumbling of voices but couldn't make out anything clearly. He lowered his head to his chest and tried to think what this was about. At first, he thought it was probably a kidnapping of what these men thought would be a wealthy tourist that they could ransom. He was concentrating so hard on his situation that he didn't hear the man approaching from behind, who swiftly slipped a black balaclava over his head, as he reached a pair of ski goggles with the lens blacked out, which were placed over his eyes so he couldn't see anything. Finally, a pair of headphones were placed on to his ears, which were playing loud white noise, so he couldn't hear anything other than the noise. As the best as he could make out, about every thirty minutes he would get doused with water, keeping him cold and damp for a short time, until the heat from the lamp would start to dry him off, and then he'd get hosed down again.

He lost all track of time; he could have been there a couple of hours or a couple of days. He hadn't had anything to eat or drink. He soiled himself twice and urinated several times. He ached. He was hungry and thirsty, and he smelled like a sewer. Flannigan was on the edge of insanity and was starting to fall off the edge, when he heard a voice coming from within his headphones, "Bill, nod if you can hear me."

Bill did as he was told; he nodded.

"Good, that's good. Now, Bill, this can all be over, and you can walk away, and we'll never bother you again, or you can play the tough guy, and then we'll start to hurt you. Nod if you understand."

Bill, again, nodded.

"Okay, Bill, all we want is for you to identify the man that you gave access to the Atlanta Zoo. The man who was responsible for the brutal death of Brittany Jones. Do you understand?"

Again, a nod.

"Good. Now, Bill, we're going to take off the hood and earphones so you can talk, okay?"

Bill nodded enthusiastically.

When the balaclava, ski mask, and headphones were finally taken off, and he slowly opened his eyes. The room wasn't bright; they had the lighting dimmed so he could adjust to his environment. Before him stood two men wearing all black and with ski masks on One was holding a truncheon in his right hand and slowly tapped it against his leg. The other man held a plastic glass with a straw sticking out of it and presented it to him, saying, "Have a drink. It's a protein shake, and it's good. Go ahead ,you need it."

Bill took a tiny sip. It was good and tasted like a banana smoothie. He then finished it off with a couple of long drags through the straw, which he wished he hadn't done because he got a killer case of brain-freeze. When he had finished, the man holding the glass dropped it onto the floor, bent down so as to look into Bill's eyes, and softly said, "So, are you going to tell us who this motherfucker is, or are we going to have to start breaking bones, pulling teeth, and hooking up some jumper cables to your nuts? What's it going to be, Bill?"

Veronica Ventura and Yum Wu couldn't have been more opposite. Veronica was five-foot-eleven, had long, blonde hair, green eyes, weighed one hundred and ten pounds—just plain beautiful—and she came from Greenwich, Connecticut. Her father was a hedge-fund banker, and the Ventura's were ranked as one of the ten richest families in America. Her father, Jonathan Ventura, was well acquainted with David Leeway; they usually would play golf together at least once every two or three months at one of the Leeway's golf resorts in West Palm Beach,

Florida. Veronica and Sasha Leeway went to the same prep school, the Greenwich Academy, when they were growing up but were wildly different in the way they saw the world. While Sasha loved killing things, Veronica volunteered at animal shelters, animal rescue centers, and local veterinary clinics.

Years later, it came as no surprise to Veronica to see that Sasha was really into big game hunting, as her family had gone on hunting parties for all of their school breaks. They once opposed each other on the issue of big game hunting while on the school's debate team. It was a spirited debate, each giving as good as they got. Emotions ran high, and what started out as a heated debate turned into a personal attack on each other, resulting in Sasha storming off the stage in a rage. That was the last time either spoke to each other, ever.

Sasha went on to graduate from The Wharton School of the University of Pennsylvania, then on to work for her father. Veronica graduated from UCLA and spent three years in the Peace Corp in Nepal, where she joined Le Gang de la Clé de Singe and recruited Yum Wu.

Yum Wu stands five-foot-four, has pitch-black hair, brown eyes, and weighs one hundred and eighty pounds. Standing side-by-side, they look like the perfect odd couple, but they are actually the perfect even pair. Yum was originally from the small town of Jinchang, the People's Republic of China. Jinchang is in the center of Gansu province, bordering Inner Mongolia to the north. It's known as China's 'Nickel Capital'.

Yum Wu's father was a miner, his father's father was a miner, and so on, and so on for eight generations. Her mother had died during her childbirth, and Yum and her father lived just outside of town on the West side of Hongshan Crossing, which literally separated the city from the rural community. The property on which they lived on was all dirt, as no plants or even trees could grow; it was a depressing existence for Yum. The only pleasure she got was from practicing target shooting for The People's Republic of China Olympic Women's 50m Rifle 3 Positions Team. The event had the athletes shoot over a distance of fifty meters in kneeling, prone, and standing positions.

In the beginning, when Yum began to try out for the team, many of the officials scoffed and laughed at her because of her physical appearance. They were all silenced when she obtained a near perfect score after only her first try.

Yum had gone hunting from an early age with her grandfather; she was an excellent shot but didn't enjoy the killing of animals. She did, however, enjoy the challenge in the precision and accuracy of hitting a target. She spent hours upon hours practicing target shooting for over twelve years, and, when she heard that the People's Republic of China Olympic trials for the Women's 50m Rifle 3 Positions Team was being held in Beijing, she and her father made the twenty-two-hour trip to Beijing by bus for the tryouts, which she aced.

While they were in Beijing, they received word that her grandfather and uncle were both killed in a major shaft collapse in the Mojiang Mine, where there had been hundreds of recent complaints from the miners of unsafe conditions. The mine owners just brushed them off as being unfounded, and the government backed the owners, bringing on no charges of neglect and stating that the miners were at fault for being careless and not heeding safe practices. When Yum stood with the miners and protested against the government, she was told to stop or she would be arrested, and she was cut from the Olympic team.

Yum and her father were arrested and spent seven months in prison. She was sent to the Provincial Women's Prison, where she was forced to work in the Jiuzhou Clothing Factory. During her time there, she was systematically beaten and raped by the prison guards.

Her father, Bohai, along with dozens of other protesters, were sent to Lanzhou Prison. It was a high-security prison that included several workshops where prisoners performed forced labor. Prisoners were deprived of food and medical care, and prisoners who did not finish their forced labor tasks were tortured. Bohai succumbed to several beatings and died after five months of imprisonment; his family was never told the truth of how he died, just that he was dead.

After Yum was released from prison, she decided to leave China. She knew that her life would be hell if she stayed, so she made her way through the twelve-hundred-mile journey, on foot, across Qinghai Province to Tibet. Qinghai was a large, sparsely populated province spread across the high-altitude Tibetan Plateau. She traveled mostly at night to avoid being seen and carried a Chinese Hanyang Arsenal Experimental Semi-Automatic Rifle that was her grandfather's—he had owned it since 1918 and kept it in excellent condition. It was the only thing she had that had any sentimental value to her. She was prepared to use it if she had to, as she had decided that she was not going to be taken alive and face prison again.

On day sixteen, she reached Amne Machin, which was a six-thousand-two-hundred-and-eighty-two-meters-high peak and part of the Kunlun Mountains, a holy site for Buddhist pilgrims. She was near death from exposure, when several Buddhist monks from the monastery Wutong found her and brought her to the monastery. There, she received medical attention and was allowed to stay under their protection for six weeks until she was fit enough to continue her journey to Katmandu. After another ten days, she finally slipped over the well-guarded border under the cover of a severe blizzard. She didn't make the journey unscathed; she suffered a severe case of frostbite—lost three toes on her left foot and two on her right foot—but she was free.

She eventually found work as a chambermaid at the Hotel Yak and Yeti, a hundred-year-old, five-star hotel in the heart of Katmandu, located on Durbar Marg Street where she learned to speak English. She worked there and, by sheer luck, met Veronica Ventura while viewing the Garden of Dreams, which, created in the 1920's, had half a dozen pavilions, several fountains, and hundreds of urns and birdhouses.

A couple of young, pre-teenage boys were teasing a dog by a small pavilion in the center of the garden. Both Veronica and Yum heard the yelping of the dog in distress and went to investigate, each approaching from opposite directions. They arrived almost at the same time, and each took actions to chase the boys away. The combination of a tall, white Anglo woman and a short, stocky Chinese woman joining forces in chasing and yelling seemed to un-nerve the lads, as they decided to run off and create mischief somewhere else. The two hit it off quickly, and, after several days, they became fast friends. After Veronica learned of Yum's talents, she recruited her into the Gang. Once the Gang found out about Yum's shooting abilities, she and Veronica were teamed up as a sniper and spotter duo. Veronica had chosen the name Sue-B in honor of her hero, Susan B. Anthony, and Yum decided to go by the name Fu Hao, an infamous Chinese female warrior from the Shang Dynasty.

Rodin and his Red Team were waiting for the fourth of Leeway's Humvees to get parallel with the IEDs in order to detonate them. Three of the vehicles were turned over on their sides by the sheer force of the explosions, and the fourth Humvee flipped up and backward, landing on top of the vehicle behind it and crushing both the driver and the man in the front. The remaining three Humvees were maneuvered into a triangular fortress formation. The men operating the mounted .50 caliber machine guns started firing in every direction, not knowing where the enemy's position was.

To Rodin's Red Team, it all looked very comical. Leeway and his remaining men scrambled out of their trucks and started to construct a basic fortification, digging foxholes and positioning themselves for what they believed to be an imminent assault.

"Cease fire! Cease fire!" Louis Armour, David Leeway's safari guide, shouted and waved his arms to the men atop the Humvee's. "You're just wasting ammunition until we know where the enemy is. Cease fire!"

After realizing that the man Leeway had hired as the leader of his security force was most likely killed while riding in the number one Humvee, and that there wasn't anyone apparently second in command, Armour took it upon himself to take charge, having served in the South African Army as a field officer in Afghanistan. Lewis took a quick survey of what he was in command of—fifteen security troops, two members of the CNN news crew, and the man responsible for the situation they were all in, Mr. David Leeway, who was pretty much useless and surely not up for command, as he was cowering behind one of the Humvee's massive bulletproof tires and had already wet himself from fear.

Armour's first thought was to seek a surrender, but, knowing the history of Le Gang de la Clé de Singe and all the reports of showing no mercy, he wasn't too hopeful. It looked like a fight to the death, but it was worth a try. What did they have to lose?

"Red Leader, this is Red Four. Over."

"Go, Red Four."

"Sir, I see a man holding a white flag approaching. Over."

"Copy that. Red Leader to all teams, hold your fire. I repeat, hold your fire. I'll go see what's up. Cover me. Stay frosty. Buster, come." Rodin and Buster walked slowly towards the man carrying the truce flag.

Louis left the safety of the Humvees and started walking slowly out aimlessly, not knowing which direction the enemy was. He turned back toward the men atop the vehicles for any sign of possible contact.

"Enemy at eight o'clock," Shouted one of the gunners, as he pointed to what looked to be a large bush rising up off the ground and walking towards them. Louis saw him and started to walk in that direction. He slightly turned his head, not taking his eyes off the figure approaching, and said, almost to himself as well as the gunner, "Cover me."

Rodin and Buster stopped when they were within three yards of the other man; he pulled up the hood of his ghillie suit, revealing his black balaclava. He didn't say anything; he just stood there. It was, after all, the other man's request for a parley.

Louis looked at the man's eyes and saw nothing—no emotion, no hatred, no warmth, nothing. Louis was sweating as the sun was starting to get warm, burning off the morning mist. There wasn't any of the natural sounds or smells that he was used to while being out on safari; these were different sounds and smells. The sounds of the vehicles on fire from the IEDs, and the sounds of moaning, of injured and dying men inside the disabled Humvees, and there was the smell from the burning gasoline, tires, and gunpowder from the machine guns. The air was full of death.

"I'm Louis Armour, David Leeway's safari guide."

The man opposite him said nothing, just stared, waiting.

"I am here to see what conditions and terms you are willing to give for our surrender."

Rodin looked at the man quizzically. "Surrender?"

"Yes, we want to surrender. We concede to you; you have won, so now we'd like to surrender."

"Is Mr. Leeway with you?"

"Yes."

"Why isn't he standing here asking for surrender?"

"Mr. Leeway isn't in any condition to be here."

"Is he wounded?"

"No, he is ill."

"Well, Mr. Armour, please tell Mr. Leeway that there are no surrender terms because there will be no surrender. Mr. Leeway, you, and everyone with you are going to die, and, most likely, some of us are going to die as well. We are willing to die for a cause we believe in. The question you should have asked yourself, Mr. Armour, is what are you willing to die for? For greed, for machismo, or for the thrill of killing? You see, Mr. Armour, we drew a line in the sand, a line you do not cross and live. You crossed that line, so no, Mr. Armour, there will be no surrender."

"Bloody hell. You're all a bunch of fanatics!"

"You know, Mr. Armour, you're right."

"His name is Angelo, Angelo Della Morte."

"Angelo Della Morte? Very funny, Bill." The man who gave Bill the shake turned to the other man in black and said, "Get the jumper cables, Bill's jerking us around."

"No, I swear on my mother's grave; it was Angelo Della Morte."

"Bill, your mother ain't dead, but she will be if you're fucking with us."

"Hey, man, I'll bet the airport's got footage in the passenger receiving area. Look at the airport security footage; I ain't lying, man. Check it out. Angelo Della Morte."

"Okay, Bill, we're going to check it out. But if you're lying, I'm going to cut your nuts off and feed them to a dog."

"Angelo Della Morte, you'll see."

"We'll be back. Just sit tight."

Bill watched them leave and shouted after them, "Funny, real funny."

The two men left Bill all alone for what seemed like hours. He had fallen asleep and was startled when one of them entered the room.

"Well, Bill, it seems that you're telling the truth about Mr. Della Morte. Now, we want to know how it came to be that you were picking him up at the airport. And what did you do and say on your way to the zoo?"

"I got a call on my cell phone. I don't usually answer numbers I don't recognize, but this was from the same area code as my mothers, so I answered it."

"Why?"

"My mother is seventy-eight, and I thought something might have happened to her, so I answered it."

"Yeah, then what?"

"This guy asked me if I was Bill Flannigan, and I said, 'Yeah.' And he asked, 'The same Bill Flannigan who works for the Atlanta zoo?' and I said, 'Yeah.' And he said, 'How would you like to make some major league money?' and so I asked, 'Who is this?' And then he said to just shut up and listen, and that all I had to do is pick up this guy from the airport, drive him to the zoo, and let him into the reptile house after hours. Then I could make a half a million dollars and a one-way ticket to anywhere I wanted to go and disappear."

"And that didn't set off any alarms, Bill?"

"Look, man, I make twelve-fifty an hour; I live in a shit hole of an apartment; I have zero social life, and some dude offers me a half a million bucks and a way outta here just to pick some guy up at the airport and let him into the zoo? Fuck alarms."

"Why did you think he wanted access to the snake house?"

"I figured he was just one of those rich freaks who was probably a private collector and wanted one of the rare snakes that we had. I didn't ask; I figured the less I knew, the better."

"Bill, have you ever heard of Le Gang de la Clé de Singe?"

"Yeah, they're that eco-terrorist group that's been wreaking havoc and killing big-game hunters."

"And what do you think of them?"

"They're okay, I guess. Some of those big-game hunters got what they deserve for going around and killing endangered animals, assholes. So what, this Della Morte-guy is one of these terrorists? I swear, I didn't know that, honest. What did he do, kill someone at the zoo?"

"What did you do after you picked him up?"

"He said he was hungry, so I took him to a BBQ joint."

"Then?

"Then I took him to the zoo, gave him a key, and left for the airport."

"Did he say anything?"

"Not really; it was just small talk. You know, about the traffic, sports, weather. Shit like that, you know?"

"How did you get paid?"

"I got a phone call that morning from HSBC Private Bank, telling me that a Swiss bank account had been opened in my name, that my opening balance was five hundred thousand U.S. Dollars, and that I needed to create a password over the phone, which I did. I checked back an hour later, just to make sure it was legit, and, sure enough, it was."

"So, you have no idea what happened at the zoo?"

"No, man. I told you, after I dropped him off and gave him the key, I drove straight back to the airport, got on a plane, headed and here, and I haven't seen or heard anything about what's going on in the world since, much less Atlanta. What happened?"

"It seems that Mr. Della Morte drugged a young woman and left her in with the fourteen-foot Green

Anaconda, who proceeded to kill her and devour her. You, my friend, are an accessory to murder."

"No fucking way, man. I didn't know anything about no murder. You got to believe me!"

"Bill, I do believe you, and I'm willing to cut you loose right now, but I need something more, anything. Think, Bill, is there anything, something else?"

Bill closed his eyes and started recalling every detail, and then something clicked.

"He got a phone call on his cell phone while we were driving. I couldn't hear too much because of the traffic, you know, but something struck me as a little odd, although I didn't think too much of it at the time."

"Yeah, what was it, Bill? What struck you as being odd?"

"When he answered the phone, he said, "Chase Madrid, go.""

"He said 'Chase Madrid'?"

The man in black walked around the room for a few minutes, stopped in front of Bill, looked at him, reached into his pocket, and took out a rather large, ominous pocket knife. He opened it and walked behind Bill. Bill was sure he was a dead man and started to weep, when he felt his ties being cut. His arms dropped to his sides. He tried to raise them, but there wasn't any strength left in them; he had been bound for over seventy-two hours. As he tried to regain some strength in his arms, the man in black plopped his clothes in front of his feet on the ground.

As the man in black left the room, he stopped, turned and said, "Goodbye, Bill."

Bumbley Bee was considered a myth-legend in the waters of Luminous Lagoon, Jamaica. Many a Jamaican considered him as much of a national treasure as Bob Marley. Bumbley was an *Epinephelus Lanceolatus*, also known as a Bumble Bee Grouper. They got their name from the Bumble Bee-like markings they had as juveniles, but, as they got older, the yellow patches eventually became green and grey or grayish brown.

It was said that author, inventor and avid scuba diver, Arthur C. Clarke, reported seeing a 20-foot-long Bumble Bee Grouper in a sunken, floating dock off the coast of Sri Lanka.

At twenty years old, Bumbley had long ago lost his Bumble Bee markings, and, at approximately one thousand six hundred pounds and over twelve feet long, he now looked more like a camo-colored 1963 rusted-out Volkswagen Beetle meandering along the ocean floor.

Bumbley spent most of his day cruising around the coral reefs of Luminous Lagoon, looking for small sharks, skates, stingrays, and pretty much anything that looked eatable. Looking at him, you wouldn't think that something that big could be very agile, but you'd be wrong. One minute there could be a four-foot Lemon Shark casually swimming nearby, and in less time than it took for you to read this sentence, no shark.

For years, there had been numerous rumors floating around the Island, totally unconfirmed, of course, that there had been the occasional snorkeler or scuba diver that had provoked the gentle giant and were never to be seen again, supposedly gobbled up in a blink of an eye. Legend has it.

The Iceman's Blue Team had collected the remaining members of Chase Madrid's team on their knees, with their hands on top of their heads, and kneeling in front of the fire next to where Dennis Wellson and Scott Mosby's bodies laid. T-Bone Bergman was standing behind the group, off to their left, holding an AK-47 on them while the other members of the Blue Team were nowhere to be seen. Anthony Johnson looked slightly behind him, towards T-Bone, and asked, "Hey, brother, what's the plan?"

T-Bone pointed his rifle at them and told them to stand up. No sooner had the words left his mouth, than, from off in the distance, eight flashes of light from eight different directions appeared in silence. In a blink of an eye, three of the four men laid dead on the ground. Moses was still on his knees when the Iceman walked back into camp.

"You can get up now, Moses. We want to thank you for all you've done for us."

"You are welcome, my friend. But tell me, why did they die like that and not just with a bullet in the head, execution style?"

"They have to look like they died in battle, not executed. Meet the murderous members of Le Gang de la Clé de Singe."

The Blue Team appeared out of the darkness and began to disassemble the campsite, loading up Moses' truck with most of the gear. They then took the bodies of Chase's team and carried them off to set the stage, so, when the Zimbabwean Army investigates the battle scene, they'll find the dead remains of Le Gang de la Clé de Singe, who they'll be able to identify.

Bumbley was the only one of his kind in those tropical waters of Jamaica. His natural habitat would normally be anywhere in the Pacific Ocean from Japan to the Hawaiian Islands, but, as luck would have it, Bumbley had been purchased illegally in 1983, when Fernando Ramos, a Spanish mariner, bought the Grouper from a local fisherman in Macau at the Red Market.

The Red Market was located at the intersection of Avenida Almirante Lacerda and Avenida Horta e Costa on the Macau Peninsula, and it was one of the most popular fish markets in Macau. Fernando had tried haggling with the elderly fisherman, who was a very crafty Chinese merchant, but the best he could do was to haggle a deal for the fish for the hefty sum of eight hundred US Dollars. Fernando reluctantly agreed but only if the hawker provided him with something to carry the weighty trophy in. The ancient Chinaman was hesitant at first, shaking his head. But when he saw that the issue was a deal breaker for the eight hundred in cash, he finally agreed.

The old man walked over to where his wife was sitting on top of an old, beat-up, cobalt blue Igloo ice cooler, smoking a spicy and aromatic blend of Black Cavendish in an old, beat-up Billard Walnut Briar pipe. The two of them got into a heated discussion for a good five minutes, when, finally, she got up, shot Fernando the stink eye, squatted down on the floor next to the cooler and gave Fernando a snarly grin, showing off her one tooth that was gold-crowned. The old man took the cooler and emptied out a half dozen dead octopuses onto the floor. He filled the ice chest to the brim with salt water and dumped the Grouper into it. To keep it sealed, the aged fishmonger grabbed a roll of yellow duct tape and proceeded to envelop and bind the chest from stem to stern. He told Fernando, in pigeon English, to get the fish into a larger container quickly, unless he was ready to have a sushi banquet.

Fernando picked up the ice chest by the side handles and struggled his way onto the crowded sidewalk on Avenida Almirante Lacerda. He gathered plenty of suspicious looks from passerby's, watching him carrying a large duct taped ice cooler as he kept bumping into people and knocking over merchant displays. He hurriedly walked through the streets, trying to flag down a cab to get him to his ship before his prized investment croaked, or before he developed a hernia.

When he finally reached the dock at the Port of Macau, he stood hidden behind a large royal blue Hanjin container, just out of sight of his ship. He waited impatiently for over an hour, until he was sure that no one was watching the gangplank. He hosted the ice cooler onto his shoulder, which, with the fish and water, weighed well over one hundred pounds and, at twenty-one hundred hours, finally sneaked Bumbley onboard the ship.

The ship was the Mairangi Bay, a German container ship that, at first glance, could have been mistaken for an oversized garbage scow. She was scheduled to sail from the Port of Macau, through the South China Seas, past Borneo and Java, and then into the Indian Ocean. From there, it sailed under the tip of the Cape of Good Hope, South Africa, out into the South Atlantic, and onto Rio Janeiro, Brazil to deliver over twenty-eight thousand tons of exotic seafood delicacies, like Chinese mitten crabs from Guangzhou, Congshao crucian carps, and the ever-popular sea worms from Shanghai.

This was not a journey for the faint of heart, especially on the Mairangi Bay. If one took the time to give the ship a close look with a critical eye, one would have noticed that the Mairangi Bay heeled severely to the starboard side. The tilting wasn't due to sloppy and improper loading of cargo; it was simply because the German owners never got around to fixing the starboard side bilge pump. Herr Adolf Schumacher, the principal owner, realized that the aging ship would be worth much more to him and his partners if she sank ; that way, they could collect the insurance. He had been greasing the pockets of the ship inspectors for over eight months in hopes that, pardon the pun, his ship would come in when his ship went down. They stood to make an access of one hundred and forty-five million dollars when, not if, it went down.

This is Josh Colman reporting under fire from Le Gang de la Clé de Singe with what's left of David Leeway's safari group. Minutes ago, four of the Humvees were destroyed with what we believe to be IEDs, and now we are under heavy fire. Lewis Armour went and met with the leader of the terrorists to try and surrender, but, apparently, they aren't willing to show any mercy. I haven't seen David

Leeway; he seems to have been hiding since the initial attack. Our only hope is that we can somehow get help, and that isn't looking likely. I believe that we are, at this moment, holding our own, but it's only a matter of time. We will continue to film and report until the end. This is Josh Colman reporting.

Josh put down his microphone and found Leeway curled up in a fetal position next to the Humvee's tire, where Armour was shouting at him to take up arms and fight back. The guide grabbed him and slapped him hard on the face, and that seemed to bring him around. "David, you've got to get a hold of yourself and start taking command. You said that you had some help out of this unit; how can we reach them?"

"Help? Right, right. Where's a walky-talky?"

Louis shouted out, "Has anyone got a walky-talky?"

One of the machine gunners tossed one down, and it landed at Louis's feet. He picked it up and handed it to Leeway. Leeway took it, activated the device, switched to the designated channel, and said, "Leeway here. Over."

"Skippy here. Over."

"Where the hell are you? We're are under fire and getting the shit kicked out of us. Over!"

"We hear fire but need to know your GPS coordinates."

Louis took the walky-talky and said, "19.1241° S, 26.5926° E. Over."

"Roger that. Hold tight, will be there in fifteen minutes. Over."

Louis shouted out to everyone, "Hey, listen up! Help is on the way. Conserve ammunition; take your shots carefully, and make every one count!"

The Iceman put the walky-talky down and relayed back to Rodin his conversation with Leeway. "Blue Leader to Red Leader. Over."

"Red Leader. Over."

"Had contact with Leeway; we're a go by thirteen forty-five. Over."

"Roger that. Remember, no fire from the Blue Team. Over."

"Roger. Watch for flares. Over."

"Roger. Over and out."

Of the original nineteen surviving members of Leeway's security force, three have been killed—two machine gunners and one rifleman. They could have taken out most of them early on, as they weren't highly professional or trained in combat techniques. They were uncoordinated in their use of their firepower, and they wasted a lot of effort with minimal effect.

Sue-B and Fu Hao had two of the three kills so far. Sue-B spotted a clear shot to David Leeway, so she radioed Red Leader. "Red Leader, this is Red Six. Over."

"Red Leader to Red Six. Over."

"I have a bead on Alfa Dog. Do we have a green light? Over."

"Negative. This is Red Leader to Red Team. Alfa Dog is off limits at this time. Please affirm. Over."

All teams responded affirmatively.

Positioned high in an Acacia tree, Sue-B spotted a rifleman peeking over the hood of a Humvee. She tapped Fu Hao's shoulder, who was sitting next to her. "Bogie, three o'clock. Distance—two-fifty, wind—two knots, drift point—three clicks, green light."

"Got 'em," Fu Hao said and then eased her hand down to caress the trigger on her M24 sniper weapon, squeezing ever so lightly. Through the scopes, both Sue-B and Fu Hao saw the fine red mist burst out of the top of the man's head as it exploded.

Josh Colman and his cameraman were huddled down next to the man when he was shot. After, he collapsed down on to his knees, and then his lifeless body slowly drifted towards Josh and came to rest against him. Josh had covered mostly nature disasters, human-interest stories, and some crime investigations, but never any hardcore combat. Sitting there, scared shitless, and now having a man's blood and brains ooze on to his lap caused within him a violent gag reflex that forced him to throw up. Unfortunately, he threw up into the dead man's brain cavity, filling the crater, which brought on even more vomiting and gagging.

Louis Armour saw what was happening with the CNN reporter, so he ran over to Josh, grabbed him by the arm, and dragged him to the other side of the small compound. There, he stood him up against the Humvee and shook him violently to bring him out of shock.

"Josh! Josh, snap out of it!" Louis shouted. He raised his hand to strike him, when Josh looked at him and lifted his hand, saying, "Yeah. Yeah. Okay, I'm okay."

Louis looked him in eye and said, "You gotta get a grip, man! This is no time to lose it. Understand? Help is on the way; we just have to keep our heads. Okay?"

"Yeah, okay. I'm good. Really."

Louis bent down, grabbed a handful of dirt, and threw it on Josh's pants to mitigate the blood and grey matter splattered on him. Josh looked down, and back to Louis, and just nodded. Things had quieted down quite a lot, and it seemed that people were taking shots only if they were sure of a hit. Leeway's forces were holding steady at twelve, and Rodin had just two wounded, luckily not seriously.

"Red Leader, Blue Leader here. Over."

Fernando Ramos was thirty-eight when he signed on as the Deck Engineer Officer on the Mairangi Bay. His job as Deck Engineer Officer meant he was responsible for maintaining, repairing, and operating deck machinery; his specialty was cargo-handling equipment like cranes, booms, and winches. He had spent over half his life on old worn out rust-buckets like the piece of crap German box-boat; he noticed, as soon as he boarded the ship, that she heeled to starboard. He was aware that the crew seemed like a bunch of bilge-sucking reprobates and that the Captain was notorious for being a renowned drunkard, so Fernando figured he had to be on one of the worst vessels of his twenty years at sea; he tried to think of a worse one, but none came to mind.

There were rumors that the Captain had lost two ships under his command—a tanker and a freighter—but, even with all the investigations, it was never proven that he was ever under the influence when the ships went down. That fact gave Fernando no comfort in knowing that the Captain wasn't a drunk, just a shitty sailor, as he figured better a drunken seaman than an inept sailor. Captain Helmut Marko's, or 'Mutt,' as the crew called him, got his nickname not because of a play on his name, but because he had saggy cheek jowls that gave him the appearance of an English Bulldog.

The Mutt was very progressive in his nautical beliefs and views, so he wasn't one to believe in the old sailor tradition of women and children first, or that the Captain goes down with the ship. No, he was more of an 'every man for himself' kind of guy. And he proved that on both occasions, as, when his ships sunk, the Mutt was the first one on the lifeboats. He proudly told investigators that he felt he could do a better job of directing the abandoning of the ship from a distance, where he could see the whole picture.

Over the course of Fernando's many years at sea, he had many friends and acquaintances around the world— most were unsavory and nefarious characters. One such acquaintance was a wealthy Brazilian restaurateur, Mateus Goncalves, who had convinced Fernando the last time they were together that he had several Japanese clients who would pay dearly for some Bumble Bee Grouper sushi. Mateus convinced Fernando that he was willing to pay him six thousand dollars for his troubles, knowing that he could conceivably see a twenty-fold return on his investment.

But as fate would have it, Bumbley was destined for much greater things than ending up on some sushi platter. It was his good fortune that a series of bad storms in the South China Seas would delay the Mairangi Bay's arrival to Rio by two weeks, which meant that, for them to stay on their schedule, all shore leave would be cancelled in order to unload their exotic cargo and bring onboard a mixed shipment of Brazilian-made Ford Escorts and containers filled with Brazilian Beef, which were headed for Kingston, Jamaica by way of Santiago de Cuba.

Being the Deck Engineer Officer and allowed one valuable perk, Fernando would have his own stateroom, which meant he didn't have to share it. Before docking in Macau, he spent several weeks of scavenging items around the ship and raiding bits and parts from the tool shop to build a makeshift aquarium to house his scaly investment. Unfortunately, the rough weather and high seas made his life miserable. His room was always wet from the water sloshing out of the aquarium due to the ship's pitching, and then he was constantly having to sneak in fresh salt water to refill the tank since he didn't have any way of oxygenating the tanks water.

If keeping Bumbley a secret and alive wasn't hard enough, feeding a growing, pubescent grouper was like feeding a teenage boy. While Bumbley was gaining two to three pounds a week, Fernando was losing about the same. His shipmates started to take notice and wondered how someone, who went through the chow line three or four times every meal, could be losing so much weight. Fernando told them that he thought he had a slight stomach condition or maybe even a tapeworm. Since taking food out of the mess hall was frowned upon, he had to be careful sneaking food out. He started wearing large, baggy denim chambray shirts and untucked and green, camouflage cargo pants with large patch pockets on the legs, which he would fill with toilet paper before he entered the mess hall. Then he would carefully swap out the toilet paper for pork chops, burgers, fried chicken, and, Bumbley's favorite, Portuguese sardines. Most of the time, he looked like the singer David Byrne wearing his 'Big Suit' in the concert movie *Stop Making Sense*. By the time they reached the waters off Jamaica, Bumbley weighed close to 120 pounds, almost as much as Fernando.

Somewhere between Cuba and Jamaica, Fernando started noticing changes in Bumbley's color; he was starting to lose the bright-colored, yellow patches, as they were beginning to turn a dull, mossy green. By now, Fernando had given up any hope of making his money back, much less of turning a profit from this google-eyed monster. Fernando didn't know anyone in Kingston to sell the fish to, and, because they were coming in from Cuba, there was a very good chance that Jamaican customs agents would board the ship—it was known to happen. Bringing in an outside wildlife species into Jamaica was a crime that carried a ten-thousand-dollar fine. Fernando decided it was time to cut his losses and get rid of this fishy Albatross from around his neck.

Since the Mairangi Bay was approaching Jamaica from the North, as luck would have it, they steamed passed Montego Bay at around 4:00AM when Fernando's fire watch was over. Not that it mattered to Fernando, but it was very fortuitous for Bumbley, for, if he had been thrown overboard deep out to sea, he would most likely have been a tasty treat for some Hammerhead or Great White Shark that swam the waters between Jamaica and Cuba.

At around 4:30AM, just as the Mairangi Bay was passing off the coast of Montego Bay, Fernando Ramos was stealthily making his way through the empty hallways of the German container ship, carrying an old burlap coffee sack slung over his shoulder, and heading up to the main deck. He was hunched over like an old man with osteoarthritis, and the fact that Bumbley was squirming and gasping for air just added to Fernando's anger and pain. As Fernando climbed the ladders leading up to the main deck, he was cursing, under his breath, those tropical storms that threw the ship off schedule, the Brazilian restaurateur for hatching the plan, his own greed, and, most of all, the stupid bug-eyed fish.

Once on deck, when he was sure it was safe, he carefully walked along the multicolored, railroad-car-sized containers stacked six stories high, making sure to stay deep within the shadows. When he was sure it was safe, he stepped out onto the walkway on the port side of the ship, where he twirled around several times, building up momentum. Finally, he let go and flung the burlap sack overboard with the grace of an Olympic hammer thrower. As he was walking back to the stairway, he turned around just in time to see the burlap bag go sailing over the side. Seconds later, he heard the splash, and then, utterly dejected, he walked back to his stateroom and went to sleep.

Inspector Volker walked out of the room where he had left Bill Flannigan, removed his balavaca, put it in his back pocket, and walked out of the warehouse to where Morris was waiting in a silver 2016 Toyota Innova. Volker got into the passenger side and said, "Got it."

"Did you kill him?"

"I decided to let him skate."

"He's one lucky motherfucker. I would have killed him."

"Then, I guess he is lucky that he got me and not you."

"So, who is it?"

"That fucker, Chase Madrid."

"No shit. Well, let's go back to HQ and find out where the asshole is." Morris dropped the Innova into drive and peeled out, heading north on Trần Não Street towards downtown.

Moments later, a weak and battered Bill Flannigan cautiously emerged from the warehouse entrance; he glanced around and saw that there wasn't anyone out on the street. He was completely disoriented and lost, and he had no idea where he was; he didn't even know if he was still in Ho Chi Minh City. He felt better once he saw a Ho Chi Minh City bus rush by, and he walked several blocks until he reached the Cho Lon Bus Station. Reaching into his pockets, he was relieved to find that his captors left him his money and wallet. Flannigan waited only minutes before a bus arrived; he boarded the bus and was back at the hotel within an hour. He went to his room, filled the tub with hot water, got in, laid back, and fell asleep.

He was awakened when the phone rang two hours later, and he didn't realize how much his body ached until he started to get out of the tub. He limped over to the phone, naked and dripping wet. "Hello?"

"Bill, do you recognize my voice?"

It was the man in black who last spoke to him. He answered with much trepidation, "Yes?"

"Bill, I just wanted to let you know that I meant what I said. You're free, but my advice to you is to go deep, become invisible. If you do not do anything to draw attention to yourself, you'll be fine. Do you understand what I'm saying?"

"I understand."

"Good."

"Why?"

"Why? I looked into who you are and what you've done, and I think you honestly didn't know what was going to happen. You're going to have to live with it, but that's between you and your God."

"Did I help?"

"Yes."

"You know, you might have just asked me."

"Yeah, no. It doesn't work like that. We find that enhanced interrogation works best."

"You mean torture."

"Potato, tomato."

"Right."

"Bye, Bill. Go deep."

Bill hung up the phone, got dressed, packed his bag, checked out, and was never heard of or seen again.

Charlie Grayson sat behind the .50 cal machine gun, on what was the last Humvee in the convoy; this was his first ever experience in a combat firefight. Prior to working for Delta Security Forces, he had served four years in the military but never saw combat. He was a photographer's mate in the U.S. Navy Air, assigned to an antisubmarine squadron based at the Naval Air Station in Key West, Florida.

Charles didn't know anything about photography before joining the Navy, and it never entered his mind that that was even an option. After taking a whole battery of skill tests and flunking all the mechanical tests, the recruiter was prepared to send him to clerical school to become a Yeomen, a pencil pusher, a paper shuffler. Then, fate took a hand in Charlie's future. There was a recruit who had been assigned to go to photography school, but he had a bunch of outstanding speeding warrants for which, when the local police caught up with him, they threw his ass in jail. This left an open slot that had to be filled. Charlie was asked if he knew anything about photography, and, of course, he didn't. But much to his credit, he lied and, the next thing he knew, he was on his way to photo school in Pensacola, Florida.

Charlie graduated at the bottom of his class and wasn't given any of the choice assignments, which was just fine by him. His motto was to never volunteer for anything and never let them know your name, just try and skate through. Because of his slacker attitude, he picked up the nickname 'Skater'.

Most days, while in Key West, Charlie could be found sleeping on the floor in the locked color-dark room. Whenever anyone would knock to try and enter, he would just shout out, "I'm in the soup, come back in twenty." He did, occasionally, have to actually do some work. Whenever there was a high ranking V.I.P. who came to the base, he would have to photograph the event for local PR. And twice a year, the Russian submarine fleet would show up in Cuba, so his outfit would fly south and play cat and mouse exercises with the Ruski's.

Once, when Charlie was sitting in the jump seat, used occasionally for a photographer when the brass wanted to have photographic evidence that they weren't just fucking around and wasting the taxpayer's money, they were about four miles off of Cuba, while tracking a Russian sub on a moonless night, when the Captain decided to buzz the sub that was cruising on the surface.

"Hey, Skater, get ready to light 'em up."

"Roger that, Captain."

"GO!"

Charlie leaned forward and hit the switch, which fired off a flare that lit up the sky so bright that, for eight seconds, it looked like high noon. As soon as the flare was released, the camera pod that was synchronized to the flare and attached to the left wing of the Grumman S-2F Tracker started taking photographs. When processed, the film revealed the Captain and several officers standing on the conning tower of a Typhoon-class looking up at their S-2F and taking photographs of them.

That was really Charlie's only notable time as a photographer in the Navy. Most of his time was spent taking photos of new people who had been assigned to the base, or photos of broken bits and pieces of equipment that needed to be attached to the reports that had to be filed in triplicate.

The only other event that people took note of was when Charlie got a call from the base commander himself, telling Charlie that he needed to go to the Monroe County Medical Examiner, because Chief Petty Officer William Scott had been involved in a head-on accident with a drunk driver and was killed. Charlie had to go photograph the deceased and both of the vehicles involved.

Charlie drove to the ME's office on Boot Key located just across the world famous seven-mile bridge. He parked his US Navy government, gray pick-up truck in the visitors parking spot and went inside. He was wearing his neatly-pressed, blue dress uniform and his "Dixie cup" hat, carrying a 4X5 Speed Graphic with an attached flash arm. The woman sitting at the reception desk barely looked up from reading the latest People Magazine. "Can I help you?" she asked.

"Hi, I'm Petty Officer Charles Grayson. I'm here to photograph the remains of William Scott."

She picked up the receiver of her desk phone, while giving him the once over, and smiled. Licking her lips, she said, "I have a Petty Officer Grayson here to take photos of William Scott. Okay."

She placed the receiver back in the cradle and pointed to the double doors to her left. "Go on back, third room on the right."

"Thank you, Miss…?"

"Miss Hanson. Rhonda Hanson. Stop by before you leave, Petty Officer Grayson."

"Charlie."

"Stop by before you leave, Charlie."

Charlie went through the double doors and entered the third room on the right, expecting to see a body on a gurney. But when he entered the room, there wasn't any gurney, just an attendant holding a silver tray measuring twenty-four inches by thirty-six inches with a white towel over it. Charlie gave a quick glance around and said to the man, "Hi, I'm here to photograph Will Scott's body."

The man pulled back the towel and revealed a pile of shredded and burnt meat, bone, hair, and gristle. There was a small portion of the glop that looked to him to resemble a face, with what seemed to be an eye and fragments of teeth and tongue. The man said, "This *is* Mister Scott."

Once Charlie's brain registered what he was looking at and combined the image and odor of death mixed with cooked human flesh, hair and gasoline, he puked all over his neatly pressed dress blues and spit-shined shoes.

The attendant placed the tray on the counter and walked out of the room. Halfway down the hall, he turned and shouted back to Charlie, "Pussy."

Charlie took several shots of Chief Petty Officer William Scott and what was left of the cars involved in the crash and burn collision, and then he headed back down to the base without ever stopping by to see Miss Hanson again.

After his four years of enlistment, Charlie decided not to re-up but to become a commercial photographer; unfortunately, Charlie's timing was off. After going deep into debt purchasing 35mm film cameras, lenses, lighting gear and renting a studio, then the dawn of digital photography emerged. Soon, Charlie was considered to be 'Old School' and was forced to sell off his photo gear just to pay back his loans. Being on the verge of total bankruptcy, a friend of his from the Navy told him that the people at Delta Security Forces were looking for ex-military men for overseas security assignments, and they were paying top dollar. The rest, as they say, is history. So, here, manning a .50 caliber machine gun atop a Humvee, and involved in a life and death firefight in Zimbabwe, Africa, sat Charlie Grayson.

Charlie was desperately trying to maintain a low profile by hunkering down behind the protective metal plates on either side of his machine gun. Occasionally, he heard and even felt the breeze of sniper fire whizzing by his head. The word had been spread that help was on the way and to keep a sharp lookout for a red flare followed by a yellow flare. That was the signal to open fire and give cover to the rescue team entering the camp.

Louis Armour made his way to everyone, who was still alive and able to fight, in order to bolster their courage and to give them hope that help was on its way; they just needed to stay strong, and, if they could, then they would make it out alive. Leeway had tried several times to contact the Zimbabwe Army to let them know that they were under attack, but, so far, all he received on his cell phone was static. Unbeknownst to him, all their communication was being monitored and jammed by the French Aerospatiale C.22 drone flying a mile overhead.

Exactly at thirteen forty-five, a red flare was seen off to the east of the Humvee encampment, shortly followed by a yellow flare. There came a series of cheers and hoorays from the men under siege that were heard by the members of the Red Team. Armour shouted for his men to open fire and cover the rescue team approaching the camp.

"Red Team, this is Red Leader. Do not return fire. Stay stealth. I repeat, stay stealth. Over."

Each member of the Red Team responded affirmatively. Veronica and Yum had a prime view of the Blue Team, disguised as Leeway's rescue team, as they artfully make their way into the camp. As the Iceman and his Blue Team entered the encampment, they spread out and assessed the opposition. Leeway and Armour met them. Leeway asked who was in charge and what happened to their leader, The Angel of Death?

"He didn't make it; he was hit as we were coming in by sniper fire."

"Is this your total team?" Armour asked.

"Yeah, but I think we're more than enough to handle this bunch, right men?"

Leeway looked at the group as they started to fan out within the encampment. Then asked the apparent leader, "What's your name, and how do you plan on getting us the hell out of here?"

"I'm sorry, Mr. Leeway; you misunderstood me when I said we're more than enough to handle this bunch. I meant your outfit. Please allow me to introduce myself; I'm known as the Iceman, and I am a representative of Le Gang de la Clé de Singe. Your support team was intercepted last night, and I'm afraid they won't be able to rescue you."

"So, they're…?"

"Dead."

"Oh, I see. So, what do you have planned now, to massacre all of us?"

The Iceman said nothing. He looked at Leeway, pulled out a whistle that was hanging from around his neck, and gave one, long blast. The members of the Blue team started shooting everyone in the encampment; most were still engaged in firing at the attackers outside the camp. Charlie Grayson was laying a barrage of fire as he was instructed to, in order to cover the rescue team, when his belt of .50 caliber ammo ran out. He dared to peer over the armor plating to see if he had been successful. Milliseconds after he raised his head up, a shot rang out from an Acacia tree. His face disappeared instantly and turned into a massive bowl-shaped concavity of goo, bone, hair and gristle, just like one William Scott of Key West. Sue-B leaned over to Fu Hao and whispered, "Nice shot."

Josh Colman and his cameraman had started to record a segment about their being rescued, as T-Bone Bergman and Gianfranco approached them, holding Glock 9mm pistols. Josh waved them over to be interviewed when the Iceman's whistle blew; they were both spared.

David Leeway and Louis Armour were the only two left alive from Leeway's safari. The Blue Leader pulled a flare gun off of his utility belt and fired off a green flare.

Within minutes, the entire Red Team entered the encampment. Rodin, with Buster by his side, walked up to the Iceman and his captives.

Rodin removed the hood of his ghillie suit, revealing his black balaclava. "Mr. Leeway, you and Mr. Armour have been found guilty of crimes against humanity and are hereby sentenced to death."

Leeway doesn't speak. He is looking around, taking in all the death, destruction and carnage surrounding him; his expression is one of shock and disbelief. His guide looks to Rodin and asks, definitely, "Under whose authority are these charges made?"

"Under the World's Nonhuman Right's Congress of 1997 and the Animal Liberation Front Council of 2006, which states that any person or persons, who knowingly kills or does harm to any endangered species, be it a creature of land, air or sea, shall be found guilty of crimes against humanity and will face the ultimate price for these discretions, if found guilty."

"We have not yet had our day in court. How can we be punished without a trail?" Louis asked.

"You have been found guilty in absentia," Rodin said, as he handed them both a copy of the trial proceedings and verdict.

Leeway scanned the papers, glanced at his watch, and defiantly said, "You won't get away with this,; my death will only make the nations of the World more resolved against you and your terrorist organization."

"Actually, Mr. Leeway, you're wrong. Eighty-eight of the nations that originally condemned us are now supporting our cause. Not necessarily our methods, of course, but the cause. We are more than willing to ease up on the violence if the results can be achieved peacefully. But until such times, I'm afraid that people like you and your spoiled, entitled children, who get great pleasure by killing animals for sport, have to die."

The Iceman noticed that Leeway kept looking at his watch and scanning the horizon, searching for something.

"They're not coming, Mr. Leeway."

David Leeway acted surprised. "I don't know who you mean."

"The Zimbabwe Army, they're not coming. Oh, they're out there, all right. But unfortunately for you, we've fed them misinformation. I'm afraid they aren't able to save you."

"Bastards!" Leeway shouted and defiantly spit in Rodin's face.

The Iceman looked at Rodin and smiled; then he gave a sideways glance at Leeway and winked. Rodin wiped the spittle off of his cheek with the sleeve of his camo-patterned, army fatigue shirt and said, "I like your style, old man. You got moxie."

Rodin, satisfied that the incident had played out, called for the Blue Team to bring out all of the kills and line them up side-by-side. There were a total of thirteen so-called 'trophies,' among them—three male Lions, two Giraffes, four Warthogs, two Zebras, one Onyx, and the prize Black Rhinoceros. As the Blue Team was displaying the animals, a portion of the Red Team that wasn't keeping lookout were recovering the bodies of Leeway's security team, laying them next to each other and placing the traditional yellow and black Le Gang de la Clé de Singe flags around their necks.

Rodin walked over to Leeway and said, "Mr. Leeway, I don't normally ask this, but is there any particular location you'd like to be placed when they find you?"

"Yes, thank you. I'd like to be laid to rest with my men."

Rodin nodded, raised his Glock 9mm and shot David Leeway, one of the world's richest men, in the forehead, sending a grapefruit-sized portion of his skull and brains spattering onto one of the parked Humvees about thirty feet away. Then, he quickly shot and killed Louis Armour in the head as well.

The Iceman turned to him and asked, "So, shall we place these two next to the others?"

As Rodin was kneeling down, placing the Le Gang de la Clé de Singe flags around Leeway and Armour's necks, he peered up to The Iceman and said, grinning, "Fuck no. Put these two assholes next to the animals they slaughtered."

After the encampment had been properly staged, Rodin and Buster walked the perimeter and did a quick inspection. They then walked out to where Chase Madrid and company had been strategically placed by the Blue Team, so as to look like members of the Gang that had been killed. Once satisfied, he called in the Air Evac Unit to evacuate both teams to their safe rendezvous point in neighboring Zambia to the North.

Within fifteen minutes, two Bell UH-1 Iroquois "Huey" helicopters arrived. Seconds later, everyone was gone; leaving behind twenty-six security force troops, Louis Armour: big game guide, Chase Madrid, his four team members and the leader, David Leeway, all dead—not to mention the seventeen animals that had been butchered. The two CNN crewmembers were the only survivors; they were told that the Zimbabwe National Army would be along in a couple of hours.

Anonymous calls were placed to the Zimbabwe National Army, CNN, AP, UP, the David Leeway Foundation and to retired SEAL Team Commander William T. "Wooch" Brown, alerting them to an altercation to which they referred to as Opération Sacs d'Argent (*Operation Money Bags*).

Bumbley had never experienced such fear and panic. One minute, he was in his small cramped environment; the next minute, he was gasping for air and fighting for his life. Then, just as he started to think that that was the end, he felt a strange sensation, nothing that he had experienced before: a weightless nothing feeling, and then a hard blow that stunned and disoriented him for a moment. All of a sudden, there was the familiar wet, coolness that allowed him to breathe again; he wiggled out of the burlap sack and was free. It took a few moments before Bumbley's natural instincts kicked in, and his little fish brain sensed the slight temperature differences in the cold and warmth of the intermingling crosscurrents off the coast of Montego Bay. He was instinctively drawn to the warmth of the Caribbean Current and started to swim towards what will become his new home, Luminous Lagoon.

Luminous Lagoon stretched along the marshlands of Trelawney, from the small community of Rock, to the town of Falmouth. Located where the Martha Brae River met the Caribbean Sea, Luminous Lagoon got its name because the salt and fresh water combined in a way that made the water to glow. In the day, the water looked brackish, however, at night, the water had a bright luminosity when disturbed, hence the name 'Luminous Lagoon.'

Somewhere in the deep dark recesses of Bumbley's brain, he never forgot his unpleasant experiences with Fernando Ramos. So for the next fifteen years, as a young fry, Bumbley consciously avoided those strange creatures that caused him so much fear and anxiety. Whenever he sensed one of those beings nearby, he would quickly swim in the opposite direction, trying to blend into the coral or hide in some of the gaps or small caves at the base of the reef. He learned, over time, that when there were very large objects that would stop above him and would not move for long periods of time, that was when those odd creatures would descend into his lagoon. Most of the time, they would just swim around the reef, and then leave. But sometimes, they would come and kill fish, his fish, and that made Bumbley scared. As time passed and he continued to observe those beings and their behavior, something strange came over him.

It was a sensation, a feeling deep inside him, that he had never experienced before: anger.

When General Charles 'the Butcher' Tshuma of the Zimbabwe National Army finally arrived at the scene, he was taken aback by what he saw. The General was a battle-hardened commander in the ZNA, with over forty years of combat service. Back in the 1980's, as a Colonel, he fought alongside the Fifth Brigade, a North Korean-trained elite unit that reported directly to the Zimbabwean Prime Minister. Under Tshuma's command, his troops and the North Koreans entered Matabeleland and massacred thousands of civilians accused of supporting 'dissidents.' An estimate of the dead during the five-year Gukurahundi campaign was believed to be eighty thousand, and thousands of others were tortured in military internment camps. The campaign officially ended in 1987, after a unity agreement was reached, and Tshuma was promoted to the rank of General for his service to the Zimbabwe African National Union-Patriotic Front.

Tshuma wasn't surprised or sickened at the carnage that lay before him. Compared to what he and his men had been known to do, this was rather tame. Instead, he was impressed at the efficient and effective display of military mastery. When they entered the makeshift compound, they found, at one end, all of the bodies laid out in a row, each man with the obligatory yellow Monkey Wrench flag around his neck. At the opposite end laid a row of several slain animal carcasses, with the bodies of two men amongst them. Tshuma recognized the two dead men; one he knew personally as the safari guide, Louis Armour, and the other from TV and newspapers as the uber-rich American, David Leeway.

He was surprised when they came across Josh Colman and his cameraman, who were still alive and sitting in one of the Humvees. He had his men escort them back to the capital to meet with the Prime Minister and the American Consultant. Once they had left, he ordered his men to bring him all the personal possessions of the dead men from the vehicles as well as what they had on them. He was especially interested in David Leeway's personal effects, which included his eighty-four-thousand-dollar Rolex watch, his eight-thousand-dollar wedding ring, and a gold chain worth nineteen grand. He also took a few bobbles from various other victims and let his men divide the rest amongst themselves.

His men also discovered the bodies of, what appeared to be, members of the Le Gang de la Clé de Singe located several meters out to the East of the compound. The General ordered them brought into the encampment; he had orders from the Prime Minister to collect all the dead and bring them back to the capital, Harare, for identification. His orders were to secure the battle scene until investigators from Zimbabwe's Central Intelligence Organization and from Interpol came to inspect the area.

"Good evening. I'm Josh Colman with CNN News. I'm reporting from Hwange National Park, where the eco-terrorist group, known as Le Gang de la Clé de Singe, has attacked and completely annihilated David Leeway's security force. I, along with my cameraman, witnessed the killing of New York millionaire David Leeway and more than twenty-five people, including his guide, Louis Armour. The entire battle, and it was a battle, lasted over four hours.

"The attack started just after dawn as the caravan of Humvees was heading east. We had been traveling for a little more than an hour, when the first four of the security force's Humvees were destroyed by several roadside IEDs, killing all of those aboard. Then, the rest of the force came under a small arms attack, forcing the remaining Humvees to triangulate into a kind of a fortress.

"During the next three hours, many members of the security forces were killed by sniper fire. Louis Armour, the world famous big game hunter and guide, took it upon himself to go under the safety of a white flag to see if he could negotiate any form of surrender, but to no avail. The word from Le Gang de la Clé de Singe was that they would show no quarter, no mercy. The only reason that Randy Gaines, my cameraman, and I were spared is that we weren't big game hunters or attached to the security force. As is their custom, they left a letter stating their reason for their actions.

"After several more hours of fighting, the Gang entered the compound and systematically killed everyone in the camp. Louis Armour and David Leeway were the last to be killed; their bodies were laid next to the slain animals that David Leeway had killed. Like I said, my cameraman, Randy Gaines, and I were allowed to live, in part, because we were just observers and because we were eyewitnesses to this carnage.

"CNN will be broadcasting footage of the firefight later tonight; there will also be an interview with one of the leaders of Le Gang de la Clé de Singe. This is Josh Colman reporting from Hwange National Park."

Olley Olsen originally came to Angola to seek his fortune in the lucrative world of diamond smuggling. The Angolan government lost over three hundred and seventy-five million dollars annually from diamond smuggling, and Olley thought he had what it took to make a killing in the illicit diamond market.

One day, while having a beer in the bar of the Hotel Princsinha where he was staying in Saurimo, the capital of the Lunda Sul province, he had overheard six Angolans, who looked to be miners at the Catoca diamond mine, hatching a scheme to rob the weekly shipment of uncut diamonds.

Olley was sitting at the bar where the six mineworkers were talking, but he seemed to be intently concentrating on the local soccer game on the TV. Unbeknownst to the mineworkers, he was casually, but attentively, listening to their conversation.

They spoke openly of their plan in front of Olley in Portuguese, the native language of Angola, thinking that he wasn't understanding them. What they didn't know was that Olley not only spoke fluent Portuguese, but he was fluent in Spanish, English, and Swedish. So, they were taken back when he told them, in fluent Portuguese, how their plan was flawed, but that he thought, with his assistance, they just might be able to pull it off.

One of the larger men got off his barstool and moved to the one to the right of Olley. In Portuguese, he asked, "What did you say?"

Olley tilted his almost empty beer stein back, finished his beer, turned to the man, and replied, "I said that your plan will never work. But I think that I might be able to help you gentlemen be successful, for a small fee, of course."

The fellow smiled, revealing that several of his front teeth were missing. He leaned over to Olley and whispered, "Let's you and me go outside and discuss your plan, mister."

Olley looked down at his stomach and saw the man was sticking the pointy end of an eight-inch knife into his side. Although Olley was on the other side of being fifty-years-old, was a mere five-foot-five, weighed two hundred and thirty pounds, and looked very pasty and doughy. Therefore, he was often mistaken to be an easy mark. Olley had an ace up his sleeve, though—he was a certified fourth-degree black belt in the art of karate.

As the two of them started to stand up from their barstools, Olley noticed the barman was nowhere to be found. Olley casually stood up, and, as quick as a flash, he pivoted to his left, grabbing the man's hand and twisting the gargantuan wrist, forcing him to drop the knife. Then, he slammed the man's forehead onto the bar, knocking him unconscious. He collapsed to the floor. Olley then started to back out of the barroom, when a man wearing an old, ragged Denver Bronco's t-shirt slowly turned, holding out his hands in a submissive gesture, and said, smiling, "Don't go, mister. You know, one can't ever be too careful, so we test you. Who are you?"

"Just a guy who might be able to help. But, if you're not interested in my help, then good day."

"Yeah, that's not good enough. Who are you?"

"My name is Olley Olsen. I'm originally from a small town in Brazil, and I'm currently in Angola to seek my fortune in diamonds anyway that I can."

"You look like a copper to me, man."

"Look, I'm not a copper. Let's just forget the whole thing."

"Yeah, that might be a good idea. Are you staying at this hotel?"

"Yes, I am."

"Well, Mister Olley, if, for some reason, we get pinched or something goes wrong, someone will be looking you up. Understand?"

"Understood."

Olley mumbled to himself, as he backed out of the bar, "Boy, that didn't go too well."

He retrieved his key from the desk clerk and went upstairs to pack and wait until the mineworkers left the bar. He had one suitcase with his personal effects and a case containing a Browning BAR MK. II Safari Grade .338 rifle when he checked out that evening. He was careful on the cab ride to be sure that the mineworkers weren't following him. The cab took him to the Win Car Rental in the center of town, where he rented a Toyota Hilux pickup 4X4 for twelve days at a cost of four hundred and twenty thousand Angolan Kwanza's, which was two thousand US Dollars. Olley had decided that he would try his hand at an alternative vocation:

the poaching of big game. He had heard from some of the locals that there was big money to be made in animal parts.

Olley decided to head south toward the national game reserve, Coutada Publica do Longa-Mavinga, on the border of Angola and Namibia. There, the wildlife had been almost completely wiped out after the civil war due to the lack of staff, resources, and support for the park. Coutada Publica do Longa-Mavinga was once home to hundreds of lions, leopards and cheetahs, but now only a few dozen of these magnificent cats survived. Olley figured that even could be a good thing, for, although there wasn't a whole lot of game, the fact that there weren't a lot of game patrols was a huge plus.

He was running low on funds and thought that, if he could bag a couple lions or some other big cat, he could get back into the game; failing wasn't an option. He considered himself to be a better than the average shot, and, right now, all he needed was one good kill

Menongue was a small town on the edge of the game reserve where Olley decided to stay for a couple of days. He drove around aimlessly for over an hour, looking for somewhere to spend the night, but most of the streets weren't marked. He was lost, so he decided to follow the railroad tracks, thinking that, eventually, he would run into a hotel, which he did. Located in an industrial area of town, he found the hotel Chik Chik Kambumne Lodge. Not exactly the Ritz, but it would be good enough for his purposes: a hot shower, a cold beer and a good night's sleep.

The next morning, Olley decided to have breakfast at the Hotel Menongue, which was located several blocks away. The streets were abandoned as he made his way to the hotel. The restaurant was full, so the hostess said that it looked to be about a half-hour wait, unless he was willing to share a table with another guest. Olley said that he was amenable to sharing and was seated with a gentleman who introduced himself as Mr. Whombosse, an exporter of rare native African artifacts. When asked, Oley told his breakfast companion that he was looking to do a bit of hunting. Mr. Whombosse inquired if Olley had obtained all of the proper paperwork needed, and that, if not, he might be able to help facilitate him in cutting through some of the red tape. Olley played ignorant and said he didn't know that he needed any paperwork other than his permit to possess and carry a firearm.

"Oh, my dear Mr. Olsen, I am afraid you are misinformed. To hunt here in Angola, one must obtain the proper license and documentation. Otherwise, you might be mistaken as a poacher, and poaching, although very lucrative, is illegal."

Olley leaned into Mr. Whombosse and slyly said, "How lucrative?"

Whombosse looked quizzically at Olley and didn't reply for several minutes, making Olley nervous. Then, he smiled and said, "Very."

It was one evening in late June, around midnight, that a small fishing boat, named BB Louie, was getting ready to head back to the docks. After having a very good night of fishing for snapper, triggerfish and grunts, it was then that they encountered the thirty-three-foot Bertram Sport Fisherman, appropriately named the "Aquaholic". At around eleven o'clock on that warm balmy evening, Marty Zuckerman, the owner of the Aquaholic, and a bunch of his friends decided that it would a fun to take the boat out for a bit of spin after consuming large quantities of Jerk Chicken, fried conch, and an exorbitant amount of Zombies.

Everyone on board was pretty much shit-faced as they left the docks at Montego Bay, heading east towards Ocho Rios. Marty, a forty-five-year-old, recently divorced insurance salesman from Boca Raton, Florida, had been trying to get into the pants of some blonde whose name he thought was Cindy or Mindy. He had met earlier that night at the Island Grill & Bar, and the blonde was a real balloon smuggler. Marty's inebriated brain thought, what better way to score with whatever-her-name-was, than to get her good and drunk, be a couple miles offshore, and then make his move? Marty figured if she said no…well, then it's, "Hey, baby, it's either put out or get out."

An hour out from the dock, Marty spotted the lights of a small fishing boat off to their starboard side. He thought it would be a real hoot to scare the crap out of the crew of that small fishing boat by heading straight at them at high speed, while blasting his air horn, and then, at the last possible second, swerve and barely miss them. It seemed like a really good idea at the time. He thought, what could go wrong? Marty shouted out, "Hey, everybody, watch this! I'm gonna scare the shit out of those yahoos." Marty cut the wheel so hard to starboard, that he knocked everyone onboard off balance and nearly threw his blonde date overboard. Just as his guests were getting back on their feet, Marty was getting ready to swing the Aquaholic to the port side, which would have missed the BB Louie's bow by a good ten feet. That was when the blonde sneaked up behind Marty, put her arms around his waist, slowly lowered her hands down to his crotch, and whispered in his ear, "Hey, Captain, is that Moby Dick in your pocket, or are you just glad to see me?"

The fishermen on board the BB Louie had just seconds to react and jump overboard before the thirty-three-foot rocket plowed into her port side. The impact sent everyone on board the Aquaholic flying; Marty and the blonde were thrown backward off the flybridge, and he ended up head first in the bait tank with her head in his crotch. His other guests were all flung overboard and into the ocean, treading water with the crew of the BB Louie. The Aquaholic came to rest on top of the fishing vessel, and, for several minutes, the two boats looked like two behemoths in some weird, contorted mating position, until the BB Louie slowly sunk and disappeared.

A few things resulted from this catastrophe. First, Captain Roscoe O'Reilly, the skipper of the BB Louie, sued Marty Zuckerman for ten million US dollars. To avoid criminal prosecution, Marty settled out of court for an undisclosed amount of cash, and Roscoe was now the proud owner of the BB Louie Too—previously known as the Aquaholic. There were eight more civil cases against Marty from the other crewmembers, and even a couple of his friends had civil cases pending. Marty had one of the cases dismissed out of court when he married his date for that night, whose real name turned out to be Delores.

And the second eventful thing that happened that night was when part of the fishing net, which was onboard the BB Louie, was severed during the collision; it drifted free for several days until it made its way into Luminous Lagoon, where it entangled one sleeping giant grouper, Bumbley Bee.

Try as he might, Bumbley could not free himself from the fishing net. In fact, the more he tried, the more entangled he got. He was getting fatigued and hungry; being all tangled up like he was, he was unable to catch anything to eat. From struggling so hard, his energy level was being sapped to the point of exhaustion. He was starting to give up hope, when one of those creatures he feared slowly approached him. The figure carefully started to remove the net that had trapped the giant fish for over eighteen hours. As he was removing the heavy net, the being gently stroked the massive aquatic creature, giving Bumbley a sensation of calm that he hadn't felt before.; it was so contrary to what he had felt at other times when he had encountered these odd creatures. After he was free, the alien being did something that none of these creatures had ever done: he gave Bumbley something to eat. That was the beginning of a beautiful friendship between Bumbley Bee and one Buzz Murdoch.

After that initial encounter, Buzz would sail out to Luminous Lagoon and hand feed the giant grouper a couple times a week. It got to where Bumbley started looking forward to his encounters with the creature—not just because of the fish it brought him, although that was a bonus, but it was the gentleness and the kindness of the being that Bumbley craved. Who really knew what went on the in those little pea-brains of fish, but, being that he was the only Bumble Bee Grouper in the Caribbean, Bumbley felt it was comforting to have another living thing around that wasn't a threat to him.

Two years later, Bumbley weighed nearly eight hundred pounds, and, with no natural enemies to speak of, and, for all intents and purposes, this was his lagoon.

Rutherford Remington Murdochski the third, a.k.a. Buzz Murdoch, was born into a very well-to-do family. The Philadelphia Murdochskis were one of Philadelphia's nouveau riche, as his grandfather had made scads of money in the post-war-banking boom of the forties and fifties. Mister Buzz Murdochski was born with a tiny silver spoon in his mouth, which he wore around his neck.

He went to the finest prep schools and was even accepted to Harvard, but he decided to go to Santa Monica City College, and then to the University of California Berkeley. He was a major activist against the Viet Nam war, where he met Todd Styles, and became a member of the SDS and multiple other anti-establishment organizations. Like so many others at the time, he was arrested on numerous occasions—mostly for petty stuff like disturbing the peace, with the odd destroying of public property, burning of draft cards, etc. He was considered to be a real character back then, and he was even part of the Sedona Seven. After his activist days were over, he literally hitchhiked around the world, and, in the late sixties and early seventies, he did a stint as a roadie for several big rock bands—The Rolling

Stones, The Grateful Dead, and even Jimi Hendrix when he appeared at Woodstock.

Then, in 1776, he took the advice of one Timothy Leary by tuning in, turning on, and dropping out. Nobody saw or heard from him for over eleven years, until he turned up at a recording studio in Jamaica as a recording engineer. He soon became the head engineer, working with all the major recording artists, from Sinatra to Santana.

When he wasn't at the studio, Buzz could be found at the Pier One Marina, on a forty-three-and-a-half-foot Spindrift Sunrise named the Sweet Mary Jane. That is, when he wasn't out sailing or scuba diving with his new best friend, Bumbley.

"This is Inspector Volker. Yes, sir, I just received it. Yes, Morris and I are booked on the next flight out to Harare."

The flight to Harare was uneventful, and they landed at Robert Gabriel International Airport late in the afternoon. There, they were met by Thomas Sawenga, Harare's Mayor, and Samuel Mzilikazi, the Chief of the Zimbabwe Republic Police. Amoung them, there were also several top officers of the Zimbabwe National Army, including General Charles Tshuma, and two agents from the FBI, Special Agents William Bradley and Charles Washington.

Special Agents William Bradley and Charles Washington had, themselves, just arrived from Washington DC hours earlier, and they had requested to wait to be briefed until Volker and Morris arrived.

After all the pleasantries and introductions were exchanged, everyone was transported to the edge of an unused runway, where there was an abandoned airplane hanger that acted as a staging area and command center.

Inside, there were makeshift walls with large area maps, hundreds of photos of the battlefield and dozens of photographs of the dead, all pinned up with numerous descriptions written under each photo. There were several tables with metal trays, each containing the personal effects of the dead and labeled with their names. For those unnamed dead, who were believed to be members of Le Gang de la Clé de Singe, they had a photograph of the person attached to the tray. There was also a long table with several platters of sandwiches, salads and a variety of hot and cold drinks, a dozen chairs seated around the table, which had name cards of everyone in attendance.

Once everyone had a few minutes to examine the maps and the photographs, and peruse the personal effects of the trays, Mayor Thomas Sawenga announced, "Gentlemen, if everyone is ready, please take your seats so we can begin."

The group slowly meandered to the table and took their seats; the mayor continued to stand until everyone was seated and all the talking had stopped. "Gentlemen, let's get started. First, I'd like to thank you all for coming. I'm sorry that it had to be under such dire circumstances. I think I'd like to start by having General Tshuma give his report. General Tshuma, if you would."

General Tshuma stood, as Mayor Sawenga took his seat. "Thank you, Mayor. Let me just reiterate the Mayor's thanks to you all; many of you have traveled very far to be here today. I will start by making a short opening statement, and then I will be more than happy to answer all of your questions.

"Last Tuesday, Army Headquarters received an anonymous call telling us that a firefight was in progress between the forces of David Leeway and the forces of, what we believe to be, Le Gang de la Clé de Singe. The caller provided us with GPS coordinates, and then they hung up before we could trace their position. We did, of course, record the call and will provide copies to both the FBI and Interpol; we're hoping that you might be able to assist us in identifying the caller.

"Once HQ received the call, I was instructed to lead an expeditionary force to confirm or deny the accuracy of the Intel. Once we arrived, my men and I took command of the battle scene and began detailing the events, trying to ascertain exactly what transpired, identify the bodies, collect evidence, as well as preserve the integrity of the battle slash crime scene. Let me show you what we found on this map. This is based on my years of experience, as well as eyewitness accounts."

Two soldiers wheeled over a large overhead satellite photograph of the area, taken several hours after the battle, which was mounted on a mobile presentation wall and placed behind the General.

Inspector Volker raised his hand and asked, "What eyewitnesses? I thought there were no survivors?"

The General said, as he moved to the map, "I'm sorry. I was sure that I had put that information into my report. There were two survivors—a cameraman and a reporter from CNN. I planned on having them brought here to be interrogated—I mean, interviewed—later, along with all of the footage that was shot that day."

He picked up a three-foot-long, wooden pointer and began. "As you can see, this is a satellite photo of the battle scene taken just hours after; let us start there." He pointed to the three Humvees that were destroyed by the IEDs.

"As you can see, the first three Humvees appear to have come under attack with several strategically placed roadside IEDs, killing all three crews immediately. Also, you'll notice the third vehicle appears to have been flipped backwards by the blast, thereby landing on top of vehicle number four, killing most of the members of their crew. When we inspected vehicle number four, it seemed that the ones that weren't killed during the initial explosion died from their injuries sometime during the battle."

"Excuse me, General, are you sure that the men trapped in vehicle number four died from their wounds and weren't assassinated?" Special Agent Washington asked.

"We didn't find any gunshot wounds to any of the men in the first four Humvees." The general paused, looking to see if anyone else had any questions. When nobody seemed to, he proceeded.

"The remaining Humvees encircled their vehicles to form a triangle, a rather smart move, except for the fact that the so-called security forces of Mr. Leeway were woefully outgunned and outmanned. The opposition had picked off the majority of them with sniper fire and, apparently, through some sort of deception, according to the CNN reporter, Josh Colman, who stated that members of Le Gang de la Clé de Singe were invited into the compound under the ruse of being a rescue team sent to help them."

You could hear a pin drop, as everyone sat in complete silence at the news that Leeway had been somehow duped into inviting members of the enemy into the encampment. Inspector Volker asserted, "We need to speak to the CNN reporter."

General Tshuma held up his hand and said, "I am almost done, Inspector, if you don't mind."

"I'm sorry, General, please continue."

"Gentlemen, over here, to the left of Leeway's encampment, you will see the only bodies of Le Gang de la Clé de Singe. We are still waiting for them to be positively identified. Their effects are over there in those metal trays. That's pretty much all that I know. Are there any questions for me before we hear from Mr. Colman?"

Special Agent William Bradley put his pen down, having finished making sketches of the battle scene and writing detailed notes. "General, I assume that post-mortems have been done?"

"Yes, we have completed them, and we have complete files and dossier that will be handed out to you now." The General waved his hand, and six soldiers entered from behind one of the partitions. They placed identical large manila envelopes, with a three-inch-thick file inside, in front of Special Agents William Bradley, Charles Washington, and Inspectors Volker and Morris.

"Now, gentlemen, let's bring in Josh Colman."

Buzz parked the Microbus at Pier One's Marina, as he had done every Saturday for over fifteen years at precisely 11:45AM. Pier One's Marina was home to several of Mo'bay's charter boat operators. It was *the* place where tourists could charter boats for deep-sea fishing, sailing, sunset cruises, or just sightseeing. There was even an underwater semi-submarine to see the underwater world without getting wet.

Buzz walked by the Waterfront Restaurant on his way to the dock, where he passed a three-hundred-and-fifty-pound Jamaican man, who handed him a large, brown paper bag containing Buzz's usual order of Whole Jamaican Peppered Shrimp, Jerk Conch with Papaya Salsa, and Rosemary-Citrus Pork Chops with a side of roasted mushrooms.

"Happy sailin', Buzz."

"Thanks, Roscoe. See ya at six, and drinks are on me tonight, man."

Buzz headed down the dock to berth sixty-six, where his forty-three-and-a-half-foot Spindrift Sunrise sailboat, named The Sweet Mary Jane, was waiting. Buzz casually casted off the stern and bowlines and slowly motored out of the channel and into open water. Then, he dropped the mainsail and the jib. The wind was kicking up, so the sea was really choppy, a lot of white caps with four to five-foot swells. Not for the faint of heart, but, for an old sea dog like Buzz, he loved any time out on the SMJ. Because of the strong winds, it only took him an hour to get to Luminous Lagoon. It looked like he had the whole lagoon to himself, probably because the water was so turbulent. On days like this, the currents could be tricky and dangerous for anyone who wasn't an experienced diver.

Bumbley was expecting his friend with fond anticipation. He saw the large object above that he associated with the creature, but, as always, he remained hidden until he was sure. Buzz gave his SCUBA gear a quick once over, before he suited up and dove in. As the two friends approached each other, Bumbley detected a scent of something very familiar. Buzz held out a bag and slowly produced two thirty-two-ounce Rosemary-Citrus Pork Chops. Buzz did a double take, because, for a brief moment, he could have sworn that he saw a smile on Bumbley's face. And you know what, he did. Bumbley got great pleasure not only from their time together, but also from the unusual treats that Buzz brought to him.

He didn't get the opportunity to taste such exotic flavors; usually, it was whole fish or tasteless chunks of mystery flesh, and that was pretty boring—filling, but boring. Buzz spent about an hour with Bumbley, petting him, a bit of grooming off the occasional barnacle, and even, for a lack of a better term, playing some 'fish games.'

Buzz tried to come to visit Bumbley three or four times a week, depending on how busy the studio was, and he, sometimes, would drop underwater speakers into the lagoon and play some Rolling Stones, which Bumbley seemed to enjoy. He wasn't too crazy about 'Angie,' but he really enjoyed 'Gimme Shelter.' Fish, Drugs and Rock & Roll, who knew?

The two "Huey" helicopters landed safely on the windward side of the island of Moot, just off the coast of Sierra Leone, which was part of the Turtle Islands. The islands were, for the most part, uninhabited, although there were a few islands that had a small village of fishermen. Rodin and his teams were dropped off and met by a small landing party from the 'Sebastes Fasciatus,' a repurposed Brazilian Newport-class tank landing ship that once fought in Vietnam.

The squadron leader of the landing team was a young woman from Ecuador, called Nekhbet. It was the name of a powerful Egyptian god, the vulture goddess, which she had chosen for herself. Nekhbet's team had been waiting on Moot for the war party to arrive for a day and a half, while the 'Sebastes Fasciatus' was sailing off the coast of Sierra Leone. Once word came that the mission had been completed, the mother ship returned and anchored off the island.

Rodin and Iceman met with Nekhbet, as their teams started to load the zodiacs for evac off the island. Rodin held out his hand and said, "It's good to see you."

She shook his hand and then Iceman's. "Hope you had a successful mission?"

"Couldn't have gone better."

"Super. Well, I've radioed the captain, and he's in position, so let's be off," She said, as she led them to their zodiac. Both the Red and Blue Teams' equipment were stowed, and they were all aboard and heading out to meet the mother ship. The three-mile journey took forty minutes due to a light fog that had started to roll in from the East, making visual contact a challenge, but uneventful. Within twenty minutes, all hands were aboard, and the 'Sebastes Fasciatus' was underway, steaming north towards Marseille.

The captain of the Sebastes Fasciatus was Captain Ehsan Khattak, a Pakistani from Karachi who had been with Le Gang de la Clé de Singe from the very beginning. He was an environmental design student, studying for his master's degree at the Sorbonne after graduating from the University of the Punjab, when he started marching against corruption and corporate greed that was destroying the environment. Khattak was one of the first to volunteer on the Gang's first anti-whaling ships, which had shadowed the Japanese whaling vessels and dared to come between the whales and the harpoon guns. As time went on, the Japanese became less and less cautious and more and more aggressive, to the point that they would go out of their way to try and injure the protesters. The incident that really solidified Le Gang de la Clé de Singe's decision to fight fire with fire was when the captain of the Kobayashi Maru deliberately rammed a zodiac with six protesters, killing all aboard except one, Ehsan Khattak. From that day on, Le Gang de la Clé de Singe declared war on any persons, companies, and entities that they deemed to be an enemy of nature—show no mercy, show no quarter.

Ehsan held just about every position on board the Sebastes Fasciatus, from Bosun Mate to Second Engineer, from Cook to First Mate, and, finally, to Captain. He knew every nook and cranny of the Sebastes Fasciatus and had, over the years, developed the respect of the entire crew. As captain, he has used his ship to run blockades, to ramming illegal fishing vessels, as well as going head-to-head with whaling ships and making them blink first. The Sebastes Fasciatus had even been used many times to transport ground troops to and from hot zones around the world.

Once everyone was safely on board, Khattak sat down with Rodin and Iceman. He told them that, when they were near Gibraltar, he would brief them on their next assignments.

Olley didn't like hunting lions with a rifle; he'd do the easy way, instead: poisoned them and waited while they died an agonizing death. Then, he would cut off the heads and paws, and if any lion cubs survived, he would capture them and sell them to Mr. Whombosse. The lion parts fetched him fourteen thousand US dollars, but the lion cubs brought a whopping thirty-five thousand each. They were usually sold to rich Arabs as novelty pets.

Olley never ventured out of his rented Toyota Hilux pickup 4X4 when he was tracking the lions or putting out the poisoned bait. The only time he would leave the safety of his vehicle was when he butchered the lions and captured any of the cubs, and he would always be armed when he did. Olley was especially cautious when he approached the dead adult lions, and he would fire at least one round into each of their bodies just to be sure that they weren't stunned or ill.

He had amassed a rather tidy sum from his poaching business, but, as time went on, he started getting nervous that the park rangers were getting wise to him. But, like most criminals, Olley figured he would pull one last big score, and then he would have a big enough bankroll to last him well into his old age.

He had been following a large pride of lions that had six females, four cubs, and two male brothers that each sported the coveted black manes. If he could bag the lot of them, he was looking at cashing in well over a quarter of a million dollars—well worth the risk.

He headed out early one morning, just after sunrise, and made his way to the spot that he had planted the poisoned Wildebeest carcass. He found the entire pride's bodies laying next to the cadaver of the Gnu, and even the cubs lay near the dead adults. Although they weren't dead, they were very ill and lethargic. He sat there in his truck for over an hour, making sure that he hadn't been followed.

When he felt safe, he proceeded to shoot the dead adults. That's when he noticed that there were only seven dead adult lions—six females and one male. One of the male lions, apparently, either hadn't eaten from the poisoned Wildebeest or wandered off and died somewhere else away from the pride. He was concerned about the condition of the cubs; that was one hundred and forty thousand dollars lost if they died, so he decided to slaughter the lions first and then gather up the cubs to take them to Whombosse, who he hoped would be able to get them healthy, or, at least, he would know someone who could.

Olley got out of the pickup and leaned his Browning rifle against the truck. He was having second thoughts about not throwing the cubs into the back of the pickup, but he could see that they weren't going anywhere, being as ill as they were, so he proceeded with his decision to start with butchering the adults.

He had actually gotten very adept at dismembering the big cats from so much on-the-job training. He started with the male's head, careful not to damage the beautiful black mane. Then he severed the paws, which were each the size of a baseball mitt. He then started on the females, and, when he had finished decapitating the last of the lionesses, he heard what sounded to him like something has fallen on top of the hood of his pickup truck.

He stood up, holding the lionesses' head in his left hand and a surgical saw in his right. As he turned around, there, sitting on the hood of the Toyota pickup, was the male lion, watching him. Olley was a good twelve feet from his rifle that leaning against the truck, but, unfortunately for him, the lion was closer to the gun than he was.

Olley started weighing his options; he could try screaming at the beast while charging at it, or he could try and distract it by throwing the lioness' head off to his left, in hopes that the male would chase after it and give him time to get to the gun or at least get inside the truck. Finally, he thought he could try and stare the big boy down; he had heard that sometimes worked. But as Olley was weighing his options, the lion was weighing his. With the option it chose, it would attack and kill the thing that was standing there and holding the head of his lover. Olley chose option one; he decided to charge the beast, screaming at the top of his lungs and waving the lionesses' head. As Olley charged the lion, the lion leaped off the hood of the pickup with a roar that could be heard for several miles. The simba slammed into

Olley, knocking him down. Olley tried to wriggle out from under the beast, but the three-hundred-pound lion had him pinned down. As the lion towered over his prey, it slowly lowered its head and seemed to grin; Olley looked into the devil's eyes and only hoped that death would come quickly. The last thing Olley saw was a blur when the lion's jaws savagely ripped his head off his shoulders. It happened so fast, but Olley actually had a last momentary thought of, *'Ain't payback a bitch.'*

When park rangers came across the abandoned Toyota pickup that afternoon, they found the butchered remains of seven adult lions with their heads and paws lying nearby, four lion cubs that were disorientated from being unwell, and a bloody human head. The head was intact and lying beside a Browning rifle that was leaning against the pickup, almost as if it was left there as a message to other poachers.

When the rangers inspected the interior of the pickup, they found the contract papers from the car rental company to one Mr. Olley Olsen. They also discovered several bills of sale for lion parts and dozens of lion cubs to a Mr. Whombosse. There was something else seen, though, that the rangers found to be humorous and totally ironic. Apparently, Mr. Olsen had been listening to a CD of John Lennon's greatest hits when he met his demise. For some strange reason, the song "Instant Karma" was looping over and over again.

A couple of hours before sunset, Buzz finished putting on the last of his SCUBA gear, checked the air supply, and rechecked the regulator. He normally dived for about an hour, but, today, he thought he needed some extra Bumbley time. He grabbed the treats and lowered himself into the lagoon. The water was a bit warmer than usual, and Buzz figured it was due to the global warming of the oceans;

despite what the right-wing science deniers claimed, the oceans were getting warmer.

Bumbley was waiting for Buzz, hiding behind a large piece of coral. He continued to be cautious of these creatures after another diver with a spear gun tried to kill him. It was just dumb luck that a six-foot barracuda swam in between the hunter and the prey. The Barracuda was hit in the tail, leaving a three-inch gouge, which was bad for both the diver and the fish. The spear strike really only pissed-off the barracuda, which, after being hit, made a beeline toward the diver and proceeded to take a five-inch chunk out of the his leg. This, in turn, attracted several Mako sharks into the area; one, of which, was a three-footer, who made the mistake of swimming past the behemoth grouper. Bumbley, spotting his dinner, made a quick juke to the left and swallowed the small Mako within a blink of an eye. Of the three of them—Bumbley, the barracuda, and the diver—only the gentle giant came out the better.

After realizing the creature was his friend, Bumbley swam up to Buzz and, like a dog, sat patiently and waited for his treat. Buzz reached into his mesh bag and pulled out something different for his friend: a whole leg of lamb, bone and all. It was devoured with one, quick sucking motion. They spent the two hours just swimming alongside each other, and, occasionally, Bumbley would stop and nudge up to Buzz.

Buzz would stop and pet the mountainous monster; it seemed to really enjoy being touched around the mouth. To a casual observer, it might have looked like the equivalent of when an animal trainer sticks his head inside a lion's mouth, but looks can be deceiving. A lion might react because of fear or maybe some sort of respect, but this was a special bond, a friendship, like that of a dog and its master. Bumbley would get sad when his friend had to go because he was the only one of his kind in the lagoon. But luckily for him, he had an attention span of a gnat and was easily distracted by living in the moment.

Buzz climbed aboard the Sweet Mary Jane as the suns last slivers were dropping over the edge of the world. When the sky was bright orange at sunset, he always remembered the sailor's lore, 'Red sky in the morning, sailor take warning. Red sky at night, sailors delight.' That usually rang true, except for tonight.

After Josh Colman finished a grueling, reliving and nine-hour download to FBI Special Agents William Bradley and Charles Washington, as well as Inspectors Volker and Morris, he was thanked and told that he may be required to give additional testimony at a later date.

Volker reminded Bradley and Washington that Interpol had jurisdiction when it came to the evidence, but they were more than willing to include the Feds in their investigation. The Interpol boys had General Tshuma's men box up all the evidence as well as all the human remains and had everything shipped to Interpol headquarters in Lyon, France, where a team of international forensic scientists was waiting to examine all of the data and materials.

The four law enforcement agents were booked on the first British Airways flight out of Robert Gabriel International Airport to London, with a connecting flight in Johannesburg. Having said their thanks and goodbyes to Mayor Sawenga, they were escorted to the airport personally by General Tshuma in his Rolls-Royce Phantom. The General then walked them to the jetway and told them that if there was anything that else that they needed, just let him know. He pulled Volker aside and asked, "Inspector Volker, one thing has been bothering me that, maybe, you can answer."

"What's that, General?"

"We were able to identify and match just about all of the fingerprints to the victims, but there is one that makes no sense. How is it possible that we found a fingerprint of Albert Einstein on one of the 50 caliber machine guns?"

"That is a conundrum, General. As soon as we figure it out, we'll let you know, sir."

"Thank you, Inspector. I would appreciate it. Again, have a safe flight."

As they entered the cabin, they noticed that Josh Colman and his cameraman were already asleep in their seats. Volker nodded to the others and said, "Poor bastards, they've really been put through the wringer."

Once they were seated in business class across from each other, Special Agent Bradley leaned over to Volker and Morris. "If you boys don't mind, I think Washington and I are going to follow Colman's lead and crash, at least until we get to Johannesburg."

Morris looked quizzically, "Crash?"

"Yeah, crash. You know, sleep."

"Oh, right. How quaint, 'crash'." Morris turned to Volker and quipped, "Bloody American slang. I never know what the hell they're talking about."

Volker smiled and whispered, "Quite right, old man. Quite right."

"This is Josh Colman, CNN News, coming to you from Robert Gabriel International Airport, Harare, Zimbabwe. It's been two days since David Leeway and his security forces were attacked by Le Gang de la Clé de Singe, where all hands were massacred; only myself and my cameraman, Randy Gaines, were allowed to live, as neither of us were hunters or part of the Leeway's armed security unit. We have hours of combat footage that is being edited, as we speak, and it will be shown in a one-hour special tomorrow night on CNN titled 'Blood of the Beast.' I will be sitting down tomorrow night for an exclusive, live interview with CNN's Walter Chancellor.

"You will see and hear, first hand, the horrors of war, along with an exclusive interview with one of the leaders of Le Gang de la Clé de Singe who led the attack. He will be giving a statement explaining the group's rationale and manifesto, in their opinion, justifies such a brutal and deadly attack. Here's a part of what the eco-terrorist said: "Le Gang de la Clé de Singe has made it clear that we are at war with all poachers, big game hunters and all big game safari outfits, as well as anybody anywhere in the world who targets, kills, profits and/or supports the killing of any animals that are endangered or hunted for sport.

"David Leeway and his children openly defied us, ignoring our warnings and, in the case of Leeway senior, openly dared us to attack him by killing these magnificent animals in hopes of getting our attention. Well, he got our attention—him, his guide, and his so-called security forces. Let me reiterate to anyone who seeks to profit from these senseless deaths: be forewarned, you do so at your peril. You will be hunted down and pay with your lives. Be it man or woman, there will be no exceptions and no mercy; we will show no quarter. You have been warned."

"I have seen things in these last few days that will haunt me for the rest of my life. The senseless killings of both man and beast—some for sport, some for revenge. This is Josh Colman reporting from Harare, Zimbabwe."

It had been several months since Detectives Johansson and Wilson of Bemidji, Minnesota's Homicide squad had any communication with Volker and Morris from Interpol. But after they had heard the news about the deadly attack on David Leeway and all the other recent activities of Le Gang de la Clé de Singe, they were expecting a call from the lads from Interpol any day.

"Detective Johansson, can I help you?"

"Detective Johansson, Inspector Volker here. I think we've got some potently good news for you, involving the Meriwether Case."

"Oh, yes?"

"It looks like we were right about the identification of the murderer; it appears to have been Chase Madrid after all. After we recovered all bodies from the Leeway massacre, including the bodies of the Le Gang de la Clé de Singe, one of them was identified as Chase Madrid, along with several other Americans. All of them were ex-military and served with or knew Mr. Madrid."

"Well, I guess that closes our case on who killed Dr. Meriwether."

"I wouldn't close it quite yet, until we've crossed all the T's and dotted all the I's, but I would say it's ninety-nine percent a certainty, old man."

"Great. I'll just wait to hear from you before we officially close the case, then. Thank you so much, Inspector Volker, for all your help, and good luck over there."

"Cheerio."

Johansson hung up the phone and called out for Wilson to come into his office. Wilson stuck his head into Detective Johansson's office door and asked, "What's up, boss?"

"Just got a call from Volker at Interpol. He said he's pretty positive that they've got the murderer of Meriwether. Chase Madrid—apparently he was one of the members of Le Gang de la Clé de Singe who was killed in the David Leeway attack in Africa."

"No shit."

"Yeah. Pardon the pun, but they said that got him dead to rights; they're just checking a few things to make sure that there isn't any doubt."

"Wow! What are the odds?"

"I'd say at least a million to one."

"Are you going to call Dr. Meriwether's family now or wait until we hear back from Interpol?"

"I thought I'd give her a heads up now. I don't want her to hear it from the news outlets."

Johansson typed a couple keys on his computer, and, when he got the number he needed, he called the doctor's home number. "Hello, Mrs. Meriwether. This is Detective Johansson."

Sometimes when things got stacked up at the studio, Buzz just needed some Bumbley time to decompress. It was two o'clock on a beautiful sunny afternoon, when The Sweet Mary Jane slipped out of the Pier One's Marina and headed east.

There were moments in everyone's life when a familiar smell could transport you back in time to a specific life-altering event. For some reason, on this day, that moment came for Buzz when the salty air hit his face out on the open sea. He broke down and cried like he hadn't done since his parents died when their KLM Flight 4805 and the Pan Am Flight 1736 crashed during takeoff from Tenerife in the Canary Islands, the worst aviation disaster in history. A total of five hundred and eighty-three people aboard both aircrafts died.

When he arrived at the lagoon, Buzz noticed there were a couple of divers already in the water while he weighed anchor. He decided to wait until everyone left, since he knew Bumbley would hide and avoid the interlopers. Besides, he wanted some quality bonding time alone with the Bee.

It was almost five o'clock when the last diver left the lagoon. Buzz was already geared up and had put on his air tank, when he first noticed what appeared to be a slow-moving squall off to the northwest that was moving in his direction. Buzz had seen hundreds of these; most would blow through and be over in an hour. This one looked like he had a couple of hours before it would hit the lagoon, so over he went. Within minutes, he spotted Bumbley and swam towards him, bringing with him his buddy's snack: a couple dozen sides of slobbered pork ribs from Biggs BBQ Restaurant, one of both Buzz and Bumbley favorites. Bumbley wasn't a big fan of their pulled pork cheesy fries, but Buzz figured it was because they probably lost some of the flavor by getting wet and soggy.

They say animals can sense human emotions, whether they're happy, angry, or even sad. It seemed to Buzz that Bumbley was extra affectionate today, as he seemed to be sensitive to Buzz by staying close by and rubbing up against him. Buzz wasn't sure if he was sensing his depression or maybe it was the BBQ ribs, but he wanted it to the former and convinced himself that he and Bumbley had developed a close psychic bond.

When Buzz reached the surface, the wind was picking up and the swells were starting to show white caps. He got underway, still wearing his wetsuit, and headed for port. He was feeling a lot better and felt able to cope with the human race again. He affectionately thought of how seeing Bumbley always cleared his head and lit up a 'fattie' on the way home. Now, life was good, at least for the moment.

Moses Kubakwashe made it back to Harare just as the news of the Leeway massacre hit the airwaves. He was driving and listening to 96.00 ZBC Radio Zimbabwe, when the announcement came on the ten o'clock world news. Although the details were sketchy and there were many gaps in the story, Moses had heard enough from the report to know the complete story.

As he arrived home and parked the van in his driveway, his cell phone rang.

"Mhoro?"

"Moses, this is Wooch. Can you talk?"

"Oh, yes, Commander. How are you?"

"I assume that you've heard about Leeway."

"Yes, sir. I just finished listening to all about it on the ten o'clock news."

"I wanted to hear from you how everything went."

"Everything went according to plan, sir."

"So, Chase and his men had no idea that they were betrayed?"

"No idea at all."

"And from what I've ascertained from my contacts at Le Gang de la Clé de Singe, Leeway bought into the whole rescue scenario, lock stock and barrel. Never did like that son of a bitch."

"Well, sir, I'm just glad that I could have been of service."

"I can't thank you enough, Moses, and rest assured that you will be well rewarded for your participation. Is there anything that you need at the moment?"

"No, sir, not that I can think of."

"Well, thank you, again. Oh, by the way, Moses, do you like whiskey?"

"Indeed, I do, sir."

"Well, I'll be sending you something special—a Yamazaki 50-Year-Old 3rd edition 2011 release."

"It sounds expensive."

"The price of anything is the amount of life you exchange for it."

"Huh?"

"Exactly."

It was about ten-thirty in the morning when Buzz reached the lagoon; it was deserted, just way he liked it. That way, he and the grouper could spend some leisurely time together without Buzz having to keep watch for other divers. He was always afraid that some jerk would kill Bumbley for sport, like a lot of those idiots who kill elephants and lions just so they can have their picture taken, to show the whole world once-and-for-all how big of an asshole they are. Whenever he could, he would try to dispel the rumors that there existed a giant grouper in the lagoon. Bumbley was like the Loch Ness Monster—people believed he existed, but there weren't any photos, at least none in focus.

Buzz climbed back on board after an hour-long dive of hanging out and feeding with his friend. Groucho and Bosco, Buzz's pet ferrets were sitting on the swim platform, waiting for him as usual. After he got out of his wetsuit, he gave the ferrets some nibbles and grabbed an icy-cold Red Stripe. He was kicking back and just soaking up some rays, when he saw a rather large vessel drop anchor about a half a mile to the east of the lagoon entrance. The ship looked to be an Armstrong-class research ship; he guessed she was close to two hundred and forty feet and looked like she was newly commissioned. He broke out his Nikon OceanPro Binocs and gave her a good once over; there was a flag flying off the aft flagpole that he didn't recognize. It was a navy-blue field with a large image of a Marlin in the center, and, beneath the fish, it read *Tynan Institute of Oceanography* in white. On the aft was the name Ogygia, which was an island mentioned in Homer's Odyssey.

He could see that there was a lot of activity; the crew was looking like they were prepping a large rubber dinghy to be lowered off the port side. Within minutes, a grey and red-striped Zodiac Bayrunner came zooming towards the lagoon with five occupants in wetsuits, heading towards him. They slowed down as they approached the Sweet Mary Jane. "Ahoy there!" the driver, who looked like a JFK look-a-like when he was in his twenties, shouted out. All five looked to Buzz like they stepped out of central casting for a Ralph Lauren catalog.

"Ahoy." Buzz smiled and flashed them a peace sign.

"Yo, bro, you come out here a lot?" the driver said.

"Yup. Can I help you, man?"

"We're with the Tynan Institute of Oceanography, a private institute that scours the great oceans for unusual marine specimens for private aquariums."

"I've never heard of private aquariums. You mean like large fish tanks for some rich dude, man?"

A young blonde woman sitting next to the driver started to laugh. "Yeah, our client has a three-hunred-thousand-gallon tank, and he's looking to fill it with the rarest species we can find."

"What kind of guy has his own aquarium?"

"I'm really not at liberty to say, but I can tell you that he's an Arab sheik."

"Well, there's nothing unusual around here. Mostly Jack, Bonito, Kingfish, and a shit load of mullet. Oh, I did see a Jewfish once, if that helps."

She looked at the others. "We heard rumors of a giant—"

Buzz took a sip of his beer and finished her sentence, "Grouper? Lady, I've lived here for almost thirty years, pretty much dived every inch of this lagoon and most of the waters in and around Jamaica. Never seen a giant grouper. I did see a tuna that would tip the scales at about five hundred pounds. You know, I've heard of a square-pants sponge named Bob, too. Don't make it real, man."

"The driver of the Zodiac said, "Who might you be, friend?"

Buzz finished his beer. "I might be Robert Redford, but I'm not, man. The name is Buzz, Buzz Murdoch. I work as a studio manager at Bitchin' Studios in Montego Bay. Who are you, man?"

The blonde woman looking at the others in the Zodiac said, "Well, Buzz, we heard that there is a monster in this lagoon, and we've traveled many hundreds of miles to check it out."

"Lady, knock your selves out."

"It's Laura, Doctor Laura Runnel. Pleased to meet you, Buzz."

"Pleasure to make your acquaintance, Doc." Buzz started to make his way to the cockpit while he continued to speak, "How do you guys search for this fish? Do you all just jump in helter-skelter and swim around, bumping into each other, man?"

"Hardly. We start in a well-organized grid pattern. We'll start in the shallows and work our way systematically, covering the entire lagoon."

As the blonde doctor was speaking, Buzz leaned down into the cockpit as to put his empty beer bottle down. When he did, he flipped a red toggle switch next to the compass. He rose up and held a full bottle of Red Stripe. "Can I offer you all a beer? It's Red Stripe, man. A local favorite."

"Maybe some other time. Buzz. We've got to get started," Doctor Runnel said, smiling.

"Sure, next time, Doc. How long you folks figure you'll be around hunting for your 'white whale'?

She laughed and said, "Good one, Buzz. Probably just a couple of days. Maybe we'll see you out here again."

"Hope so. You all be safe. See you kids on the flip side, man."

As they headed towards the beach, Buzz stood there, waving and smiling.

Mark Landreth, one of the convicted members of the West Texas Shooters Association of Pecos, in what is commonly known as the 'French Wrench Abattage,' was housed at the James Lynaugh Unit in Fort Stockton. He arrived in prison as somewhat of a celebrity; a member of the Aryan Brotherhood, a white supremacist gang, approached him one day while walking by himself around the yard. The man, who was called Dog, was about thirty years old, weighed two hundred and twenty-five pounds, was covered in prison tattoos, and had a shaved head. Mark noticed the man approaching and tried to maneuver away from him, but to no avail. Dog walked right in front of him and stopped, looked Mark in the eye, and said, "Hey meat, what's your name?"

"Mark Landreth."

"Yeah, I heard of you. You're one of the dudes that blasted the shit out of those Frenchies."

Not wanting to explain the whole mistaking-identity-thing for the umpteenth time, he said, "Yeah, that's me."

"My name is Roger, but everyone calls me Dog," he claimed, as he held out his hand.

"Nice to meet you, Dog."

"Listen man, I'm guessing this is your first time in the prison. Am I right?"

"Yeah."

"How long?"

"Twenty to life."

"Rough. Me, I'm doing all day and a night."

"Huh?"

"Life without parole. Yeah, it sucks, but at least I got the Brotherhood."

"The Brotherhood?"

"The Aryan Brotherhood. Listen man, you ain't going to make it twenty years, much less twenty days, without some friends, some protection. Now, you see that group of beaners over there? Those are the Mexikanemi, the Texas Mexican Mafia, and that large group of Africoons by the weights, thems the Mandingo Warriors.

What'dya gonna do when they come to fuck with ya, steal your shit, or rape your ass? Cause sooner or later, they'll get ya ass. Shit, they'd probably just kill your ass so's you won't snitch on them.

That's why you need a family, people that will watch over you. They ever fuck with you, then we fuck them up, see, because you're part of a family—the Brotherhood."

"But, I don't want trouble."

"Dude, just being here, you're in trouble. You don't even have to do anything to get into trouble. You could be walking along and accidentally bump into some dude, and, next thing you know, you got a shiv sticking out of your ass. Or you're standing in the shower, minding your own business, and some three-hundred-pound Chicano decides he wants you to blow him. Next thing you know, you're on your knees with this guy's dick in your mouth, and now you're his bitch. Is that what you want?"

"God, no."

"All right, then. Come on, and I'll introduce you to your brothers." Dog put his arm around Mark's and walked him over to a group of men, all with their heads shaved and tattooed with mostly swastikas, eagles, and skulls.

"Hey, bros. This here's Mark. He's the motherfucker that wasted all those French assholes couple years back. He wants to be part of the Brotherhood. Right, Mark?"

"Right."

A man with a tattoo across his chest of a Nazi eagle holding a swastika with an SS symbol on each side of the eagle walked over to Mark and said, "Is that right? You want to join the Brotherhood?"

"Yeah."

"Well, Mark, you got to prove yourself, so we know that you got our backs."

Mark looked at the group and back to the man, and then he said, "Well, what do I have to do?"

"Ya see that fat ass beaner all by his lonesome over there, leaning against that wall smoking?"

"Yeah."

"Well, I want you to take this shank and go over there and stab him. Dog will go over with you."

"What'd he do?"

"Okay. Now, Mark, when you're in the Brotherhood, you don't be asking questions. You asked to do something, you do it. Ya dig?"

Mark looked at Dog, and Dog smiled. "Come on, I'll be with ya. It'll be okay."

Mark took the weapon from the tattooed man and started to walk over to the large Hispanic man, who was casually leaning against the wall. Dog was walking alongside him, pretending to laugh and look unassuming. He whispered to Mark, "Listen, as we walk past him, just lunge and stab him as many times as you can. Then, keep walking. If anything happens, I'll be right next to you. But, know this: you're going to get punished by getting thrown into solitary for several months. Just keep your mouth shut and don't say nothing about the Brotherhood. Just tell them he tried to rape you, and that you had to defend yourself. If you bring the Brotherhood into it, the Badger will kill you."

"Wh-who the fuck is the Badger?"

"That guy who gave you the shank. He's the head of the Brotherhood. Hey, don't worry. Just think of this asshole as a Frenchy."

Mark wanted to break down and cry, but he knew he couldn't show weakness, not with these guys. He was way in too deep. He had twenty years ahead of him; he realized that his life, as he knew it, was dead. Now it was all about surviving one day at a time, and this was day one of seventy thousand and three hundred.

"Hey, amigo," He said, as he lunged.

Over the past twelve years, to keep Bumbley safe, Buzz had spent hundreds of hours training the gentle giant to swim out of the lagoon and migrate down to the White Bay National Coral Preserve, where, because of the fragility of the reef, no divers were allowed.

Buzz had devised a Pavlovian response technique to get Bumbley out of danger. He had installed twin underwater

Bose speakers that emitted a high-frequency sound, not perceived by the human ear. He had a remote that he would use underwater when he would dive with Bumbley. Whenever Buzz would set off the alarm, he would then coax the fish to move into the direction he wanted. Bumbley would get a special treat whenever he successfully accomplished the journey. It took over twelve years to have Bumbley make the connection, but he did, and it was on a Saturday in March. On that day, Buzz set off the alarm, set sail out of the Lagoon to White Bay, and waited. And waited, and waited.

But after three hours, while Buzz sat on the swim platform and peered into an underwater viewing, sniping scope, he saw the mammoth grouper sauntering up to the coral reef. It stopped under the Sweet Mary Jane and waited. Buzz dropped a twenty-two-pound Mackerel as a reward, which Bumbley inhaled in milliseconds.

At least once a week, Buzz and Bumbley made the secret trek from Luminous Lagoon to White Bay National Coral Preserve and back again, because you never knew. But Buzz always knew this day would come, when Bumbley's rumored fame would bring people out to try and find him to either kill him for 'sport' or capture him as a prize. Buzz decided he was prepared to go to extremes to keep his friend safe, even if it meant going all sea-sheppard on them.

Buzz kept watch over Bumbley that night and the next day too. He decided he'd give the good doctor at least two days to search the lagoon. Buzz made sure to keep Bumbley all treated up at the White Bay National Coral Preserve so he wouldn't be tempted to head back to his old stomping grounds. Buzz called Bobby at the studio just to check in, although he was pretty sure there weren't any big projects on the horizon that he had to get back for. Bobby told him just to relax and chill out, nothing cooking until the end of the next week. Buzz was anything but chilled out, though; he was on high alert and planning for a battle royale.

Doctor Laura Runnel and her team had spent two full days scouring the lagoon; they searched from the beach, out towards the ocean, and back again. After four times, nothing. At sundown, the doctor and her team were sitting out on the deck, having some beers and nachos and going over some of the data they had collected over the last couple days. They were deciding whether or not to give up the search for the elusive giant grouper.

Jack Williams, better known as 'Black Jack,' her most experienced diver, thought that the rumors were probably just that: rumors. "It makes for a good legend, but to find an *Epinephelus Lanceolatus* in these waters is unheard of. There has never even been a reported case of one ever seen in the Atlantic, much less in these waters. I say we weigh anchor and head down to Rio to snag a *Brachyplatystoma Filamentosum*. The sheik doesn't have one of those, and they're real."

Laura, who was sitting facing the lagoon, took a sip of her Corona while looking past Jack, who was leaning against the railing. She said, to no one in particular, "What was the name of that old hippie we meet out on the lagoon when we first got here? I thought it began with a B. Bud? Bob? Bill?"

Someone from behind, hidden within the group, said, "Skip."

"Skip?" Laura looked at Mike Rogers, the driver of the Zodiac, "Skip!"

"Just kidding. It was Buzz."

"Buzz. Yeah, Buzz. I'd like to talk to him one more time before we pull out of here. It might be worth having a beer or six with the old coot."

Jack stood up off the rail. "You're not serious. He's just some old, burned out hippie from the sixties. He's the poster boy for 'this is your brain on drugs.' For crying out loud, the name of his boat was the Sweet Mary Jane. The only reason I can see that you're going to find out from this old guy is where to score some righteous ganja."

"Don't be such a stick in the mud. It won't hurt to hang around a day or two, and then we'll head down to Rio to get his highness his precious *Piraíba*. Maybe we'll even throw in a couple *Jacundas* and *Bicuda o Picudas* for good measure," She said smiling. "Now, what was the name of that studio he worked at?"

After three days at sea, the Sebastes Fasciatus was six miles off the coast of the Canary Islands amd heading towards the Strait of Gibraltar. Captain Ehsan Khattak summoned Rodin and the Iceman to his cabin.

"Gentleman, I've asked you here to brief you on your next assignments. Iceman, you've been instructed to take your team to Brazil. You and your team will be airdropped into Jaú National Park; it's a national park located in the state of Amazonas. It is also one of the largest forest reserves in South America South and part of a UNESCO World Heritage Site.

Your mission is to track down a man, Joao Ferreyra. He is an extremely wealthy man, who illegally entered Jaú National Park. While there, he shot, cooked, and ate a highly endangered black leopard. Because of his wealth and connections, his poaching may go unpunished." He handed a thick folder with all of his instructions—a complete dossier on the subject, maps, names of local contacts, and all the legal papers he and his team would need—to the Iceman.

The Iceman took the folder, turned, and looked at Rodin. "What's with these rich fucks? They think, just because their rich, that they can get away with shit. Well, I'm going to have a special treat for Mr. Ferreyra."

Rodin winked and said, "I can't wait to read all about it."

Captain Khattak handed Rodin his folder and said, "It seems that an old friend of yours is in need of some special Monkey Wrench help."

"A friend?"

"Does the name Buzz Murdock ring a bell?"

"Buzz! I wonder what kind of trouble he's gotten himself into now?"

"Apparently, it has something to do with a sixteen-hundred-pound Grouper and some evil oceanographers down Jamaica way."

"Well, if Buzz is involved, you can be sure it's going to be a wacky adventure. You see, Buzz was one of the original Hippie Flower Children from the sixties and has never grown up. He's a really great guy—weird, but great."

The Iceman smiled. "Sex and Drugs."

"And don't forget Rock & Roll."

It had been days since David Leeway had gotten his ass shot off in Zimbabwe, and, back in Atlanta, Detectives Steve Matchet and Charlie Davis hadn't heard jack squat from those two café-society, super sleuths from Interpol. It was starting to piss them off.

Matchet was complaining to Davis, when Davis said, "Well, Hells Bells. Why don't you just call them?"

"Hell no! They're supposed to be the almighty crime experts. They should be calling us, God Dammit!"

"Hey, Steve, you got a call from London holding on two," Detective Delores Dotter, from Burglary and sitting four desks down, shouted out.

"Thanks, Dot." He looked at Davis and grinned. "See, I told ya they'd call."

Davis just rolled his eyes, and then came and sat on the corner of Matchet's desk. Steve picked up the phone and punched the button for line two.

"This is Matchet."

"I say, old man, Volker here. Sorry we haven't been in touch sooner, but I must tell you, as you can well image, we've been up to our asses in dead bodies while trying to sort everything out."

"Hey, no problem. We understand."

"Well, thank you. I think we've got some good news for you. It seems like the man responsible for Brittany's murder is a man named Chase Madrid; he went by the alias of Angelo Della Morte when he met her on the flight back from Africa—which, by the way, the name Angelo Della Morte is 'Angel of Death' in Italian. This man has used several of these types of aliases; he is also responsible for the death and decapitation of a dentist up in Minnesota that you may have heard about. It seems that Mr. Madrid is known to be a member of the French eco-terrorist group Le Gang de la Clé de Singe."

"Where is Mr. Madrid now?"

"He is resting comfortably downstairs in our morgue with multiple gunshot wounds, which he received while participating in the David Leeway attack."

"Well, that's a shame. I would've loved to have him stand trial here in the States so we could have had the pleasure of frying his ass in the electric chair."

"I do quite understand how you feel, old man, but I guess you could say justice has been served."

"So, what now? I've never had to deal with international red tape. Do we get the body or any type of evidence?"

"You will receive a complete dossier of all the evidence, the ME's report, fingerprints, photo's, and, of course, all files and records pertaining to Mr. Chase. I am afraid that we at Interpol must keep the remains of the deceased, as he was killed in the commission of an international felony. Sorry, old chap. Oh, and just a thought, you may want to request any information that your FBI might have on Mr. Madrid as well."

"Well, I want to thank you, Inspector, for all your help. We at Atlanta PD appreciate all you've done. I don't suppose we'll be talking to each other again soon, so goodbye and thanks."

"It was our pleasure, old man. Cheerio."

Once the Sebastes Fasciatus had docked in Marseille, Rodin asked Sue-B and Fu Hao to meet him in the galley at zero-eight-hundred hours for a special assignment. The two women entered the galley on time, where they found Rodin sitting alone in a booth near the coffee machines and drinking a glass of milk. He waved them over when he saw them enter.

"Ladies, won't you join me? Can I get you something to drink—coffee, tea, milk?"

They looked at one another and shook their heads no. Sue-B said, "No, thank you. What's up?"

"Well, ladies, I have an assignment that I think you might enjoy. You would be acting as an independent solo-action team, with back up support, of course. Think you might be interested?"

"Maybe. What is it, and what are we talking as far as back up?" asked Fu Hao.

"Good. Never jump into anything until you know everything. Well, what it is, is we want to start scaring the shit out of those bastard sealers that club baby Harp seals to death for their fur. And by scaring the shit out them, I mean to blast the shit out of them. Those twisted hunters, and I use the term 'hunters' loosely, club thousands of defenseless baby seals to death as part of the barbaric and senseless annual sealing season.

Last week, a commercial vessel rammed an inflatable boat filled with protesters, and the crew, laughing at the injured protesters, threw seal guts on them. It's payback time.

These fuckers use a hakapik or club; it's a four to five-foot wooden pole with a bent metal spike affixed to the end. It's the club of choice, because it's much easier to aim a blow directly at the seal pup's head with it. One swing from a hakapik will usually kill a pup right away. They keep clubbing the seal in the forehead, though, until they know for sure that it's dead. They're supposed to 'palpate' a pup's skull after they've clubbed it to feel the caved-in bone beneath the skin and blubber, or they perform the 'blink reflex' test, which consists of touching the seal's eyeball—if it blinks, they have another excuse to club it again.

As far as back up, I'm planning on sending Aleppo and Lu Wei with you. You will be transported to your targets on a forty-seven-foot Motor Lifeboat; it's designed to weather hurricane-force winds and heavy seas. And, God forbid you guys capsize, it self-rights in less than ten seconds with all equipment fully functional. This puppy comes armed with an M240 machine gun, but I'm also sending along a French Aerospatiale C.22 drone armed with two Aster missiles, just in case things get hairy out there."

Sue-B looked at Fu Hao and stated, "Well, you can count me in."

"Me too," Fu Hao agreed. "Unfortunately, for these assholes, they're bringing a hakapik to a gun fight."

It was getting dark fast, and, had they been looking off to the East, they might have made out a silhouette of a sailboat slowly making its way back into the lagoon. Buzz had spotted the outline of the Ogygia; she was hard to miss, as not too many ships her size hung out in these waters. Buzz slowed down to a crawl, so he could slip into the lagoon undetected. He actually turned off his running lights, which is a big no-no, and he slowly slipped into the lagoon unnoticed. Buzz watched the activity on the research vessel until eleven o'clock to see if there was a chance of a night dive. When he was satisfied that nothing was going to happen, he set up his hammock on deck and went to sleep.

Buzz woke up just as the sun was peaking over the horizon, around five-thirty in the morning. He broke down and stowed the hammock, and went below deck to hit the head and grab his binocs, before he went back topside and checked if there was anything going on over on the Ogygia. As he was scanning the ship from bow to aft, he spotted the good doctor looking back at him with her binoculars. They were top of the line Nikon Ocean Pro 7 x 50's; they were nitrogen-filled and O-ring-sealed for waterproof, shockproof, and fog proof viewing. Buzz was impressed and said to himself, "I would expect no less." He lowered his binocs, waved, and gestured for her to come over. He peered back to see that she was nodding yes. She pointed to her watch as to ask what time, and he flashed semaphore signals indicating ten o'clock. He was impressed, but not surprised, that she knew the telegraphy system.

Buzz saw the doctor piloting the Zodiac, leaving the Ogygia at a quarter-to-ten and heading his way; she was alone. He made a mental note to keep an eye out for the other members of her team. He didn't want her to distract him while the others snooped around down below.

As she pulled up, Buzz yelled, "Ahoy there!"

The Zodiac slowly inched toward the port side, and the doctor threw Buzz a line, which he caught and tied off. As he was helping her from the Zodiac and onto the yacht, she said, "Permission to come aboard, Captain?"

"Permission granted. Welcome aboard, Doctor."

She looked very nautical, wearing navy-blue, twill cropped pants and a striped, navy and white, linen spilt-neckline top. Her hair was straight, blond, and about shoulder length. She was wearing tortoiseshell Chanel sunglasses, which she removed to unveil blue eyes the color of the lagoon. She was beautiful and looked like the type of woman Hollywood would have cast to play the unscrupulous evil doctor in a James Bond film; Buzz figured her to be in her mid to late thirties. And the one thing Buzz knew more than anything in this world was that he had to careful with this woman, with that coy smile of hers, the flip of her hair and the twinkle in her eyes; this woman was dangerous. He figured she was going to try to play him like an old Gibson guitar.

She suddenly grabbed his arm, as she seemed to lose her balance. "Sorry." She held on for just a beat too long, as to send a subtle message. She smiled. "I'm glad you signaled for me to come over. I was hoping to see you before we left."

Having been in the music business for over forty years, Buzz knew a thing or two about timing; so far, he was just enjoying this artful dance of seduction. He held up a Red Stripe and asked, "Beer?"

"At ten o'clock in the morning?"

He held it out to her. "It's five o'clock somewhere, man."

She smiled and shrugged, taking the bottle. She said, "True enough."

"So, any luck finding the infamous Luminous Lagoon monster?" Buzzed motioned for her to have a seat, while he sat behind the wheel on an angle so he could nonchalantly give a glance to the Ogygia.

"No. We did four complete grid explorations and didn't find anything interesting, not even a Jew Fish."

"That's a bummer, man."

"Yeah, that is a bummer. Tell me, Buzz, you say you've lived here a long time. How do you think this legend of a giant grouper got started?"

"As far as I can remember—and I don't remember too much—it seemed to have started about ten or fifteen years ago, when a diver claimed he came face to face with a large fish that scared the pee out of him. When he said it reminded him of some sort of grouper class he had never seen before, I think he probably saw the endangered Atlantic goliath grouper, aka *Epinephelus Itajara*."

"*Epinephelus Itajara?* Buzz, I'm impressed."

"Not bad for an old stoner, huh? I guess that I lied to you when we first met; I have seen a couple of big groupers in these waters, young ones. The biggest one I ever saw here was about two hundred pounds, not the monster grouper you're searching for. They usually only stick around until they get three or four years old, then they head out to deeper water." Buzz stood up and opened the cooler next to him, swapping his empty for another Red Stripe while giving a quick glance over to the Ogygia. "You care for another?"

She held up her bottle. "Still working this one, thanks."

"So, after that kid's encounter, the storyies started to be fueled mostly by the locals to get tourists interested in the lagoon. You see, that restaurant bar and dock over there? That's the result of local lore and stories, man. Once, a guy snorkel diving drowned in the lagoon about six years ago; it must be the giant grouper. Or a small boat tipped over, the giant grouper. Yeah, that fish must have caused every mishap, misfortune, and misadventure not only in this lagoon, but I've heard story's down in Kingston blamed on the giant grouper as well."

"Well, I guess it was worth checking out. Stranger things have been known to happen."

"If you're into strange things, I could take you on a snipe hunt if you want to. I hear they're up in those hills, along with some duppies."

"No thanks, my dad took me on a snipe hunt when I was eight. But what are duppies?"

"A Duppy is a Jamaican word from West Africa, meaning a ghost or spirit. They are said to live at the roots of cotton trees and bamboo thickets, from where they emerge during the nights or at midday."

She straight up and leaned in, seeming to be really intent on not missing a single word. She said, "Fascinating. Go on."

"Well, Duppies are generally considered malicious. The Duppy can linger around or be summoned by an obeah. That's a man or woman from the graveyard to do harm in exchange for payment of food or drink, especially rum. According to legend, one can tell if a 'Duppy' is around if certain signs are observed, such as a dog whines or howls or even a spider web across your face, especially at night. So, why were you glad that I signaled you to come over?"

Laura was so enthralled with Duppies, she was caught off guard by Buzz's question. She stumbled, trying to come back with an answer. "Well, ah, I guess I thought you might shed some light on the tale of the grouper, and I was right. Plus, I got an unexpected lesson in Duppies. Why did you ask me to come over?"

Buzz was about to answer, when Bosco and Groucho scurried on deck, giving the doctor a bit of a start. "Oh, cute, a couple of *Mustela putorius furos*. What are their names?"

"Bosco and Groucho. Boys, say hello to the doctor." He gave a short whistle, and they ran over to her. Bosco jumped right onto her lap. "Bosco, down!"

"No. He's fine." She started to pet the animal as he settled into her lap. Bosco started making a kind of purring sound and even rolled on his back for some tummy rubs, which the doctor obliged gladly. "So, Buzz, why did you want me to come over this morning?"

"I was curious how you search was going."

"Is that all?" she said with just a hint of seduction, as she slid her sunglasses back on.

"Well, Doc, it has been a long time since I entertained anyone as charming as you onboard the Sweet Mary Jane. Most of the folks I have onboard are old rock & rollers, who aren't too interested in stimulating conversation, man. Most of the time, I barely remember most of it, if you know what I mean and I think you do."

She started to giggle. "Yes, I think I do." The doctor tilted the bottle back and finished her beer.

"Care for another?"

"Sure, why not?"

As Buzz got another Red Stripe from the cooler, he shot a glance to the Ogygia, still nothing. He walked over and handed the doctor the beer. "So, what's your next port of call?"

"Brazil."

"Wow! Brazil. I've never been, you?"

"Oh, yeah. I once did a six-month expedition about three years ago. Up the Amazon."

"What were you doing for six months? Were you stocking some rich dude's aquarium?""

"No, I was working for the Cousteau Society at the time. We were studying *Serrasalmus manueli.*" She waited to see how knowledgeable the old man was.

Buzz didn't disappoint. "Piranhas, that's awesome. Are they as vicious as everyone thinks?"

She was blown away that this ex-flower child was so damn smart, smarter than some of her colleagues and definitely more interesting. "Very good! I am truly impressed, Buzz."

"Thanks. It's amazing what you pick up from listening to NPR. Are they?"

"Are they what?"

"Are they as vicious as everyone thinks?"

"Oh, they can be. Depends on if there's blood in the water, or if they're just in a shitty mood."

"Sounds like some people I know."

The music of Madam Butterfly started to play, and the doctor reached for her cell phone from her pocket. She looked at the number and said, "Excuse me."

"No problemo."

As she spoke, she turned slightly away and lowered her voice. Buzz wasn't really interested in her conversation; it gave him a chance to scope out the Ogygia. This time, he did notice that there was activity; it appeared that they were gearing up for a dive. There were about six or seven in wetsuits loading up a Zodiac with tanks, spear guns, and what looked to Buzz to be some sort of scientific gear. The doctor was facing the shoreline with her back to him, so he took the opportunity to flip the toggle alarm to let Bumbley start migrating.

She finished up her call. "Sorry about that."

"It's cool, man. Hey, I really like your ringtone. I love what Malcolm McLaren did with 'Un Bel Di Vendremo'."

"Buzz, you continue to amaze me."

"Far out."

"Listen, I have to head back to the ship; we're going to give the lagoon one last going over before shipping out for Brazil. I'd love to see again before we head out."

"How about dinner?"

She gave him a big smile and touched his arm. "I'd love to. What time?"

"Well, I got to go meet a friend this afternoon. How about we say around seven?

"Where should I meet you?"

"The Sweet Mary Jane. I make a mean Ackee and Saltfish."

"Fabulous. I look forward to it."

Buzz offered her his hand to help her back onto the Zodiac, but she waved him off. "That's okay, Buzz. I'm good."

He untied the line and tossed it to her. She waved as she headed back to meet the other divers. Buzz held his hand up and went down into the cockpit to weigh anchor. Then, he was headed off to the White Bay National Coral Preserve to meet up with Bumbley. Buzz had trained his buddy to stay in the preserve until he gave the signal to return to the lagoon. Over the years, Buzz had tried to think of any and all possibilities. So far, it had worked.

Mark sat in isolation for nearly eight months for the attempted murder of Pedro Pascal; he also received an additional six years tacked onto his original twenty to life. While in solitary, he received numerous death threats from the Mexikanemi's, and notes would be slipped under his cell door with messages like, *"We're gonna fuck you, man.", "You're DEAD!" and "Dead Man Walking"*. Sometimes, he would hear them whisper death threats as someone would walk by his cell. He was afraid to eat anything that wasn't sealed or in a can, for fear of being poisoned.

When he did get released and walked, escorted by two prison guards, out to the Yard, there stood Dog and the other members of the Aryan Brotherhood to greet him.

Dog walked up to him, put his arm around him, and whispered, "Welcome to the Brotherhood, man. You did it, man. You're now part of the family. No one's going to fuck with you, right Badger?"

"You got that right, Dog. Hey, Birdman, we got to give our new friend here an official name. What'dya think?"

The Birdman was the man who delegated new brothers with thier Aryan Brotherhood moniker. He was one of the original members of the Brotherhood, while serving ten years for armed robbery in San Quentin. He too, like all the other members, was covered with Aryan tattoos. The most notable one was on his back, and it was a large eagle sitting atop a swastika with the word 'birdman,' all in caps, arcing around the eagle.

He looked Mark up and down and asked, "What did you do before you came here?"

"I owned a hardware store."

"Hardware store, huh? Well, from now on, you're the Hammer!" Birdman proclaimed.

Badger slapped Mark on the back and said, "Hammer, I like it. From now on, you're the Hammer. Now, Hammer, we got to start getting you inked up. I know, how about a swastika made of hammers. What do ya think, Dog?"

"That would be awesome. What do ya think, Hammer?"

Mark said, pointing to his left arm, "Yeah, okay. How about here?"

Badger shook his head and pointed to his chest. "No, man. It's got to go here and big, so everyone knows you're the Hammer!"

All the Brothers agreed and off they went to have the Butcher, the Aryan Brotherhoods tattoo artist, start what everyone figured would be the Hammers first of many prison tattoos.

Tattooing was illegal in prison, but, like so many illegal things in prison, there were ways around such restrictions—like bribes, threats, and even quid pro quo with other gangs. After nine hours of excruciating pain, Hammer's first prison tat was completed.

As Mark looked in the mirror, he thought, except for the subject matter, it was actually a fairly decent looking tattoo. But unfortunately for Mark, getting a tattoo in prison, which isn't the most hygienic of environments, and the fact that the Butcher's tattoo gun hadn't been sterilized properly, all added up to Mark the Hammer contracting a raging staph infection. It ended up killing him in less than a week.

It came as a bit of a blow to the members of the Aryan Brotherhood. Badger summed it up rather poetically, "Aw. fuck it. Well, shit happens."

Black Jack Williams had been with Tynan Institute of Oceanography for about four years as the lead diver and the go-to guy to get things done. Most of the time it was within the confines of the law, but occasionally it wasn't, which is how he got the nickname, 'Black Jack.' When 9/11 occurred, he was a college freshman at Santa Monica City College majoring in fun times. But after seeing the towers fall, he ran down to the local Navy recruiter and signed up for the SEAL program. On the bus down to Coronado, California, the home of the Naval Special Warfare Command, all the recruits were fired up to go over to Afghanistan and kill them a bunch of those camel fuckers. They were going to finish what George W's daddy didn't finish in Operation Desert Storm.

The first day was a real eye-opener. As the band Talking Heads proclaimed, "This ain't no party, this ain't no disco, this ain't no fooling around. This ain't no party, this ain't no disco, this ain't no fooling around. This ain't no Mudd Club or C. B. G. B., I ain't got time for that now." Whatever they thought, they thought wrong. The Navy was planning on weeding out the weak in a hurry. A couple of hours were the usual military routine every recruit goes through—an ultra close buzz haircut, getting their uniforms, settling into the barracks, filling out a shitload of paperwork and meeting their SEAL instructor, First Class Petty Officer Robert "Kilo" Watts.

In August 1990, Watts was part of the first western forces to deploy to the Persian Gulf as part of Operation Desert Shield. His team of six infiltrated the capital city of Kuwait within hours of the invasion, gathered intelligence and developed plans to rescue US embassy staff, should they become hostages. His SEAL team was also the first to capture Iraqi Prisoners of War when they assaulted nine Kuwaiti Oil platforms on 19 January 1991.

In March 1991, he was one of the members of a six-man SEAL team led by Lieutenant Jimmy "Wags" Porraski, who launched a mission to trick the Iraqi military into thinking an amphibious assault on Kuwait by coalition forces was imminent by setting off explosives and placing marking buoys five hundred meters off the Kuwaiti coast. The mission was a success, and Iraqi forces were diverted east away from the true coalition offensive. Petty Officer Robert Watts was wounded during a firefight with Saddam Husain's elite Revolutionary Guard, where he received the Purple Heart, Bronze Star, and the Navy Cross.

Since then, he had served in Somali, where he was deployed to Mogadishu to work alongside Delta Force as part of Task Force Ranger in the search for Somali warlord Mohammed Farrah El Aydah. He was involved in at least eight black ops missions to mostly Arab speaking countries from 1993 to 1999, and it was then, in 2000, that he assigned to be a Navy SEAL instructor.

The screaming started immediately once they got off the bus. Jack Williams and the others couldn't think straight, and that was the whole point—to keep everyone disorientated, confused, and dazed. As the group of two hundred lined up outside of their barracks, Petty Officer Robert Watts stood facing the group of recruits, waiting for the other instructors to give him the sign that they were ready. Petty Officer Willie "Hog" Hibler shouted, "Attention!"

Watts counted to ten before he spoke. "Greetings, ladies. My name is SEAL Instructor Watts; that is SEAL Instructor Hibler, and this is SEAL Instructor Lopez. I want you all to look to your left. Now look to your right. Odds are, the person on either side of you will not make the cut and will ring the bell. Only about ten of you will be a SEAL. You are going to start with five weeks of Indoctrination and Pre-Training, and then you'll go through three phases of BUD/S, Basic Underwater Demolition/SEAL training. You can quit at any time, no questions asked. Is there anyone of you who wants to quit now?"

There was a unanimous, "Sir, no, sir!"

"I can't hear you!"

"Sir, no,, sir!"

"Hog, get these boots fed and bed."

"Aye, Aye."

By the time he fell into bed, Jack was exhausted and he hadn't even done anything yet; it was all the mental stress he was feeling. He was asleep as soon as his head hit the pillow. It seemed that he had just laid down, when he woke with a start as lights were flashing and someone was screaming and banging a garbage can. "Get your asses up! Let's go, let's go! Get dressed and get your ass outside! Now! T-shirts and shorts. Move it! Last one out gets my boot up his ass!"

Jack jumped up, got dressed and ran outside into the dark, where Petty Officer Watts was standing exactly in the place that he stood just seven hours ago. It was four-thirty in the morning; it was dark, cold, and there was a heavy layer of fog making everything out of focus.

"Today, at least ten of you will be gone. We are going to complete the Physical Screening Test, PST. It is designed to see if you have what it takes to enter SEAL training. To pass this test, you must be able to complete the following regimen: swim five-hundred-yard breast or side stroke in a minimum of twelve minutes, complete at least fourty-two push-ups in two minutes and fifty push-ups in two minutes, run one and a half miles in eleven minutes, and complete at least six pull-ups. Anyone want to quit?"

"Sir, no, sir!"

"I can't hear you!"

"Sir, no, sir!"

Jack had been a long-distance runner on his track team in high school, and he had competed in a couple of marathons and even a triathlon while in college. He thought that he was in good physical shape, but, after the fifty sit-ups, he was thinking that he might not be cut out for the SEALs. He handled the run relatively easily, and then it was onto the pull-up. With those, the only thing that saved him was there wasn't a time limit. At the end of the PST, they were down to one hundred and eighty-five. They lost fifteen that day, and the attrition continued over the next five weeks until, at the end of the initial training program, only one hundred and sixteen boots moved into phase one.

First Phase was the toughest. It consisted of eight weeks of Basic Conditioning, which peaked with a grueling segment called 'Hell Week,' where they were tested to their limits. Hell Week was a test of physical endurance, mental tenacity and true teamwork, where much of the class 'rang the bell.' Physical discomfort and pain caused many to say, "Fuck this shit; it just isn't worth it." The miserable, wet-cold, approaching hypothermia made others quit. Sheer fatigue and sleep deprivation caused every candidate left to question their core values, motivations, limits, and everything they're made of and stand for. Jack hung tough; the more the SEAL Instructors screamed and yelled at him and tried to get him to quit, the more he dug deep and refused to yield. Then, one day, he heard Petty Officer Watts yell the longed-for words, "Hell Week is secured!" While the twelve Boot survivors left from a class of two hundred started cheering and hugging each other, Jack dropped to one knee and cried.

The First Phase was all about basic conditioning and separating the wannabes from the ones who could cut the mustard. The Second Phase concentrated on diving; it covered SCUBA skills. The Boots learned open and closed circuit combat diving and how to complete long-distance underwater transit dives. Finally, the Third Phase was learning the art of land warfare, which included land navigation, small-unit tactics, rappelling, military land and underwater explosives, and weapons training.

Once Jack completed the initial SEAL training, he went on to the advanced training program, which included foreign language training, SEAL tactical communications training, Sniper, Military Free-fall Parachuting, Jump Master, Explosive Breacher, Parachute Training, and Diving medicine and medical skills.

After all the training, Jack did two tours in Iraq and Afghanistan. On 12 April 2009, in response to a hostage-taking incident off of the coast of Somalia by Somalian pirates, his Navy SEAL Team engaged and killed the three pirates who were closely holding the Captain of the freighter ship, the Maersk Alabama. The pirates and their hostage were being towed in a lifeboat approximately one hundred yards behind the USS Bainbridge, when each of the pirates was killed by a different SEAL with a single shot to the head.

After that, he decided to call it a day and retired from the Navy. He went back home to California, decided to go back to college, enrolled in Cal State Long Beach, and started taking classes in oceanography. In his senior year, he did an internship at the Tynan Institute of Oceanography and felt that he found his calling.

There was the adventure of diving with just a hint of danger that went along with some of the assignments. The Institute occasionally operated in the gray area of the law, which was okay with Jack, and, besides that, there was Doctor Runnel. He usually got his way with women, but the Doc wasn't giving in so easily. One thing about Jack: he did love a challenge.

The Iceman and his team said their goodbyes to Rodin and the Red Team, before heading off to Brazil to find Joao Ferreyra and make him pay for his sins.

Their flight would take almost twenty hours, flying from Marseille to Frankfort, Germany on Lufthansa, then from Frankfurt to Sao Paulo, Sao Paulo to Manaus, the capital of the vast state of Amazonas and where the wealthy Brazilian CEO of Amazonas Oil illegally entered the UNESCO World Heritage forest of Jaú National Park and proceeded to shoot, cook, and eat a highly rare and endangered black leopard. Because of his wealth and connections, he believed that his poaching would go unpunished.

Forest rangers found Ferreyra and two of his associates illegally camped in Jaú National Park Wildlife Sanctuary with multiple rifles, hundreds of rounds of ammunition *and* the bullet-riddled carcasses of eleven protected animals, including a female black leopard. There were only one thousand breeding pairs remaining in all of Brazil.

Forensic evidence revealed that the small female leopard died slowly and in agony after being shot six times by Ferreyra's rifle. When she finally died, the bastard skinned her body and consumed her flesh in a leopard stew that the rangers found cooking in a pot.

If convicted of the multiple charges against them, Ferreyra and his buddies should have gone to jail for twenty-eight years. But because of his vast wealth and government connections as CEO of one of the largest oil companies in Brazil, he got away unpunished.

While out on bail, he had already attempted to bribe court officials into ignoring his crimes—other previous cases against the rich and powerful had dragged on for years as the authorities stalled and got rich off of kickbacks.

When the Blue Team landed at Manau International Airport AM Eduardo Gomes at seven in the morning, they were met by their local contact, a young woman in her mid-twenties, Aceline Hernandez.

Aceline stood at the arrival reception area holding a sign that read "*Bem Vinda Johnny Cubo de Gelo*," translated as "*Welcome Johnny Ice Cube*." The Iceman approached the young woman and said, "Voce fala Ingles?"

She smiled and she replied, "Sim. Yes, I do."

"Great, because asking where the bathroom is and 'I would like a beer' pretty much covers the extent of my Portuguese."

"No worries. I believe I speak enough English, so it shouldn't be a problem. What shall I call you? Johnny or the Iceman?"

"Let's go with Johnny. I'll introduce everyone when we get to the car, if that's all right."

"Yes, of course. Follow me."

Aceline led the group of four out of the arrival doors and to her Ford Troller T4 parked at the curb. After stashing their gear into the back of the SUV, the Iceman took the front seat, while Willie Tyler, Gianfranco, and T-Bone climbed into the backseat.

Once they all were aboard the van and all the introductions were made, Aceline headed east on Avenue Santos Dumont, then south on Avenue Constantino Nery toward the Porto de Manaus area, to their hotel, Hotel Colonial. The ride only took forty minutes, but, by the time they arrived, Willie and Gianfranco were fast asleep. It was no surprise after their twenty-plus-hour flight.

Aceline had registered everyone prior to their arrival, and, as they were getting their room keys, she asked if they would all like to grab a bite at the café next door just to go over some details and a couple of new developments.

The Iceman said, "Sounds good. Give us fifteen minutes to drop our stuff off and splash some cold water on our faces, and we'll meet back here in the lobby."

"Bem, okay. Vemos entao."

The Iceman looked perplexed, so she said, smiling, "See you then."

He repeated, "Vemos entao."

Aceline Hernandez was born and raised in Manaus twenty-four years ago. Her father worked at the shipyard Estaleiro Jurua, which was across the Rio Negro that separated the city of Manaus from the rural province of Iranduba. Her father, Ayrton Hernandez, had been building floating petrol stations for twenty-four years, while her mother, Maria, taught music at the Conservatorio de Musica do Amazonas.

When Aceline was eighteen, she joined the Guarda-Florestal at the Jaú National Park Wildlife Sanctuary. During her time as park ranger, she had seen the rich and powerful abuse the prohibited hunting of endangered species by bribing park officials and having them turn a blind eye to their illegal hunting excursions. When she complained to her superiors, she was taken out of the field and stuck behind a desk to shuffle papers all day long. That's when she became an underground member of Le Gang de la Clé de Singe.

She was the one who alerted 'the Gang' about Joao Ferreyra killing the leopard. She and a small group of loyal conservationists have meddled, sabotaged, and foiled many illegal hunting parties, but without much success. She was hoping that this revenge against such a wealthy man would bring attention to the plight of the endangered animals of the park.

She was having a cup of coffee, when the Iceman and the Blue team entered the café. The café had only a few people having breakfast, so they sat down at a large table in the corner opposite the entrance. The waitress took their order, but since breakfast isn't the biggest or most important meal of the day, they ordered what the locals were having: some coffee and pao na chapa, a skillet-toasted French bread roll with butter and a variety of locally grown fruit.

Aceline waited until the waitress brought breakfast and left to ask, "Are you thinking of taking care of business today?"

The Iceman smiled and said, "That might raise a few eyebrows if four strangers fly in on the same day as Mr. Joao Ferreyra goes missing, don't you think?"

"Yes, of course."

"I think we should be seen doing some tourist-type activities for a couple of days. Got any suggestions?"

"Sure, there are a lot of great things to do and see."

"Great, what don't you set up some things, tours and activities for us to do and see, and be sure to include a tour of Jaú."

After eating breakfast, the Iceman looked at his team and said to Aceline, "While you're doing that, I think me and the boys are pretty knackered from that killer flight, so I think we'll go and grab us a little shut-eye."

"Shut-eye?"

"Sleep."

"Oh, okay. What time do you think you'd like to get together?"

He looked at his watch and held up five fingers.

Aceline stood up, shook all their hands, and said, "I'll see you at five. You all have a nice nap. Tchau, bye."

"Good evening, ladies and gentlemen, and welcome to a CNN special, 'Blood of the Beast.' I'm your host, Walter Chancellor, and we'll be joined with our correspondent, Josh Colman, who was with the David Leeway safari during what is now being called 'a massacre.' After our interview with Josh, he and his cameraman, Randy Gaines, have put together a documentary of the fateful day. So be sure to stick around for that. Welcome, Josh, and thank you for taking the time to be here."

"Thanks, Walter, my pleasure."

"Now, Josh, you were with David Leeway from the very beginning of the safari, is that right?"

"That's right. I contacted Mr. Leeway's office and asked if I might be able to join and document the safari, and they agreed. Providing we didn't get in the way, of course, which we assured them that that wouldn't be a problem."

"Now, the safari was in Zimbabwe."

"Yes, my cameraman and I met up with the safari in Hwange National Park, Zimbabwe. By the time we joined them, the security forces were already there, along with Louis Armour, the safari guide. Mr. Leeway was in the

process of planning his hunting campaign and developing a tactical plan in case of an attack, which he had counted on. He was actually looking forward to engaging with members of Le Gang de la Clé de Singe.

"He was seeking revenge for the killing of his two sons, David Thorndike Leeway and Richard 'Skippy' Leeway, and his daughter, Sasha Alexis Leeway. The three of them were killed while hunting big game in Africa by Le Gang de la Clé de Singe."

"Yes, The Gang claimed that they had killed a couple animals that had been placed on the endangered species list, so they were all killed after one of the Leeway sons, Skippy, reportedly shot a lion cub."

"That's true, Walter. They later released a video showing Richard 'Skippy' Leeway actually shooting the lion cub, then, a split second later, everyone in the hunting party was killed, with the exception of the porters and hired staff."

"So, Josh, tell us about David Leeway's hunting safari leading up to the attack."

"We were out on safari for about a week; David Leeway was keen on finding a particular elephant, Castor, who is a legend in those parts. He felt that if he could kill the notorious beast, he would coax Le Gang de la Clé de Singe out and deal with them on his terms. During the week before the attack, Mr. Leeway killed a male lion, two giraffes, four warthogs, and a Black Rhinoceros. He didn't seem to be enjoying himself, as he never did emote any real joy in either the hunting, tracking, or killing."

"What can you tell us about the day of the attack?"

"Well, his guide, Louis Armour, had gotten word that Castor, the elephant, had been seen recently in a certain area of the park the day before, so the whole caravan of armed Humvees started to head toward the GPS coordinates relayed to Armour. Which, in hindsight, they appear to have been a trap sent by Le Gang de la Clé de Singe, because they were laying in wait for us. No one seemed to be on edge or *on heightened alert; it seemed to be just another leisurely drive through the beautiful nature preserve, when, all of a sudden, there were a series of explosions set off by numerous roadside IED's. They destroyed the first four armored vehicles, killing or wounding all the members of the security forces in those Humvees."*

"So, Josh, this was totally unexpected? Neither Leeway nor the security team had any idea that you were in danger?"

"No. We all believed that nothing would happen until Leeway had killed Castor, the elephant. Everyone firmly believed that the confrontation wouldn't occur until after the death of Castor. They did send scouts out in advance, but, after more than a week of not finding any evidence of potential danger, the security forces became lazy and lax in their duty. They paid the price."

"Now, tell us what happened next. The first four vehicles had been destroyed, and then..."

"Well, the remaining three vehicles maneuvered into a circling of the wagons to create a sort of crude fortification. Leeway and Armour were in the fifth vehicle, and my cameraman and I were in the sixth. We all got out and hunkered down inside behind the tires of the vehicles because we were under heavy fire. The safari guide, Louis Armour, had taken charge, giving orders and overall taken command. David Leeway seemed to be in shock and, for the longest time, was unresponsive. Armour tried to negotiate with Le Gang de la Clé de Singe, and he went out to meet with them under a flag of truce, but to no avail. They said that there were to be no terms of surrender, no quarter shown, that anyone who was part of the safari security forces, hunters, or guides were destined to die. The only reason that Randy and myself were spared was that we had no involvement in the killing of any animals.

When Armour returned to the encampment, we were informed that this was a fatal situation, and that's when

Leeway remembered that he had arranged for an extra security support team that was supposed to aid if and when we were in trouble. He then contacted them, and, within an hour, there was a red flare that was fired. That was supposed to be the signal that help had arrived. By that time, most of our security team had been killed by sniper fire. Leeway arranged with what he believed to be our rescue team to enter the compound, but, as it turned out, they were in fact members of Le Gang de la Clé de Singe, who had killed the original members of the rescue team and were posing as them. In effect, David Leeway opened the door and let the killers in, They did just that; they entered the compound and killed all the remaining members of the security forces, Louis Armour, and David Leeway. Like I said, Randy and I were spared. They lined up all the animals that Leeway had killed and placed him and his guide beside them. Le Gang de la Clé de Singe then placed all of the other dead bodies side-by-side and put the traditional yellow Monkey Wrench flags around their necks."

"How were you and your cameraman treated once you were captured?"

"We were treated with kindness and were checked over by a medic. We were even able to speak with one of the leaders on camera, which you will see as part of my documentary, Blood of the Beast, *to be shown after my interview with Walter. After I spoke with the leader, they put us in one of the Hummvee's with enough food and water to last us five days, plus they gave us a pistol and ammunition for protection. We were told that someone should be arriving within a day or two, probably the Zimbabwean Army. Then, a couple of unmarked Huey helicopters arrived, and, in minutes, they were gone."*

"How long did you and Randy have to wait before the Zimbabwean Army came?"

"It was about two in the afternoon of the following day that a couple of Zimbabwean Army scouts came across

us. During the night, a herd of hyenas started to invade the compound, so Randy and I took turns firing shots at them through the night. We actually had to kill a couple so that they would go after their own instead of the people in the encampment. Once we were rescued, the Zimbabwean Army, Interpol, and the FBI interviewed us. Apparently, there were several members of Le Gang de la Clé de Singe that had been killed; it is my understanding that some, if not all, have been identified. We have also learned that several are Americans and that, once all the families have been notifie,; their names will be released."

"That is an amazing story, Josh, and we are all thankful that you are here and able to share it with us. Now, ladies and gentlemen, we are going to show Josh's documentary, titled Blood of the Beast. *We must warn you that some viewers might find some scenes disturbing; viewer discretion is advised."*

As Buzz headed out of the lagoon, heading towards White Bay to check on Bumbley, he called Bobby, his studio manager. "Hey, man, it's Buzz. What's up, brother?"

"Pretty slow, Buzz. How you doing?"

"Chilin like a villain. Any reason for me to come in, or are you guys cool, man?"

"We're all good here. You out on the boat?"

"Yeah, going out to see my buddy. I'll tell him you say hi."

"You do that and be careful."

"No worries, man. Love to all."

Buzz was weary of the Doc and her team, so he sailed out of the lagoon and headed in the opposite direction of the preserve towards Montego Bay. After about an hour, he was pretty sure he wasn't being followed, but he was still paranoid that they could be tracking him on radar. So, he waited until two similar sized yachts were passing in opposite directions, and then he changed course by pulling, basically, a U-turn and followed the eastbound yacht back towards White Bay. Bumbley was there waiting for him. Buzz didn't stop. Instead, he slowed down to a crawl and dropped him a four-foot sand shark that he had just caught fishing while making his way to the preserve. Buzz scanned the horizon to be sure he was alone and then continued sailing east for another half an hour just to be safe. He then made a sweeping arc westward, so as he could come back into the lagoon from the east. As he sailed past the Ogygia, there was no activity on deck that he could see. The sun was starting to dip behind the mountains, which bathed the lagoon in a soft-focus light; the clouds were a bright orange-red that gave the whole lagoon a golden aura.

Buzz went below to the galley and started to prepare dinner for the doctor. He lit up a doobie, getting his mellow on listening to CSN&Y and singing along to Suite Judy Blues Eyes. Bosco and Groucho, his ferrets, sat on the booth seats across from where Buzz was cutting up the veggies for his Caesar salad. Every now and then, he would toss them some scraps, which they patiently waited for and would even share with one another. Bosco stood on his hind legs and ran topside, then ran back and pawed at Buzz's leg. Buzz peered out the cabin window and saw that his dinner guest was on her way. Bosco had an acute sense of sound that Buzz had come to rely on to alert him, especially as he was a super sound sleeper. Although the waters were relatively safe, there had been the occasional incidence of piracy.

He helped Laura aboard, who was wearing a white classic tank dress with black brushstroke stripes and a slit up the side that was just south of modesty. She was wearing her hair up with simple pearl earrings. Buzz looked her up and down and said, "You look lovely this evening, Doc."

"Why thank you, Buzz. You look…rather fetching yourself."

Buzz had made the minimal effort to spiff himself up; he was wearing a faded blue chambray shirt, paint-stained khakis, and blue converse sneakers. He looked down at himself and back to her and said, "I try. Would you care for something to drink?"

"That would be nice."

"Right this way." He showed her below to the galley, where Bosco and Groucho popped their heads from under the captain's table. Buzz gestured for her to have a seat. "You two, scat," Buzz said with a wave of his hand. Both ferrets jumped down, scurried towards the guest cabin, and disappeared.

"What would you care to drink?"

"Oh, I'll have whatever you're having."

"Well, normally I would just have a beer, but, tonight, let's get crazy. How about a White Russian, my choice for special events?"

"White Russian sounds great. The table looks nice."

He had his back to her, mixing the drinks, so he peered over his shoulder in her direction. "Thanks. Dinner will be ready in about twenty minutes. Just enough time for us to get better acquainted." He placed her drink in front of her, as he slid into the bench facing her. He held up his drink. "Cheers."

"Cheers."

The glasses clinked, and they smiled at each other. With each one trying to size up the other, it was going to be an interesting game of cat and mouse. The question was: who was going to be the cat and who was going to be the mouse? Buzz decided to make the first move. "Any luck today?"

"Sadly, no."

"Ah, that's too bad. For you."

"What do you mean?"

"Bad for you, good for the fish, man."

"You don't approve of aquariums?"

"No, I do. Public aquariums but not for the pleasure and bragging rights of some rich fucks who could find better use of their money, man. I mean…" He stopped, took a drink, and smiled. "Sorry, didn't mean to go off on a rant."

She reached over and touched his hand. "It's okay. I understand, totally. You're a man of principles, and I respect that. But, it's an unfair world we live in, Buzz, and some of us get caught up in it."

"So, it's go along to get along, man?"

"Something like that," She said with a hint of embarrassment and shame.

Buzz was looking hard at her to see if she was giving off any tells of sincerity or deceit, but there was nothing. He thought to himself, she's trying to give the impression of being a victim of circumstance, caught up in something she has little control over. So far, he wasn't sold.

He smiled, as he pushed himself up from the bench. "Ready for some salad?"

She blinked as if she was coming out of a trance. "Yes, please."

He set her Caesar salad in front of her and his at his place, as he sat across from her. "Hope you like it."

She wasn't expecting much as she took a bite, but she stopped after one bite and said, "Last time I had an authentic Caesar salad was in New York. Buzz, I'm impressed."

"Aw, shucks. Twern't nothing."

"No, really, this is fabulous."

"Well, I'm glad you like it, man."

"Mmmm, I can't wait for the main course."

"Ackee and Saltfish, one of my especialalities."

"Buzz, you're amazing."

While Buzz and the good doctor were occupied with dinner, Black Jack and his team of six divers were making a final night search of the lagoon. At one point during their dinner, Buzz excused himself to go to the head. There, peaked out the porthole and saw lights in the depths of the lagoon. He was smiling when he returned to the table.

Aside from a few curious nurse sharks, there wasn't anything larger than Jacks' hand, so their dive lasted a little longer than an hour. When Jack got back onboard the mothership, he called the 'doctor' to report what they didn't find. Her cell phone rang. "Hello?"

Buzz stood and started to clear the table, placing the dirty dishes in the sink. He tried to nonchalantly listen in, but she held the phone tightly against her ear. All he heard from her was a lot of uhuh's and okay's. He could tell she was disappointed by her body language. When she hung up, she looked up at him and turned on a smile. "That was the Captain of the Ogygia, letting me know that we're all set to set sail tomorrow."

"That's a bummer, man."

"Well, there's no reason to stay if the giant grouper is just a legend." She stood up, walked over to him, and put her arms around his waist. "Is it only a legend, Buzz?"

"It's just a legend, Doc."

She pulled him close to her and gave him a long, slow kiss. Buzz was thinking, now she's dangerous, as she was counting on him to be seduced and let down his guard. She started to unbutton his chambray shirt. "Buzz, tell me about Bumbley." Buzz figured this was where he knew the evening would eventually come to, that proverbial fork in the road. And he remembered what Yogi Berra said: when you came to a fork in the road, take it. So he decided to take it. He started to unzip her dress, asking "What do you want to know?"

She stopped and looked into his eyes; she was a bit surprised that he gave in so easy and so quick. "Tell me everything."

As they made their way to his cabin, they were both losing articles of clothing—a shirt here, a bra there. By the time they covered the fifteen feet from the galley to the bed, they were both completely naked.

Sue-B and Fu Hao had been lying on a sheet of ice for a couple of hours, waiting for the sealers; they were lying within three hundred yards of a herd of sixty baby Harp seals. They were dressed in ECWCS, Extreme Cold Weather Clothing System that the United States Marines wore for winter combat. The outfit had a disruptive digitized snow camouflage print that was effective in various winter environments. They were going to be virtually invisible to the sealers at the distance they were positioned.

The French Aerospatiale C.22 drone was circling high above operated by Aleppo and Lu Wei aboard the forty-seven-foot Motor Lifeboat named King Edward I, which was skippered by Captain Snowy White, a French Canadian who captained a River Patrol Boat for three tours in Vietnam. Snowy was wounded twice and received the Star of Military Valour, the second highest military decoration one can receive, three times. He was a war legend in Quebec and even had his own statue in Melocheville standing next to the Canadian Vietnam Veterans Monument.

The sealing ship, the Lady Jane, was coming into sight of Sue-B and Fu Hao; they had been alerted to it by Lu Wei forty-five minutes earlier. The two ladies were ready to take action as soon as the sealers jumped off the ship and onto the ice floats where the baby Harp seal lay helpless. They waited until all fifteen sealers, each carrying a hakapikor club, started to advance towards the seal pups. As the first man raised his arm to strike and brought the club down, there was a large splatter of blood that covered the ice. But it wasn't seal blood; it was the hunters this time and not the hunted. It wasn't until the third man had fallen next to the intended victim that the other hunters realize that something was wrong. They all started screaming for the sealing ship to come and retrieve them off of the ice, but, one-by-one, they were all struck down.

Donald Dennison, the captain of the Lady Jane, called in a Mayday and for the Coast Guard to send help, that there were people being killed out on the ice flows. Moments after, he sent out his message: Allepo fired one of the AGM-12 Bullpup air-to-surface missiles, and the Lady Jane was no more.

The King Edward I picked up Sue-B and Fu Hao and took them to where each of their fifteen victims lay. Most lay feet if not inches from the baby Harp seals that they had intended to bash their heads in. The snipers gingerly placed the traditional yellow Monkey Wrench flags around each of the sealers necks, along with a note stating that the war on hunters has been expanded.

The CCGS Polaris, one of the fisheries patrol vessels that was assigned to patrol the Queen Elizabeth Islands of northern Canada in the Arctic Ocean, arrived at the coordinates north of Borden Island, which were provided in the distress signal that was sent by Captain Dennison of the Lady Jane. There, they only found a large oil slick on the surface of the water and a lot of floating debris. As they continued towards the ice flows, that's when they discovered the dead bodies of the fifteen sealers with the mark of Le Gang de la Clé de Singe placed around their necks.

The skipper of the Polaris, Captain Philippe Arnoux, ordered that the crew bring aboard all the dead sealers and their hakapikor clubs, plus any other evidence that they found brought onboard to present to the Royal Canadian Mounties for forensic analysis. Then, they were have their bodies covered and lay them side-by-side on the top deck. Once all the victims had been secured on deck, the first mate, Howard Johnston, reported to the captain that his orders had been completed. He handed Arnoux all fifteen Monkey Wrench flags that had been placed around their necks and fifteen copies of the letters put into each of the deceased's pockets.

Let it be known that, from this day forth, Le Gang de la Clé de Singe has expanded our declaration of war to sealer. Today marks the end of the fallacy that we humans were given divine dominion over the birds of the skies, the animals on land, and the creatures in the sea. Be forewarned, do so at your peril. You have been warned.

After reading the proclamation, he radioed back to Rankin Inlet, the search and rescue station on the Kudlulik Peninsula located on the northwestern Hudson Bay. It was between Chesterfield Inlet and Arviat, which is the regional center for the Kivalliq Region. The station was almost one thousand and two hundred miles away, so any assistance would be days away. Captain Arnoux was instructed to carry on a search of the area for the killers and to warn any other ships carrying out sealing that they too could come under attack.

The doctor cuddled up to Buzz and kissed him on the cheek, "Buzz, that was epic. Wow."

"Not bad for an old dude."

"I'll say. Not bad at all. I guess experience does count."

"Thank you, and I must say you were, in a word, incredible. That was nice."

She leaned up and rested her head on his chest, looking at him. "Bumbley?"

"Ah, yes, Bumbley. Tell me what you've heard."

"Well, we've heard of a giant grouper that lives in this lagoon. Apparently, it's very elusive. No one has ever taken a photograph of it, and there have been rare glimpses of it. Of course, there are the rumors that it has eaten divers who get too close or provoke it."

"And you believe that there is such a creature here in this lagoon after all your searches?"

"I believe that within every rumor, there is a grain of truth."

"Like werewolves and vampires?"

"Come on, Buzz. Those are just myths."

He just looked at her and smiled. "Okay, get ready for the ride of your life. Back in the twenties, during Prohibition, there was a Captain Roscoe Mackoy who began bringing rum from Montego Bay and the rest of Jamaica into south Florida through Governmant Cut. Although the buying and selling of rum was not illegal here, Roscoe thought that he could make a ton more dough bootlegging his own cheap, rotgut rum. Story has it, he would mix in any and everything he could find to spice it up, man. He used fish heads, toads, old sailing ropes and even liquor slop from the bar he owned in Kingston, called the "The Real Mackoy."

His stills were up in those hills above this lagoon, and he was producing hundreds of gallons of, quote, rum, unquote. He needed a place where he could stash his booze where people couldn't steal it. So, he filled watertight barrels with his liquor and kept them under the water here in this lagoon, man. And even if there was some leakage, it was common for captains to add water to the bottles to stretch their profits. They built, basically, corrals to keep the barrels contained, as I'm sure you and your team saw the remains of what looks like rebar fencing in your searches at the deeper end of the lagoon. Mackoy also stationed a couple of yachts with armed goons and machine guns mounted on their decks, setting both inside the lagoon and just outside in the open water, man.

Captain MacKoy had a rival, his nemesis, Havana Joe, who began a turf war. And they went at it tooth and nail; a lot of guys were killed. There was a big gun battle just outside the lagoon here, where Havana Joe teamed up with Al Capone to try and get rid of MacKoy and his gang. But Roscoe got a tipoff from one of Capone's guys that Havana Joe was planning on sending in a bunch of divers to blow up MacKoy's stash of rum. So a couple of days before the battle, he had his men chum the waters of the lagoon with cows blood, which naturally drew dozens of sharks. Capone's men never stood a chance. The story goes that only one diver survived, a guy named Skiff Tufnell, who lost his right hand in a fight with a nine-foot Hammerhead, only to be shot in a gunfight up in the hills behind us."

"All very fascinating, but what does all that have to do with the *Epinephelus Lanceolatus*?"

"I'm getting there, man. You got to learn to lighten up, Doc."

"Sorry," She said sheepishly.

"So, like from then on, this lagoon was dubbed Blood Lagoon. As you can imagine, it wasn't a big draw for the tourist crowd. By the end of Prohibition, MacKoy and his boys were either all killed or arrested, and the rum corrals were blown up by the US Navy, but the moniker for the lagoon stuck for decades. If you don't believe me, check it out on the Google, man."

He got out of bed. "Gotta pee, be back. Need anything?"

"No, hurry back."

The head was across from the guest cabin; when he closed the door, he didn't turn on the light. Instead, he peaked out the porthole to see if her divers were still searching. He didn't see anything, so he hoped that this would be the last of it." As he was returning to bed, he heard she was on the phone. "Yeah, I'll be back in the morning before we weigh anchor. Okay, okay, you just worry about yourself. Right. Bye."

"Everything cool?"

"Oh, yeah. Just letting Jack know that it's all good."

"Jack?"

"Jack, he's my team leader and den mother."

"Cool."

She sat up,crossed her legs, and put her arms on knees. Leaning forward, she rested her head on her hands, "Go on with your story."

"Would you like me to throw something over you; are you cold?"

"I'm fine. Does my being naked bother you?"

"Well, it is a bit distracting," He admitted, as he looked down.

"Oh, yeah. I see. Well, all the more reason to finish the story."

Buzz laid on the bed with his back against the headboard, resting his head on his crossed arms behind him. "Well, the lagoon remained Blood Lagoon until 1948, when Americans really took an interest in the Caribbean, and Jamaica and Cuba became hot destinations. So, skip forward to 1962, when the Governor-General, a dude named Sir Kenneth Blackburn, was given a kick in the ass from good old Queen Elizabeth II. She told him to get off his pompous butt and make Jamaica THE place to go, since Castro put the kibosh on travel to Cuba. Sir Blackburn called a meeting of all his cabinet members to gather ideas of shit they could do to make Jamaica the number one tourist destination. One of the first things they did was hire an American ad agency, Doyle Dane Bernbach outta New York, the hottest shop at the time."

"Oh, yeah. I've heard of them. They did those cool VW ads, 'Think Small and Lemon'."

"Right on, man. Well, one of the first things they told Sir Blackburn was he had to rewrite a bit of history. They told them that Americans weren't going to bring the kiddies to a beach called Blood Lagoon, for example. They said, 'hey you just might want to give it a warm and fuzzy name,' hence Luminous Lagoon. Sir Kenny and his crew set about homogenizing names and places so as not to frighten off the Americans. But, no matter how the tried, there was an underground tale of something freaky that happened in the lagoon. In 1983, Sir Floizel Glasspole was appointed Governor-General, and it just so happened that his Minister of Tourism was a cat named Boswell Bumbley the third. I'm not shitting you, look it up, man. Old Boswell had an idea that, instead of a shitload of sharks, one big fish would be more palatable. So, he leaked to the press and several other venues; he even paid several individuals to say that they saw a mysterious large fish that resembled a Goliath Bass Grouper. The locals named it Bumbley after the good Minister of Tourism, and there you have the story. And over the years, whenever anything unusual happened, they blamed it on the grouper— a diver has problems, a kayaker gets tipped over or a tourist drowns, it was Bumbley."

The Doc sat upright and slowly clapped. "Buzz, good story."

"Look it up, man. In fact, I'd be surprised if you hadn't."

"Well, to be honest, we did."

"So why did you have me go through it all, man?"

"Just checking; it's part of the job."

"And was this part of the job, too?"

"Oh, no, this was not job-related. In fact, I'm off the clock and could use some more personal recreational time if you're up to it, and I can see that you are."

Buzz saw the doctor off the Sweet Mary Jane around five-thirty, just as the sun was climbing above the horizon. He watched her as she climbed aboard the Ogygia, and he sat there smoking his pre-breakfast doobie as the ship silently headed west. He looked to see if he could see her; he thought that she might be standing by the railing and waving goodbye, but, alas, no. He wasn't one-hundred-percent sure she bought that load of crap that he told her last night, but they were leaving. About two years ago, he had salted Wikipedia with the story about MacKoy, Capone, Havana Joe, Boswell Bumbley and the whole thing, just in case something like this might happen.

Buzz waited until the Ogygia was completely gone before he set sail to go retrieve his friend. Buzz made his way out to White Bay, all the while searching for anybody that might be following him. Just because you're paranoid doesn't mean you're crazy. He couldn't shake the feeling that he was being observed; he scanned the horizon several times with his binoculars but didn't see anything. He heard a loud commotion from above; a couple of seagulls seemed to attack something. He looked up with his binocs and saw that the gulls were attacking a small drone about eight or nine-hundred-feet overhead. He hadn't seen it, because the drone was flying with the sun behind it. Buzz checked his location and started to let the yacht do a slow drift out to sea. As the SMJ slipped further out, he went below and loaded his Mossberg 500 Tactical shotgun. The ads say the 500 was built for military, police and law-abiding citizens, who were mission-ready for any scenario. Buzz wondered if the downing of a drone was ever considered in any of the scenarios the fine folks at Mossberg considered.

Buzz went topside, concealing the weapon, and checked his position readings—three point six seven miles into international waters. He raised his weapon and fired six rapid shots at the aerial menace. The drone fell like a stone and plopped into the water about a hundred yards to his starboard side; it just bobbed and just floated there until he retrieved it with a shrimp net.

On the left side of the small black drone was printed in large letters: *PROPERTY OF TYNAN INSTITUTE OF OCEANOGRAPHY*. Buzz checked the internet and found that the drone was an xFold Dragon X12 RTF U11 Drone with a 2x Radio Transmitter, retailing for about thirty-two thousand, and that's before the camera—nothing but the best for the good doctor. The damn thing was very sophisticated. Buzz wasn't sure that the transmitter would keep tracking him if he kept the damn thing on board, and he couldn't figure out how to shut it down, so he secured a lead weight to it and dropped it to the bottom of the sea. He thought maybe they could still observe some sea life, and, if they couldn't, fuck 'em.

About fifteen minutes later, his cell phone rang. "Hey, Buzz. Nice shooting."

"Yeah, thanks, man. Sorry about your drone, Doc."

"Where were you headed, Buzz? To meet up with Bumbley? You didn't really think I bought that cock & bull story of your's, did you?"

"Hey, man, you believe what you want."

"I don't give up that easy."

"I don't either."

"Buzz, you seem like a nice guy. You have no idea what you're going up against."

"Bring it on, Doc."

"We'll be seeing you, Buzz."

"Look forward to it, man."

When he got to the preserve, he hit the signal switch. In just a few minutes, Bumbley arose to just below the surface. Buzz tossed overboard two six-pound pork roasts, which were gone almost as soon as they the hit the water. A half-hour later, Buzz made sure his buddy was safe and all settled in. Then he set sail back to the dock and Bitchin Studios.

Aceline sat on a park bench in the Praca Sao Sebastia facing the Amazon Theatre, most commonly known as the grand opera house in the rainforest. She was eating her lunch and enjoying people watching, when the Iceman and team arrived.

She smiled at the four of them trying really hard to look like tourists; they were all wearing shorts and colorful Hawaiian shirts, some were carrying maps, two of them had cameras slung around their necks, and all were wearing baseball caps with sunglasses.

The Iceman smiled and waved, saying, "Boa tarde."

Aceline nodded and replied, "And a good afternoon to you, too. Have you all been enjoying your visit to the beauty of my city?"

Willie Tyler sat down next to her and said, "Yeah, my favorite site was the Meeting of Waters."

"Yes, it is quite unusual. The fact that when the Negro River's dark water and the Solimeoes River's murky water come together to form the Amazonas River, but that both rivers waters run side by side without mixing for over three miles, is amazingly beautiful. And the reason isn't totally clear."

Gianfranco said, "Yeah, that was pretty cool, but I'm a zoo guy myself, and I was really bummed out when we went to the CIGS Zoo; it's really a strange place, for sure. The fact that it's part of the army's jungle warfare-training center and soldiers on patrol captured many of the animals, just is freaky. I have to say that the animal enclosures range from the worst I've ever seen to some of the most sophisticated."

She agreed, saying, "I know, it's quite a paradox. The big cat collection is especially tremendous: black and spotted jaguars, cougars, leopards, and smaller cats. They also have toucans and macaws, but the harpy eagles are stuck in heartbreakingly small enclosures. And yet the monkey habitat is wide and well done; I don't get it."

The Iceman brought the subject back to why they were there. "Speaking of leopards, I think we've played the tourists long enough. I believe its time to go to work. Can you get us Mr. Joao Ferreyra's itinerary?"

She handed him a piece of paper with Ferreyra's schedule for the next three days. She explained that the man never travels alone; he always has at least one bodyguard, sometimes two.

The Iceman smiled and looked at his team. "The more the merrier, right, boys?"

They all laughed and agreed.

"Well, I want to thank you for everything, Aceline. We'll take it from here."

"What, that's it?"

"Listen, Aceline, we appreciate all your help, but things are going to get very ugly, and if something goes wrong…"

"I understand. I'd just get in the way."

"I'm not saying that. It's just, when the shit starts flying, we've all worked together in the past, so it just becomes an instinct, a split decision, a reaction. And having a new member can just kind of throw things off. Look, everyone plays a part in the success of a mission; we wouldn't be able to do this without you, so don't feel let down."

"I do understand, but it doesn't make it any less disappointing. Will I see you all again?"

"Probably not right away." He leaned down and gave her a hug and a kiss on the cheek. "You take care of yourself and, who knows, with all the assholes in the world, I'm sure there's a good chance we'll run into each other soon."

"Please be careful." She gave everyone a hug and a kiss, and then they were gone.

"Inspector Volker, I'm going to put you on speaker phone, if that's alright? I'd like Detective Davis to hear this too," Detective Matchet asked.

"Of course."

Matchet punched the speaker button on the fifty-year-old antiquated Western Electric black, plastic office desk phone that has never, other than a light dusting, been properly cleaned. "Okay, we're both here."

"Greetings to you both. I have some good news for you. I'm sure you've undoubtedly heard about the fatal attack on the David Leeway safari. Well, I just wanted to let you know that the killer in the Brittany Jones murder has been identified as Chase Madrid. As you know, he happened to be a member of the notorious Le Gang de la Clé de Singe, just as we suspected. He was, among other things, the murderer of the Minnesota dentist, Doctor Jimmy J.

Meriwether, who was beheaded and then had his head mounted on his office wall among his prized big game trophies."

"Yeah, we had heard about that. That's one sick puppy to carry out such heinous and vile crimes. How sick do you have to be to chop someone's head off and then feed another human being to a snake to be eaten alive? I just hope he suffered."

"I must say, I concur. Although, we have come to discover that his alias was the 'Angel of Death,' which seems quite appropriate under the circumstances. As far as did he suffer, I really couldn't say; we do know, though, that he died from multiple gunshot wounds."

" 'Angel of Death,' huh? Motherfucker. Any news about his accomplice, Bill Flannigan?"

"Actually, we feel he was pretty much an unwitting participant who seemed to have been duped into helping this man, and, at this point in time, we haven't been able to locate him. When we do, we will be sure to keep you abreast of any new developments as to his whereabouts."

"Well, we want to thank you for all of your assistance, Inspector Volker, and thank you for the news."

"You're quite welcome, chaps, and thank you for all your cooperation. Ciao."

When Volker hung up, his partner, Inspector Morris, asked, "Why did you tell them that?"

"Tell them what?"

"Well, we don't know definitely that Madrid did either of those murders, and we do know about Flannigan."

"Look, old man, everything points to Madrid, he fits the bill. Everything we know about him and his background; he was angry about being the fall guy in the military. We've heard from our profilers, and they believe that there is a very high probability that this is the guy. And you know that with this group unless somebody really screws the pooch, which they haven't yet, there is zero chance of making a definitive call as to who actually committed these crimes."

"Okay, well, what about Flannigan?"

"I know you didn't approve my handling of him, but don't you agree he was duped into helping Chase?"

"Duped? No, he had to have known something was hinky. When someone offers that kind of money, they're not going to be doing something charitable. He might not have to know the details, but no one is that stupid."

"Well, maybe you're right. But, without him, we wouldn't have gotten Madrid."

"Like I said, he was lucky having dealt with you and not me."

"Oh, I don't know. Living on the run, having to always look over your shoulder, isn't my idea of lucky.

Todd Styles and Buzz went way back to their days protesting the Viet Nam War while attending Santa Monica City College. Buzz was more of the peaceful protester, while Todd was the more aggressive activist. While Buzz would march and hand out protest leaflets, Todd would break into the ROTC building and set fire to files and throw bricks at the 'fascist pigs.' They both felt they were on the right side of history, and both had been arrested numerous times for various charges, but it was Todd who was involved in a bombing of a draft board facility in which several people were injured. Todd decided that he had to go underground before he was arrested, but he met with Buzz just before he disappeared. They met down in the Haight-Ashbury district at the Drugstore Café; Buzz didn't recognize Todd at first, as he was wearing a suit and had cut his hair. Todd sat down at the table across from him and held up a menu so that it hid his face; he kept looking around, being very paranoid. Buzz reached over and lowered Todd's menu. "Relax, man. You're freaking me out, man."

"Sorry, Buzz, but the man's after me, and I gotta get out of town, fast. Ya dig?"

"Where are you going to go?"

"I have an uncle in Montreal, thought I'd go up there for now."

"Is there anything I can do, man?"

"Can you lend me some bread, man?"

"How much you need?"

"Whatever you can spare."

"I brought $2,500. I figured you might need some help. Here ya go, man." Buzz slid the wad of cash over to Todd.

"Thanks, brother. I will repay you, I promise."

"Whatever, man. I just want you to be safe. Just let me know that you're doing okay whenever you can."

"Whenever you hear from your 'Cousin Jeffery,' that's me."

"Cousin Jeffery, got it. Now get the fuck outta here." Buzz and Todd stood up and gave each other a hug. As Todd walked out, he turned and gave Buzz a peace sign.

That was the last time he saw Todd.

Lu Wei and Aleppo sat at the controls in a small cabin just off the galley, operating the Aerospatiale C.22 drone; they had been keeping track of the Canadian Coast Guard cutter, Polaris, when Captain White ducked his head in the doorway and asked, "How's it going, boys?

Aleppo, still staring at the monitor, gave the captain a thumbs up and said, "All good, Captain."

"Where is the Polaris?"

"She's approximately forty nautical miles south-southeast. She looks to be stationary for the moment, however we've spotted another sealer heading our way; it should be within range in less than an hour."

"Thanks, I'll let the ladies know," He said, as he made his way to the main cabin where Sue-B and Fu Hao were seated at the table, cleaning their sniper rifles and adjusting the scopes.

"Ladies, I've just been informed by the flyboys that there's a sealer approaching. Should be arriving within an hour. Care to engage?"

Fu Hao snapped the scope into place, looked at Sue-B, who nodded, and said, "Let's rock 'n' roll."

"Great. I'll get you ladies into the ice with the pups when you're ready."

"Give us twenty minutes," Sue-B said, as she stood and zipped up her parka.

Sue-B and Fu Hao sat in the front of the zodiac as Weezer, the first-mate who took his alias from the band, manned the helm and slowly pulled up to a sheet of ice over thirty feet long and fifteen feet wide. They shared the ice with but one seal pup, who looked at them with wide-eyed wonder as they climbed onto the floating iceberg. They were situated in an excellent position, less than a hundred yards from the ice sheets that held dozens of seal pups, and, more importantly, they were downwind of where the sealer would be. As they got themselves into position, the seal pup slowly bounced its way closer until it snuggled up against Sue-B's leg.

Sue-B started to rub the little fur ball, which seemed to enjoy the attention so much that it rolled on to its back and allowed her to give it some belly rubs. Fu Hao smiled and said, "I don't understand how anyone could walk up with a club and bash its brains in. And for what, their fur? With all the man-made synthetic furs, it's criminal."

"Sealers approaching. Stay sharp, ladies," Lu Wei whispered into their earpieces.

They watched as the sealers' launch boat dropped off the hunters onto nine different sheets of ice; they counted twenty-two men on the ice. When the launch had pulled away and was sitting off away from the floating killing fields, Fu Hao took aim and fired her first shot, killing the helmsman of the launch and stranding the sealer on the ice flows.

She and Sue-B turned their attention at the marooned sealers. A few, seeing what was happening, decided to try and swim to the launch boat. But with it being too far and the water freezing at twenty-eight point eight degrees Fahrenheit, they all died of hypothermia within less than ten minutes.

Shortly after Sue-B and Fu Hao had been brought back onboard, Captain Snowy White heard the sealers' mothership send out an SOS distress call. Once it had been acknowledged he gave the order to Lu Wei to blow it out of the water.

By the time the Polaris reached the crime scene, the King Edward I was miles away. Captain Arnoux and his men, once again, found dead sealers with the yellow monkey wrench flags about their necks and notes declaring war on sealers and the like. The launch boat was still adrift with the bodies of the drowned men on board; there was a lot of debris floating nearby from their mother ship, the Louisa May.

One of the sealers had managed to kill one of the seal pups before he was gunned down, and there was something out of the ordinary about the scene that hadn't occurred before. They found a black & white Polaroid Photo of the dead baby seal lying next to the dead sealer, with a hand-printed note inscribed on the back: "*Do Good, Reap Good: Do Evil, Reap Evil.*" And upon close examination, there seemed to be a single clear fingerprint. Captain Arnoux smiled to himself and thought, got you.

Buzz headed back to the Sweet Mary Jane to check on Bumbley; he made a couple stops along the way.

His first stop was to the Burger King on the corner of Church Lane and St. James Street, where he had a Double Whopper, fries, and a chocolate shake. Then, he took a short walk up St James Street to his P.O. Box at the Post Office to pay some bills and get his mail. Then, there was another five-minute walk down to the Hi-Lo Supermarket on Orange Street to pick up some supplies for him and his buddy. Finally, after a quick in-and-out at the Western Union office, he made his way back to his van, where he loaded his stuff into the back and headed over to Tactical Accessories & Innovation in Postville Plaza to load up on ammo and sundry items of mass destruction. The old Hippie was ready to get it on with the 'Man,' but, this time, he wanted this to end by any means necessary.

He was aware that he had been followed since he left Bitchin Studios; he had spotted at least two of the tails. One, in a beat-up black 1990 Mercedes 190 E 2.5, and the other was riding a Honda Valkyrie motorcycle with flames painted on the tank and fenders; neither one was trying to be conspicuous. He thought they wanted him to know that he was under surveillance; that way he would get scared and make some slipups. Buzz decided to have some fun with them, though, so he drove over to the Freeport Police Station. Buzz got out of the van, flashed a peace sign to his followers, and smiled as he walked into the station. Buzz waited in the lobby for a few minutes until his old friend, Detective Clarke, came out. "Buzz! What do I owe the pleasure? Is there anything wrong?"

"I was just down at the Hi-Lo, man, and heading back to the dock, so I thought I'd stop by and say hello."

"Well, I'm glad you did. It's good to see you."

"Working on any interesting cases?"

"Just the usual police business, nothing exciting."

"I guess that could be a good thing, man."

"Buzz, are you sure everything is okay?"

"No, man, everything is cool. Well, like I said, just checking in. You be cool, and I'll check you later, man."

"Yeah, see ya, Buzz. You let me know if there's anything you need."

Buzz walked back to his van, waved to his tails, and then headed to the dock. As soon as he got onboard, he noticed that someone had been on the boat. But, as far as he could tell, nothing was missing. He figured that Black Jack and the boys had been on board and had installed some electronic gadgets and tracking devices. Buzz was under no illusions that they would do anything to get their hands on Bumbley. He thought of calling Detective Clarke, but thought better of it; he figured that, at some point, it could get messy with the cops involved. Besides, he had a couple of super sleuths already on board, Groucho and Bosco.

The two ferrets were very sensitive to strangers and anything that was new and out of the ordinary onboard the boat. They were acting extremely agitated, and, within minutes, they had pointed out nine different locations where various devices had been hidden. There was everything from a homing tracker to listening apparatuses, but Buzz decided to leave everything alone and just either work around them or try and use them to his advantage. He finished stowing away his supplies, grabbed a Red Stripe and headed topside to enjoy the evening. He laid down in his hammock, sipped his beer, and slowly drifted off to sleep with the gentle rocking of the boat in the marina. At two o'clock in the morning, his cell phone rang and woke him from a deep sleep. "Hello? Hey, man! Wow, man, it's been too long."

By first light, Buzz headed out of the marina, heading west, and sailed to Runaway Bay as a test to see if he could see who and how they were tracking him. He dropped anchor just off the Jewel Paradise Cove Resort & Spa and waited. He went below, away from prying eyes, and turned on some of his new toys that he purchased. First, he checked his Humminbird Helix 10 Sonar to see they were tracking him from below. Then, to see if they had eyes in the sky, he checked the Simrad 4G Broadband Radar, which could spy over thirty-two nautical miles in all directions. There didn't seem to be anyone anywhere, but he knew they had all those gadgets on board to know exactly where he was. He sat there fishing for over an hour, when he heard beeps coming from the radar. He went below and saw a blip on the screen heading his way from the east, and it was airborne and coming in fast and at about six hundred feet high. Buzz went back outside and continued to fish. He waited until he was sure they were spying on him, and then he got naked and dived into the water.

Afterward, he spread a towel on the deck and laid bare ass naked, sunbathing, and he actually fell asleep for about a half-hour. When he woke up, he went below to check the radar and sonar; he was alone. It was about one in the afternoon, so he decided to sail towards Ocho-Rios and stop at Reggae Beach. He arrived just before 3 o'clock, and, again, he dropped anchor. Sure enough, after an hour, the alarm from the radar alerted Buzz that the drone was present. Buzz made stops at White Bay National Coral Preserve and Luminous Lagoon, then back to the Marina. He repeated a random pattern of stops every day for over a week, so as not to give the impression that Bumbley was at any particular spot.

Bumbley wasn't use to all this moving from one location to another, although he did enjoy the rewards that came after each relocation. Besides the usual bill of fare of fish, octopus and sharks, there were also pork roasts, leg of lamb, and beef ribs. He enjoyed the treats, but he did miss his contact with his creature; it had been a long time. Not that he could tell time like a human, but he felt an emptiness, or maybe, like so many animals, there was just a routine that he was used to.

He had just returned to the lagoon and was getting settled within the coral reef after he received and finished off two pork shanks. He was tired after his swim from the White Bay National Coral Preserve all the way to Cousins Cove; it was a good four-hour trek, so he wasn't as alert as he normally would have been. He didn't notice the six divers heading in from the direction of the cove inlet, nor did he notice the other five divers approaching from the direction of the beach. Within minutes, he was snared within a net and being taken towards the surface. The creatures kept him there, immobile, until they hauled him out and plopped him into a small tank. They, then, transported him to the mothership, where they once again transferred him to another environment. Bumbley was getting stressed out with all the changes and unfamiliar sounds and sensations; he longed for his creature to comfort him.

"There he is," Gianfranco said, as he spotted the target exiting the restaurant CoCo Bambu Manaus. It was after midnight when he and three other men, who all appeared to be enjoying themselves way too much and looked to be slightly inebriated, stumbled out onto the sidewalk. They were gathered just off to the side of the restaurant, joking and laughing, waiting for their limos to pick them up. One-by-one, limos came and picked up the other men, and Ferreyra was getting annoyed that he was the last to be picked up. He kept looking at his watch, and, just as he reached for his cell phone, his limo arrived. He opened the door and got in.

"Ruben, where the hell have you been? I've been waiting for over ten minutes," He snarled, and then realized that the man driving the car wasn't Ruben. Bewildered, he asked, "You're not Ruben. Who the hell are you?"

As the limo pulled away from the restaurant and headed north on Avenue Coronel Teixerira, the driver turned to Ferreyra, smiled, and said, "Ruben got detained. My name is Johnny, Johnny Cubo de Gelo."

"Johnny Cubo de Gelo. Johnny Ice cube?"

"Right you are, but you can call me 'the Iceman'."

"What's going on?"

"Oh, just relax, Joao. We're going for a little fish dinner."

"I've just had dinner, and I don't like fish. I demand that you pull this car over and let me out right now!"

The Iceman pulled the car over, and, as Ferreyra tried to exit the car, Willie Gianfranco got into the vehicle. He forced Ferreyra back into the backseat, as T-Bone jumped into the front passenger seat.

T-Bone turned and said, "So, you're the dude who likes to eat leopards. You know, my Uncle Louie used to drive a Jaguar, and my cousin Billy once played for the Carolina Panthers. I also know a lot of rich dudes who think of themselves as 'fat cats,' but I ain't never heard of anyone eating one. Was it good?"

"I demand that you let me out of this car right now!"

T-Bone grinned and said, "You hear that fellas? The leopard eater demands that we let him out of the car. That's cute."

Willie, sitting to the left of Ferreyra, took his elbow and smashed it into his face, breaking his nose. He said, "Just sit there and shut the fuck up."

Ferreyra was seeing stars, as he held his hands up to his bleeding nose; he looked at the man sitting in the passenger seat and asked, "Just tell me what is it you want. Money? I can get you money. Just tell me that you're not going to hurt me."

T-Bone shook his head and said, "Well, Mr. Ferreyra, I'm afraid that's exactly what we're going to do. We're going to hurt you, bad."

But why? What did I ever do to you?"

"Have you ever heard of Le Gang de la Clé de Singe?"

Ferreyra nodded. "Is that what this is about, the leopard? If you let me go, I promise I will never do anything like that again, promise."

"Well, I'm afraid it doesn't work like that. You see, we have a strict rule: there are no do over's, no mulligan's, no second chances. You fuck up, you die."

"But, I have money. I can pay. You all will be rich."

"Well, you see, Mr. Ferreyra, that's the problem right there. The world can always get more money, but once there aren't any more leopards, well, then that's it. No more. You dig?"

"Isn't there anything I can say or do?"

The Iceman looked in the review mirror and said, "You can die with dignity, like the leopard you killed."

The limo stopped at an empty parking lot next to the Marina Do Davi, where they made their way to a twenty-foot Boston Whaler 210 Montauk, which appeared to be all decked out for an evening of fishing. The Iceman showed Ferreyra the Glock 9mm he had in his hand, as he told him to get aboard. Ferreyra did as he was told and took a seat in the stern of the boat, sitting next to T-Bone and Willie. Gianfranco untied the lines, as the Iceman started up the engine and steered the Whaler out of the marina. They snaked their way to the small fishing village of Barcelos.

Having slipped past Barcelos unnoticed, they sailed past the little petrol station at Santo Antonio. Then, they motored on for another six miles off onto the small tributary of Rio Cuiuni, where they finally cut the engine and dropped anchor. There was a full moon showing itself every now and then, peeking through the clouds. And, for at least fifteen minutes, it showed brightly and revealed a structure sticking up out of the water. It consisted of two upright posts with a crossbar connecting them; it resembled an American football goal post, but it was sitting in the middle of the narrow rivulet.

Willie stood up and gestured for Ferreyra to do the same. "Okay, Ferreyra, strip."

"Strip?"

"That's right, strip, everything off."

Ferreyra started crying and begging, as he unbuttoned his shirt. "Please, I beg you. Please."

Willie was about to punch Ferreyra again, when the Iceman said, "Willie, no! Mr. Ferreyra, what you did was beyond cruel; that leopard sacrificed its life for your glutinous pleasure. If there is one thing that you might take away from this, it is that maybe your death will be sending a message to all the other thoughtless assholes like yourself to think twice before committing such atrocities against Mother Nature. So, in a way, think of this as you sacrificing your life to save other leopards. Quite a noble cause, don't you think?"

Ferreyra stood naked and shivering, as Willie and T-Bone placed a gag into his mouth. They, then, fitted him into a six-inch leather harness strap that went around his chest and under his arms. It buckled in the back and attached to a rope, which ran through a pulley connected to the center beam. As they began to host him up, he was desperately trying to keep his feet on the boat deck, but to no avail. In seconds, his flailing swung away from the Whaler. He was swinging back and forth under the crossbeam, swaying three-feet above the water between the two upright posts. He swung there, kicking wildly for a few minutes, until he tired to get himself out. Then, he just hung there like a life-sized piñata.

Gianfranco weighed anchor, and the Whaler slowly drifted towards Ferreyra. When they were next to him, the Iceman pulled out an eight-inch fishing fillet knife and made several deep cuts to Ferreyra's legs. That's when he realized what manner of death he was in for: piranhas. Ferreyra's eyes bugged out, and he tried screaming. But for all his effort, hardly a sound was heard due to the gag.

The boat drifted away from Ferreyra, who was now so terrified that he actually soiled himself. As Willie started to slowly lower Ferreyra into the river, the droplets of blood were causing the water to seem to churn and bubble due to the waiting devilfish's excitement. Ferreyra was kicking frantically; his muffled screams were desperately hysterical. Each time his legs came out of the water, the more they were bleeding where the piranhas had bitten him. Occasionally, a fish would even still be attached, gnawing at the flesh and muscle. Willie continued lowering Ferreyra's body into the river, down to the waist, and then tied him off so only his upper torso was above water. The piranhas were in such a frenzy, they were now jumping out of the water and taking chunks of flesh out of his chest and arms; after four minutes, Joao Ferreyra was dead, as half his body had been eaten away.

The Iceman placed the traditional yellow monkey wrench flag around his neck and nailed a letter to the cross beam above his head. Then, they sailed down the river and back to the Marina Do Davi unnoticed. They arrived at the airport by six o'clock in the morning to catch their flight to Jamaica.

As he passed through customs, the customs agent, while examining the Iceman's passport, inquired, "Did you enjoy your stay here in Manaus?"

"Yes, very much."

"What did you enjoy the most?"

"The fishing," he said with a grin.

"Good evening. I'm Nigel Williams, and this is the BBC World News. Our top story this hour is from Manaus, Brazil. The half-eaten body of Joao Ferreyra was discovered this morning, suspended between two posts in a tributary of the Rio Cuiuni River. Authorities believe that he was lowered into piranha-infested waters and allowed to be eaten alive. The eco-terrorist group Le Gang de la Clé de Singe has taken responsibility, claiming that this action was taken in response to Mr. Ferreura having killed an endangered leopard. He then made a leopard stew from the animal, ate it, and then went on social media and bragged about it, saying he looked forward to doing it again.

"This is the latest incident in a string of such a brutal nature, that the United Nations have unanimously declared

war on the organization; this is the first time that every member nation, except for the tiny island nation of Kiribati, has agreed to form a unified coalition to take arms against a single foe.

"The group Le Gang de la Clé de Singe has released a response, stating that they will continue their war against anyone or any nation who pursues what Le Gang de la Clé de Singe considers to be acts of aggression against nature and the Earth.

"Their exact quote was, 'Bring it on!' "

As Buzz was heading back to the marina, the sun setting over the mountains above Montego Bay, his cell phone rang. "Buzz."

"Hey, Doc."

"Buzz, I just wanted to say goodbye. This time, we're really leaving."

"Really?"

"Yes, we're really going."

"Why?"

"Buzz, we got what we came for."

"Bullshit, man!"

"I'm afraid not. We found Bumbley in Cousins Cove."

Buzz felt like his gut had been shot. "Leave him alone; he doesn't deserve to live his life in a glass bowl, man."

"Sorry, Buzz. I really am, but business is business. He'll have a great life where he's going."

"Fuck!"

"I've called to ask if you'd like to see him before we go?"

"Where are you?"

"We're anchored just off Sandy Bay. We're shoving off around midnight for Brazil."

"I don't know, man. I don't think I could stand to see him like that."

"Well, if you change your mind…"

"Yeah."

"Buzz? I really am sorry."

Buzz ended the call and placed another. "Cousin Jeffrey?"

Aboard the Polaris, Captain Arnoux was awaiting the results of the single fingerprint that they found on the photograph left behind by the killers of the sealers, which he had sent to Canadian Naval Intelligence for identification.

He had been informed that the Canadian Coast Guard was sending an additional six patrol boats and a light cruiser to patrol the waters in and around the Queen Elizabeth Islands. His orders were to seek out, capture, and/or destroy those terrorists. Unfortunately, the group of islands allowed for plenty of hiding places and small inlets in which a small craft could easily hide. Conversely, there weren't any villages to stock up on supplies or any refueling opportunities. So with the current weather conditions seeming to take turn to the worst, things looked like they might work out in Canada's favor.

Meanwhile, Captain Snowy White was well aware of the shortcomings of the environment, so, a month before the expedition, he had laid supplies and hidden fuel in a small fjord on the north side of Little Cornwallis Island. It was not visible if one would be passing by and was only accessible to a small craft no larger than fifty feet. He had been keying in on the communications between the Coast Guard and Captain Arnoux, so he was well aware that the opposition was starting to be more aggressive. From then on, the use of the drone was a two-edged sword; on one hand, it would've allowed them to keep track of the enemy, and yet, if they weren't extremely vigilant and careful, the Canadians could've used it to track and destroy them. As the weather started to turn bad, all they could do was sit tight and wait out the storm, knowing that the sealers and the Coast Guard would have to do the same. The inlet where they sat was going to give them fairly good shelter from the storm, which was expected to last for five to six days. There was nothing to do except ride the storm out, so it was a good thing they had plenty of DVD's, books, and interesting company to keep them occupied.

Snowy went down below to the galley, where he saw Sue-B and Fu Hao talking with Aleppo and Lu Wei. It looked like they were going over the latest aerial photos that the drone had taken as to the location of the seal pups and the sealers. Due to the pending storm, the seal pups were, for the time being, safe.

When Sue-B noticed Snowy, she asked, "Hey, Cap, what's the good word?"

"Well, looks like we're all going to be in for a bit of foul weather, but we shouldn't get too must up. We're sitting in a good spot; the storm is coming in from the south, and, since we've got the island to our back, it shouldn't be bad at all. Now you know things can change, and we'll be keeping our eye on it, but I don't expect too much trouble."

"And what about the sealers?" Fu Hao inquired.

"Well, I suspect they and our Coast Guard friends will be having a bit of a rough go of it, being stuck out to sea."

"Aw, boo fucking hoo," Sue-B said, smiling.

Lu Wei interjected with some concern, "You know, Captain, with no drone, we don't know who's where."

"I know. We're going to have to do things old school until the storm passes. You shouldn't be concerned, though. It's true we can't see them, but they can't see us either. Plus, we're sitting still while they're moving, so we can track them with sonar and satellite imaging. Unless they have an idea where we are, it's going to be near impossible for them to locate us. So, I wouldn't lose any sleep over it."

Black Jack walked up to Doctor Runnel, who was standing at the port-side rail just outside the bridge. "You didn't really think he'd come, did you?"

"Actually, I did."

"He fought the good fight, but the old hippie didn't stand a chance."

"I'm just glad nobody was hurt like last time."

"Hey, that asshole shouldn't have pulled a gun."

"You're lucky you got out alive, never mind not getting arrested."

"Listen, Doc, I do whatever it takes. That's what you pay me for."

"Not murder!"

"I say it was self-defense."

She looked at her watch. "Go tell the Captain to set sail."

Jose Perez was born into the second wealthiest family in Mexico in 1958. The Perez family acquired its wealth as Mexico's largest private Copper Mine owner. Jose was expected to follow the tradition of following in his father's footsteps and eventually taking over the reins of the family business, but he had other plans.

Jose lived a privileged life, went to the best private prep schools in Switzerland, and then to Harvard Business School. As a young boy growing up in Mexico, he became an excellent horseman, learning to play polo at the age of five on his family's five hundred-thousand-acre ranch, called Rancho Cabeza de Cobre, located three hundred miles west of Mexico City.

During his days at the prestigious prep school, the Collège Champittet, which was located just minutes away from Lake Geneva, he played on the varsity polo team. That landed him a full scholarship to Harvard. He was offered scholarships to Yale and Cornell but chose Harvard, in part, because they had oldest intercollegiate polo program in the

U.S, the Harvard Polo Club, which built a tradition of polo at the University dating back to 1883.

Because of his outstanding abilities, he was voted captain of the Harvard polo team as a freshman, which was unheard of, and led the Harvard Crimson to three straight UDPA National Intercollegiate Championships. Because of his dedication and passion, he earned the nickname of JoLo, which he wore as a badge of honor.

After graduating with honors from Harvard, he joined the Mexican National Polo Team, while slowly getting involved in the family copper business. Polo was his first priority, though, and, in his second year, they won nearly every possible tournament in the game, including the Argentinean Triple Crown of Hurlingham, Tortuguitas, and Palermo. That same year, he also won the US Open and the British Open Gold Cup, becoming the only the fourth player in history to win the Grand Slam of Polo.

While playing in Argentina, he met a young woman, Micaela Sanchez, who was enjoying some time off from working as a climatologist with the World Wildlife Fund, where she was studying the effects of climate change on the Green Turtle populations of the Galapagos Islands.

Micaela found, while researching the effects of climate change, that the bigger issue was the illegal trade for their meat, eggs, or shells. She was so enraged that she wrote an article that was published in the National Academy of Sciences, decrying the plight of not only the Galapagos Islands Green Turtles but also the Iguanas, the Blue-footed Booby, and the Galapagos Giant Tortoise.

Several days later, she received an email stating that a man, who went by the username Cadillac, had read her article and said that he was in a position to help if she indeed wanted this poaching to come to an end. She replied that she indeed wanted to put an end to the poaching and would appreciate any assistance they could provide. She asked, *"by the way, who are you?"*

Three days later, a forty-seven-foot catamaran cruiser, named the Queen Anne's Revenge, after the pirate Blackbeard's ship, anchored off the island of Puerto Baquerizo Moreno, the capital of Galapagos Province. Its aluminum hull was painted black with pitch black sails, and atop its mainsail flew a bright yellow flag with a black skull and two black crossed monkey wrenches. Once anchored in Shipwreck Bay harbor, three men headed to shore in a zodiac, where they tied off at the pier of hotel Casa Opuntia.

After they checked in to the hotel, they headed over to the Mockingbird Café & Internet, where they had arranged to meet with Micaela for lunch. When they arrived, she was sitting at a table in a corner, drinking a Colada Morada and eating an order of the Carne Fritas. The three men introduced themselves; the one who called himself Cadillac was tall, muscular, and resembled the actor Andy Garcia. The second man was shorter and not in as good of shape; he had shaggy blond hair with a Van Dyke beard. He called himself Street. The third man looked to be over fifty, short, and dumpy. He just nodded and smiled, but it turned out that he was a deaf-mute, named Mickey. They sat down on either side of her, and each ordered the Pescado ala plancha with a bottle of the local beer, Amaru.

Cadillac took a sip of his cerveza and asked, "Have you ever heard of Le Gang de la Clé de Singe?"

She nodded and said, "I have heard that you take revenge on poachers so as to send a message to others that there will be a price to pay for the stealing and killing on creatures for profit. Am I right?"

Street took a bite of his grilled fish and said, "Right you are. But, we always want to let people know just what they could be getting themselves into by associating themselves with us. We have been declared terrorists by most countries in the world, and, if we're caught, we will be shown no mercy, just as we show no mercy to the people that we capture and kill. You understand that's what we're going to do to anyone we catch poaching the animals of the Galapagos? We're going to kill them, and, sometimes, in a brutal way so as to send a powerful message to the world."

"I understand, but, so far, nothing else has worked. There just aren't enough government patrols to put a dent into the amount of poaching. Plus, if they do get caught, it's usually a small fine or a slap on the wrist as far as jail time. Something has to be done to save these animals."

Cadillac asked, "Do you know any of these poachers, and could you point some of them out to us, discreetly?"

"I do. I thought you might want to know, so I made a list here in my purse."

"Don't pass it to us now; wait until we get outside. We want you to not to be too involved, so as to protect you as much as possible. Once you've given us the list, we won't be contacting you again. If you need to reach us, let me give you my business card." He handed her a plain white business card with the name Buster Harrington, and below his name was an international phone number.

The four of them got up and walked out of the café. As they shook hands goodbye, she slipped Street a folded piece of paper with six names on it. As the trio walked away, she noticed Street signing to Mickey, letting him know what transpired. After they went their separate ways, she never saw any of them again.

Eight months had passed since her encounter with Cadillac and Street, and nothing. There was nothing in the newspapers, nothing on the radio, and nothing on TV. She figured that something more important probably had taken priority, and, soon, she got busy with her projects, forgetting alll about it and planning a vacation to Argentina. For two weeks in Buenos Aires, she had it all planned out—day trips to the National Museum of Fine Arts, The Metropolitan Cathedral, Teatro Colon Opera House, the Evita Museum, and, of course, the Argentinean Triple Crown of Hurlingham polo match.

Micaela wasn't model beautiful, but there was elegance, charisma, and a natural beauty that attracted Jose Perez to her. She was sitting alone at the bar in the Restaurante i Latina, enjoying an order of Mollejas en Aji Panka Y Naranja, when Jose, while trying to avoid bumping into the waitress, bumped into Micaela spilled her Red Pepper Margarita.

"I am so sorry, Miss. Please excuse me."

"It's quite all right; accidents do happen."

"Please, let me buy you another drink." As he sat down beside her, he waved to the bartender. "Sir! Another drink for the young lady, and I'll have a Negroni."

He smiled, held out his hand, and said, "Hi, I'm Jose, Jose Perez."

She shook his hand and replied, "Hi, I'm Micaela Sanchez."

"Are you from Buenos Aires?"

"No, are you familiar with Argentina?"

He shook his head.

"Well, I'm from a small fishing village called Puerto Deseado, about seventeen hundred kilometers south. And you, where are you from?"

"Mexico City. Have you've ever been?"

"No, I've never been north of the Equator. What brings you to Buenos Aires?"

"Polo. I play on the Mexican National Polo Team; we're here to play at Hurlingham, tomorrow. Do you like polo?"

"Yes, I do. In fact, I have a ticket for tomorrow's match."

The bartender came and brought the drinks. As he set them down, Jose said to him, "Can I get what the lady is having? It looks delicious." He turned to her and asked, "If you don't mind?"

She smiled and said, "I would love it."

"What do you do, Micaela Sanchez?"

"I'm a climatologist with the World Wildlife Fund, currently studying the effects of climate change on the Galapagos Islands."

"Wow, I'm truly impressed. That sounds like very rewarding work. Not like someone riding around on a horse and trying to hit a little, white ball. Although, I am involved in running my family's business."

"Oh, what kind of business?"

"My family has one of the largest copper mines in all of Mexico. And, I might add, one of the most environmentally friendly and safest mines in the world."

"Wow, now I am impressed. And here I thought your only talent was to be able to hit a ball while atop a horse, muy bien."

"Gracias. I would be honored if you would be my personal guest at tomorrows match."

"That's very kind of you. I would love it, Mr. Perez."

"Jose, please. Well, actually, my closest friends call me JoLo."

"Well, JoLo, my friends call me Micaela."

At about one o'clock in the morning, the Ogygia finally got underway; she was sailing along the west coast, passing Lucea, Orange Bay, and then she headed down to Negril, where she was going to take a hard turn to the southeast towards Aruba. Continuing, she followed the coast of Venezuela past Guyana, Suriname, French Guiana, and on to Rio. That was the plan, but it was funny how some plans never turned out how you thought they should.

Sitting just off the coast of Little Bay, on the southern tip of western Jamaica, were twelve Scorpio Stealth Zodiacs. Each had six heavily armed mercenaries, who were all dressed in black, wearing balaclavas, and waiting for the Ogugia to pass by.

At four-thirty in the morning, the Ogugia came into sight, the order was given, and the twelve teams of eco-warriors launched their Zodiacs. There was a new moon, so the night was pitch black; there wasn't any night watch on deck, and, on the bridge, there was only the first mate sitting at the wheel and half asleep. The first Zodiac reached the stern of the vessel and unloaded its team with ease, and each of the other teams successfully boarded the Ogugia without any problems. They all had been thoroughly briefed as to their assignments and went into action with weapons drawn, much like a SWAT or SEAL team on a mission.

The Red and Blue teams were assigned to take control of the vessel; the Red team moved up to the bridge and secured it, as well as the communication room, whereas the Blue team got control of the engine room. It was up to the other teams to round up the crew and bring them all to the mess hall, which they did. All assignments were completed by five-twenty.

Black Jack Williams was awoken from a sound sleep in the bed of marine biologist Tia Guarascio, a twenty-two-year-old grad student from USC on her first summer internship with Tynan Institute of Oceanography. Doctor Runnel, at first, thought that this was some kind of stupid prank perpetrated by Jack and some of the others but soon came to realize that this was no joke. She had heard of the terrorist group Le Gang de la Clé de Singe and knew they were not to be trifled with; they were known to kill those who resisted.

When she was brought into the mess hall with everyone else they were made to sit at the dining tables with their hands in front of them; their hands were to remain flat on the tables, no exceptions and no arguments. Any resistance would be met with swift punishment. The leader spoke with an American accent that had just a hint of French. They communicated with each other primarily through hand signals.

As they sat at the tables, one of the intruders was calling their names off of a roster list, and, as they acknowledged themselves, someone would put a black cover over their heads. Since Jack Williams was one of the last names to be called, so he tried to glean as much information to give to the authorities as possible. Ss he was making his observation, he noticed that there something familiar about one of the terrorists, something about his eyes, the way he moved. After he acknowledged his name, though, everything went black.

There was silence for what seemed to be ten minutes, before the leader spoke, "Listen up! We are Le Gang de la Clé de Singe, or, in English, The Monkey Wrench Gang. You are all prisoners of war; you will be treated as such. We have no intention of harming you as long as you obey our orders. But, if you resist or interfere in any way, you will be dealt with harshly. There will be no talking unless we engage you, and you will keep your hands flat on the table in front of you. Any deviation will result in punishment. If you have any special needs, such as the use of medication or having to use the bathroom, slowly, and I repeat, slowly, raise your right hand. Someone will come and assist you. We will not answer any questions. Once again, any attempt to interfere with our mission will result in swift repercussions."

Down below, where they kept the specimens, the Green team, a specialized team of marine biologists, was inspecting the marine captives. When they were satisfied, they radioed up to Rodin, "We're good to go."

"Copy that, Green team." He scanned the mess hall to see if all was good; then he held up his right arm with a clenched fist and gave a pumping up and down motion. Half of the Red and Blue teams silently slipped out of the mess hall and went down to give a hand with the Green team's preparation to transport the specimens to the ship that was now coming alongside the Ogugia.

Rodin walked out to the starboard side railing and radioed the captain of the Maximilien Robespierre, a specially equipped cargo vessel that was used primarily to rescue and care for all forms of marine life, including mammals. When pursuing and intercepting Japanese whaling ships, they performed rescues and had given medical attention to wounded whales.

"Mike • Uniform • Romeo. This is Bravo • Uniform • Zulu • Zulu, do you read me? Over."

"Bravo • Uniform • Zulu • Zulu, this is Mike • Uniform • Romeo, we read you loud and clear. Over."

"We are a Go! Over."

"Copy that, Go. Over"

A team from the Robespierre fired a series of repelling ropes over to the Yellow team, who was waiting on the Ogugia to secure the ropes in order to transport the captured specimens from the Ogugia to the Robespierre where they would be examined, cared for, and then released back into their natural habitats.

Buzz was standing by the large glass tank, where his old friend was being held. He wondered if Bumbley knew it was him all dressed in black. He pulled off his balaclava but got no reaction from the large fish. Buzz heard steps of someone approaching and quickly pulled his balaclava back on. "Relax, it's just me," He heard his old friend say, as he put his hand on Buzz's shoulder.

"I can't thank you enough for doing this for me, man."

"Well, mon ami, it wasn't just for you. We do it for these magnificent creatures."

"I know."

"So, have you decided what we're going to do with this beast?"

"What do you mean, man?"

"Well, we could put him back in the lagoon, but what's going to stop another organization from coming for Bumbley, and, maybe the next time, they won't be interested in just capturing him?"

Buzz hadn't thought about that, as he was so focused on just saving his friend. "I don't know, man."

Rodin said, "Buzz, you've got some time to think about it. In fact, once we get all these safely on board the other ship, I'll have you talk to one of our specialists. Okay? But we got to start offloading these puppies to the mother ship. The clock is ticking; it will be light in a couple hours. Why don't you come on up to the mess hall with me and let these guys do what they do best?"

"Okay."

As they headed topside to the mess hall, Rodin asked Buzz, "Would you consider joining the team? We could always use a good man in the gang."

Buzz paused and thought for a few moments before he answered, "I don't know, man. That's some heavy shit to think about."

"That's cool. I wouldn't want you to commit without thinking it through."

After their meeting with Micaela, Cadillac, Street, and Mickey nosed around some of the less high-brow drinking establishments and picked up some scuttlebutt about a gathering of poached items that might be going on the market on a nearby Island. So, the next day, the Queen Anne's Revenge sailed southwest to the tiny island of Isla Floreana, where she dropped anchor just off the rocky beach of Puerto Velazco Ibarra.

Cadillac and Street went ashore, and Mickey stayed on board to keep things ready just in case they needed to make a quick getaway. They headed to a small café, La Canchalagua, where they sat at the bar and ordered the local favorite, Chaquinan IPA, on tap. After several more rounds of cervezas, two men came into the café and asked the bartender where they might find a man called Carlos Obando. Carlos Obando was one of the names on the list that Micaela had given them; the bartender leaned close to the two men and whispered, "Habitacion Cinco. Hospedaje El Pajad." One of the men, then, handed the bartender a US Twenty Dollar bill, and then they left.

After ten minutes, Street and Cadillac finished their beers and paid the tab. They bid the bartender goodbye and headed towards the Hospedaje El Pajad, which was clear on the other side of town, about four blocks away.

The Hospedaje El Pajad was unique because the rooms were actually open spaces without beds and with hammocks suspended from the ceiling, instead. There was no need for air conditioning, as there was a continuous ocean breeze blowing. It was rather nice, except for in the rainy season when they dropped some canvas screens to keep most of the rain out—not all, but most.

Street and Cadillac rented the 'room' next to where the meeting of eight men was going on. As they were setting up their room, they hanged the hammocks and acted like they weren't eavesdropping. The men were speaking Spanish and watching the two strangers to see if they were able to understand what they were saying. At one point, one of the men asked the others if they should kill the two gringos who were listening. But Cadillac and Street, although they did speak and understand Spanish, played dumb and didn't react to any of the taunts and threats. After they set up their room, they tested out the hammocks, which were surprisingly comfortable. After a few minutes, they decided to leave, as they had picked up all the information they needed to complete their mission. As they were leaving, they waved to their neighbors, and Street said, "Bye, guys. See you later."

The meeting wasn't about buying and selling poached items; it was a plan for that night's raid on a Green Turtle hatchery beach on the neighboring island of Isla Espanola. Their plan was to sail to the north side of the island to the beach of Bahia Gardner, wait until midnight when the full moon would be at its brightest, and be ready for when the newly hatched turtles would scamper towards the ocean.

There, they would be waiting to scoop them up by the hundreds.

The Queen Anne's Revenge weighed anchor as soon as Street and Cadillac got onboard and set sail for the island of Isla Espanola. When they arrived, Mickey dropped Street and Cadillac off onto the beach, and he took the Queen Anne's Revenge and sailed her to the little island of Isla Gardner, which sat less than a mile off of Bahia Gardner beach, and dropped anchor.

Bahia Gardner beach was crescent-shaped, and the hatched turtles were located at the west end of the beach, so Street and Cadillac positioned themselves down on the very east end, hunkered down, and waited. They waited close to three hours, before Mickey spotted the poachers boat and alerted Street and Cadillac by using Morris Code on the wireless.

Street and Cadillac started making their way west, towards the poachers; the beach was very bright from the full moon, so they hugged the line of heavy vegetation and edged the beach so as not to be noticed. As they inched closer, they saw the men had started a bonfire and were starting to drink guarapo, a fermented alcoholic drink made from sugarcane.

By the time Street and Cadillac were within striking distance, the six men were pretty well shit-faced and in no condition to resist. Cadillac held them prisoner with his Smith & Wesson M2.0 9mm pistol, while Street tied their hands behind their backs and bound their feet together. They asked each man his name and checked their names off of the list of known poachers that Micaela had provided them.

They asked them in Spanish if the had heard of Le Gang de la Clé de Singe, which they all said they had. Street, then, placed the traditional monkey wrench flags around their necks and a letter within a plastic bag in each of their pants pockets. Street and Cadillac then proceeded to dig six holes in the sand near the water's edge. The tide was at its low ebb, so they placed each man to stand in their own separate hole. They buried them each up to the neck, so only their heads remained above ground. The men were all pleading for forgiveness and leniency, but Street told them that Le Gang de la Clé de Singe never gave and never expected mercy.

As Street and Cadillac started to take the poachers boat back to the Queen Anne's Revenge, they noticed, as the tide had started to come in, that the newly hatched baby Green Turtles were beginning to make their journey to the sea. By the time Street and Cadillac were on board the Queen Anne's Revenge, the cries from the poachers went silent, as the rising tide had risen about their heads. Onboard the poachers boat, the federales found the fingerprints of the poachers and one single fingerprint of Che Guevara on a note that simply read, *"Viva la Revolucion"*.

The storm had sat over the Queen Elizabeth Islands for over a week, pounding the ships out at sea. Their main course of action was just to survive, as the storm was categorized as a Category Five, with winds exceeding one hundred and fifty-six miles per hour and seas with waves breaking at over seventy feet high on top of the puny Coast Guard ships for five days straight. There were times when Captain Arnoux was sure they were going to flounder and go down, which would have surely meant all hands would have been lost. But, with a bit of luck and the skill of his Helmsmen, they managed to ride the beast out. Even the most hardened salty sailors admitted to being scared shitless at times, but only to themselves.

On board the King Edward I, Captain Snowy White and crew actually had a relativity calm week, as they were sheltered from the storm while sitting in the inlet. Snowy figured it would be another week before the sealers would be back out. Everyone was getting itchy to be back out there, though, as they had checked and rechecked their equipment and were ready to go. Aleppo and Lu Wei asked and received permission from Snowy to send the drone up and see what was going on, just in case there were a couple of eager sealers wanting to get a jump on the others.

In just under two hours, they discovered that there were, in fact, two sealing ships not all that far away, heading in their direction towards a large ice flow with several hundred seal pups. Captain White gave the order to set sail for the flows. They would reach the ice flows hours ahead of the sealers, giving them plenty of time to get Sue-B and Fu Hao in position.

"Captain, we just downloaded some images from the drone; it showed a small vessel heading out from an inlet on the north side of Little Cornwallis Island. She seems to be heading towards a large body of ice flows, which appears to have a large colony of baby Harp seals. There looks to be two sealing ships that are heading in that direction, as well."

"Thank you, Lieutenant." Captain Arnoux turned to the Helmsmen at the wheel and shouted orders, "Helmsmen, set a new course for Little Cornwallis Island."

"Aye, Aye, Captain."

The Lieutenant waited until the Captain finished giving his orders to tell him, "Captain, we just received word from RNC Intelligence that they've identified the fingerprint found on that photograph."

"Great, whose was it?"

"You're not going to believe it, Sir. Gordie Howe."

"Gordie Howe, the hockey player? But he's dead."

During those two weeks in Buenos Aires, Joe and Micaela spent every day together. She went to all the polo matches and practices with him, and he went to all the tourist attractions with her. They had realized that this was more than a summer romance; it had the potential to become much more than that. His polo season was coming to an end in three months, and they talked about his coming to visit her in the Galapagos Islands after the season was over.

One night, after dinner, they went back to his hotel. While they were lying in bed together, after making love, he couldn't go to sleep, so he asked if she would mind if he watched a little television. As he was surfing through the channels, he happened to stop on CNN World News, where there was a breaking news story about how Ecuadorian Police discovered the bodies of six men who were known poachers of Galapagos wildlife.

As Jose was about to change channels, Micaela sat up and said she had to hear this. The story, as best as the local police could piece together, was that all six men's feet and hands were bound tight, and they were placed into holes dug into the sand, buried with only their heads exposed. They were buried at low tide, so, when the tide rose, they were slowly drowned and died an agonizing death. The beach that they were buried on was a known Green Turtle hatchery. All six were found with Le Gang de la Clé de Singe trademark skull and crossed monkey wrench yellow flags, which were placed around their necks and accompanied with a note stating that all poachers beware, for the same fate awaited them if they continued their evil ways.

Micaela started to cry, and Jose tried to console her, asking, "Micaela, did you know these men?"

She confided in him and swore that she had no idea that they would do such a thing. She only thought that they would frighten them, not kill them. She asked if should turn herself into the police. Jose said definitely not, and that those type of men were destroying the environment and looting the world of these beautiful creatures for profit. He felt that, sometimes, a message like the one Le Gang de la Clé de Singe was sending was the only kind of message that those type of men understood. He asked her if she thought that she could make contact with this group again, and he told her that he was inspired by her courageous actions. He possibly even wanted to get involved. She asked him, "Do you think you are capable of doing such a thing as personally taking a life?"

"No, but I feel that there may be other ways to help. I might be able to help in the financing, or maybe the logistics; these coordinated actions cannot be cheap. They travel the world, combating these evil deeds, so somebody, or some corporations, and maybe even some governments, must be helping. Micaela, I feel like you do, that our world is running out of time when it comes to the mass extinction of the world's wildlife, the pollution, and destruction of our planet. You shouldn't feel guilty; just think of all the Green Turtles and other animals' lives you helped save."

"Inspector Volker is here."

"Please show him in."

"Mr. Perez, thank you for seeing me and taking time out of your busy schedule of running one of the largest copper mines in Mexico."

"Like I said on the phone, Inspector, I really don't know anything about those killings in the Galapagos Islands. I'm afraid you might have traveled all this way to Mexico for nothing."

"I don't think so, Mr. Perez. Might I ask if you happen to be the same Jose Perez, the international polo legend, JoLo?"

"Well, I don't know about legend, but I do play polo."

"It's quite an honor to meet you, Mr. Perez. I'm a huge fan."

"Thank you, and, please, call me Joe."

"Would it be presumptuous of me to call you JoLo?"

"Not at all, Inspector. Please do."

"Fantastic, the boys at Interpol will be so jealous. Ah, but I digress. The reason I'm here, actually, is that it's my understanding that you're currently involved with a Micaela

Sanchez, who works with the World Wildlife Foundation, is that correct?"

"Yes, that is correct."

"Isn't Ms. Sanchez currently studying the effects of climate change on the Green Turtle population in the Galapagos?"

"Yes, but—"

"We believe that those men, those poachers, were killed because they were involved in poaching Green Turtles, and Ms. Sanchez is involved in Green Turtles. We know that Micaela Sanchez contacted Le Gang de la Clé de Singe and gave their agents the names of the six poachers that she wanted to be targeted."

"Inspector, I can assure you that Micaela Sanchez would never."

Volker held up his hand and smiled. "I also know that you've expressed interested in aiding and abetting Le Gang de la Clé de Singe, am I right, JoLo?

"I think I would like a lawyer."

"You know, Le Gang de la Clé de Singe depends on men like you, powerful men who want to help save the environment, men who feel that they can help more by staying anonymous, working behind the scenes and financing the frontline troops. Men like you, JoLo, and men like me. Am I right?"

"I don't understand. Whose side are you on, Inspector?"

"If you're serious about helping, there is someone I'd like you to speak to."

"I am interested."

He took a burner phone out of his coat pocket and dialed a number. "Hello. Yes, I do believe he is interested. Okay, hold on." Volker handed the phone to Jose and whispered, "Its United States SEAL Team Commander William T. "Wooch" Brown."

Jose took the phone, still unsure, and said, "Hello?"

"Wooch here."

Bumbley stared out of his tank, looking at the creatures moving all about. He couldn't distinguish one from another, although he noticed that one of them was moving up towards the surface of his tank. He slowly moved away from the creature and headed towards the opposite end of the tank, when he noticed the creature was partially in the water. After a few minutes, he experienced a familiar scent. He cautiously moved towards the creature, when, all of a sudden, a large leg of lamb plopped into the water; Bumbley consumed it in a flash and approached the creature, realizing that it was his friend. He came up to Buzz's feet, and Buzz began rubbing his feet on Bumbley's back. The large fish liked it, as it gave him a sense of calm.

When it came time for the extraction team to move the grouper, Buzz made sure that they treated the mammoth beast with extra care. Bumbley's tank was covered, so he couldn't see anything; it was complete darkness. It took less than a half an hour for Bumbley to be safe aboard the Robespierre. Once they got confirmation that he was secure, Buzz and Rodin started to make their way up to the bridge.

Sitting with his hands flat on the table, Black Jack had formulated a plan of resistance. He wasn't the type to sit idly by and let shit happen without a fight. He raised his hands and waited for someone to come; he didn't have to wait long. A male voice asked what he wanted. "I have to use the head," Jack said. The man took hold of his shirt and said, "Okay, just take it easy. I'll guide you," as he lifted on Jacks shirt. Jack slowly got up, swung his legs over the bench, and started slowly moving towards the head. His captor was being very gentle with him; there wasn't any manhandling of him, which Jack hoped would work in his favor. He could tell, by the smell, that they were in the head. He was led to the urinal, and the man said, "Here you go; the urinal is right in front of you. Sorry, I can't free your hands. You'll just have to manage."

"Thanks." Jack was counting on the fact that the man wouldn't watch him too closely as he relieved himself. He unzipped his fly and started to pee. At the same time, he slowly moved his hands to his belt buckle, which contained a Bowen wide double-edged knife. He maneuvered the knife in his hands and cut the tie almost all the way. He wasn't sure, if he cut it completely, if the guard would notice, so he erred on the side of caution. Jack strained to hear if there was anyone else nearby; he didn't hear anything.

After he zipped up his pants, he felt the guard's hands on his shoulders, guiding him to turn around to head back to the mess hall; that's when he struck. He cut the ties off his wrists and spun around, jabbing the blade into the guard's neck, while covering the man's mouth so as to not allow his screams to be heard. The guard let out a muffled cry and was dead within seconds. Jack quickly lowered the dead man and ripped off his black cover. Then went to the bathroom door and peeked out, ready to attack, but the corridor was clear.

He checked the guard for weapons and was surprised that all the man had was a truncheon. Well, as he learned in the SEALS, you make the best out of what you have. He, then, dragged the guard into one of the two stalls and set him down. Sitting on the toilet, he locked the door from the inside, climbed over the stall, and started toward the bridge. As he was making his way to the upper deck, he heard a couple of voices approaching from behind him; he quickly darted into a storage cabin and waited.

As Rodin and Buzz reached the corridor, which split off to either head up to the bridge or straight to go to the mess hall, they stopped just short of the cabin where Jack hid. "Why don't you head back to the mess hall, and I'll come to get you in a few minutes. Then we can discuss what you want to do," Rodin said.

"Far out, man. I'll see you later."

Jack's eyes got as big as saucers, and then a fiery rage set in when he heard that voice; it was that fucking hippie, he said to himself. Just as Buzz passed the cabin door, he felt a hand grab his shoulder and drag him into the room. "Hey man, careful!" Buzz yelled as he fell to the deck. Rodin was halfway down the hall when he heard something. He quickly turned around and didn't see Buzz. A bad feeling came over him, as he pulled his 9mm Glock 17 with mounted suppressor and red-dot sight; he, then, slowly started easing down the corridor, when he heard voices.

"Hey, asshole! Remember me?" Jack asked, as he ripped the balaclava from Buzz's head.

"How could I forget you, man?"

"Come on, get up, you old hippie freak." He grabbed Buzz and put a chokehold on him from behind with his left arm, while holding the knife blade against his neck with his right hand, and led him out into the corridor to where all the specimens were stored. The area was clear, as the transfer of the specimens hadn't begun yet. They were walking on a gangway above all the tanks, and they stopped over the tank holding Bumbley. Black Jack held the knife to Buzz's throat and said, "So, you're responsible for all this just because we stole that fucking fish?"

Buzz could see that Bumbley had swum up towards the surface, looking up at them, when he said, "That's right, asshole."

They heard the sound of a 9mm Glock being cocked and turned to see a commando figure, who stepped out from a connecting passageway and held a revolver at eye level. "Let him go, and no one will get hurt." Jack could see the gun had a red dot mount and sensed the dot focusing on him. Jack pushed the blade ever so slightly into Buzz's neck to draw some blood and accentuate that he was in the catbird's seat. "Either you drop the gun, or the hippie dies."

Rodin stood motionless, processing his options.

Jack pushed the knife a little further into Buzz's neck. "Last chance, or he dies."

Rodin smiled and whispered, "Fuck you."

Buzz saw a flash, heard a pop, and then felt a misty spray on his face. The chokehold loosened, and then he was standing there alone. Jack's body staggered backwards and started to fall into the tank where Bumbley was; the mammoth fish dropped down below the surface, turned and got a running start upwards, his mammoth mouth wide open. As Black Jack hit the water, Bumbley swallowed the man whole. Then he meandered downward to the bottom, leaving Buzz and Rodin totally gobsmacked. Buzz turned to his friend and said, "That's fucking weird, man; that's fucking weird. He has done nothing like that before. I guess there's just no accounting for taste."

Rodin walked up to Buzz, looked at the wound on his neck, and talked into the radio attached to his shoulder, "This is Rainbow Leader. I need a medic on B Deck A-SAP." He patted Buzz's face. "You'll be fine. It's no biggie, just a precaution."

"Did you see that man?"

"Fuck him. That dick killed one of my men. I'm sure he would have killed you, too."

"Thanks, man."

The medic came running down the passageway. She knelt down by Jack's lifeless body and felt for a pulse She shook her head, stood up, and looked at Buzz. "Looks like you'll need a couple stitches, come with me." As she took him away, Buzz looked back at his friend and flashed a peace sign.

Rodin nodded. "See you on the bridge in a few minutes."

Rodin entered the mess hall. All of the crew of the Ogygia were seated quietly with their hands flat on the tables in front of them, with the exception of one empty chair. He moved to the center of the room. "Can I have your attention, please!" He could see that everyone's body stiffened. "Our mission is almost done here. We will be leaving your ship shortly, however we will be leaving a small contingency onboard until the majority are safely away. We are going to set a timer in here. When that timer alarm goes off, you will be free to get up. Do not attempt to get up before the timer goes off. If you do, and my men are still onboard, you will be shot! Is that understood? I want a verbal acknowledgment from each of you. Do you understand?" In unison, they all said yes and nodded their heads.

"Good! Red leader, proceed."

"Aye, aye, sir."

Rodin made his way up to the bridge where Buzz and a half a dozen members of Le Gang de la Clé de Singe, along with the Captain and first mate of the Ogygia, were waiting. Rodin went over to the Captain and said, "Captain, we are returning your vessel back to you. We have temporarily disabled your communication capabilities, and all cell phone calls will be blocked, which will last for six hours; you should also know that we have placed several explosive and monitoring devices onboard your ship. If we find out that you have tried to communicate with anyone, or if you deviate from the course that we have set for you, your ship will be sunk. We disavow any responsibility of injury or deaths if you do not follow these orders exactly as I have stated. Do you understand?"

"Yes, I understand."

"Good. Red leader, move your men out. Captain, I have informed the crew seated in the mess hall that they are not to leave until a signal has been given. I want you and your first mate to stay on the bridge and not leave for at least one hour, you're being watched."

"I understand."

With that, the team from Le Gang de la Clé de Singe left the Ogygia and made their way to the Maximilien Robespierre, at which point all lines were severed and the ship steamed off towards Cuba. Rodin went up to the bridge and called down to the TelCom room, "This is Rainbow leader. Status on the Ogygia?"

"Rainbow leader, they are behaving. No rouge actions detected."

"Roger. Keep an eye on them. Over."

"Roger that."

Then Rodin switched on the ship's intercom. "This Rainbow leader, may I have your attention, please? I just wanted to congratulate everyone on a job well done. Unfortunately, during our mission, we lost one of our own, Fonte Mwanajuma, who served with Le Gang de la Clé de Singe for more than six years. He will be missed. Please join us on deck at eighteen hundred hours to bid farewell to our brave comrade in arms. Over."

He then headed down to the ships mess hall, looking for Buzz. "Hey, buddy, how you doing? Let's see that neck." He tilted Buzz's head to the left. "I think you'll live."

"Thanks again, man."

"So, have you given any thought to the Bee?"

"I'm torn, man. I just don't know."

"Well, why don't you talk to one of our oceanographers? I can have somebody come on, and you two can figure it out. We have to decide pretty quickly, as we have a mission down in the Antarctic. Those fucking Japanese are down there killing whales again, so we're going to send some Japanese scrap iron to the bottom of the sea."

"I would like someone to talk to; I want to do what's best for Bumbley."

"Okay, sit tight and I'll have her come right up. Her name is Doctor Alcosta." With that, he got up and left the mess hall. Buzz sat in a booth tucked away in a corner, drinking a hot cup of Bosco in honor of his ferrets. Buzz was feeling tired and drowsy, when a middle-aged woman wearing what looked to Buzz to be a khaki uniform. She walked over to him and held out her hand. "Buzz, I'm Doctor

Alcosta. I understand you have some questions. I hope I can help."

Buzz proceeded to tell her the saga of Bumbley Bee, about how they came to meet and the friendship, at least on his part, with the giant grouper. Was he crazy to think that the fish might have some sort of feeling for him, or was that all in his head and wishful thinking? He told her of the plot to capture the behemoth, and that and wasn't sure what he should do; he just wanted to what was best for Bumbley. She sat patiently listening, smiling, and being very sympathetic; she could see that he was emotionally connected to the grouper and knew that he genuinely wanted what would be best for Bumbley.

"Buzz, would you say that Bumbley was dependent upon you, or do you think he could survive by himself?"

"Well, he did survive before I meet him, so I would have to say he'd be fine without me."

"From what I can tell, he is a magnificent specimen and one that could help the gene pool, if you know what I mean."

"Sorta put him out to stud, as it were?"

"Exactly. We're on our way to the Antarctic and will pass by some of the best breeding grounds for *Epinephelus Lanceolatus*. If you decide to let us release him there, I'm sure he will have a very good life, but, remember, it's out where mother nature can be cruel. He'd have to make it on his own—no BBQ ribs or leg of lamb out there. I just want you to go in with all the facts."

"Thanks, Doc, I appreciate it. I think he deserves a little of the wildlife. He's a tough old bird like me, and I believe he should have his shot with the ladies. He's quite the looker, am I right?"

"He is that, Buzz. He is that."

Tā moko is the marking of the face and body as traditionally practiced by Maori, the indigenous people of

New Zealand. It is different from tattooing, in that the skin is carved, not punctured. The tattoos are usually spirals in a symmetrical pattern, and each one is unique unto itself.

Around the 1860's, men stopped performing Tā moko with the change in fashion and acceptance, but, in 1990, there was a resurgence in both men and women, as a sign of cultural identity and a reflection of the general revival of the language and culture.

On Iraia Ngata's eighteenth birthday, he shaved his head and went to see his village's Tohunga-ta-moko, or their 'tattooist,' to receive his facial moko. His face was marked from forehead to throat, creating a mask-like effect, which enhanced his face's bone structure, strengthened his features, and confirmed him as a warrior.

Iraia was a large boy, at six foot three and weighing two hundred and eighty pounds, he was a star high school rugby player with ambitions to one day play on New Zealand's national rugby union team, the All Blacks. Unfortunately, two days before he was to try out for the Junior All Blacks team, while surfing off of Papamoa Beach, he was attacked by a fifteen-foot Tiger Shark that tore a softball size chunk out of his left calf, ending his dreams of ever playing professional rugby.

During the long days of hospitalization and rehabilitation, Iraia got bored sitting around all day watching TV and playing video games, so he started reading. The first book he chose was Herman Melville's *Moby Dick*; the fictional character of Queequeg, the son of a South Sea chieftain who left home to explore the world, captivated Iraia, especially once he was aboard the whaling ship, Pequod, and became a harpooner.

Although Queequeg was supposed to come from the fictional island of Rokovoko, the way Melville described the native made Iraia feel a strange kinship to the tattooed cannibal. When he eventually joined Le Gang de la Clé de Singe, he chose the name Queequeg.

It happened shortly after he was released from the rehab center. He had taken a trip to Wellington to visit his great-grandfather, when, by chance, he was approached by a Greenpeace volunteer, who was asking for donations to help aid in their "war" against Japan's whaling operations in the Antarctica Ocean. It just so happened that Greenpeace's Rainbow Warrior was in Wellington for refueling and taking on supplies. Iraia went down to where the ship was docked and signed up as a deckhand.

Iraia enjoyed his time with Greenpeace, but he always felt a bit frustrated while they played by the rules; the other guys didn't. So, when he heard about Le Gang de la Clé de Singe and how they said, 'Fuck the rules; there are no rules, just results,' he switched parties and went with the bad boys of the environmental wars.

During a campaign against a group of poachers, who were killing and stealing kiwis and their eggs for private collectors, Queequeg met and worked with the Iceman and his team. They were successful in ending the poaching epidemic, and they captured two of the poachers who had a dozen kiwi eggs and three of the dead birds, which they were carrying in backpacks. The Iceman had Queequeg saw the beaks off of the birds and bring them and the tiny bodies to him, where the two captives were gagged and bound against a Kauri tree, their pants and underwear down around their ankles. The Iceman had taken the gags off, momentarily, to stuff the dead kiwis into their mouths. He, then, duct taped their mouths and had one of the female members of the team induce the poachers to have an erection, where he inserted a four-inch kiwi beak up into each man's penis.

They left the men bound to the trees with the yellow monkey wrench flags around their necks and a note, which stated that this and more would happen to kiwi poachers. Four days later, the men were found dead and news spread like wildfire. Four and a half days later, all poaching stopped.

Days after the assignment, Queequeg realized that, while handling the dead birds, he had inadvertently cut his left index finger, and it had gotten infected. Since the team's deployment for their next operation wasn't scheduled for another week, Queequeg took the opportunity to go to a clinic for stitches and some antibiotics.

"Good evening. This is Josh Colman, CNN Breaking News. Tonight, we bring you the stories of three revenge killings from the notorious international group of eco-terrorists, Le Gang de la Clé de Singe.

"We will start with the killing in Manaus, Brazil of Joao Ferreyra, who had boasted of killing an endangered leopard before making it into a stew and eating it. The killers abducted Mr. Ferreyra after attending a dinner with friends; they, then, took him to a boat in the Marina Do Davi and sailed up the Rio Cuiuni, where they hung him in between two poles and lowered his body halfway into the piranha-infested waters. He was eaten alive.

"The second recent killing spree took place off the Queen Elizabeth Islands in the waters of the Arctic in Northern Canada. Over thirty men, known as sealers, were shot to death, and two sealing ships were sunk with all hands onboard. The men hunted baby Harp seals; they used a club called a hakapik to bash the baby seals brains to a pulp until they were dead. Le Gang de la Clé de Singe has declared that the killing of these sealers was far more humane than the method they use for killing the baby seals and are unregretful.

"And the third killing involved six known turtle poachers, who were bound by the hands and feet, and then buried up to their necks on the beach of the island Isla Espanola at low tide. When the tide came in, they were drowned to death. The beach, Bahia Gardner, is known as a Green Turtle hatchery. It is off limits to the public this time

of year because of the turtle's eggs hatching and migrating to the sea.

of year because of the turtle's eggs hatching and migrating to the sea.

"Stay tuned for a discussion with our panel of experts, right after the break."

Snowy and the crew of the King Edward I were sailing away from the ice flow where Sue-B and Fu Hao had taken a position, when Lu Wei called up to the bridge.

"Captain, Lu Wei here. We have received photos from the drone that a coast guard vessel has been spotted; it is estimated to be three to four hours from here. It looks like it is definitely heading in our direction."

"Copy that. What is the ETA of the sealers?"

"Looks to be within the half hour, sir."

"Well, I think we should be in good shape to get the job done and get the hell out of Dodge. Keep me posted if things change."

"Aye, aye, sir."

Sue-B and Fu Hao were in position; they were separated by a hundred yards, and each was on ice flows that gave them the high ground overlooking the colonies of baby seals. They maintained their positions for over an hour, when the sealer ship came into view. Fu Hao spotted them first and radioed Sue-B, "Here they come."

"Roger that. I see them."

"Wait for my signal."

"Roger."

The sealer ship lowered two zodiacs, with twelve to fifteen men in each launch. As the first launch headed toward the colony of baby seals, Sue-B noticed that two of the men in each of the boats were armed with AR-15's. She alerted Fu Hao, and they quickly decided that the first course of action was to take the armed guards before disposing of the others.

Fu Hao whispered into her headset, "We'll take out the closest hunters first, because the first group will have become more spread out and will be farther from their launch."

"Right. That will give us more time, so we won't feel rushed."

The first group of twelve sealers landed onto an ice flow where a colony of forty seals lay. The two men with AR-15's stood at the ready while the sealers, armed with their hakapiks, headed towards the baby seals. Moments later, the second group of sealers landed on an ice flow three hundred feet to the right of the first group. Again, as with the first group, the two armed men with AR-15's landed first while the sealers got out of the zodiac and moved towards the colony of baby seals.

Fu Hao took aim on the armed men on ice flow number one and said to Sue-B, "I'll take the one wearing the fur hat; you take the one with the red jacket. Then, you go for the armed man closest to us wearing the red and black pea coat, and I'll take the other one. After they're down, just open fire."

Sue-B lined up the man in the red jacket and answered, "Roger."

As she squeezed the trigger, Fu Hao said, "Go."

The two men stood motionless, as their heads emitted a fine red mist that drifted down around them, coloring the bright white snow blood red. They both fell forward onto their knees and then dropped face-down onto the ground. The second team of armed men was unaware of what had occurred behind them, same as the men on the ice flow. One started to react to seeing their armed guards lying dead, just as the two armed guards succumbed to the same fate, dropping down to the ground with the backs of their heads blown away.

The female assassins started their assault on the sealers, who were running towards the zodiacs. As Fu Hao was shooting at the sealers, Sue-B took out both of the pilots of the zodiacs, leaving the sealers stranded on the ice flows.

Several of the trapped men picked up baby seals and were holding them up as shields, hoping that the snipers wouldn't try and shoot at them. Unfortunately for them, Fu Hao was such an excellent shot that it was said she could split an atom. The only harm that came to the baby seals that were used as shields was that a few of their furs were no longer pristine white.

Again, like before, the ice flows were littered with a mixture of baby Harp seals and dead sealers. This time, no one even got close to try for the zodiacs. The French Aerospatiale C.22 drone that was circling high above, watching over Sue-B and Fu Hao, once again fired on the sealer's ship, the Summer Breeze, striking her just below the water line on the starboard side. She sank in under nine minutes. As far as they could tell, there were only three survivors clinging to bits of debris in the freezing waters.

Captain White was about to give full discretion to Fu Hao and Sue-B as to let these survivors live or not, when he got an urgent call from Aleppo, saying that they spotted a Coast Guard Cutter steaming in their direction. Snowy radioed the two ladies of the ice fields and told them to get ready to be picked up, as they had been spotted and were prepared to get underway ASAP. Weezer was there in minutes, piloting the zodiac, and they were all onboard and under full sail within eight minutes. As they were leaving the area, Fu Hao climbed up the mainsail to the crow's nest and killed all three while sailing away from the scene.

Weezer looked at Snowy and said, "You don't ever want to fuck with her."

"Amen, brother. Amen.

The Maximilien Robespierre had sailed between the Paracel Islands and Da Nang, Viet Nam and was sitting just off Vinh Van Phong Sea, waiting to rendezvous with a small yacht, the Sweet Mary Jane.

After what was called the Ogygia Massacre, Buzz returned to his yacht to undertake an eleven-month journey, sailing halfway around the world to meet up with the mother ship, Maximilien Robespierre, off the coast of Vietnam. There, they were going to release Bumbley Bee back to the waters of his birth.

Buzz hadn't seen his old friend, Rodin, since he had saved his life or his buddy the Bee either. He wondered if Bumbley would remember him. Once aboard, he met with Doctor Alcosta and discussed the procedure of release. Before they released Bumbley, Buzz donned a wetsuit and scuba gear and got into the tank. He entered the water and presented the behemoth with something very special: twelve pounds of Vietnamese stewed pork stomach, which Bumbley scoffed down in a nano-second, and then Buzz gave the big boy a long-awaited back scratch.

Buzz and Rodin spent the night before Bumbley's release sharing some beers and a few joints, enjoying their time together while knowing that this might be the last time they see each other. Buzz was planning on staying in Vinh Van Phong, keeping an eye on Bumbley and out of trouble. Rodin thought that it might be Bumbley who would be keeping Buzz out of trouble.

As for Rodin, he had to fly out the next day. He had a score to settle with a gentleman in Switzerland, and then he accepted a new assignment in Indonesia, taking care of some Komodo Dragon poachers.

They stayed up all night, and, when the sun came up, Buzz took Rodin ashore to make his way to Ho Chi Minh City and catch his flight to Geneva.

"You take care of yourself and that oversized sardine. Hopefully, we'll see each other soon, my friend."

"May the force be with you, brother. I love ya, man. We'll be waiting for you."

Rodin waved as Buzz took the zodiac back to the Sweet Mary Jane to await the reintroduction of the

Epinephelus Lanceolatus back into its natural habitat. By the time he got onboard, Rodin was gone.

Later that morning, Dr. Alcosta and crew released Bumbley into the waters off Hon Lon Island. They planted a special transmitter on Bumbley in hopes that Buzz would be able to keep track of him. Once they had facilitated Bumbley's release, they said their goodbyes to Buzz and set sail down to the Timor Sea off of Australia's Northern Territory. There, they were scheduled to release other species that were taken for the private aquarium.

After six hours of searching for a signal from Bumbley, Buzz finally picked up one pretty much where Doctor Alcosta said he would. Finding the signal was one thing, seeing if he could re-establish a permanent relationship with the Bumble Bee Grouper after all these months was another. Buzz hit the switch that emitted the high-frequency sound that he used to train Bumbley with and waited. He waited for nearly sixteen hours, and then he saw a large grey-green mass slowly rise towards the surface. It was his old friend coming to visit him.

The Azuma Maru, the Japanese whaler factory ship, had six minke whales transferred on board by the whaling vessel Sanda Maru; that brought the total number killed for the season to over three hundred.

The Japanese claimed that they were conducting the whale hunts for scientific research and not commercial, but the International Court of Justice ruled that the hunt was commercial in nature and ordered them to stop. The Japanese hadn't complied and stood by their claim that the slaughtering of whales was strictly for research, and yet all the meat ended up in gourmet shops all across Japan. Le Gang de la Clé de Singe decided that if Japan won't listen to international diplomacy, maybe they would listen to threats and intimidation.

Sailing into the waters of the Antarctic was Le Gang de la Clé de Singe's flagship of the anti-whaling fleet, the Attila the Hun. The Island Class Patrol vessel was one hundred and ninety-four feet, with a max speed of twenty-two knots, six knots faster than the Azuma Maru. She was painted primarily in a black with blue and white razzle dazzle camouflage paint scheme. And painted in a bright yellow on either side were twelve-foot letters that read, '*Eat Shit And Die!*'. She flew two flags, the skull and cross monkey wrench flag on a yellow field and a banner flag that read, '*Death to All Whalers*'. She also carried a McDonnell Douglas MH-6 Little Bird Helicopter, which was equipped with one 30mm M230 Chain Machine Gun and two LAU-68D/A rocket pods armed with Hydra 70 rockets.

Before sailing out of their homeport of Hobart, Tasmania, they received the new crew rotation assignments. Coming to take command of the combat assignment was the Blue Team headed up by the Iceman. Once they were out in international waters, heading south to encounter the Azuma Maru, the captain, Captain Robert Hunter, and the Iceman assembled the entire crew in the mess hall to inform them of what to expect of the upcoming campaign.

They entered to mess hall together. Captain Hunter, was a Toronto native who joined the Sierra Club at the age of fourteen to protest against nuclear testing. He was an early and influential member of the Canadian branch of Greenpeace, protesting the hunting of Arctic Wolfs and Polar Bears. When he was eighteen, he joined the Canadian Coast Guard, where he served aboard weather ships, search and rescue hovercrafts, and buoy tenders. After being discharged, he signed up as a merchant seaman with the French Consulate in Vancouver and shipped out on the thirty-five thousand ton bulk carrier Seinte Cruz as a deckhand. Once in Paris, he witnessed a protest against the State-sponsored oil companies staged by Le Gang de la Clé de Singe and got involved. He worked his way up from a deckhand to obtain the position of captain of the Attila the Hun; he was a six-year veteran of the whale wars.

"Ladies and gentlemen, most of you know me and have sailed with me. For those who are new, I am Captain Robert Hunter, and this is the Iceman. While I will be in charge of the ship, Iceman will be heading up the combat campaign. We will be going to interrupt and put an end to the Japanese whaling season. Just so you know, we are going to be, basically, committing high crimes and piracy on the sea. I mention that just to be clear, as I want you all to know exactly what you'll be getting your selfves into if we get caught. It's, at a minimum, jail time, and there is a strong possibility of death. I'm not going to sugarcoat it; we are going to out there to stop the killing of whales, even if it means we die trying. So, if any of you might be having second thoughts, now is the time to say something before we're too far from shore. Because once this meeting is over, it's over. Anybody?"

Everyone looked around the room at each other, but no one moved.

"Excellent. I'm proud of all of you. Now, I'd like to introduce my compatriot, the Iceman, who will be leading the Blue Team. They are all veterans of many successful combat missions, most recently the victorious assault of the David Leeway massacre, as the mainstream and even the not so mainstream media called it, so I think I can honestly say we're in good hands. Iceman, anything to say?"

"Thank you, Captain Hunter. My team and I are proud to be a part of this crew and this assignment. Over the next few days and weeks, we will all have time to swap war stories, but, for now, I just want to say that my team and I are here to support you any way we can. I believe that I speak for the entire Blue Team when I say we're proud to serve with such heroic souls, Captain."

"Alright, any questions, statements, speeches? No? Good, let's rock 'n' roll. Dismissed."

As Captain Hunter and the Iceman were heading back up to the bridge, the captain asked about the young man with the native markings on his face.

"Oh, that's Queequeg. Good man."

"Queequeg, like in Moby Dick?"

"They must be tracking us by drones," Lu Wei informed Captain White.

"What can we do?" Snowy inquired.

Aleppo smiled and said, "A drone war. We'll launch our armed C.22 and bring theirs down."

"Can you do that? How will you even know where theirs is?"

Lu Wei thought for a moment and answered, "It won't be easy. I'm sure their drone has an integrated drone detection system as does ours. Once we send ours up, their drone should automatically trigger alerts and then send signals as countermeasure. What we need to devise, and fast, is a cloaking device that will make our drone stealth."

Aleppo said, "We'll enhance the cloaking capabilities by attaching a nozzle that will spread the exhaust and help mix the hot exhaust with cooler air. We can't eliminate all of the noise or heat, but we can reduce it. We'll have to convert our existing turbofan into a more efficient engine, so the exhaust will spread out as much as possible, masking both heat and noise."

Snowy said, "You're talking Greek to me; just tell me how long will it take. I'm afraid that they might not want to engage us, but just take us out."

Lu Wei and Aleppo mumbled to each other for a few minutes and then, almost in unison, said, "Four hours."

Snowy said, "Go!"

While the two drone heads went down below to augment the C.22, Snowy went into the mess cabin where his lady snipers were sitting, drinking hot tea and warming themselves up. He told them of the situation and said there's a good chance that they might, at some point, encounter the Coast Guard. In that event, the choice would either be surrender or fight, which would probably mean to the death. Or they could, at some point, get blasted out of the water unexpectedly by a drone strike. He asked them, if and when they did encounter the Coast Guard, what did they think, of the two options, were they prepared to choose.

Fu Hao and Sue-B both thought for several minutes. Fu Hao, who sat with her eyes closed, spoke softly. "I can not image spending the rest of my life in prison, and I am sure that the authorities would seek the death penalty after some enhanced interrogations to see if I would reveal what I know and who I know. For me, I choose going out like a lion, not a lamb."

Sue-B nodded and said, "That's how I would like to die, like a warrior, not a slave."

Snowy slapped his knees as he stood up and said, "Well, let's hope that Lu Wei and Aleppo can work their magic, and we won't have to make the ultimate sacrifice. Because, for me, I'd prefer to go out dying in my sleep when I'm ninety-something."

Rodin's plane landed at Geneva International Airport at five-fifteen in the afternoon. He passed through customs and was sitting in a cab on the way to 4278 Chemin de Plonjon, a private residence that was located next door to the Mission Corée République Populaire démocratique or, translated, the Democratic People's Republic of Korea.

The ride was a short twenty minutes, but Rodin asked the cab driver not to let him out as it appeared that no one was home. Instead, he requested that the cabbie drop him off a few blocks away at Bateau Genève. The MS Genève was the oldest paddle ship of Lake Geneva, which was converted into a historical restaurant moored at Eaux-Vives dock.

Rodin sat enjoying a glass of Chambertin Clos-de-Bèze Grand Cru, a mere hundred and ninety dollars a glass, watching the sunset over the Swiss Alps. At seven o'clock, he strolled along the south-side promenade of Lake Geneva, the Quai Gustave Ador to Chemin de Plonjon, where he turned right and walked past the North Korean Consultant to the large estate, 4278, next door.

The home was dark when he entered illegally; it seemed very cold and dank, and there were dozens of stuffed trophies of exotic animals mounted on the walls, along with a number of animal skins covering the floors. It was definitely a man's home, as no woman could stand to be surrounded by so much death. He placed himself strategically facing the front entrance in what seemed to be the owner's chair and waited.

It was nearly two in the morning, when he heard the front door open. He could see the man backlit from the front porch light, a short dumpy figure. The man closed the door and turned on the entrance hall light, where he removed his overcoat, hung it up in the coat closet, and then started to walk into the main living room, unaware of the unexpected guest.

Ten steps into the main room, the man froze. Sensing something was amiss, he looked around the room and noticed someone sitting in his chair. He slowly walked towards the figure asking, "Who are you? What do you want?"

"Good evening, Herr Drumpf, we meet again," Rodin said, holding his Glock 9mm waist high at the man.

"Who are you? Do I know you?"

"I'm disappointed that you don't remember me. Think back, Singapore. Did you think I was kidding when I said we'd met again?"

"Listen, I'm a wealthy man; I can pay you. You name your price. How much do you want?" Drumpf asked with fear in his voice.

"Oh, I don't want any money, Mr. Drumpf. Might I ask, what is your profession?"

"I deal in the buying and selling of precious metals—gold, silver, etc."

"Like this?" Rodin reached behind him and produced a gold bar from his bag; he held it up into the man's face. It was quite heavy, weighing twenty-five pounds with the Nazi eagle and swastika symbol imprinted in it. There was the name 'Deutsche Reichsbank' and the weight amount, along with a serial number.

"Yes, that is correct. That is legal to own."

"Where did you obtain it?"

"I can not remember."

"Is it a family heirloom? I know that your family got rich off of the possessions of the Jews that were sent off to the camps to die. For example, I see that you have quite a collection of fine paintings, many from the masters like that Van Gogh and that Matisse. Oh, I particularly like that Picasso drawing over there."

"Do you? Then it's yours. Please, take it."

"Yes, it is mine." Rodin handed him a worn out, tattered, faded photograph of an orthodox Jewish family posing in their living room, and in the background, hanging on the wall, was the exact same Picasso that was hanging on Drumpf's wall.

"Sit down over here, Herr Drumpf." Rodin directed him to a straight back wooden chair that he found in the hall leading to the library.

He did as he was told, and Rodin bound his hands behind the chair and his legs together. He then placed a gag in his mouth, and, just for good measure, he bound his captive to the chair itself.

"Whatever you want, just don't hurt me. Take it, please, and just go. And the gold, too."

"No, not the gold. That, I think, you should keep. You know, the Nazi's forced the prisoners in those death camps to pull the gold teeth from the corpses after they gassed them. Ever wondered how many dead Jews it took to make this bar of gold?"

"Please, don't hurt me."

"Nah, I'm thinking it never crossed your mind, and, even if it did, you wouldn't give a shit. After all, they were just a bunch of dirty, filthy Jews."

Rodin held up a device that he took from his bag. It resembled an industrial food mixer. He showed his hostage, asking, "Do you know what this is?"

Drumpf nodded and tried to speak, but Rodin held up his hand, saying, "Sure you do, and it's a portable melting furnace. This little puppy has the capability to melt gold. You wouldn't think that this little thing could reach temperatures of one thousand and ninety-three degrees. Amazing. What will they think of next."

Rodin proceeded to plug it in, place a gold bar into the graphite crucible, and turn the portable furnace on. As the gauge started to display the rising temperature, there appeared a warm glow emanating from within the cylinder containing the gold bar. Within minutes, the gold bar started to liquefy into what looked like a bright golden elixir of life. Rodin reached into his bag and produced a thick leather strap, which he placed around Drumpf's forehead and pulled his head back, until his head was looking straight up towards the ceiling. Then, he attached the strap to the chair so his head could not move.

Rodin leaned down to the fat man's ear and whispered, "I read that the Aztecs devised this method of death for Cortez's men in the 1500's, who, like you, were greedy, selfish, and avaricious towards people who they thought were less than human. People who live and breath covetousness. "

Drumpf's eye bulged almost out of his head, and he started to squirm and shake from left to right, trying to break free from the chair. Rodin punched him hard in the stomach and said, "Sit tight, asshole!"

He slumped down into himself, and Rodin pulled him back straight by the shoulder. He, then, took a large funnel from his bag and ripped the gag out of Drumpf's mouth. Shoving the funnel down his throat, Rodin began pouring the molten gold down his trachea, filling his lungs and windpipe with the liquid gold, and forming an eerily beautiful golden organic sculpture within Drumpf that only a select few outside the M.E. and law enforcement officials would ever see. The room was filled with the stench of burnt flesh and melted gold; Rodin had to damp out the fire that emitted from Drumpf's throat with a rag.

The lifeless body sat rigidly straight in the chair. Because of the gold in his torso, he was incapable of bending. Rodin left the scorched body, with its cooking insides, sitting in the chair, while he clinically cleaned the crime scene and packed up his equipment. He placed the yellow monkey wrench flag around Drumpf's neck, and he, then, placed the traditional celebrity fingerprint—this time, it would be of the world famous Swiss architect and designer, Le Corbusier, on the side of a twelve-thousand-dollar Rombach & Haas walnut cuckoo clock, which was hanging opposite of Herr Drumpf's body. Then, he inserted the accompanying note in the mouth of the cuckoo. Lastly, he removed the Picasso drawing off the wall, took it out of the frame, rolled it up, and placed into a mailing tube that was stamped and addressed. He walked out the front door, locking it as he left.

He walked back along the Quai Gustave Ador to the Geneve-Quai Gustave Ador ferry terminal, where, before boarding the ferry, he placed the tube containing the Picasso in a mailbox and proceeded take the ferry to the other side of La Rade Bay to the Geneve-Paquis ferry terminal. Somewhere along the way, he deposited his bag into the waters of Lake Geneva.

It was just a short walk from the ferry terminal to the Grand Hotel Kempinski Geneve, where he checked in for the night. The next day, he was off to Indonesia to connect with the Red Team and start dealing with a group of Komodo dragon poachers.

Captain Haruka Nakamura was a hard-line whaler, he had commanded the Azuma Maru for the last six whaling seasons and had his fill of those so-called 'eco-terrorists.' They were through playing nice; the Japanese government had given them permission to retaliate if fired upon with whatever means he felt appropriate.

The Azuma Maru was now armed with four mounted twin M2HB machine guns, two on each side, plus two World War 2 Oerlikon 20mm cannons, one mounted on the stern and the other on the bow, making the Azuma Maru a very formidable foe.

Sitting about halfway between the continents of Africa, Antarctica, and Australia laid the Kerguelen Islands, French Southern and Antarctic Lands in the south Indian Ocean. A tiny flyspeck on the world map, Port-aux-Francais was the capital settlement, which consisted of two major roads—Route Rouen that intersected with Route 66. The small town also boasted two unique features; one was Church of Our Lady of the Winds, and the other was the movie theater, CineKer, that featured the latest films from five years ago. The island's primary purpose was for meteorological and geophysical research, so it had but a handful of inhabitants and was visited mostly by researchers studying the native fauna. There was a small hospital that existed in Port-aux-Francais, which was why the Attila the Hun sat in Morbihan Bay.

Walter Hardcastle, the ship's corpsman, had seen all types of accidents, sicknesses, and maladies during his eight years sailing onboard the Attila the Hun, but he had never had to deal with an amputation.

Bobby Jackson, an American from San Diego, signed on as a deckhand who occasionally would help out in the engine room. Two weeks prior, while doing some routine maintenance on the number two engine, he slipped and suffered a deep gash to his right calf. It got infected after not reporting the injury to Walter for treatment, for fear of being put ashore and not being able to continue the campaign. He tried to cover the fact he was hurt, and, by the time he went to seek medical treatment, the infection had gotten so bad that gangrene had set in. Walter immediately alerted Captain Hunter, and they set a course to the nearest port with the proper hospital facilities, that being Port-aux-Francais, where doctors were prepared and waiting.

Unfortunately, the Jackson tragedy placed the Attila the Hun behind schedule in tracking down and encountering the Azuma Maru, which meant whales were going to die. They spent three days at Port-aux-Francais, waiting for Bobby's prognosis. Sadly, he lost his leg from just above the kneecap, and he was going to be air evacuated to Perth, Australia the next morning. It would turn out to be that Bobby was the lucky one.

As the Attila the Hun pulled out of port, the crew saw Bobby's flight take off and head east towards Perth. Now, the hunt was on for the Azuma Maru, and finding the factory ship involved more luck than skill. Captain Hunter's skill in knowing the migratory patterns of the minke whales was legend and would play a huge factor in the hunt, but an even bigger factor would be sheer luck. The Indian Ocean was over twenty-seven million square miles; finding one lone ship was like looking for a needle in a haystack.

There was an old saying, 'I'd rather be lucky than good,' and Captain Hunter was both. On the ninth day out from Port-aux-Francais, the sonar picked up a blip traveling south approximately fifteen miles away. It was definitely a large vessel, but, to verify if it was the Azuma Maru, they would need visual confirmation. So, they would send up the Little Bird, flying below radar detection, and see what was what.

David 'Doc' Holiday was a veteran with four tours of duty in Iraq and Afghanistan, where he flew Apache helicopters in over a hundred combat missions against the Taliban. He was shot down twice but never captured, and he joined Le Gang de la Clé de Singe after his last tour of duty when he helped save dozens of mistreated animals from the Kabul Zoo, where people were forced to come to watch live animals being fed to lions and tigers for the Taliban's amusement.

Doc took off with the Iceman riding shotgun, flying what seemed to be inches off the surface of the water. Every now and then, they would clip the top of a white cap with the landing skids and lose visibility for a second or two from the spray that would envelop the cockpit's bubble window.

Twenty minutes into the flight, they spotted the Azuma Maru. They had a GoPro mounted on Doc's helmet, which was sending back a live feed to the crew of the Attila the Hun. Doc radioed back, "Are you guys seeing this?"

"Roger that, Doc. That's her. Better head on back before they spot you."

"Copy that. We're on our way home. Over."

The Little Bird landed safely back on board the Attila the Hun, and the Iceman thanked Doc and said, "That was a hoot, Doc. Love to do again real soon."

"Glad you liked it, anytime."

The Iceman, the Doc, and Captain Hunter all met up in the captain's cabin to strategize next steps. The Iceman had a plan and wanted to bounce it off them to get their thoughts.

He wanted to take three zodiacs out tonight and attack the Azuma Maru. Two of the zodiacs would be acting as decoys to draw the crew's attention by trying to drop fishing nets in front of the bow to try and tangle their propellers. They would be attacking from the port side, while, on the starboard side, the third zodiac would try and land a small group of commandos on board to plant timed explosives strategically below the waterline.

Unbeknownst to anyone on the Attila the Hun, the Azuma Maru had undergone heavy-duty rearmament. Captain Hunter thought it might be a good idea, before sending anyone to attack the Azuma Maru, to have Doc take a closer inspection to see just what we might be up against.

Captain Hunter said, "Every year, that fucking Nakamura always brings something new to the fight. Last year, they threw grappling hooks out to try and snag our crewmembers, and they even fired rifles, wounding two of our men. So, let's be sure what surprises might be in store for us this year."

Doc Holiday took off, and, again, the Iceman wanted to go along for the ride. They stayed low below the radar scan, not because they didn't want to be detected but because they enjoyed skimming over the tops of the waves. Once they could see the Azuma Maru, they lifted up and began to circle the vessel. The Iceman noticed the armaments straight away, as did the Doc.

The Iceman exclaimed, "Holy shit, are you guys seeing this? We're talking major firepower here."

Doc said, "These guys are loaded for bear."

"Have they spotted you?" asked Captain Hunter.

"Yeah, they're manning the guns, but no shots fired," Doc answered.

"Okay, come on back. We'll talk about it when you get back."

"Roger that," Doc said, as he did one more fly by, then turned tail, and got the hell out of there. "So, what do you think?" he asked the Iceman.

"Oh, I got something special planned for Captain Nakamura and the boys from the rising sun. We're going party hardy."

Lu Wei nodded to Aleppo, who then launched the C.22 drone, and the crew of the King Edward I watched as the gray monstrosity flew straight up and out of their sight. The French Aerospatiale C.22 drone originally was a sleek, streamlined, and nimble flying machine. But, after Lu Wei and Aleppo customized it to become a stealthy silent drone killer, it had a Frankenstein appearance.

Snowy stuck his head into the drone command room and asked, "So?"

Aleppo smiled and replied, "In theory, it should be invisible. We'll know soon enough, as we just picked up the Coast Guard drone. She's about six miles away."

Snowy headed up to the bridge and got on the ship's PA. "Can I have everyone's attention? I'm going on the assumption that we're going to be victorious in the war of the drones. So, as soon as we're up to speed, we're setting sail. I would advise everyone to be ready for engagement, just in case. If we're lucky, the drone boys will have gotten us out of a tight jam. If not, then we'll go down kicking some ass."

The Canadian drone was cruising at an altitude of fifteen thousand feet, when, from up above, the C.22 approached, undetected, and fired one of its two Aster 15 missiles, blowing the Canadian's Fulmar X mini-UAV drone out of the sky. Lu Wei shouted so loudly that everyone on board the King Edward I heard, "We got her!" The whole crew hooped and hollered and hugged one another like they all had won the lottery.

Captain White gave the command, "Weezer, let's get the hell out of here. Strike the Monkey Wrench flag and hoist the Greenland flag."

Sue-B and Fu Hao had come up to the bridge after having some tea and asked why the Greenland flag.

"That's where we'll be heading—Nuuk, Greenland. I have a couple of old navy buddies there who will shelter us until things cool down."

As they threaded their way through the Queen Elizabeth Islands and down into the Northwestern Passages, they slipped in with a fleet of fishing boats making their way out into the Atlantic. From there, the King Edward I made the crossover to Greenland.

Varanus komodoensis, better known as the Komodo dragon, were the largest living lizards in the world. They were only found on the Indonesian islands of Komodo, Pinca, Flores, Gili Montang, and Padar.

The average size of a male Komodo dragon was eight to nine feet long and about three hundred pounds. They had a unique way of killing their prey; if they captured the prey, they used their teeth to shred it to death. If the prey escaped with just a bite wound, it usually died within twenty-four hours of blood poisoning because the Komodo's saliva contained about fifty strains of bacteria. With its fantastic sense of smell, the Komodo would find the dead animal and finish its meal.

Rodin's Thai Airways fight landed in Ngurah Rai International Airport on the island of Bali at six in the morning. After passing through customs, he was greeted at the airport by two members of the Red Team—Odin and Lu Wei. Hazael and Vulcan were waiting at the Ritz-Carlton, Bali with their local guide, Cahya Kusumo, who used to work for one of the islands largest Komodo Dragon tourist companies before joining Le Gang de la Clé de Singe.

The targeted poachers were a group known as the Ghost Riders, who operated out of the fishing village of Waingapu on the island of Pulau Sumba, south of the Komodo Islands. They trapped, killed, and skinned the dragons, leaving the carcasses for the other dragons to eat. Occasionally, they captured one and sold it to a private collector or zoo. It was believed that they continued to operate because of payoffs to government officials.

Rodin checked into his room at the Ritz after having a breakfast of lobster scrambled eggs and two cups of black coffee during a meeting with the entire Red Team. Cahya believed, from the information he has been able to glean, that the Ghost Riders were going on a dragon raid on Rinca Island in the next two or three days. He procured a 1978 twenty-nine-foot Ranger Tugs commercial fishing trawler, which was gassed up and ready to go. All necessary gear had been checked out and was onboard, so he and the boat were ready to go at a moment's notice. It was decided that they would leave before sunset. The plan was for Cahya to drop the team off on to the island at dusk, where they would look for any poaching activity during the night until dawn, and, if there were no encounters, then he would pick them up late in the morning and shuttle them back to the trawler to rest until he would drop them off again at dusk.

Loh Buaya Komodo National Park sat on the northeast arm of Rinca Island, tucked inside the Toro Buaya inlet; it was not easily visible from the open sea. There was a small boat ramp where visitors could tie up, but the inlet was not deep enough for large vessels, so most visitors usually used shallow-bottom boats, or zodiacs, and launch boats. To the west of Loh Buaya Komodo National Park, there was a small peninsula jutting out a few hundred yards, and that's where Rodin and his Red Team came ashore and made their way over the hills to the national park. There, they waited for the Ghost Riders.

Since Komodo dragons were cold-blooded and had a body temperature varying with that of their environment, they were sluggish in the early morning and around dusk and were the most active during the mid-day hours. Mid-day was prime time for tourists to come and observe the dragons.

Attacks on humans were rare, but they have been responsible for several human deaths in the past. Between 1974 and 2012, there had been twenty-four reported attacks on humans, with five being deadly. That was why all tours were conducted in a specially equipped bus; no one ever walked or got out of the vehicle. Not long ago, a young boy snuck off the tourist bus to go to the bathroom behind some bushes, and a dragon lunged at the boy, biting him in the leg. By the time the guides and rangers arrived to help the boy and get the dragon to release its grip, he was dead from massive bleeding from the torso. The coroner's report stated that the boy was bitten in half.

On the trip over to Rinca Island, Cahya warned the team about how vigilant they had to be while on the island. There were over thirteen hundred dragons on the island, and they were fearless and tenacious. He told them about a group of divers that were stranded for two days and nights after their diving boat had sunk and they were swept ashore of Rinca Island by the infamously strong currents surrounding the island. They were attacked immediately and repeatedly, day and night, until, on the third day, they were spotted by chance from a passing fishing boat.

To combat the dragons, Rodin and the Red Team brought backpack canisters containing a pungent mixture of gasoline and citrus acid, which they would spray at the giant lizards to keep them at bay. As the sun got ready to set on the island of Rinca, the Red Team was dropped off by Cahya and made their way to the national park. On their arrival, they had been greeted by two aggressive, nine-foot dragons, who were dissuaded from following—closely, at least—by the use of the 'Dragon Juice,' as Cahya called it.

It was the same thing for the next two nights. They were constantly being harassed and followed by dozens of giant lizards, and, sometimes, they would find themselves encircled. They had to be overly cautious because a bite could lead to certain death, or, even if it's a slight wound, it could mean months of agonizing pain and possible amputation. After the first night, Vulcan devised several anti-dragon devices using a six-foot pole with tasers attached to the ends; it had just enough zap to keep the monsters away but not kill them.

On the third night, close to three in the morning. Rodin received a radio transmission from Cahya, alerting them that he spotted a small boat heading into the Toro Buaya inlet. Rodin broke his team into two groups. Odin, Hazel, and Vulcan would make their way east, past the boat dock and past the tourist welcome center, while he and Lu Wei would stay on the west side of the landing. Rodin could see that there were five men wearing personal headlamps, all of them concentrating their beams to the shore and looking for any sign of dragons lying in wait.

As the men got off the boat, Rodin could see that they were heavily armed, which he communicated to Odin. The group's headlamps were shining in all directions, keeping a sharp lookout for any dragons. As they made their way towards the welcome center, they stopped and talked amongst themselves, trying to decide on which way to go, when one of them spotted a juvenile Komodo about four feet long. One of the men raised his revolver and was getting ready to shoot, when Rodin gave the order to open fire. Regrettably, the man got his shot off and killed the adolescent lizard before he, himself, was wounded. Of the five poachers, four were killed outright, but the man who killed the dragon was only wounded in the shoulder.
Rodin and the Red Team approached the Ghost Riders, weapons raised. Rodin shouted out to the wounded man, "Drop your weapon, now!"

"Don't shoot," The injured man pleaded, as he raised his hands.

Vulcan and Hazael started to position the dead men next to each other, placing the yellow monkey wrench flags around their necks, while Lu Wei retrieved the carcass of the dead Komodo dragon and placed it next to the bodies of the poachers. Vulcan then nailed a flag to the door of the welcome center, along with a proclamation letter, so there would be some indication of what happened. They knew that, by the time anyone would discover them, there might not be anything left to be discovered of the men and the young lizard, let alone the flags and letters, after the dragons finished with them.

Odin helped the wounded man to his feet, and, as he put a flag around the man's neck, Rodin bent down and picked up the poacher's revolver. The revolver was a Smith 7 Wesson Model 19 Classic 357 Magnum six shot, and Rodin emptied the cylinder of all but one bullet. He handed the revolver back to the bleeding man and said, "You have one shot; use it wisely."

The man pointed the gun at Rodin and sneered, "If I die, you die."

Rodin held up his hand to his team, who were pointing their weapons at the man, and said, "Friend, what is your name?"

"Satria."

"Satria, your killing me will not change your fate one way or another. My men will not shoot you, even if you kill me. Satria, you are destined to die, and now you have a hard choice to make. You can kill me and try surviving until someone finds you, but, in your condition, that doesn't seem too likely. Your killing me might give you some satisfaction, but you will die a horrible death being eating alive by these monsters. Otherwise, you can do the only sensible thing and man up."

Satria looked around and saw that the smell of blood had attracted several large dragons, which were starting to make their way towards him and his dead compadres; he lowered the revolver. Rodin and his men left him standing there, and they made their way down to the dock where the Ghost Riders' boat was secured.

The dragons approached the lifeless bodies of men and of the Komodo dragon lying on the ground yards away from Satria. Once they realized that there would be no opposition, they began devouring the dead. Eating clothes, meat and even bones, there would be nothing left but a rather large, bloody stain on the concrete sidewalk. Satria thought for an instant that, with all the dragon's attention on consuming his friends, he just might be able to survive. He turned to make a dash to a grove of trees situated behind him, when he saw a group of the giant reptiles galloping towards him. For a split second, his reaction was to point the gun at them and start shooting, but then he remembered he had but one bullet. He put the gun in his mouth.

About the time the team reached the launch, they heard a single shot ring out.

Rodin turned to Odin and said, "Dinner is served."

Captain Hunter, Doc Holiday, and the Iceman were sitting around Hunter's desk in his cabin, going over how to best combat the Azuma Maru. The Iceman was still in favor of trying to get men on board the Azuma Maru to plant explosives. The big question was how, and would the decoys be put into undue danger trying to draw the Japanese's attention onto the port side, while the boarding party would try and sneak on board from the starboard side?

There would be a new moon the next night, so, with limited visibility working in their favor and with everyone wearing black and traveling in the black zodiacs, they felt that it might be their best chance of bringing the Azuma Maru down. They would also have Doc Holiday harassing them, as well with all the commotion on the port side, so hopefully they would be able to keep their attention away from the starboard side, where the Iceman and Queequeg would board the Japanese mothership. Captain Hunter picked up the mic and announced, on the ship's address system, that there would be an all-hands meeting right after that evening's mess in the mess hall at eighteen hundred hours.

Queequeg was on the top deck, assembling explosive devices, when Iceman approached him; he sat down next to him and told Queequeg about the proposed attack plans for the Azuma Maru. After going over the strategy, he asked for his thoughts. Queequeg thought a moment and said, "Sounds like it should work, but…"

"But what?"

"Well, I think I should board the ship alone."

"No way. This is a two-man operation."

"I think you'll agree that this is pretty much a suicide mission. Once we're on board and we're spotted, they're not going to be looking to take any prisoners, and, knowing you, you're not going to surrender. Am I wrong?"

"Yes, you're wrong. One, if all goes to plan, they won't spot us, and, two…well, hell at least we'll die trying, and we sure won't be going in alone."

"I've been thinking of a less chancy way, which I feel will be fool-proof."

"And that would be?"

"I go on board wearing a suicide vest plainly visible, and the device would be rigged with a pressure release switch. So, once I'm onboard, I pull the safety lock pin to arm the firing pin, and, if for any reason I release the pressure on the detonator, the explosives go off. Once they realize that—even if they shoot me—once my finger loses pressure…boom!"

"But, Queequeg, that really is a suicide mission. At least my plan is optimistic that we'll survive. Why would you want to go to certain death?"

"Brother, I am already facing certain death. Remember when I cut myself when we tangled with those kiwi poachers, and I went to the clinic for some stitches?"

"Yeah, but that was just for a couple of stitches."

"Right, but they did routine blood work on me and found that I have stage four acute myeloid leukemia; it's cancer of the blood and bone marrow. Seems my bone marrow makes abnormal white blood cells. Ain't that a kick in the dick?"

"Shit, man, why are you waiting till now to tell me? We could have gotten you into a program back in Wellington. You should have told me, man!"

"Well, from what the doctors told me, I have anywhere from a couple months to a few weeks, and, man, I don't want to go through what's comin., I'd rather go out in a blaze of glory."

"Are you sure about this?"

"You just get me on the Azuma Maru tomorrow night."

"Good evening. I'm Nigel Williams, and this is BBC World News. Our top story this hour tonight, once again, is about the eco-terrorist group that calls themselves Le Gang de la Clé de Singe; there have been several incidents recently reported that they have laid claim to.

"There were reports of another attack on seal hunters near the Queen Elizabeth Island just below the Arctic Ocean. Over twenty men were killed in the latest ambush. Apparently, the killers were able to escape capture by the shooting down of a Canadian military drone that was tracking them.

"In Geneva, there were reports of an unusually gruesome death of Baron Von Drumpf, an international dealer of precious metals, who was murdered last night. Authorities aren't giving out too much information,n but one unidentified source said that molten gold was involved. His link for revenge from the Le Gang de la Clé de Singe is unclear at this time.

"And, finally, there are details of the deaths of several men who were known to be poacher. They were killed and, apparently, eaten by dozens of the giant lizards, known as Komodo Dragon,s on the Indonesian Island of Rinca. Le Gang de la Clé de Singe called into BBC, stating

that these men were known poachers of the dragons, killing them and selling their skins on the black market. The killers said that it seemed only fitting that, since the men made their living off of the death of the dragons, the dragons should make there living off of the death of the poachers.

"Le Gang de la Clé de Singe reiterated that this campaign will continue until the senseless killing of these animals has come to a stop.

"And now for the scores from today's cricket matches."

The Attila the Hun had been hounding the Azuma Maru for two days by staying uncomfortably close to the ship. They hadn't launched any real threatening attacks against the whalers, just some cursory ones so as not to endanger any of the crew or zodiacs. No one aside from the Iceman, Doc Holiday, and Captain Hunter were aware of what Queequeg was destined to do once onboard. Each member of the decoy attack crews was prepared to try and keep the Japanese whalers' attention to the port side of the Azuma Maru by making as much noise and chaos as possible, but without putting themselves into any undue danger.

The night was pitch black, except for the running lights aboard the Azuma Maru. If you looked into the heavens, there wasn't a cloud in the sky and you could see billions and billions of stars twinkling. The Attila the Hun had its starboard side facing the Whaling factory ship, so the Iceman and his Blue Team started lowering the zodiac's off of the port side to remain undetected. Once all the crews were in the water, the two decoy zodiacs headed out first, going past the bow of the Attila the Hun while the zodiac carrying the Iceman and Queequeg scooted around the stern of the ship. Each of the zodiacs was powered by two Torqeedo Cruise 10.0R electric outboard motors. They were extremely fast and, best of all, silent.

Each zodiac had two members of the Blue Team. T-Bone piloted boat number one, and Bellator was assigned to fire a modified t-shirt cannon that was refitted to be able to fire canisters of butyric acid. Bottled and fired onto the decks of the Azuma Maru, it spoiled any whale meat it came into contact with and made it almost impossible to work on the deck.

Gianfranco piloted boat number two, and Cowboy tried to draw the attention of the Azuma Maru crew by dropping a tow line in front of the ship so as to snag the ship's propellers. If successful, the ship would be dead in the water until they were able to untangle it.

Doc Holiday took off solo and flew without running lights, staying off to the Azuma Maru's port side as an additional distraction. Iceman steered the boarding boat, while Queequeg attempted to board the Azuma Maru and make his way to the bridge to confront Captain Haruka Nakamura. Once onboard, Iceman had Hunter call the Azuma Maru and alert them to the fact that they had a man on board wearing a suicide jacket, and that any attempt to interfere with him would mean certain death for a majority of the Japanese crew.

T-Bone and Bellator drew first blood; Bellator fired and landed six canisters of butyric acid on the main deck where they cut up the whales and harvested the meat. Within seconds of the attack, the Azuma Maru had turned on several powerful spotlights that lit up the surrounding area about the size of a football field. There was an alarm that was sounded, and the people in the zodiacs could see a lot of activity onboard the ship. The Japanese crew started throwing out grappling hooks to try and snag people or the zodiacs. Either way, the chance of serious injury or even death was possible.

Gianfranco and Cowboy made their way up towards the bow to start dropping the towline in front of the vessel in hopes of having it get entangled with the propeller. As Gianfranco steered the boat across the bow, while Cowboy was letting the heavy towrope overboard, one of the Japanese sailors threw a grappling hook that caught the Cowboy's left shoulder and lifted him right out of the zodiac and into the icy water in front of the oncoming ship. The vortex of the ship sucked him down and under the bow, as the tension and force of the grappling hook ripped his arm off of his body. When the sailor reeled in the line with the hook, the Cowboy's arm was still attached.

Meanwhile, the Iceman and Queequeg took advantage of the chaos happening on the port side of the Azuma Maru to get Queequeg onboard undetected. Once onboard, Queequeg found a secluded spot on at the stern of the ship and waited to hear from the Iceman that the captain of the ship had been alerted to his presence. He removed his life jacket, revealing his All Black Rugby jersey; he, then, pulled the safety pin from his device and tossed it overboard.

The Iceman slowed the zodiac and radioed Hunter, "Mother, this is sonny boy. Do you read? Over."

"Sonny boy, this mother. We read you loud and clear. Over."

"Mother, the kiwi has landed. Make the call. Over."

"Copy that."

"Blue Team, this is Blue Leader. Mission accomplished. Return to mother. Over."

"Blue Leader, this is Blue One. Copy," T-Bone said.

"Blue Leader, this is Blue Two. Cowboy is lost, taken overboard by a grappling hook."

"Blue Team, let the Azuma Maru pass and see if we can spot Cowboy."

The Iceman and the other two zodiacs turned on their portable spotlights and started skimming the black water to see if they could spot the body of their friend, but to no avail.

"This is the Captain of the Attila the Hun to Captain Nakamura. Do you read me? Over." He waited for a few minutes, and then he repeated, "This is the Captain of the

Attila the Hun to Captain Nakamura. Do you read me? Over."

"This is Captain Nakamura. That was a very foolish thing that you have done. I believe that because of your act of aggression, one of your men has perished. Over."

"Captain, all my people are willing to die for what they believe in. The question for you is, are your people ready to die for the killing of whales? First, I must tell you that all of your communication systems have been blocked. You are unable to send or receive any radio or telecommunications, and we've jammed your internet and satellite service, as well. Secondly, we have a man on board the Azuma Maru right now; he is wearing a suicide vest that will be sent-off if pressure is released from the trigger. Meaning that, any attempt to capture, wound, or kill the man will only result in setting off the explosive device. Do you understand?"

"Yes, I understand. What is it you want?"

"The destruction of the Azuma Maru and the death of all whalers."

"You realize that this is an act of murder and piracy?"

Captain Hunter and the crew of the Attila the Hun could hear the abandon ship alarm coming from the Azuma Maru and the muffled sound of Captain Nakamura making an announcement over the ships address system.

Captain Nakamura picked up the receiver to the ships public address system and spoke in a calm and direct manner in Japanese, "Attention, attention. This is Captain Nakamura. We have an intruder on board who is wearing a suicide vest. Under no circumstance must you interfere with this man; it is my understanding that any attempt to capture or harm him will result in the device going off. Abandon ship before the bomb is to go off."

He then spoke English, "To the intruder on board, this is Captain Nakamura speaking. Please, make your way up to the bridge or call me on any phone."

Queequeg started to make his way to the engine room, when he saw a phone. He picked it up and spoke to the bridge, "I want to speak to the Captain."

"Captain Nakamura."

"If you want to speak to me, you better hurry on down to the engine room now."

He, then, radioed the Iceman, "Iceman, this is Queequeg. I'm down in the engine room. I just wanted to say that it's been an honor and privilege working with you, the team, and being part of Le Gang de la Clé de Singe."

"Queequeg, thank you for your sacrifice. God speed, brother."

Queequeg was going to say more, but he lost radio contact being down so far below the water line and with all of the interference with the engine. The engines were still roaring, pounding in his ears. Then, all of a sudden, the engines stopped. He assumed that the Captain had shut them down. The Azuma Maru went eerily quiet, and there was just the creaking and moaning of the ships natural expanding and contraction.

Queequeg stood in between the two enormous engines, leaning against a railing, when the Captain appeared. He was holding his arms in front of him, signaling for the tattooed bomber not to release the trigger.

"Please, wait. What is your name?"

"Queequeg."

"Queequeg, like the character in Moby Dick?"

"Just like in Moby Dick. And just like Moby Dick, he and I are both going to die because of whales. He died hunting them, but I'm going to die to save them."

"Is there nothing I can say to convince you not to do such a foolish act?"

Queequeg shook his head and proceeded to start his war haka. He bent his knees, crossed his arms in front of his chest, and made his scariest warrior face. He opened his eyes wide, contorted his face and stuck out his tongue, as he began vigorous movements and stamping his feet with rhythmic shouting of the All Black haka chant.

> *"Taringa whakarongo*
> *Kia   rite!   Kia   rite!   Kia   mau!*
> *Hi!*
> *Kia   whakawhenua   au   i   ahau!*
> *Hi, aue! Hi!*
> *Ko   Aotearoa,   e   ngunguru   nei!*
> *Hi, au! Au! Aue, ha! H!*
> *Ko   kapa   o   pango,   e   ngunguru   nei!*
> *Hi, au! Au! Aue, ha! Hi!*
> *I ahaha!*
> *Ka tu te ihi-ihi*
> *Ka tu te wanawana*
> *Ki runga i te rangi, e tu iho nei, tu iho nei, hi!*
> *Ponga ra!*
> *Kapa o pango! Aue, hi!*
> *Ponga ra!*
> *Kapa o pango! Aue, hi!*
> *Ha!"*

<u>*TRANSLATION*</u>

> "Let me go back to my first gasp of breath
> Let my life force return to the earth
> It is New Zealand that thunders now
> And it is my time!
> It is my moment!
> The passion ignites!
> This defines us as the All Blacks
> And it is my time!
> It is my moment!
> The anticipation explodes!
> Feel the power
> Our dominance rises

Our supremacy emerges
To be placed on high
Silver fern!
All Blacks!
Silver fern!
All Blacks!
Aue hi!"

Queequeg peered at the Captain, who seemed mesmerized by his haka. Then he looked up, closed his eyes, and screamed as loud and with as much power as his lungs could generate, "All Blacks!" He removed his thumb from the trigger.

The entire crew of the Attila the Hun was on deck, and all eyes were fixated on the Azuma Maru. They suddenly heard the engines stop, and then they felt a concussion wave, followed by the sounds of the explosions. Then, there was a giant fireball shooting hundreds of feet straight up into the blackness, seeming to illuminate the sky as far as the eye could see. And then the Azuma Maru was gone, and there was nothing but silence.

Out of the nothingness, came a lone cry from the distance for help. It turned out to be the one survivor of the Azuma Maru, who was clinging to a lifesaver. Bellator and T-Bone took one of the zodiacs and fished him out of the icy waters. He appeared to be about twenty-years-old, covered in oil from head to toe, and scared shitless. Before he was brought onboard, all the crewmembers had donned their black balaclavas so they could not be identified. Doc Holiday wrapped him in a blanket, brought him down to the mess hall, sat him down, and gave him a hot cup of tea. Captain Hunter sent everyone back to their stations, while he and the Iceman went down to the mess hall to talk to the survivor. The Captain asked if he understood English, which he indicated that he did but only a little. He told them that his name was Takuma Yahama.

The Iceman asked, "Takuma, do you know Le Gang de la Clé de Singe?"

"Hai."

"What do you know of us?"

"You very bad. You kill people."

"That's right, we do, but only people who do bad things to animals."

"But me not hogei-sen," He said, pantomiming the action of somebody throwing a harpoon. "Me kukku. Ah, kook."

"Cook?"

"Hai, cook." He looked around at Hunter, Doc Holiday and the Iceman, and asked, "You kill Takuma?"

The Iceman shook his head and said, "No, Takuma. We not going to kill you."

While the sole survivor of the Azuma Maru was below deck sleeping, the crew of the Attila the Hun got busy painting the ship. In case they were stopped by a warship, they painted over the large 'Eat Shit and Die' message on both sides of the ship and replaced it with a giant Greenpeace. After they were through, the Attila the Hun looked like the sister ship of the Greenpeace's Arctic Surprise, called the Arctic Breeze. They also flew the Dutch flag and had documentation that stated that this ship was, in fact, registered to Greenpeace.

The next evening, they outfitted Takuma with an ultra-bright orange SeaArctic immersion survival suit, which provided buoyancy and protected against heat loss, thus increasing the survival time in cold water. Then, they placed him in a fully equipped zodiac and sent him on his way. Before they released him, they attached a flexible makeshift flagpole with the bright yellow monkey wrench flag and a letter placed inside his survival suit. Then, they called in an SOS to any ships in the area.

Takuma spent eleven days floating around the Antarctic Ocean in relative calm seas, before an Australian air and sea rescue helicopter found him, alive. When interviewed, all he could recall was that there was a suicide bomber who had made his way onboard, and that one minute he was preparing a typical Japanese meal of a bowl of rice, a bowl of miso, pickled vegetables, and some tuna steaks with a side of udon noodles, and the next thing he knows he's clinging to a lifesaver and freezing his *O shiri* off.

He had been saved shortly after the ship sank. When asked about the pirates, he told the authorities that everyone was wearing ski masks and that he was unable to provide them with any description of any of the people who claimed to be from Le Gang de la Clé de Singe.

Takuma was flown back to Japan, where he was given a hero's welcome and had his picture taken with the Prime Minister. Takuma never went back to the sea; he opened a small sushi restaurant in the Tokyo Ginza Subway Station, called Kujira no Koibito, or 'Whale Lover.'

When the Japanese authorities sent the letter that Le Gang de la Clé de Singe had placed inside his survival suit, their forensic crime lab discovered a single fingerprint; it was that of Emperor Hirohito.

"Good evening. I'm Nigel Williams and this is BBC World News. Our top story this hour is the sinking of the Japanese Whaling ship, the Azuma Maru. The apparent suicide bomber killed himself and all hands on board, with the exception of Takuma Yahama, the ships cook who managed to abandon ship prior to the detonation. Takuma Yahama was saved by Le Gang de la Clé de Singe, the very people responsible for this horrendous act of piracy.

"He told authorities that he was well treated once rescued. After two days of recuperation and medical attention, they outfitted Takuma with an ultra-bright orange survival suit, placed him in a zodiac with four weeks of survival supplies, and then they set him adrift in the frozen waters of Antarctica. Once they cast him off, they called in

an SOS to any ships in the area. When found, eleven days later, Mr. Yamada was in remarkable condition for someone who had gone through such a traumatic experience.

"The United Nations issued a statement saying that the World's navies are on high alert searching for these criminals and will not rest until these killers are brought to justice

"The Japanese government has placed a ten million dollar reward for the capture of these individuals.

"Also, in the news, America's President Martin L.K. Washington has announced that the United States and the United Nations Department of Peacekeeping Operations has agreed to commit over sixty thousand troops, worldwide, to combat Le Gang de la Clé de Singe. All the members of the Security Council have agreed to provide troops in an effort to bring these outlaws to justice. President Washington said that those responsible can never be at peace and will all be made to answer for their crimes. America and the rest of the world will never stop hunting these terrorists until every one of them is either captured or killed.

"And, in local politics…"

Two months after the sinking of Azuma Maru and the end of whaling season, the Iceman took command of both the Red and Blue Teams, with Odin as his second in command. They had received a new assignment—to infiltrate and destroy the organization Worldwide Affiliates of Safari Partners, or better known as *W.A.S.P.*

W.A.S.P.'s public mission statement was that they're the world's leader in protecting the freedom to hunt while promoting wildlife conservation worldwide. In fact, they had become a powerful political force in Washington, D.C. and other world capitals, but they were really only interested in hunting while playing lip service to wildlife conservation. It was decided for Iceman and his team to start reeking havoc and to bring some Hell to their doorstep.

Rodin was to be a lone rogue agent, working on special assignments and concentrating on those particularly egregious individuals who need a little extra special attention. His next mission involved a Le Gang de la Clé de Singe leader, named Icarus, who had been captured while on assignment in Botswana and was going to put on trial for murder. If found guilty, he would be hung, and Rodin wasn't about to let that happen.

The United Nations had officially declared war on Le Gang de la Clé de Singe and seeked to destroy and dismantle the outlaw organization, bringing all those responsible to justice.

The sun was just cresting over the horizon, and a light breeze was blowing in from the east as Buzz lit up a fattie. The Sweet Mary Jane was anchored off the small island, Hon Lon, less than a mile off the coast of South Vietnam in the Vinh Van Phong Sea. Buzz sat on the edge of the boat swim platform with his feet hanging over the side. Bosco and Groucho were sitting next to him; he opened a canvas bag sitting next to him and threw a four-pound hunk of beef and two fried chickens overboard. Within minutes, he spotted Bumbley coming up to visit him. Buzz slowly lowered himself into the water and started to swim; the gargantuan followed alongside.

On the boat stereo, Bob Marley and the Wailers were singing "One Love". Buzz started to sing along, *"One Love, One Heart. Let's get together and feel all right. Hear the children crying. Hear the children crying. Sayin' give thanks and praise to the Lord, and I will feel all right. Sayin' let's get together and feel all right."*

Buzz stopped swimming and turned over onto his back. As he was floating, he reached over and petted Bumbley, saying, "To quote the Grateful Dead, 'what a long, strange trip it's been, man'."

THE END
for now